Invasion of the Dykes to Watch Out For

Also by Alison Bechdel

DYKES TO WATCH OUT FOR

MORE DYKES TO WATCH OUT FOR

NEW, IMPROVED DYKES TO WATCH OUT FOR

DYKES TO WATCH OUT FOR: THE SEQUEL

SPAWN OF DYKES TO WATCH OUT FOR

UNNATURAL DYKES TO WATCH OUT FOR

HOT, THROBBING DYKES TO WATCH OUT FOR

SPLIT-LEVEL DYKES TO WATCH OUT FOR

THE INDELIBLE ALISON BECHDEL

POST-DYKES TO WATCH OUT FOR

DYKES AND SUNDRY OTHER CARBON-BASED LIFE-FORMS TO WATCH OUT FOR

Invasion of the Dykes to Watch Out For

by

Alison Bechdel

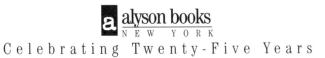
alyson books
NEW YORK
Celebrating Twenty-Five Years

All characters in this book are fictitious. Any resemblance to real individuals—either living or dead—is strictly coincidental.

Manufactured in the United States of America.

This trade paperback original is published by Alyson Books,
P.O. Box 1253, Old Chelsea Station, New York, New York 10113-1251.
Distribution in the United Kingdom by Turnaround Publisher Services Ltd.,
Unit 3, Olympia Trading Estate, Coburg Road, Wood Green,
London N22 6TZ England.

05 06 07 08 09 10 a 10 9 8 7 6 5 4 3 2

ISBN 1-55583-833-2
ISBN-13 978-1-55583-833-1

Library of Congress Cataloging-in-Publication Data

Bechdel, Alison, 1960–
[Dykes to watch out for. Selections]
Invasion of the dykes to watch out for / by Alison Bechdel.—1st ed.
ISBN 1-55583-833-2; ISBN-13 978-1-55583-833-1
1. Comic books, strips, etc. I. Title.
PN6728.D94B48 2005
741.5'973—dc22 2005049715

...WHERE WERE WE?

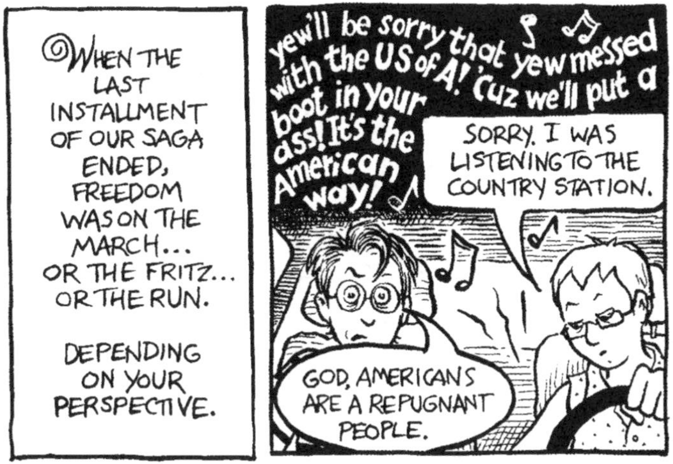
WHEN THE LAST INSTALLMENT OF OUR SAGA ENDED, FREEDOM WAS ON THE MARCH... OR THE FRITZ... OR THE RUN.
DEPENDING ON YOUR PERSPECTIVE.
yew'll be sorry that yew messed with the US of A! 'Cuz we'll put a boot in your ass! It's the American way!
GOD, AMERICANS ARE A REPUGNANT PEOPLE.
SORRY. I WAS LISTENING TO THE COUNTRY STATION.

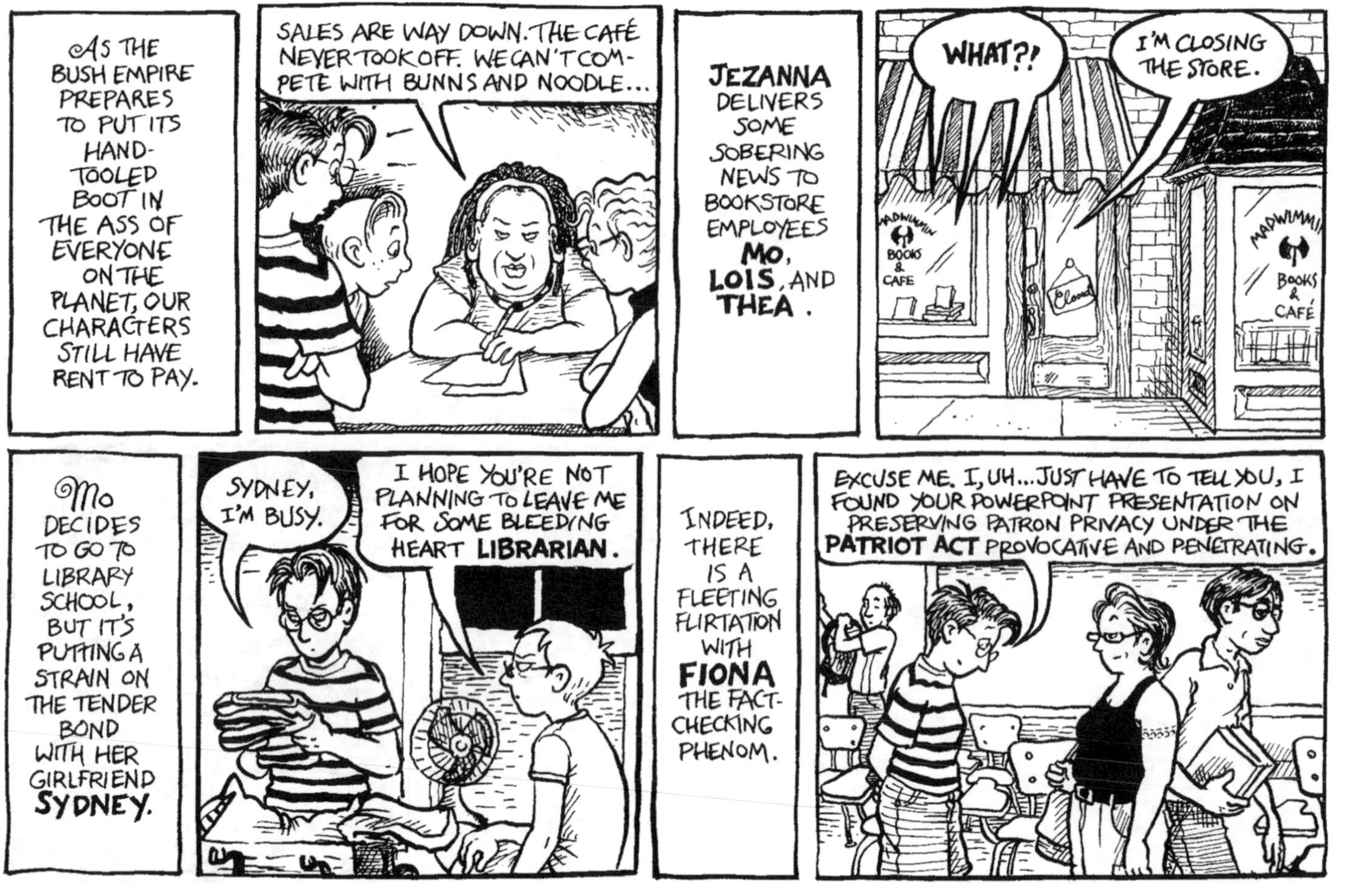
AS THE BUSH EMPIRE PREPARES TO PUT ITS HAND-TOOLED BOOT IN THE ASS OF EVERYONE ON THE PLANET, OUR CHARACTERS STILL HAVE RENT TO PAY.
SALES ARE WAY DOWN. THE CAFÉ NEVER TOOK OFF. WE CAN'T COMPETE WITH BUNNS AND NOODLE...
JEZANNA DELIVERS SOME SOBERING NEWS TO BOOKSTORE EMPLOYEES MO, LOIS, AND THEA.
WHAT?!
I'M CLOSING THE STORE.
BOOKS & CAFE
Closed
BOOKS & CAFÉ
MO DECIDES TO GO TO LIBRARY SCHOOL, BUT IT'S PUTTING A STRAIN ON THE TENDER BOND WITH HER GIRLFRIEND SYDNEY.
SYDNEY, I'M BUSY.
I HOPE YOU'RE NOT PLANNING TO LEAVE ME FOR SOME BLEEDING HEART LIBRARIAN.
INDEED, THERE IS A FLEETING FLIRTATION WITH FIONA THE FACT-CHECKING PHENOM.
EXCUSE ME. I, UH... JUST HAVE TO TELL YOU, I FOUND YOUR POWERPOINT PRESENTATION ON PRESERVING PATRON PRIVACY UNDER THE PATRIOT ACT PROVOCATIVE AND PENETRATING.

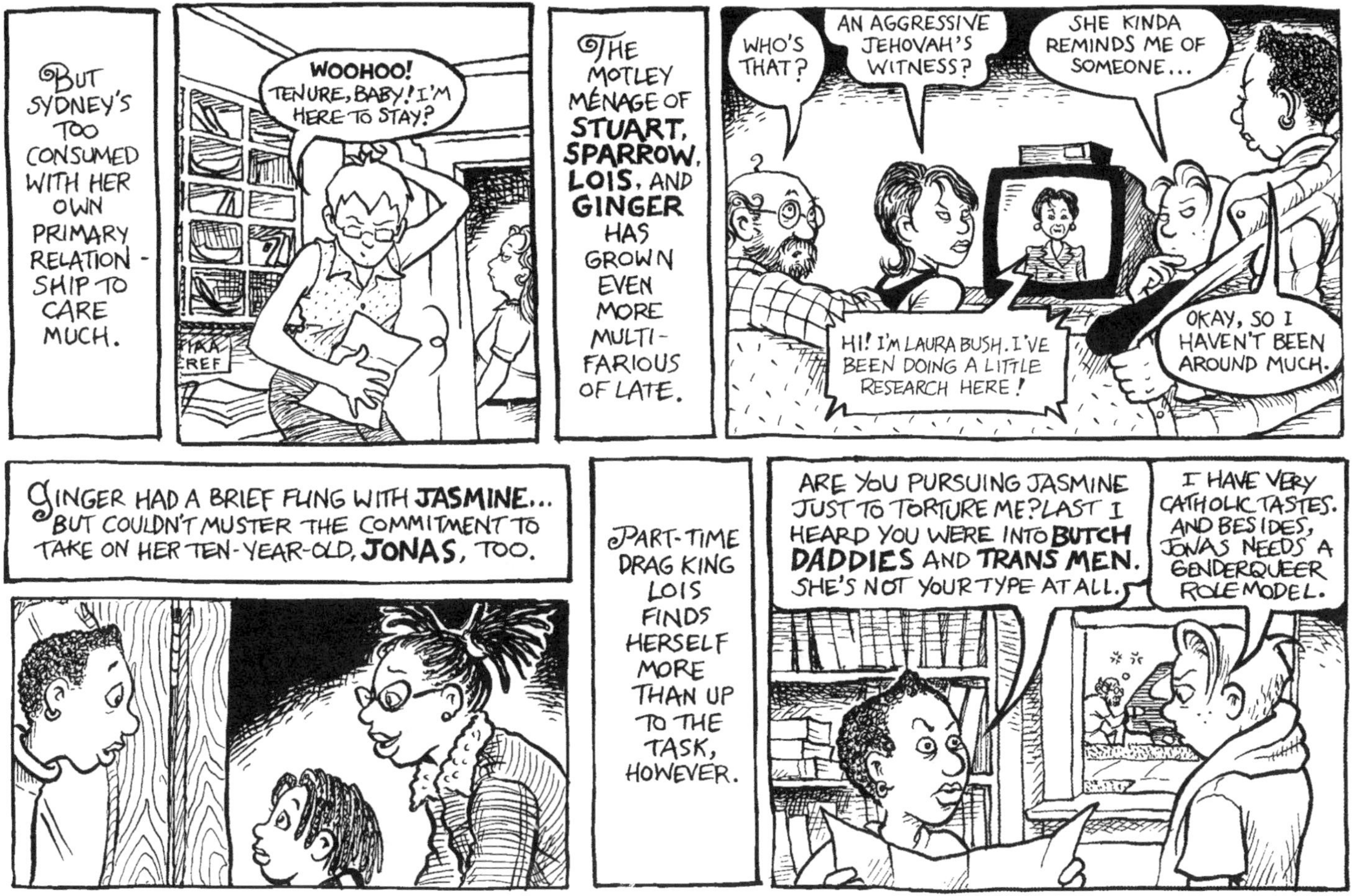

BUT SYDNEY'S TOO CONSUMED WITH HER OWN PRIMARY RELATIONSHIP TO CARE MUCH.
WOOHOO! TENURE, BABY! I'M HERE TO STAY!
TIAA CREF
THE MOTLEY MÉNAGE OF STUART, SPARROW, LOIS, AND GINGER HAS GROWN EVEN MORE MULTIFARIOUS OF LATE.
WHO'S THAT?
AN AGGRESSIVE JEHOVAH'S WITNESS?
SHE KINDA REMINDS ME OF SOMEONE...
HI! I'M LAURA BUSH. I'VE BEEN DOING A LITTLE RESEARCH HERE!
OKAY, SO I HAVEN'T BEEN AROUND MUCH.
GINGER HAD A BRIEF FLING WITH JASMINE... BUT COULDN'T MUSTER THE COMMITMENT TO TAKE ON HER TEN-YEAR-OLD, JONAS, TOO.
PART-TIME DRAG KING LOIS FINDS HERSELF MORE THAN UP TO THE TASK, HOWEVER.
ARE YOU PURSUING JASMINE JUST TO TORTURE ME? LAST I HEARD YOU WERE INTO BUTCH DADDIES AND TRANS MEN. SHE'S NOT YOUR TYPE AT ALL.
I HAVE VERY CATHOLIC TASTES. AND BESIDES, JONAS NEEDS A GENDERQUEER ROLE MODEL.

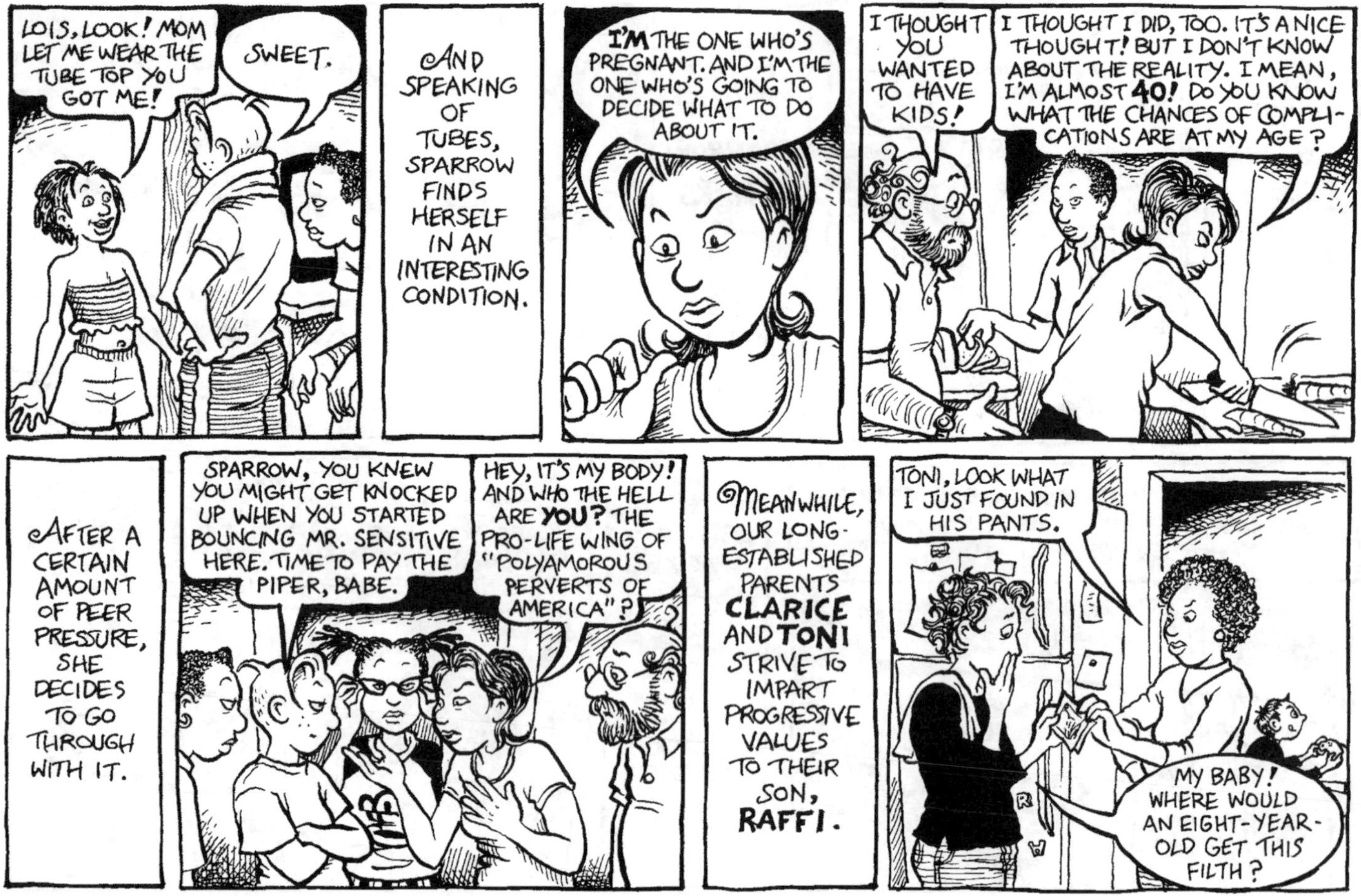
LOIS, LOOK! MOM LET ME WEAR THE TUBE TOP YOU GOT ME!
SWEET.
AND SPEAKING OF TUBES, SPARROW FINDS HERSELF IN AN INTERESTING CONDITION.
I'M THE ONE WHO'S PREGNANT. AND I'M THE ONE WHO'S GOING TO DECIDE WHAT TO DO ABOUT IT.
I THOUGHT YOU WANTED TO HAVE KIDS!
I THOUGHT I DID, TOO. IT'S A NICE THOUGHT! BUT I DON'T KNOW ABOUT THE REALITY. I MEAN, I'M ALMOST 40! DO YOU KNOW WHAT THE CHANCES OF COMPLICATIONS ARE AT MY AGE?
AFTER A CERTAIN AMOUNT OF PEER PRESSURE, SHE DECIDES TO GO THROUGH WITH IT.
SPARROW, YOU KNEW YOU MIGHT GET KNOCKED UP WHEN YOU STARTED BOUNCING MR. SENSITIVE HERE. TIME TO PAY THE PIPER, BABE.
HEY, IT'S MY BODY! AND WHO THE HELL ARE YOU? THE PRO-LIFE WING OF "POLYAMOROUS PERVERTS OF AMERICA"?
MEANWHILE, OUR LONG-ESTABLISHED PARENTS CLARICE AND TONI STRIVE TO IMPART PROGRESSIVE VALUES TO THEIR SON, RAFFI.
TONI, LOOK WHAT I JUST FOUND IN HIS PANTS.
MY BABY! WHERE WOULD AN EIGHT-YEAR-OLD GET THIS FILTH?

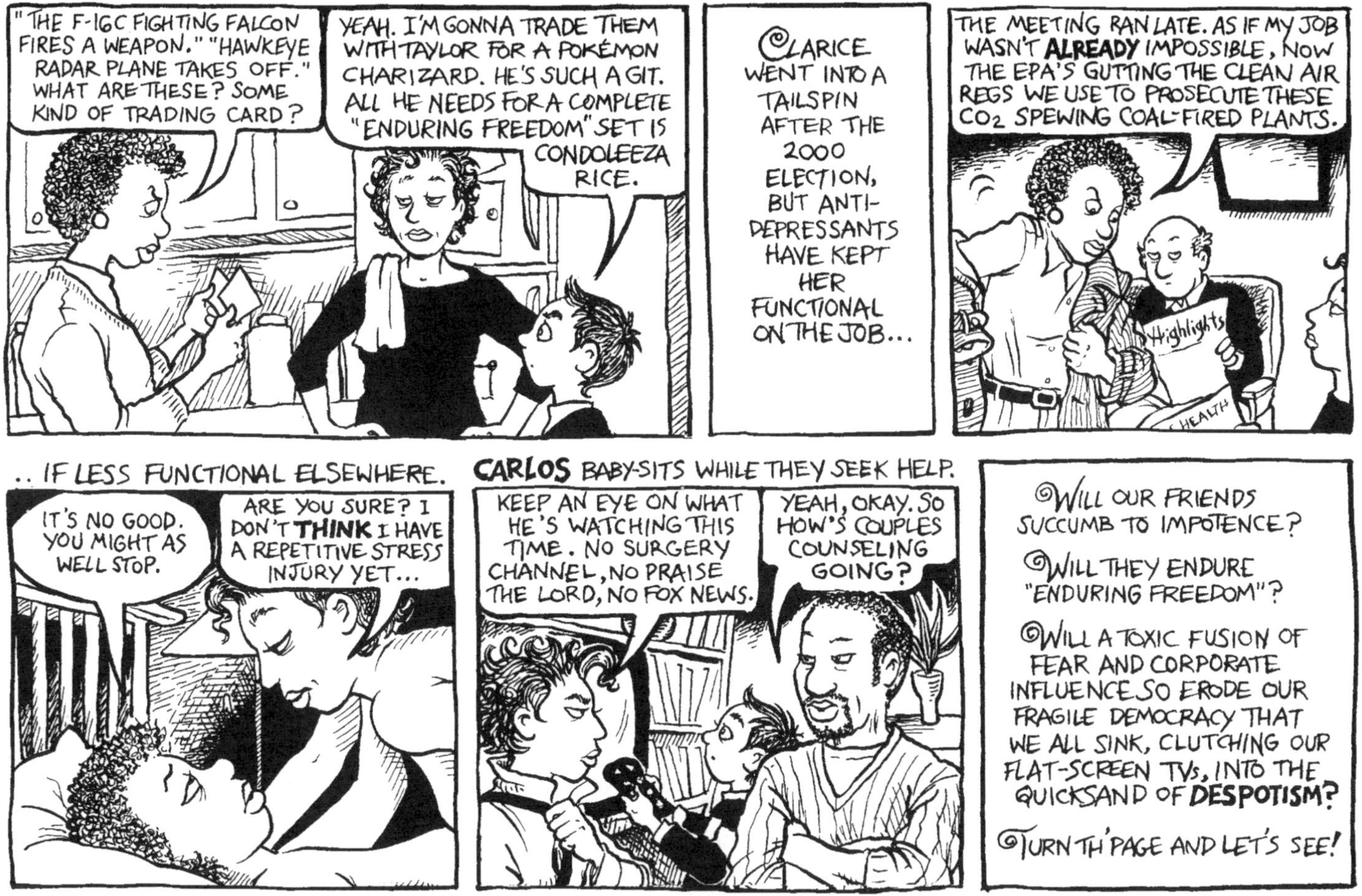
"THE F-16C FIGHTING FALCON FIRES A WEAPON." "HAWKEYE RADAR PLANE TAKES OFF." WHAT ARE THESE? SOME KIND OF TRADING CARD?
YEAH. I'M GONNA TRADE THEM WITH TAYLOR FOR A POKÉMON CHARIZARD. HE'S SUCH A GIT. ALL HE NEEDS FOR A COMPLETE "ENDURING FREEDOM" SET IS CONDOLEEZA RICE.
CLARICE WENT INTO A TAILSPIN AFTER THE 2000 ELECTION, BUT ANTI-DEPRESSANTS HAVE KEPT HER FUNCTIONAL ON THE JOB...
THE MEETING RAN LATE. AS IF MY JOB WASN'T **ALREADY** IMPOSSIBLE, NOW THE EPA'S GUTTING THE CLEAN AIR REGS WE USE TO PROSECUTE THESE CO_2 SPEWING COAL-FIRED PLANTS.
Highlights
HEALTH
.. IF LESS FUNCTIONAL ELSEWHERE.
IT'S NO GOOD. YOU MIGHT AS WELL STOP.
ARE YOU SURE? I DON'T **THINK** I HAVE A REPETITIVE STRESS INJURY YET...
CARLOS BABY-SITS WHILE THEY SEEK HELP.
KEEP AN EYE ON WHAT HE'S WATCHING THIS TIME. NO SURGERY CHANNEL, NO PRAISE THE LORD, NO FOX NEWS.
YEAH, OKAY. SO HOW'S COUPLES COUNSELING GOING?
WILL OUR FRIENDS SUCCUMB TO IMPOTENCE?
WILL THEY ENDURE "ENDURING FREEDOM"?
WILL A TOXIC FUSION OF FEAR AND CORPORATE INFLUENCE SO ERODE OUR FRAGILE DEMOCRACY THAT WE ALL SINK, CLUTCHING OUR FLAT-SCREEN TVs, INTO THE QUICKSAND OF **DESPOTISM**?
TURN TH' PAGE AND LET'S SEE!

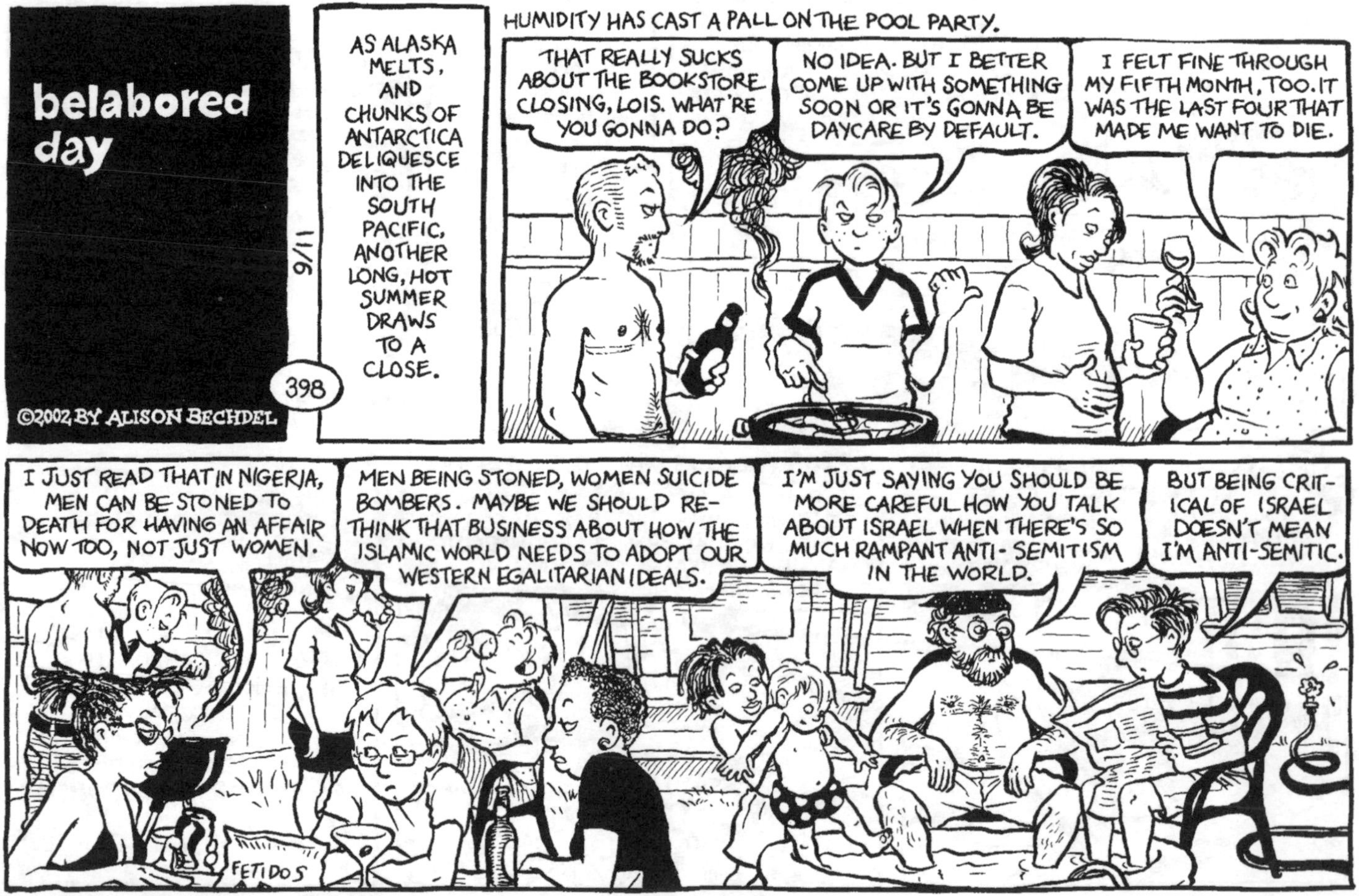

belabored day
©2002 BY ALISON BECHDEL
398
9/11
AS ALASKA MELTS, AND CHUNKS OF ANTARCTICA DELIQUESCE INTO THE SOUTH PACIFIC, ANOTHER LONG, HOT SUMMER DRAWS TO A CLOSE.
HUMIDITY HAS CAST A PALL ON THE POOL PARTY.
THAT REALLY SUCKS ABOUT THE BOOKSTORE CLOSING, LOIS. WHAT'RE YOU GONNA DO?
NO IDEA. BUT I BETTER COME UP WITH SOMETHING SOON OR IT'S GONNA BE DAYCARE BY DEFAULT.
I FELT FINE THROUGH MY FIFTH MONTH, TOO. IT WAS THE LAST FOUR THAT MADE ME WANT TO DIE.
I JUST READ THAT IN NIGERIA, MEN CAN BE STONED TO DEATH FOR HAVING AN AFFAIR NOW TOO, NOT JUST WOMEN.
MEN BEING STONED, WOMEN SUICIDE BOMBERS. MAYBE WE SHOULD RE-THINK THAT BUSINESS ABOUT HOW THE ISLAMIC WORLD NEEDS TO ADOPT OUR WESTERN EGALITARIAN IDEALS.
I'M JUST SAYING YOU SHOULD BE MORE CAREFUL HOW YOU TALK ABOUT ISRAEL WHEN THERE'S SO MUCH RAMPANT ANTI-SEMITISM IN THE WORLD.
BUT BEING CRIT-ICAL OF ISRAEL DOESN'T MEAN I'M ANTI-SEMITIC.
FETIDOS

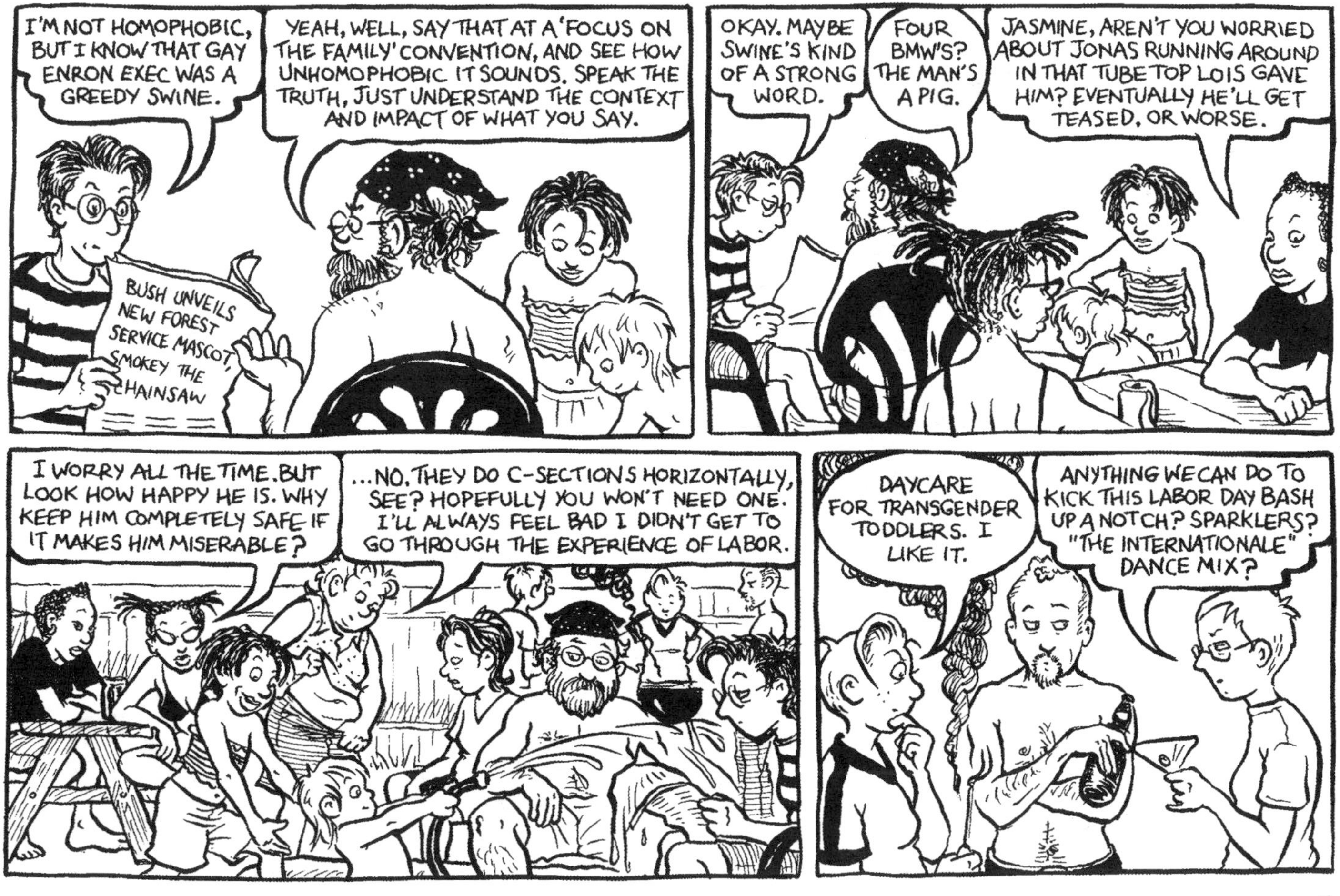

I'M NOT HOMOPHOBIC, BUT I KNOW THAT GAY ENRON EXEC WAS A GREEDY SWINE.
YEAH, WELL, SAY THAT AT A 'FOCUS ON THE FAMILY' CONVENTION, AND SEE HOW UNHOMOPHOBIC IT SOUNDS. SPEAK THE TRUTH, JUST UNDERSTAND THE CONTEXT AND IMPACT OF WHAT YOU SAY.
BUSH UNVEILS NEW FOREST SERVICE MASCOT, SMOKEY THE CHAINSAW
OKAY. MAYBE SWINE'S KIND OF A STRONG WORD.
FOUR BMW'S? THE MAN'S A PIG.
JASMINE, AREN'T YOU WORRIED ABOUT JONAS RUNNING AROUND IN THAT TUBE TOP LOIS GAVE HIM? EVENTUALLY HE'LL GET TEASED, OR WORSE.
I WORRY ALL THE TIME. BUT LOOK HOW HAPPY HE IS. WHY KEEP HIM COMPLETELY SAFE IF IT MAKES HIM MISERABLE?
...NO. THEY DO C-SECTIONS HORIZONTALLY, SEE? HOPEFULLY YOU WON'T NEED ONE. I'LL ALWAYS FEEL BAD I DIDN'T GET TO GO THROUGH THE EXPERIENCE OF LABOR.
DAYCARE FOR TRANSGENDER TODDLERS. I LIKE IT.
ANYTHING WE CAN DO TO KICK THIS LABOR DAY BASH UP A NOTCH? SPARKLERS? "THE INTERNATIONALE" DANCE MIX?

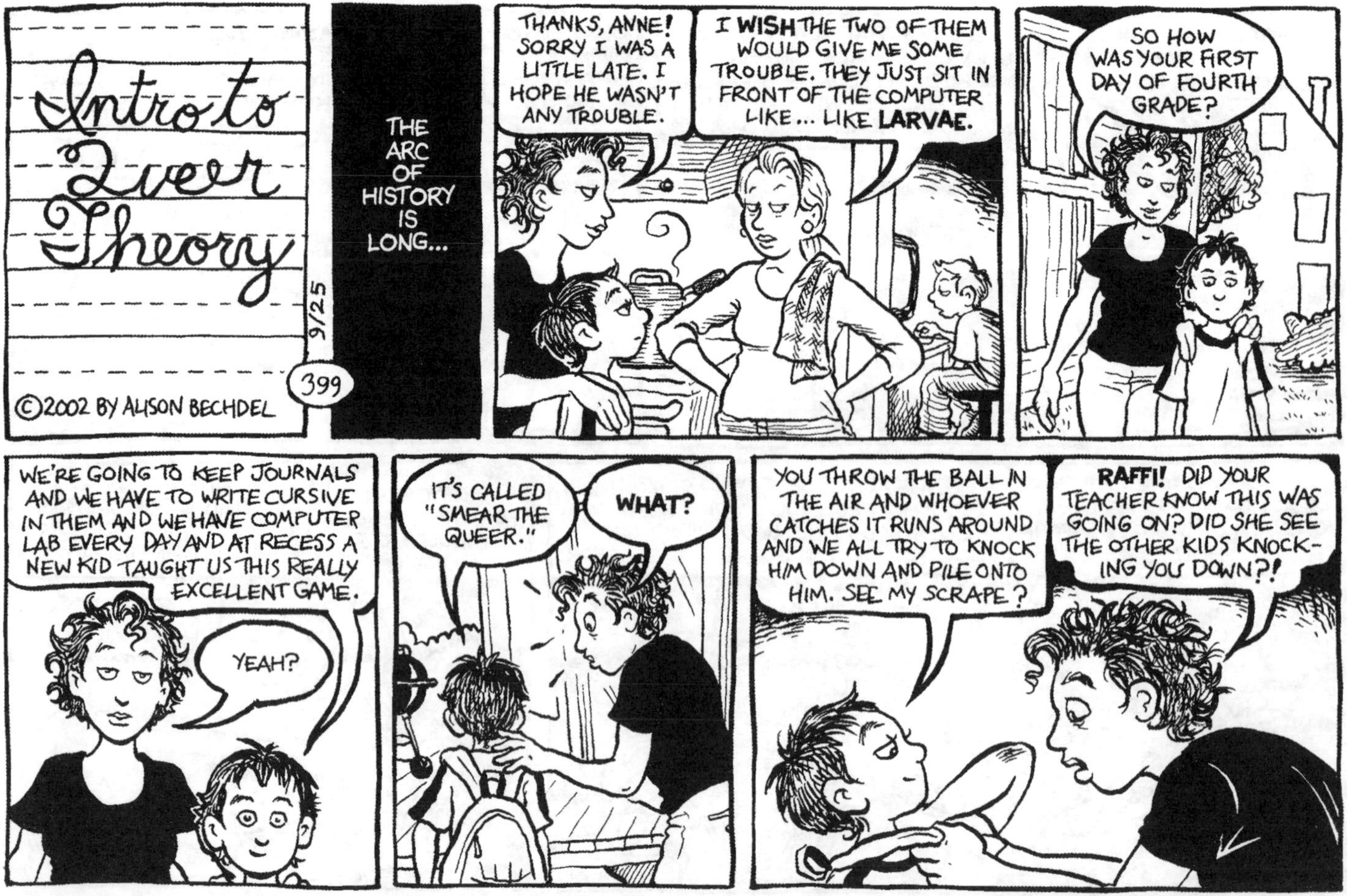
Intro to Queer Theory
9/25
399
©2002 BY ALISON BECHDEL
THE ARC OF HISTORY IS LONG...
THANKS, ANNE! SORRY I WAS A LITTLE LATE. I HOPE HE WASN'T ANY TROUBLE.
I WISH THE TWO OF THEM WOULD GIVE ME SOME TROUBLE. THEY JUST SIT IN FRONT OF THE COMPUTER LIKE... LIKE LARVAE.
SO HOW WAS YOUR FIRST DAY OF FOURTH GRADE?
WE'RE GOING TO KEEP JOURNALS AND WE HAVE TO WRITE CURSIVE IN THEM AND WE HAVE COMPUTER LAB EVERY DAY AND AT RECESS A NEW KID TAUGHT US THIS REALLY EXCELLENT GAME.
YEAH?
IT'S CALLED "SMEAR THE QUEER."
WHAT?
YOU THROW THE BALL IN THE AIR AND WHOEVER CATCHES IT RUNS AROUND AND WE ALL TRY TO KNOCK HIM DOWN AND PILE ONTO HIM. SEE MY SCRAPE?
RAFFI! DID YOUR TEACHER KNOW THIS WAS GOING ON? DID SHE SEE THE OTHER KIDS KNOCKING YOU DOWN?!

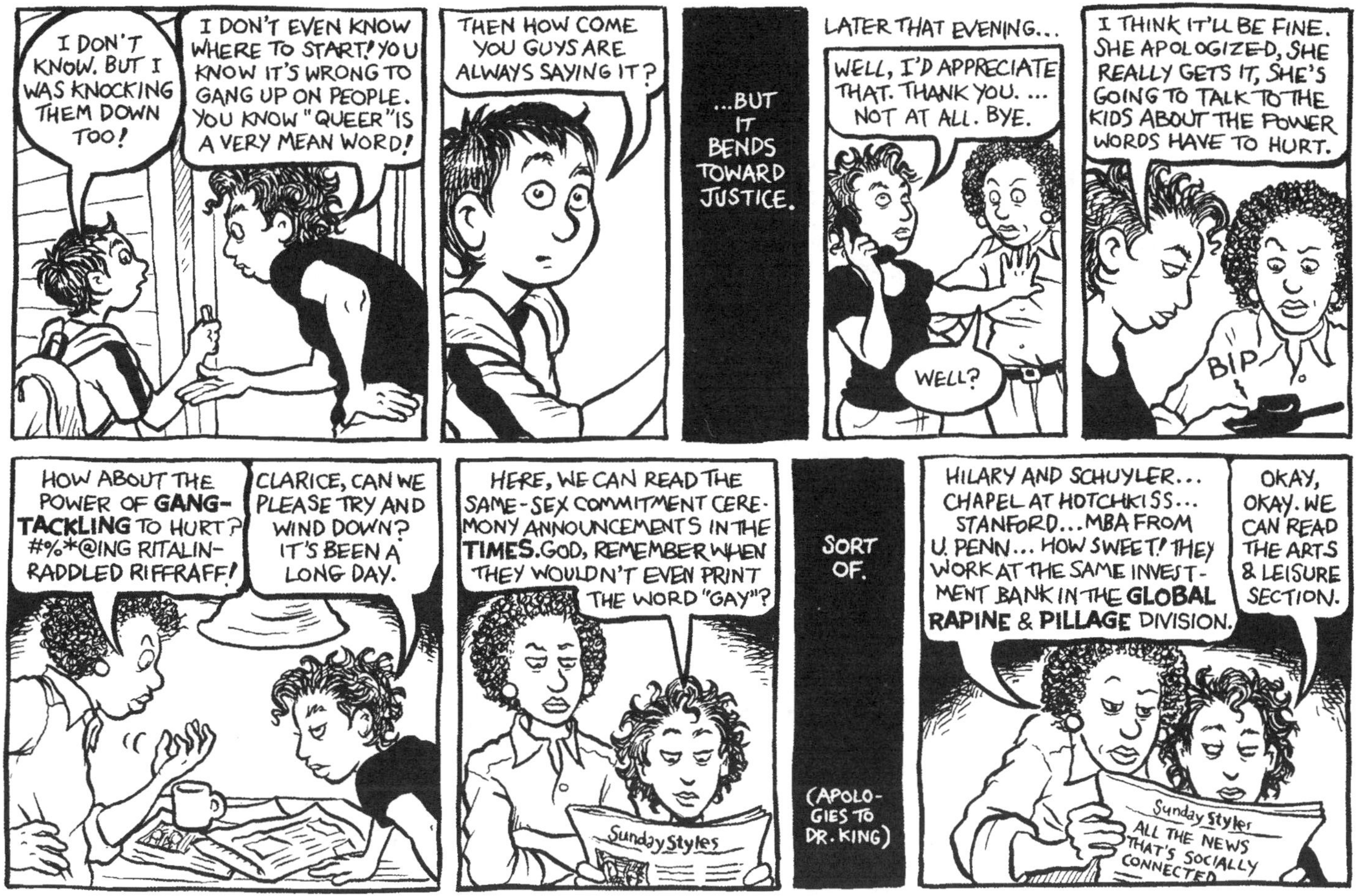
I DON'T KNOW. BUT I WAS KNOCKING THEM DOWN TOO!
I DON'T EVEN KNOW WHERE TO START! YOU KNOW IT'S WRONG TO GANG UP ON PEOPLE. YOU KNOW "QUEER" IS A VERY MEAN WORD!
THEN HOW COME YOU GUYS ARE ALWAYS SAYING IT?
...BUT IT BENDS TOWARD JUSTICE.
LATER THAT EVENING...
WELL, I'D APPRECIATE THAT. THANK YOU. ... NOT AT ALL. BYE.
WELL?
I THINK IT'LL BE FINE. SHE APOLOGIZED, SHE REALLY GETS IT, SHE'S GOING TO TALK TO THE KIDS ABOUT THE POWER WORDS HAVE TO HURT.
BIP
HOW ABOUT THE POWER OF **GANG-TACKLING** TO HURT? #%*@ING RITALIN-RADDLED RIFFRAFF!
CLARICE, CAN WE PLEASE TRY AND WIND DOWN? IT'S BEEN A LONG DAY.
HERE, WE CAN READ THE SAME-SEX COMMITMENT CEREMONY ANNOUNCEMENTS IN THE **TIMES.** GOD, REMEMBER WHEN THEY WOULDN'T EVEN PRINT THE WORD "GAY"?
Sunday Styles
SORT OF.
(APOLOGIES TO DR. KING)
HILARY AND SCHUYLER... CHAPEL AT HOTCHKISS... STANFORD... MBA FROM U. PENN... HOW SWEET! THEY WORK AT THE SAME INVESTMENT BANK IN THE **GLOBAL RAPINE** & **PILLAGE** DIVISION.
OKAY, OKAY. WE CAN READ THE ARTS & LEISURE SECTION.
Sunday Styles
ALL THE NEWS THAT'S SOCIALLY CONNECTED

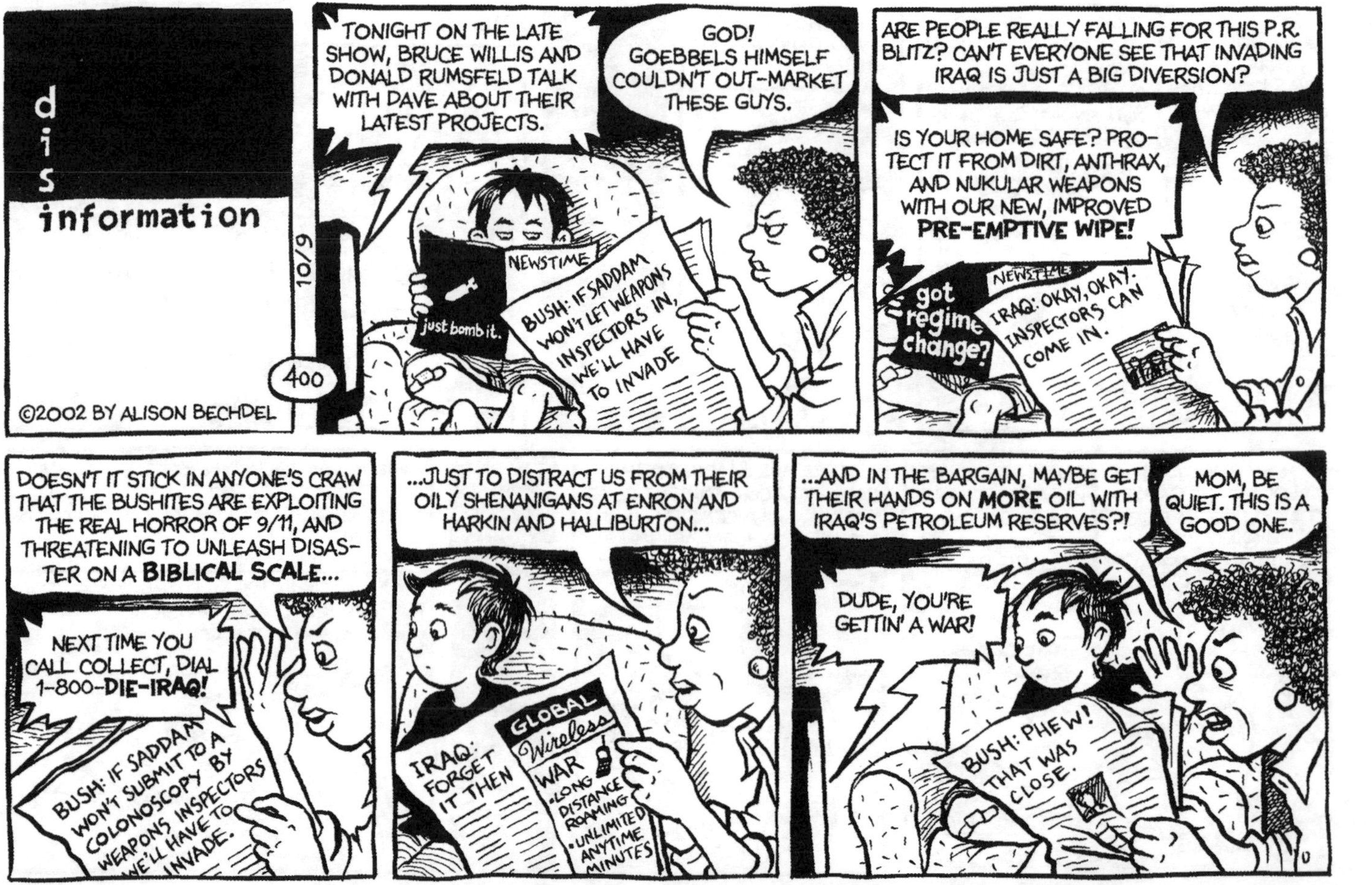

dis
information
10/9
400
©2002 BY ALISON BECHDEL
TONIGHT ON THE LATE SHOW, BRUCE WILLIS AND DONALD RUMSFELD TALK WITH DAVE ABOUT THEIR LATEST PROJECTS.
GOD! GOEBBELS HIMSELF COULDN'T OUT-MARKET THESE GUYS.
just bomb it.
NEWSTIME
BUSH: IF SADDAM WON'T LET WEAPONS INSPECTORS IN, WE'LL HAVE TO INVADE
ARE PEOPLE REALLY FALLING FOR THIS P.R. BLITZ? CAN'T EVERYONE SEE THAT INVADING IRAQ IS JUST A BIG DIVERSION?
IS YOUR HOME SAFE? PROTECT IT FROM DIRT, ANTHRAX, AND NUKULAR WEAPONS WITH OUR NEW, IMPROVED PRE-EMPTIVE WIPE!
got regime change?
IRAQ: OKAY, OKAY. INSPECTORS CAN COME IN.
DOESN'T IT STICK IN ANYONE'S CRAW THAT THE BUSHITES ARE EXPLOITING THE REAL HORROR OF 9/11, AND THREATENING TO UNLEASH DISASTER ON A BIBLICAL SCALE...
NEXT TIME YOU CALL COLLECT, DIAL 1-800-DIE-IRAQ!
BUSH: IF SADDAM WON'T SUBMIT TO A COLONOSCOPY BY WEAPONS INSPECTORS WE'LL HAVE TO INVADE.
...JUST TO DISTRACT US FROM THEIR OILY SHENANIGANS AT ENRON AND HARKIN AND HALLIBURTON...
IRAQ: FORGET IT THEN
GLOBAL Wireless WAR
•LONG DISTANCE ROAMING
•UNLIMITED ANYTIME MINUTES
...AND IN THE BARGAIN, MAYBE GET THEIR HANDS ON MORE OIL WITH IRAQ'S PETROLEUM RESERVES?!
MOM, BE QUIET. THIS IS A GOOD ONE.
DUDE, YOU'RE GETTIN' A WAR!
BUSH: PHEW! THAT WAS CLOSE.

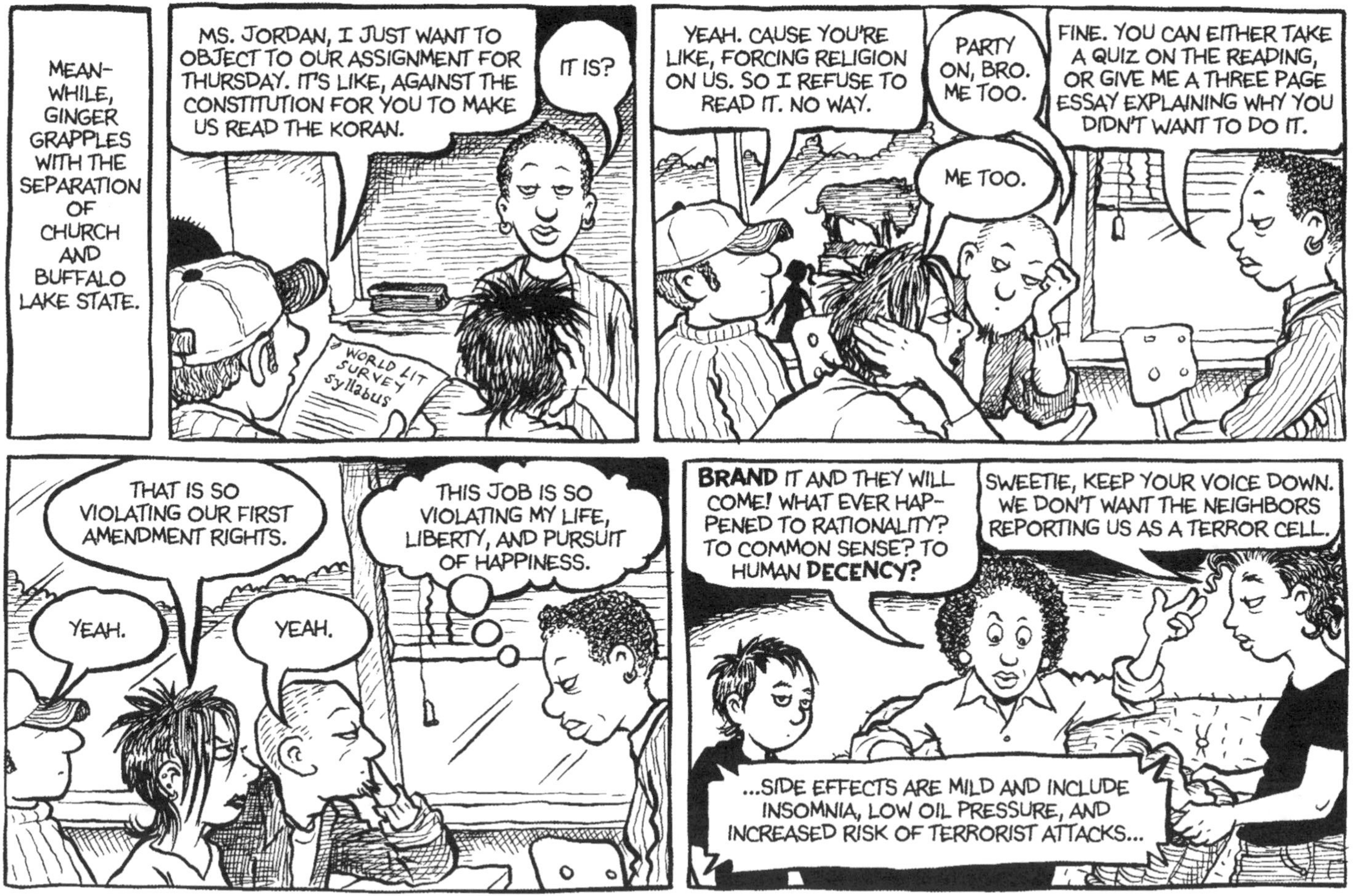
MEAN-WHILE, GINGER GRAPPLES WITH THE SEPARATION OF CHURCH AND BUFFALO LAKE STATE.
MS. JORDAN, I JUST WANT TO OBJECT TO OUR ASSIGNMENT FOR THURSDAY. IT'S LIKE, AGAINST THE CONSTITUTION FOR YOU TO MAKE US READ THE KORAN.
IT IS?
WORLD LIT SURVEY syllabus
YEAH. CAUSE YOU'RE LIKE, FORCING RELIGION ON US. SO I REFUSE TO READ IT. NO WAY.
PARTY ON, BRO. ME TOO.
ME TOO.
FINE. YOU CAN EITHER TAKE A QUIZ ON THE READING, OR GIVE ME A THREE PAGE ESSAY EXPLAINING WHY YOU DIDN'T WANT TO DO IT.
THAT IS SO VIOLATING OUR FIRST AMENDMENT RIGHTS.
YEAH.
YEAH.
THIS JOB IS SO VIOLATING MY LIFE, LIBERTY, AND PURSUIT OF HAPPINESS.
BRAND IT AND THEY WILL COME! WHAT EVER HAPPENED TO RATIONALITY? TO COMMON SENSE? TO HUMAN DECENCY?
SWEETIE, KEEP YOUR VOICE DOWN. WE DON'T WANT THE NEIGHBORS REPORTING US AS A TERROR CELL.
...SIDE EFFECTS ARE MILD AND INCLUDE INSOMNIA, LOW OIL PRESSURE, AND INCREASED RISK OF TERRORIST ATTACKS...

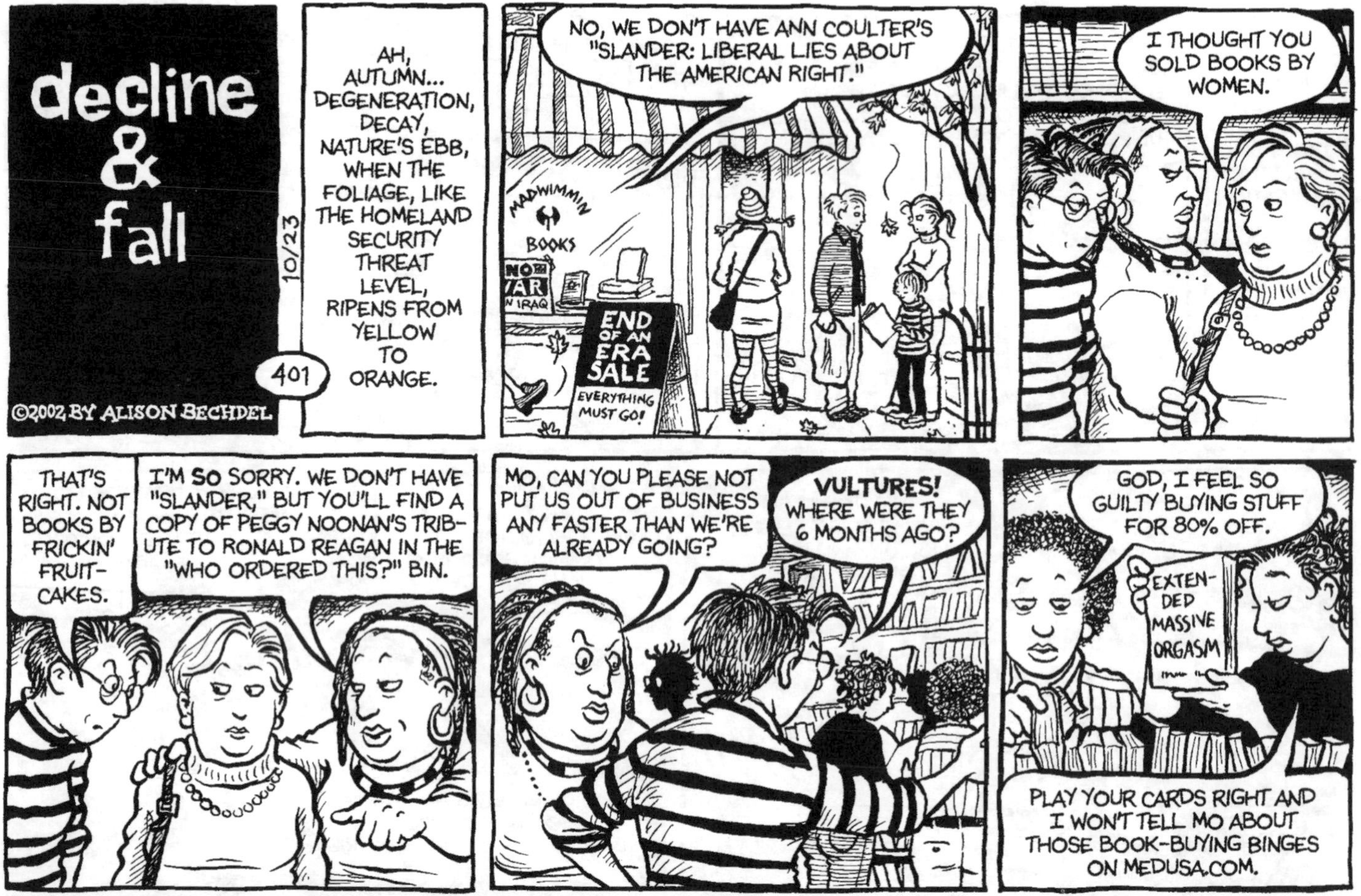

decline & fall
©2002 BY ALISON BECHDEL
10/23
401
AH, AUTUMN... DEGENERATION, DECAY, NATURE'S EBB, WHEN THE FOLIAGE, LIKE THE HOMELAND SECURITY THREAT LEVEL, RIPENS FROM YELLOW TO ORANGE.
NO, WE DON'T HAVE ANN COULTER'S "SLANDER: LIBERAL LIES ABOUT THE AMERICAN RIGHT."
MADWIMMIN BOOKS
NO WAR IN IRAQ
END OF AN ERA SALE
EVERYTHING MUST GO!
I THOUGHT YOU SOLD BOOKS BY WOMEN.
THAT'S RIGHT. NOT BOOKS BY FRICKIN' FRUIT-CAKES.
I'M **SO** SORRY. WE DON'T HAVE "SLANDER," BUT YOU'LL FIND A COPY OF PEGGY NOONAN'S TRIB-UTE TO RONALD REAGAN IN THE "WHO ORDERED THIS?" BIN.
MO, CAN YOU PLEASE NOT PUT US OUT OF BUSINESS ANY FASTER THAN WE'RE ALREADY GOING?
VULTURES! WHERE WERE THEY 6 MONTHS AGO?
GOD, I FEEL SO GUILTY BUYING STUFF FOR 80% OFF.
EXTEN-DED MASSIVE ORGASM
PLAY YOUR CARDS RIGHT AND I WON'T TELL MO ABOUT THOSE BOOK-BUYING BINGES ON MEDUSA.COM.

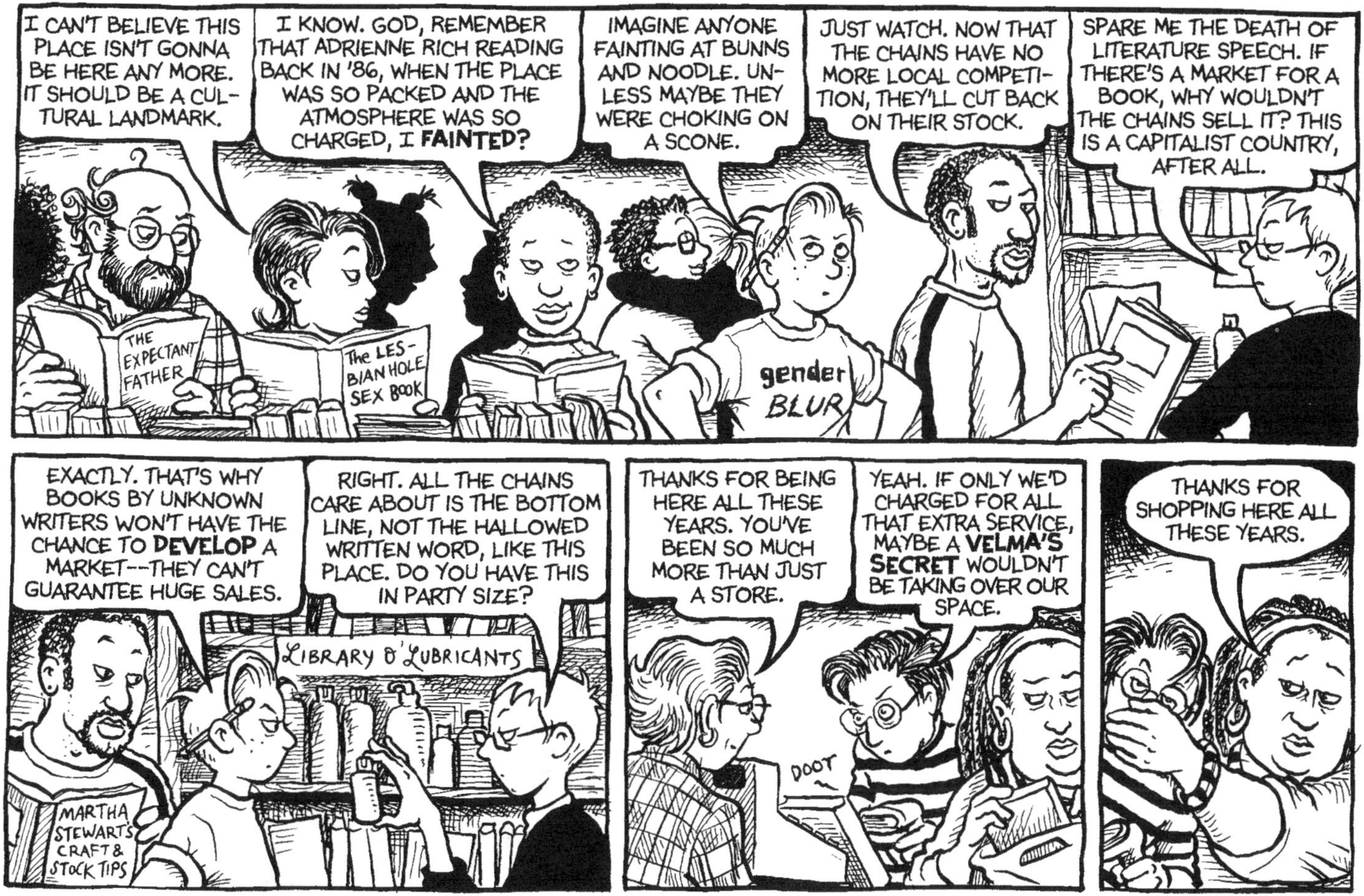
I CAN'T BELIEVE THIS PLACE ISN'T GONNA BE HERE ANY MORE. IT SHOULD BE A CULTURAL LANDMARK.
I KNOW. GOD, REMEMBER THAT ADRIENNE RICH READING BACK IN '86, WHEN THE PLACE WAS SO PACKED AND THE ATMOSPHERE WAS SO CHARGED, I **FAINTED?**
IMAGINE ANYONE FAINTING AT BUNNS AND NOODLE. UNLESS MAYBE THEY WERE CHOKING ON A SCONE.
JUST WATCH. NOW THAT THE CHAINS HAVE NO MORE LOCAL COMPETITION, THEY'LL CUT BACK ON THEIR STOCK.
SPARE ME THE DEATH OF LITERATURE SPEECH. IF THERE'S A MARKET FOR A BOOK, WHY WOULDN'T THE CHAINS SELL IT? THIS IS A CAPITALIST COUNTRY, AFTER ALL.
THE EXPECTANT FATHER
The LESBIAN HOLE SEX BOOK
gender BLUR
EXACTLY. THAT'S WHY BOOKS BY UNKNOWN WRITERS WON'T HAVE THE CHANCE TO **DEVELOP** A MARKET--THEY CAN'T GUARANTEE HUGE SALES.
RIGHT. ALL THE CHAINS CARE ABOUT IS THE BOTTOM LINE, NOT THE HALLOWED WRITTEN WORD, LIKE THIS PLACE. DO YOU HAVE THIS IN PARTY SIZE?
LIBRARY O' LUBRICANTS
MARTHA STEWART'S CRAFT & STOCK TIPS
THANKS FOR BEING HERE ALL THESE YEARS. YOU'VE BEEN SO MUCH MORE THAN JUST A STORE.
YEAH. IF ONLY WE'D CHARGED FOR ALL THAT EXTRA SERVICE, MAYBE A **VELMA'S SECRET** WOULDN'T BE TAKING OVER OUR SPACE.
DOOT
THANKS FOR SHOPPING HERE ALL THESE YEARS.

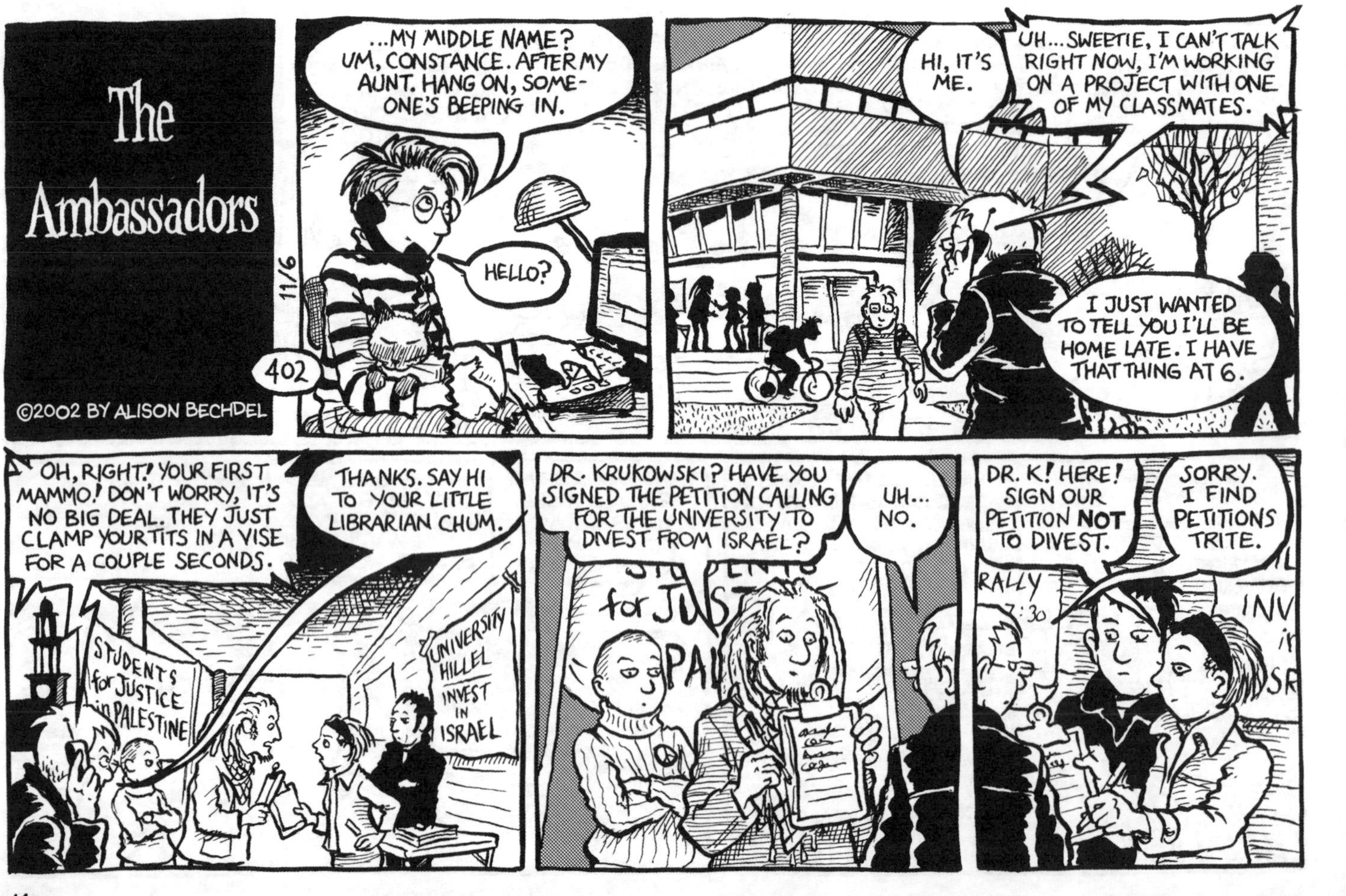
The Ambassadors
©2002 BY ALISON BECHDEL
11/6
402
...MY MIDDLE NAME? UM, CONSTANCE. AFTER MY AUNT. HANG ON, SOME-ONE'S BEEPING IN.
HELLO?
HI, IT'S ME.
UH... SWEETIE, I CAN'T TALK RIGHT NOW, I'M WORKING ON A PROJECT WITH ONE OF MY CLASSMATES.
I JUST WANTED TO TELL YOU I'LL BE HOME LATE. I HAVE THAT THING AT 6.
OH, RIGHT! YOUR FIRST MAMMO! DON'T WORRY, IT'S NO BIG DEAL. THEY JUST CLAMP YOUR TITS IN A VISE FOR A COUPLE SECONDS.
THANKS. SAY HI TO YOUR LITTLE LIBRARIAN CHUM.
STUDENTS for JUSTICE in PALESTINE
UNIVERSITY HILLEL
INVEST IN ISRAEL
DR. KRUKOWSKI? HAVE YOU SIGNED THE PETITION CALLING FOR THE UNIVERSITY TO DIVEST FROM ISRAEL?
UH... NO.
DR. K! HERE! SIGN OUR PETITION **NOT** TO DIVEST.
SORRY. I FIND PETITIONS TRITE.
RALLY
7:30

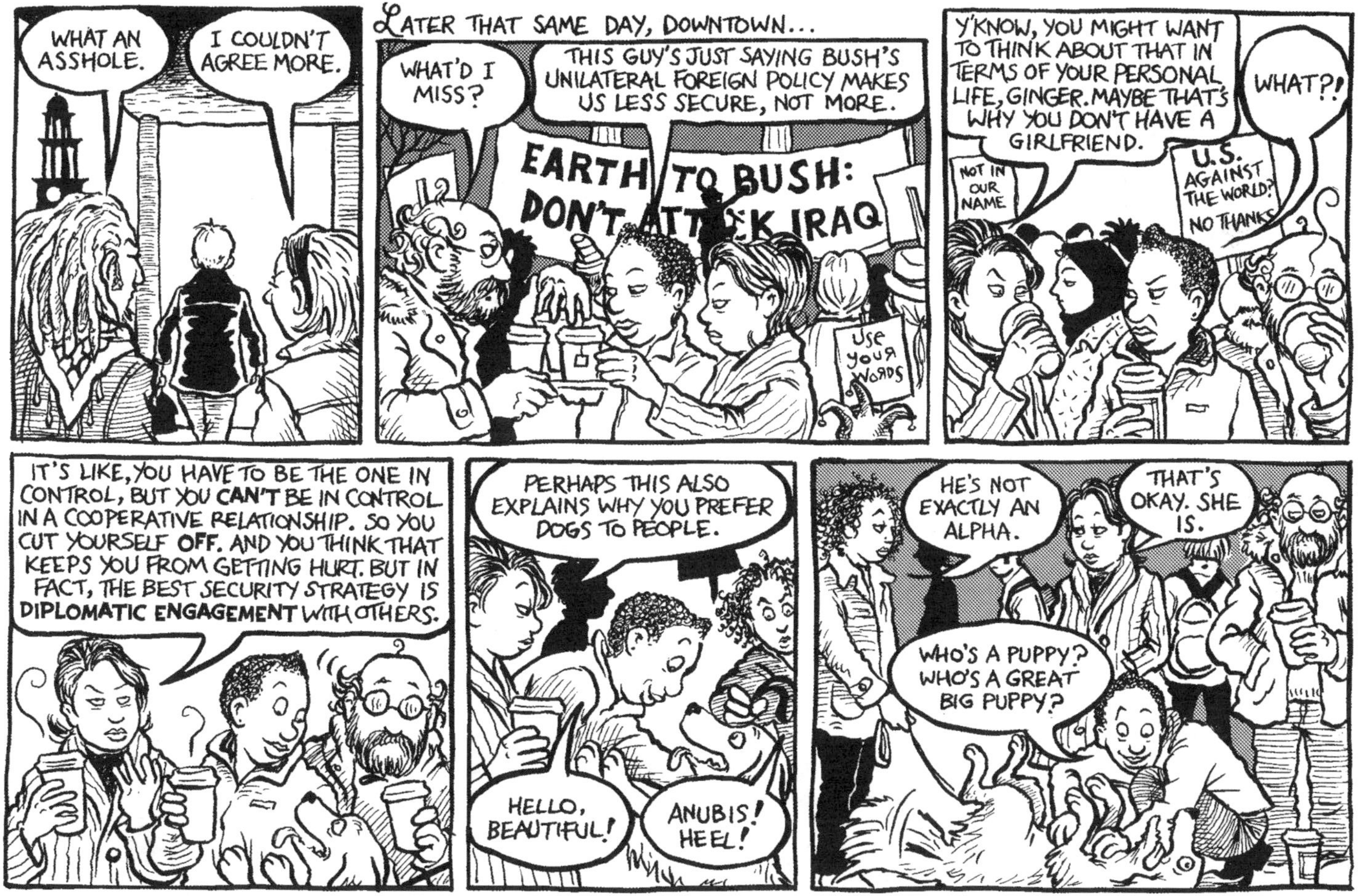
WHAT AN ASSHOLE.
I COULDN'T AGREE MORE.
LATER THAT SAME DAY, DOWNTOWN...
WHAT'D I MISS?
THIS GUY'S JUST SAYING BUSH'S UNILATERAL FOREIGN POLICY MAKES US LESS SECURE, NOT MORE.
EARTH TO BUSH: DON'T ATT K IRAQ
USE YOUR WORDS
Y'KNOW, YOU MIGHT WANT TO THINK ABOUT THAT IN TERMS OF YOUR PERSONAL LIFE, GINGER. MAYBE THAT'S WHY YOU DON'T HAVE A GIRLFRIEND.
WHAT?!
NOT IN OUR NAME
U.S. AGAINST THE WORLD? NO THANKS
IT'S LIKE, YOU HAVE TO BE THE ONE IN CONTROL, BUT YOU CAN'T BE IN CONTROL IN A COOPERATIVE RELATIONSHIP. SO YOU CUT YOURSELF OFF. AND YOU THINK THAT KEEPS YOU FROM GETTING HURT. BUT IN FACT, THE BEST SECURITY STRATEGY IS DIPLOMATIC ENGAGEMENT WITH OTHERS.
PERHAPS THIS ALSO EXPLAINS WHY YOU PREFER DOGS TO PEOPLE.
HELLO, BEAUTIFUL!
ANUBIS! HEEL!
HE'S NOT EXACTLY AN ALPHA.
THAT'S OKAY. SHE IS.
WHO'S A PUPPY? WHO'S A GREAT BIG PUPPY?

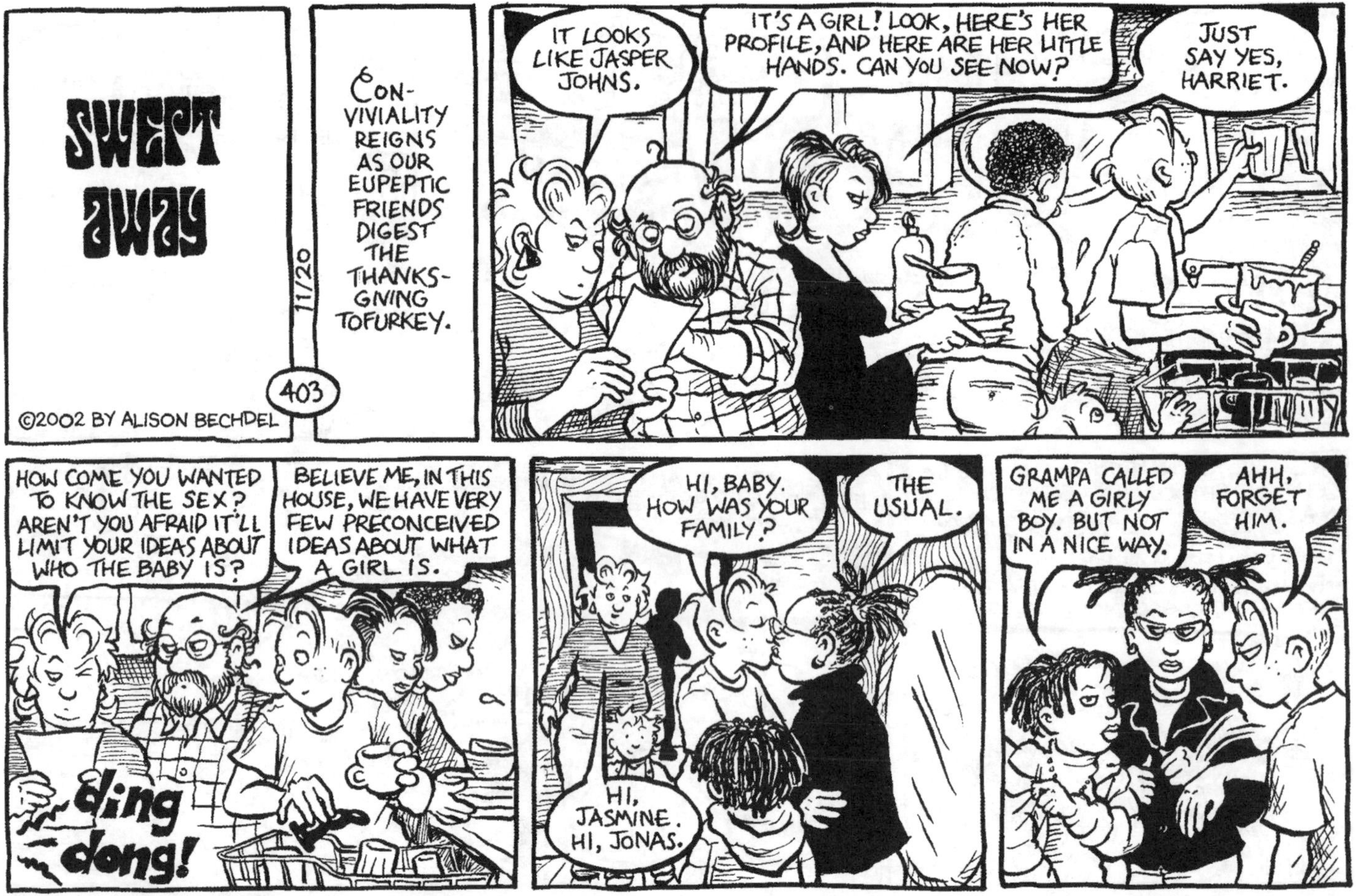
SWEPT AWAY
©2002 BY ALISON BECHDEL
403
11/20
CONVIVIALITY REIGNS AS OUR EUPEPTIC FRIENDS DIGEST THE THANKSGIVING TOFURKEY.
IT LOOKS LIKE JASPER JOHNS.
IT'S A GIRL! LOOK, HERE'S HER PROFILE, AND HERE ARE HER LITTLE HANDS. CAN YOU SEE NOW?
JUST SAY YES, HARRIET.
HOW COME YOU WANTED TO KNOW THE SEX? AREN'T YOU AFRAID IT'LL LIMIT YOUR IDEAS ABOUT WHO THE BABY IS?
BELIEVE ME, IN THIS HOUSE, WE HAVE VERY FEW PRECONCEIVED IDEAS ABOUT WHAT A GIRL IS.
ding dong!
HI, BABY. HOW WAS YOUR FAMILY?
THE USUAL.
HI, JASMINE. HI, JONAS.
GRAMPA CALLED ME A GIRLY BOY. BUT NOT IN A NICE WAY.
AHH, FORGET HIM.

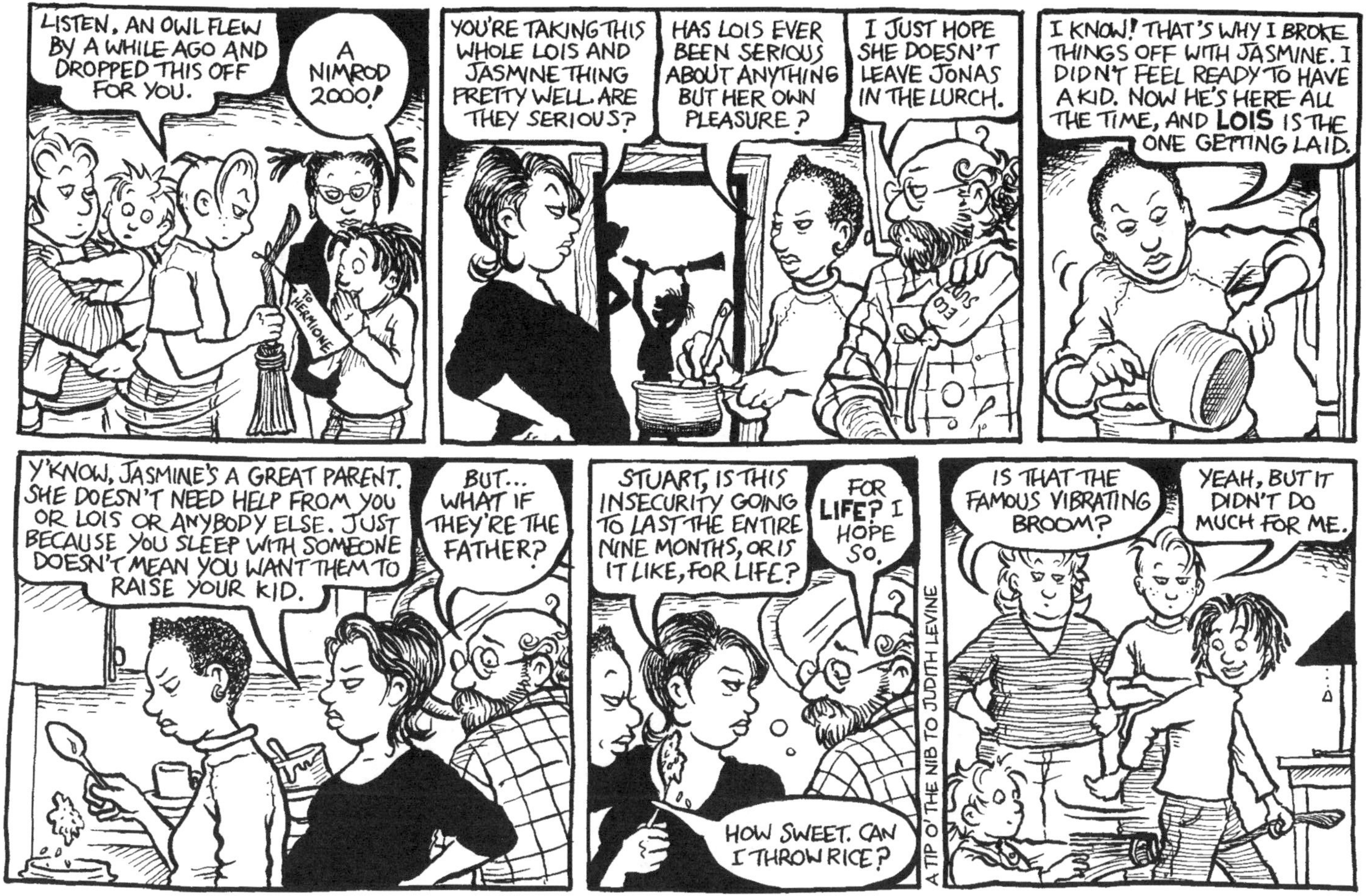
LISTEN, AN OWL FLEW BY A WHILE AGO AND DROPPED THIS OFF FOR YOU.
A NIMROD 2000!
TO HERMIONE
YOU'RE TAKING THIS WHOLE LOIS AND JASMINE THING PRETTY WELL. ARE THEY SERIOUS?
HAS LOIS EVER BEEN SERIOUS ABOUT ANYTHING BUT HER OWN PLEASURE?
I JUST HOPE SHE DOESN'T LEAVE JONAS IN THE LURCH.
ECO SUDS
I KNOW! THAT'S WHY I BROKE THINGS OFF WITH JASMINE. I DIDN'T FEEL READY TO HAVE A KID. NOW HE'S HERE ALL THE TIME, AND LOIS IS THE ONE GETTING LAID.
Y'KNOW, JASMINE'S A GREAT PARENT. SHE DOESN'T NEED HELP FROM YOU OR LOIS OR ANYBODY ELSE. JUST BECAUSE YOU SLEEP WITH SOMEONE DOESN'T MEAN YOU WANT THEM TO RAISE YOUR KID.
BUT... WHAT IF THEY'RE THE FATHER?
STUART, IS THIS INSECURITY GOING TO LAST THE ENTIRE NINE MONTHS, OR IS IT LIKE, FOR LIFE?
FOR LIFE? I HOPE SO.
HOW SWEET. CAN I THROW RICE?
A TIP O' THE NIB TO JUDITH LEVINE
IS THAT THE FAMOUS VIBRATING BROOM?
YEAH, BUT IT DIDN'T DO MUCH FOR ME.

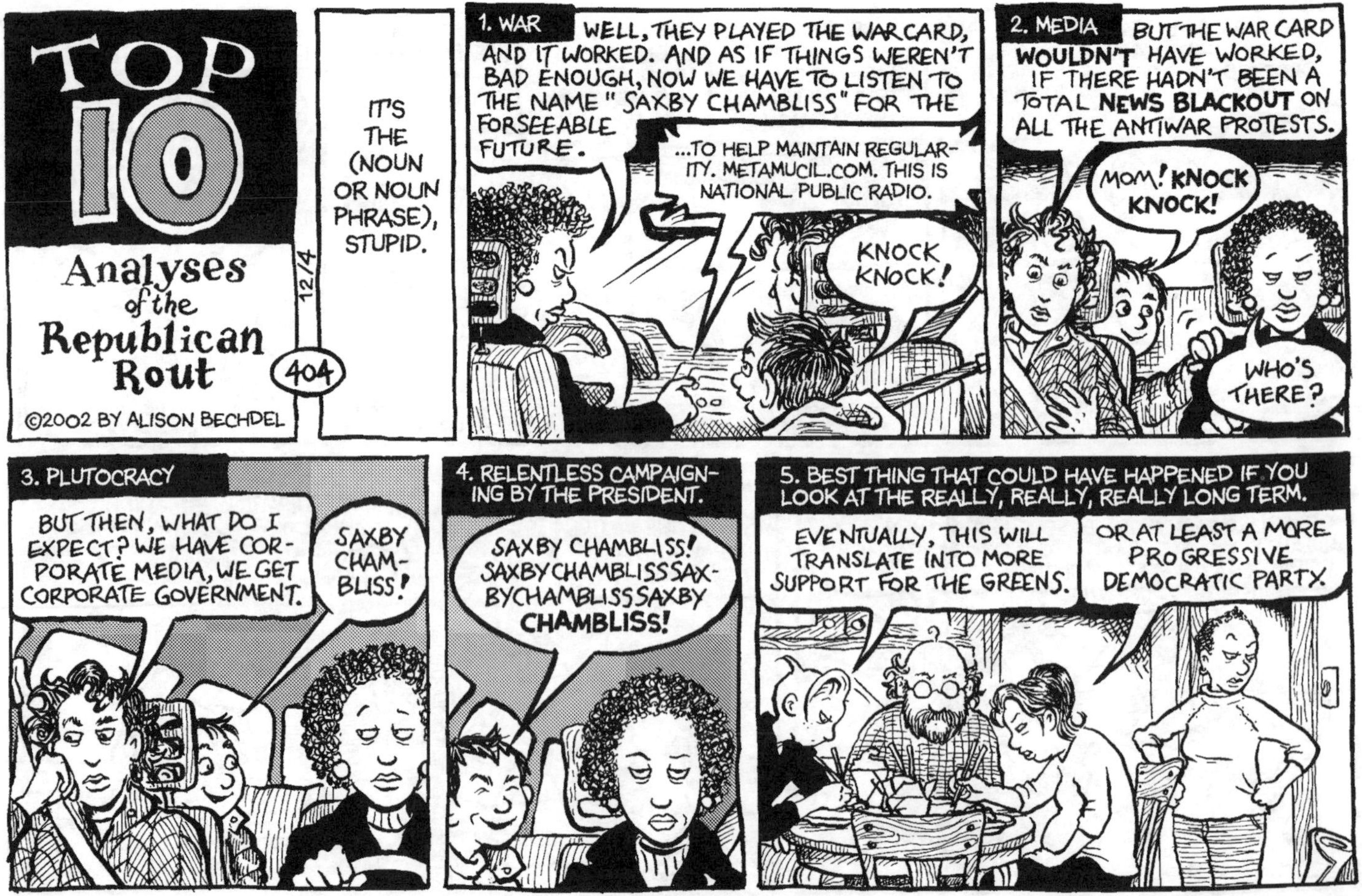

TOP 10
Analyses of the Republican Rout
©2002 BY ALISON BECHDEL
12/4
404
IT'S THE (NOUN OR NOUN PHRASE), STUPID.
1. WAR
WELL, THEY PLAYED THE WAR CARD, AND IT WORKED. AND AS IF THINGS WEREN'T BAD ENOUGH, NOW WE HAVE TO LISTEN TO THE NAME "SAXBY CHAMBLISS" FOR THE FORSEEABLE FUTURE.
...TO HELP MAINTAIN REGULARITY. METAMUCIL.COM. THIS IS NATIONAL PUBLIC RADIO.
KNOCK KNOCK!
2. MEDIA
BUT THE WAR CARD **WOULDN'T** HAVE WORKED, IF THERE HADN'T BEEN A TOTAL **NEWS BLACKOUT** ON ALL THE ANTIWAR PROTESTS.
MOM! **KNOCK KNOCK!**
WHO'S THERE?
3. PLUTOCRACY
BUT THEN, WHAT DO I EXPECT? WE HAVE CORPORATE MEDIA, WE GET CORPORATE GOVERNMENT.
SAXBY CHAMBLISS!
4. RELENTLESS CAMPAIGNING BY THE PRESIDENT.
SAXBY CHAMBLISS! SAXBYCHAMBLISSSAXBYCHAMBLISSSAXBY **CHAMBLISS!**
5. BEST THING THAT COULD HAVE HAPPENED IF YOU LOOK AT THE REALLY, REALLY, REALLY LONG TERM.
EVENTUALLY, THIS WILL TRANSLATE INTO MORE SUPPORT FOR THE GREENS.
OR AT LEAST A MORE PROGRESSIVE DEMOCRATIC PARTY.

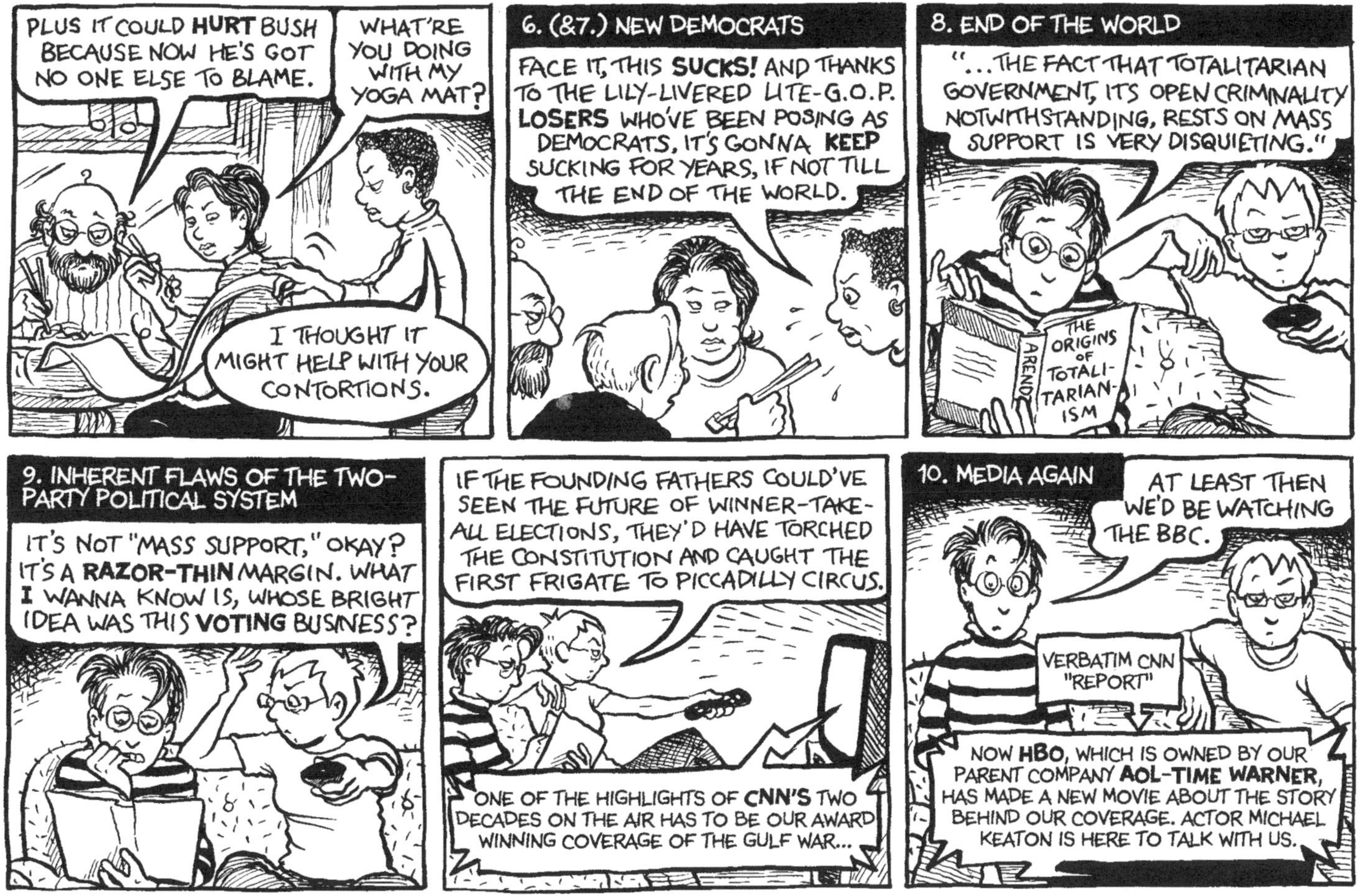

PLUS IT COULD HURT BUSH BECAUSE NOW HE'S GOT NO ONE ELSE TO BLAME.
WHAT'RE YOU DOING WITH MY YOGA MAT?
I THOUGHT IT MIGHT HELP WITH YOUR CONTORTIONS.
6. (&7.) NEW DEMOCRATS
FACE IT, THIS SUCKS! AND THANKS TO THE LILY-LIVERED LITE-G.O.P. LOSERS WHO'VE BEEN POSING AS DEMOCRATS, IT'S GONNA KEEP SUCKING FOR YEARS, IF NOT TILL THE END OF THE WORLD.
8. END OF THE WORLD
"...THE FACT THAT TOTALITARIAN GOVERNMENT, ITS OPEN CRIMINALITY NOTWITHSTANDING, RESTS ON MASS SUPPORT IS VERY DISQUIETING."
ARENDT
THE ORIGINS OF TOTALITARIANISM
9. INHERENT FLAWS OF THE TWO-PARTY POLITICAL SYSTEM
IT'S NOT "MASS SUPPORT," OKAY? IT'S A RAZOR-THIN MARGIN. WHAT I WANNA KNOW IS, WHOSE BRIGHT IDEA WAS THIS VOTING BUSINESS?
IF THE FOUNDING FATHERS COULD'VE SEEN THE FUTURE OF WINNER-TAKE-ALL ELECTIONS, THEY'D HAVE TORCHED THE CONSTITUTION AND CAUGHT THE FIRST FRIGATE TO PICCADILLY CIRCUS.
ONE OF THE HIGHLIGHTS OF CNN'S TWO DECADES ON THE AIR HAS TO BE OUR AWARD WINNING COVERAGE OF THE GULF WAR...
10. MEDIA AGAIN
AT LEAST THEN WE'D BE WATCHING THE BBC.
VERBATIM CNN "REPORT"
NOW HBO, WHICH IS OWNED BY OUR PARENT COMPANY AOL-TIME WARNER, HAS MADE A NEW MOVIE ABOUT THE STORY BEHIND OUR COVERAGE. ACTOR MICHAEL KEATON IS HERE TO TALK WITH US.

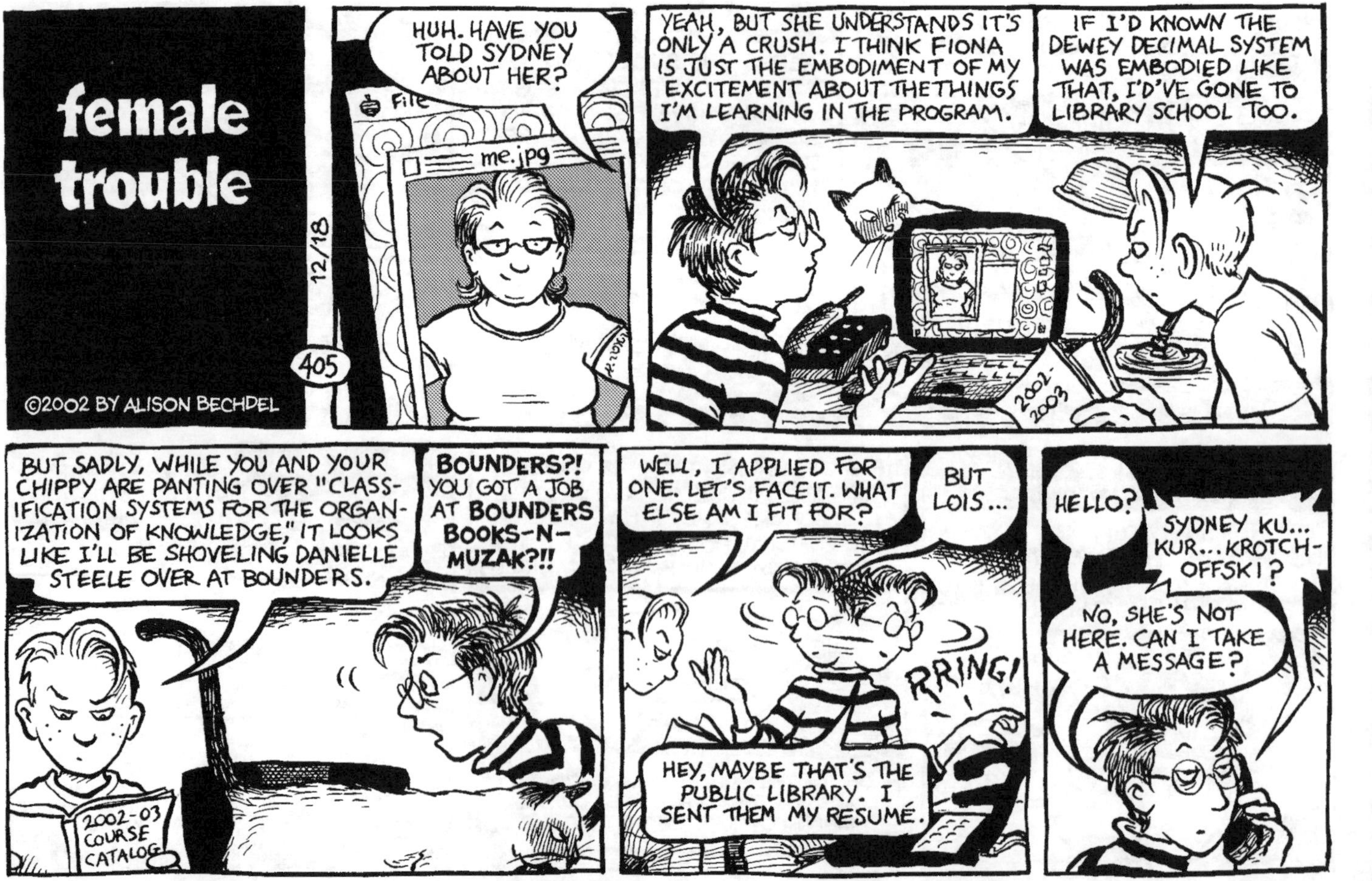
female trouble
©2002 BY ALISON BECHDEL
405
12/18
HUH. HAVE YOU TOLD SYDNEY ABOUT HER?
File
me.jpg
YEAH, BUT SHE UNDERSTANDS IT'S ONLY A CRUSH. I THINK FIONA IS JUST THE EMBODIMENT OF MY EXCITEMENT ABOUT THE THINGS I'M LEARNING IN THE PROGRAM.
IF I'D KNOWN THE DEWEY DECIMAL SYSTEM WAS EMBODIED LIKE THAT, I'D'VE GONE TO LIBRARY SCHOOL TOO.
2002-2003
BUT SADLY, WHILE YOU AND YOUR CHIPPY ARE PANTING OVER "CLASSIFICATION SYSTEMS FOR THE ORGANIZATION OF KNOWLEDGE," IT LOOKS LIKE I'LL BE SHOVELING DANIELLE STEELE OVER AT BOUNDERS.
BOUNDERS?! YOU GOT A JOB AT **BOUNDERS BOOKS-N-MUZAK?!!**
2002-03 COURSE CATALOG
WELL, I APPLIED FOR ONE. LET'S FACE IT. WHAT ELSE AM I FIT FOR?
BUT LOIS...
RRING!
HEY, MAYBE THAT'S THE PUBLIC LIBRARY. I SENT THEM MY RESUMÉ.
HELLO?
SYDNEY KU... KUR... KROTCHOFFSKI?
NO, SHE'S NOT HERE. CAN I TAKE A MESSAGE?

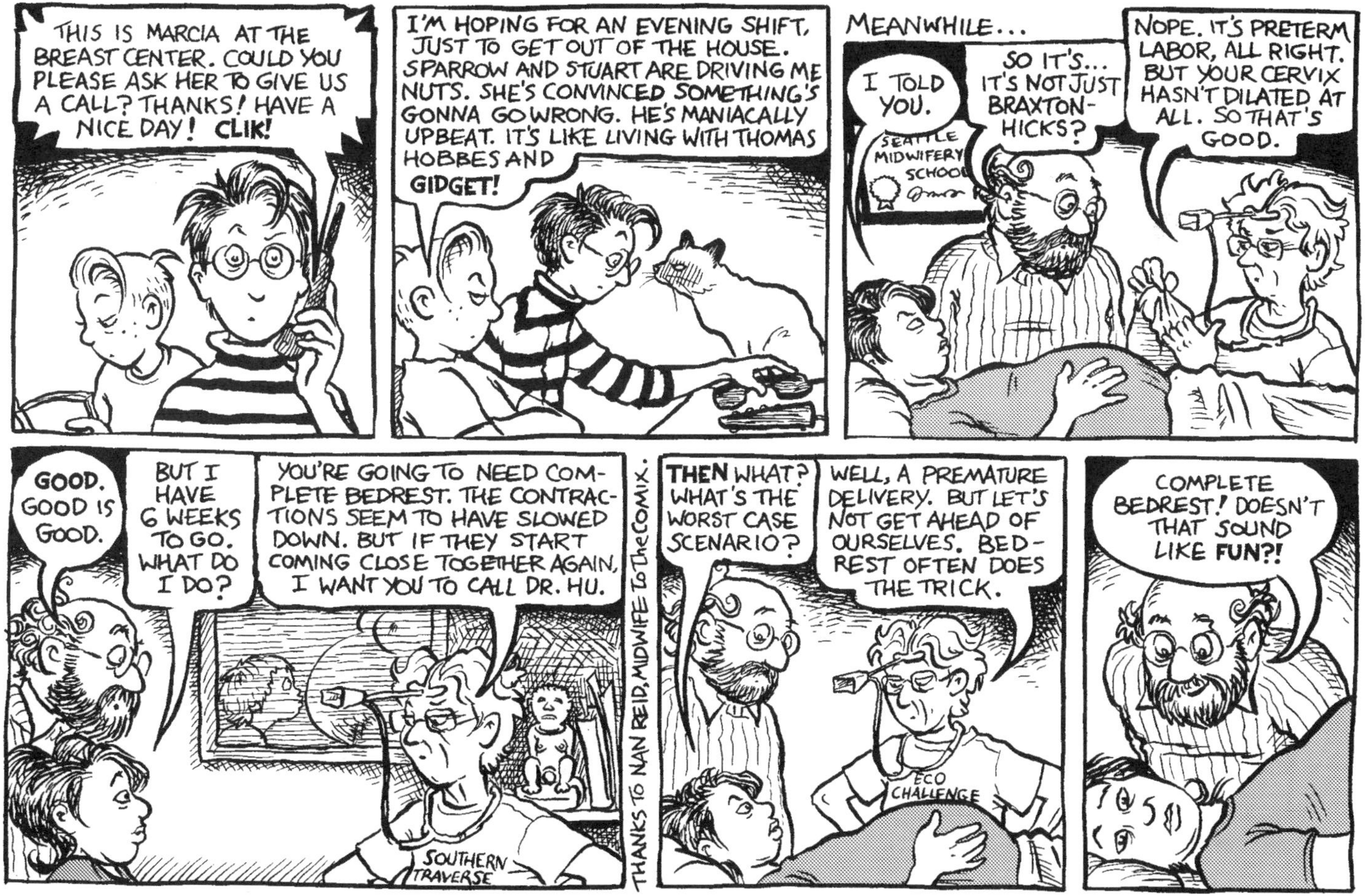
THIS IS MARCIA AT THE BREAST CENTER. COULD YOU PLEASE ASK HER TO GIVE US A CALL? THANKS! HAVE A NICE DAY! CLIK!
I'M HOPING FOR AN EVENING SHIFT, JUST TO GET OUT OF THE HOUSE. SPARROW AND STUART ARE DRIVING ME NUTS. SHE'S CONVINCED SOMETHING'S GONNA GO WRONG. HE'S MANIACALLY UPBEAT. IT'S LIKE LIVING WITH THOMAS HOBBES AND GIDGET!
MEANWHILE...
I TOLD YOU.
SO IT'S... IT'S NOT JUST BRAXTON-HICKS?
NOPE. IT'S PRETERM LABOR, ALL RIGHT. BUT YOUR CERVIX HASN'T DILATED AT ALL. SO THAT'S GOOD.
SEATTLE MIDWIFERY SCHOOL
GOOD. GOOD IS GOOD.
BUT I HAVE 6 WEEKS TO GO. WHAT DO I DO?
YOU'RE GOING TO NEED COMPLETE BEDREST. THE CONTRACTIONS SEEM TO HAVE SLOWED DOWN. BUT IF THEY START COMING CLOSE TOGETHER AGAIN, I WANT YOU TO CALL DR. HU.
SOUTHERN TRAVERSE
THANKS TO NAN REID, MIDWIFE TO THE COMIX.
THEN WHAT? WHAT'S THE WORST CASE SCENARIO?
WELL, A PREMATURE DELIVERY. BUT LET'S NOT GET AHEAD OF OURSELVES. BEDREST OFTEN DOES THE TRICK.
ECO CHALLENGE
COMPLETE BEDREST! DOESN'T THAT SOUND LIKE FUN?!

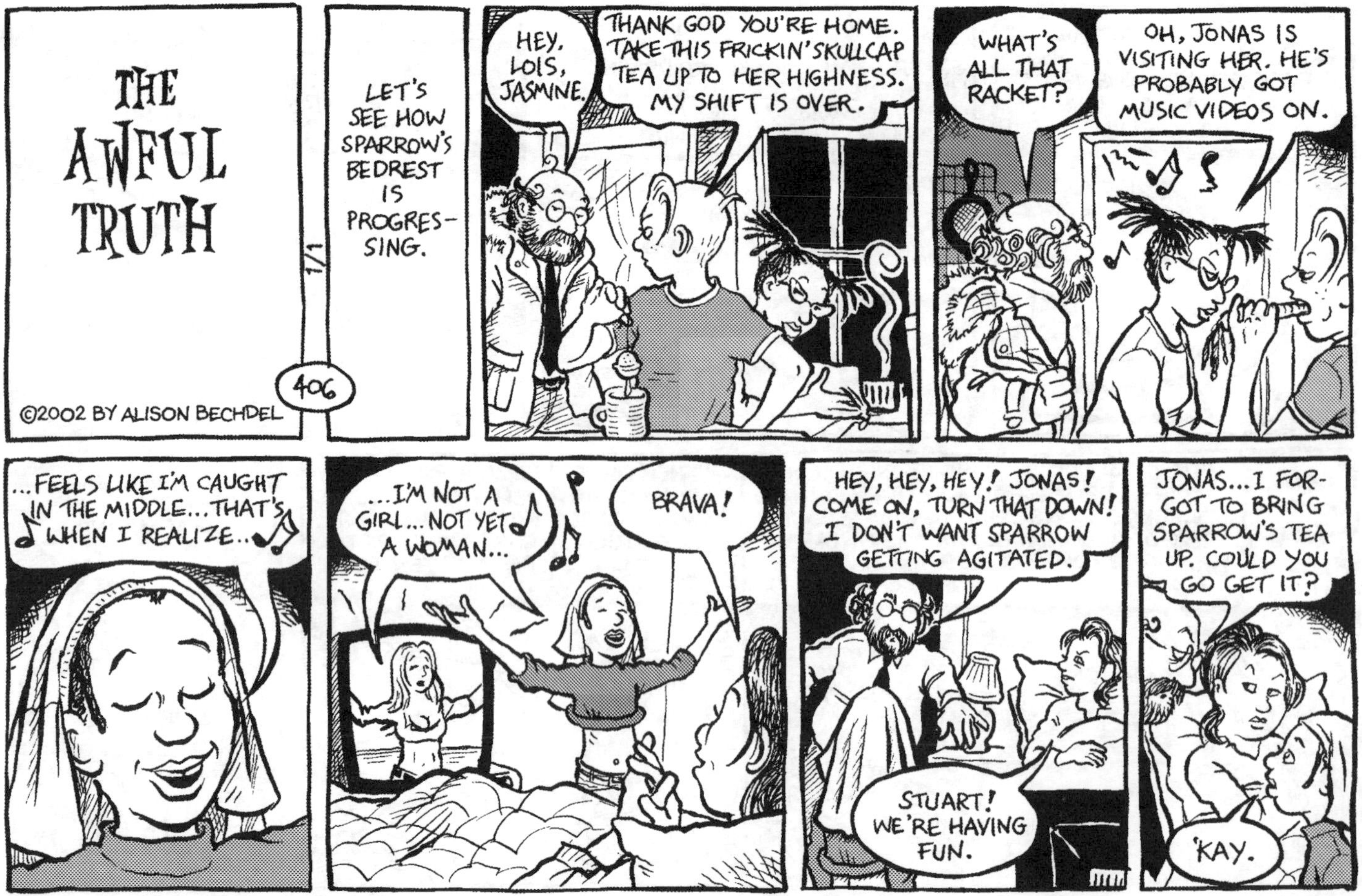
THE AWFUL TRUTH
©2002 BY ALISON BECHDEL
406
1/1
LET'S SEE HOW SPARROW'S BEDREST IS PROGRES-SING.
HEY, LOIS, JASMINE.
THANK GOD YOU'RE HOME. TAKE THIS FRICKIN' SKULLCAP TEA UP TO HER HIGHNESS. MY SHIFT IS OVER.
WHAT'S ALL THAT RACKET?
OH, JONAS IS VISITING HER. HE'S PROBABLY GOT MUSIC VIDEOS ON.
...FEELS LIKE I'M CAUGHT IN THE MIDDLE...THAT'S WHEN I REALIZE...
...I'M NOT A GIRL...NOT YET A WOMAN...
BRAVA!
HEY, HEY, HEY! JONAS! COME ON, TURN THAT DOWN! I DON'T WANT SPARROW GETTING AGITATED.
STUART! WE'RE HAVING FUN.
JONAS...I FOR-GOT TO BRING SPARROW'S TEA UP. COULD YOU GO GET IT?
'KAY.

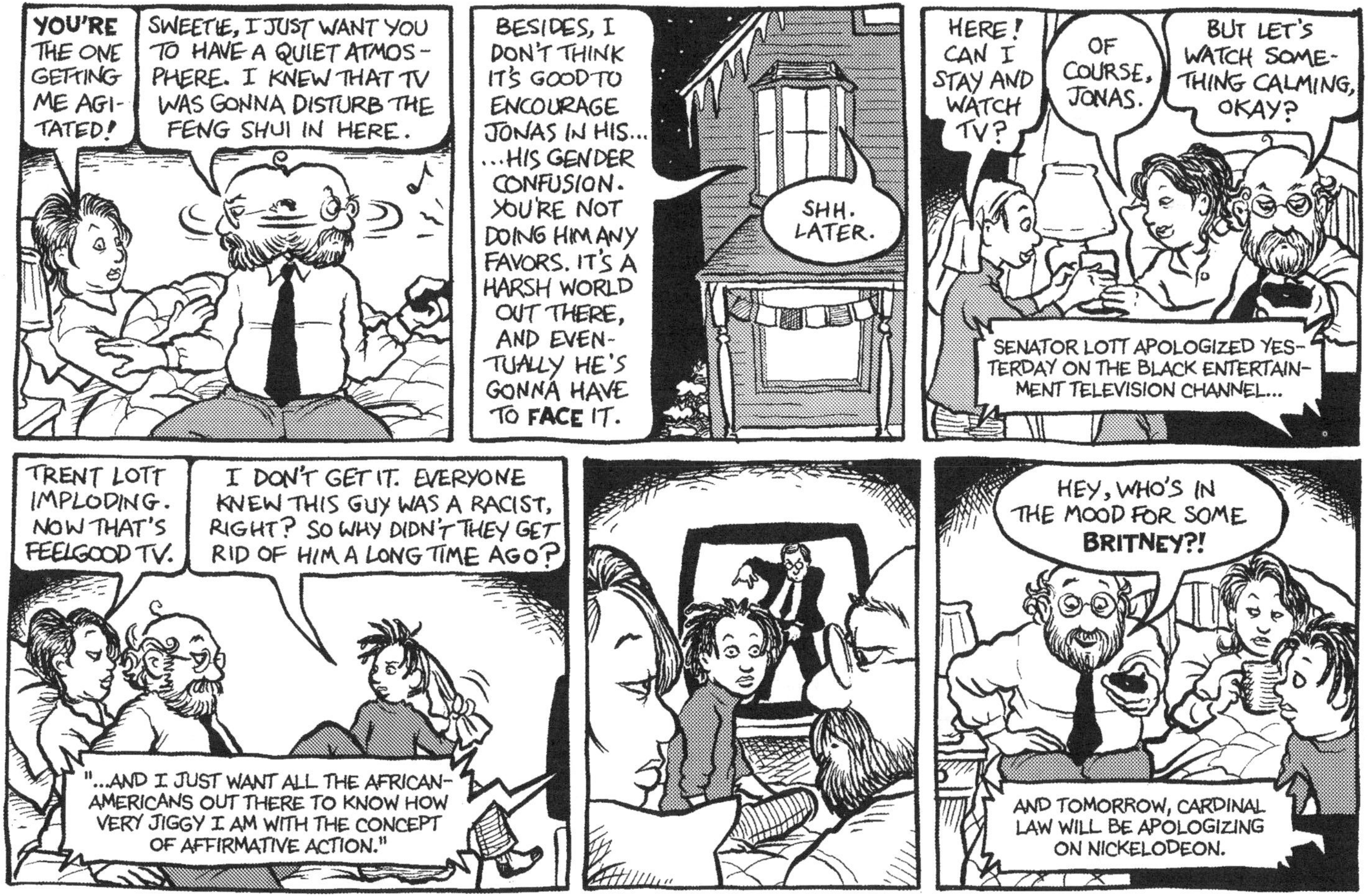
YOU'RE THE ONE GETTING ME AGITATED!
SWEETIE, I JUST WANT YOU TO HAVE A QUIET ATMOSPHERE. I KNEW THAT TV WAS GONNA DISTURB THE FENG SHUI IN HERE.
BESIDES, I DON'T THINK IT'S GOOD TO ENCOURAGE JONAS IN HIS... ...HIS GENDER CONFUSION. YOU'RE NOT DOING HIM ANY FAVORS. IT'S A HARSH WORLD OUT THERE, AND EVENTUALLY HE'S GONNA HAVE TO FACE IT.
SHH. LATER.
HERE! CAN I STAY AND WATCH TV?
OF COURSE, JONAS.
BUT LET'S WATCH SOMETHING CALMING, OKAY?
SENATOR LOTT APOLOGIZED YESTERDAY ON THE BLACK ENTERTAINMENT TELEVISION CHANNEL...
TRENT LOTT IMPLODING. NOW THAT'S FEELGOOD TV.
I DON'T GET IT. EVERYONE KNEW THIS GUY WAS A RACIST, RIGHT? SO WHY DIDN'T THEY GET RID OF HIM A LONG TIME AGO?
"...AND I JUST WANT ALL THE AFRICAN-AMERICANS OUT THERE TO KNOW HOW VERY JIGGY I AM WITH THE CONCEPT OF AFFIRMATIVE ACTION."
HEY, WHO'S IN THE MOOD FOR SOME BRITNEY?!
AND TOMORROW, CARDINAL LAW WILL BE APOLOGIZING ON NICKELODEON.

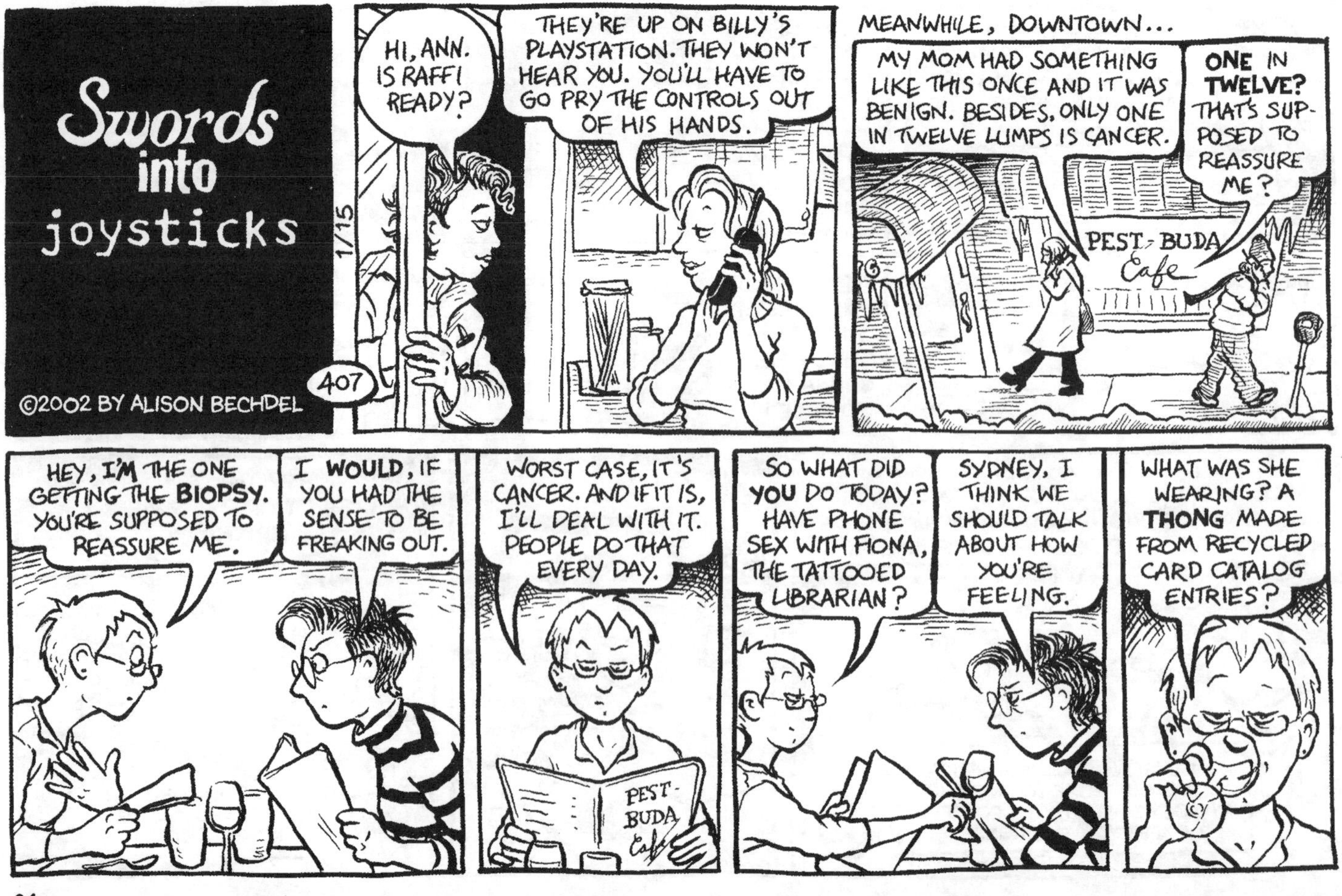

Swords into joysticks
©2002 BY ALISON BECHDEL
407
1/15
HI, ANN. IS RAFFI READY?
THEY'RE UP ON BILLY'S PLAYSTATION. THEY WON'T HEAR YOU. YOU'LL HAVE TO GO PRY THE CONTROLS OUT OF HIS HANDS.
MEANWHILE, DOWNTOWN...
MY MOM HAD SOMETHING LIKE THIS ONCE AND IT WAS BENIGN. BESIDES, ONLY ONE IN TWELVE LUMPS IS CANCER.
ONE IN TWELVE? THAT'S SUPPOSED TO REASSURE ME?
PEST-BUDA Cafe
HEY, I'M THE ONE GETTING THE BIOPSY. YOU'RE SUPPOSED TO REASSURE ME.
I WOULD, IF YOU HAD THE SENSE TO BE FREAKING OUT.
WORST CASE, IT'S CANCER. AND IF IT IS, I'LL DEAL WITH IT. PEOPLE DO THAT EVERY DAY.
PEST-BUDA Cafe
SO WHAT DID YOU DO TODAY? HAVE PHONE SEX WITH FIONA, THE TATTOOED LIBRARIAN?
SYDNEY, I THINK WE SHOULD TALK ABOUT HOW YOU'RE FEELING.
WHAT WAS SHE WEARING? A THONG MADE FROM RECYCLED CARD CATALOG ENTRIES?

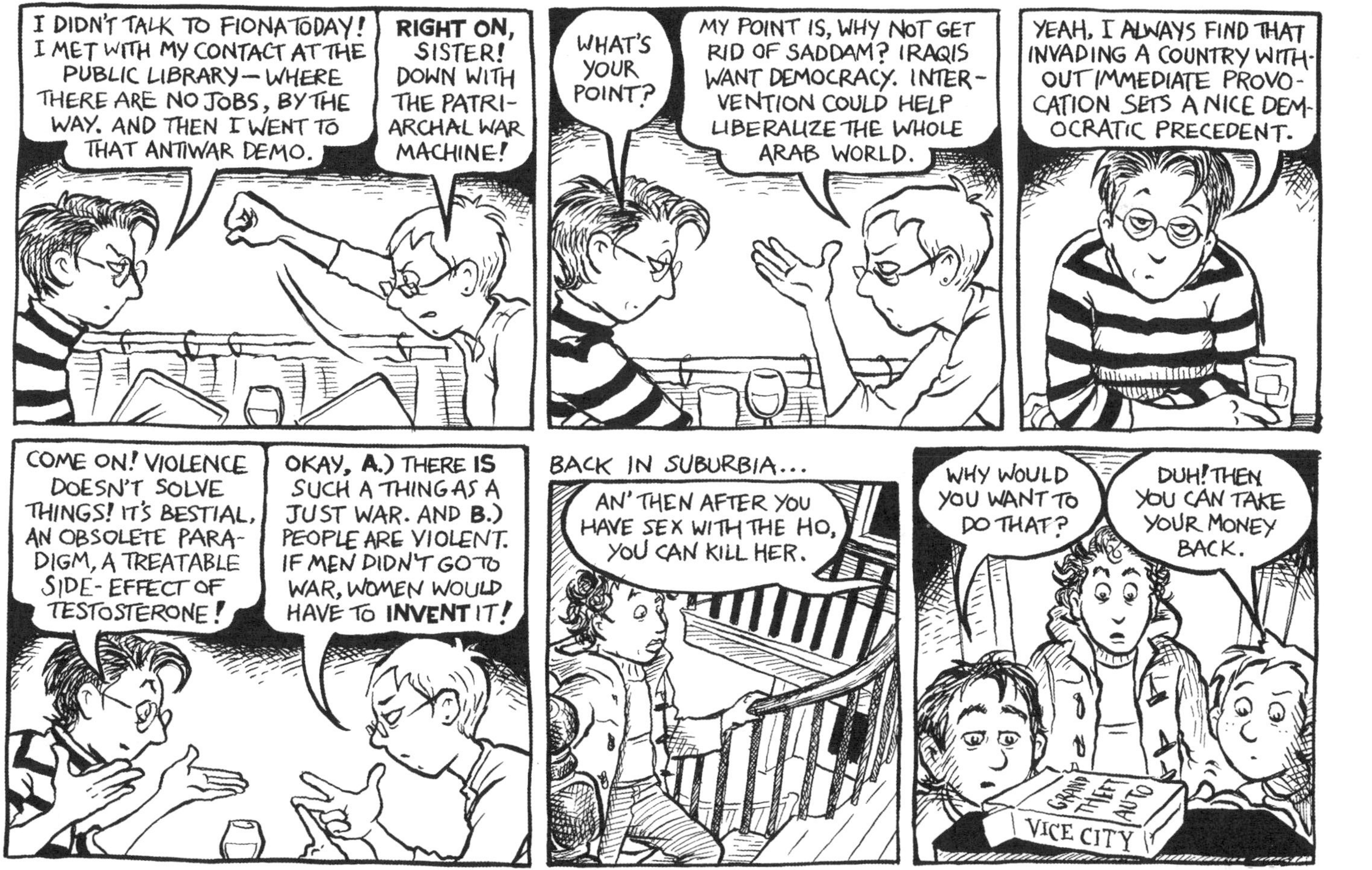
I DIDN'T TALK TO FIONA TODAY! I MET WITH MY CONTACT AT THE PUBLIC LIBRARY— WHERE THERE ARE NO JOBS, BY THE WAY. AND THEN I WENT TO THAT ANTIWAR DEMO.
RIGHT ON, SISTER! DOWN WITH THE PATRIARCHAL WAR MACHINE!
WHAT'S YOUR POINT?
MY POINT IS, WHY NOT GET RID OF SADDAM? IRAQIS WANT DEMOCRACY. INTERVENTION COULD HELP LIBERALIZE THE WHOLE ARAB WORLD.
YEAH, I ALWAYS FIND THAT INVADING A COUNTRY WITHOUT IMMEDIATE PROVOCATION SETS A NICE DEMOCRATIC PRECEDENT.
COME ON! VIOLENCE DOESN'T SOLVE THINGS! IT'S BESTIAL, AN OBSOLETE PARADIGM, A TREATABLE SIDE-EFFECT OF TESTOSTERONE!
OKAY, A.) THERE IS SUCH A THING AS A JUST WAR. AND B.) PEOPLE ARE VIOLENT. IF MEN DIDN'T GO TO WAR, WOMEN WOULD HAVE TO INVENT IT!
BACK IN SUBURBIA...
AN' THEN AFTER YOU HAVE SEX WITH THE HO, YOU CAN KILL HER.
WHY WOULD YOU WANT TO DO THAT?
DUH! THEN YOU CAN TAKE YOUR MONEY BACK.
GRAND THEFT AUTO
VICE CITY

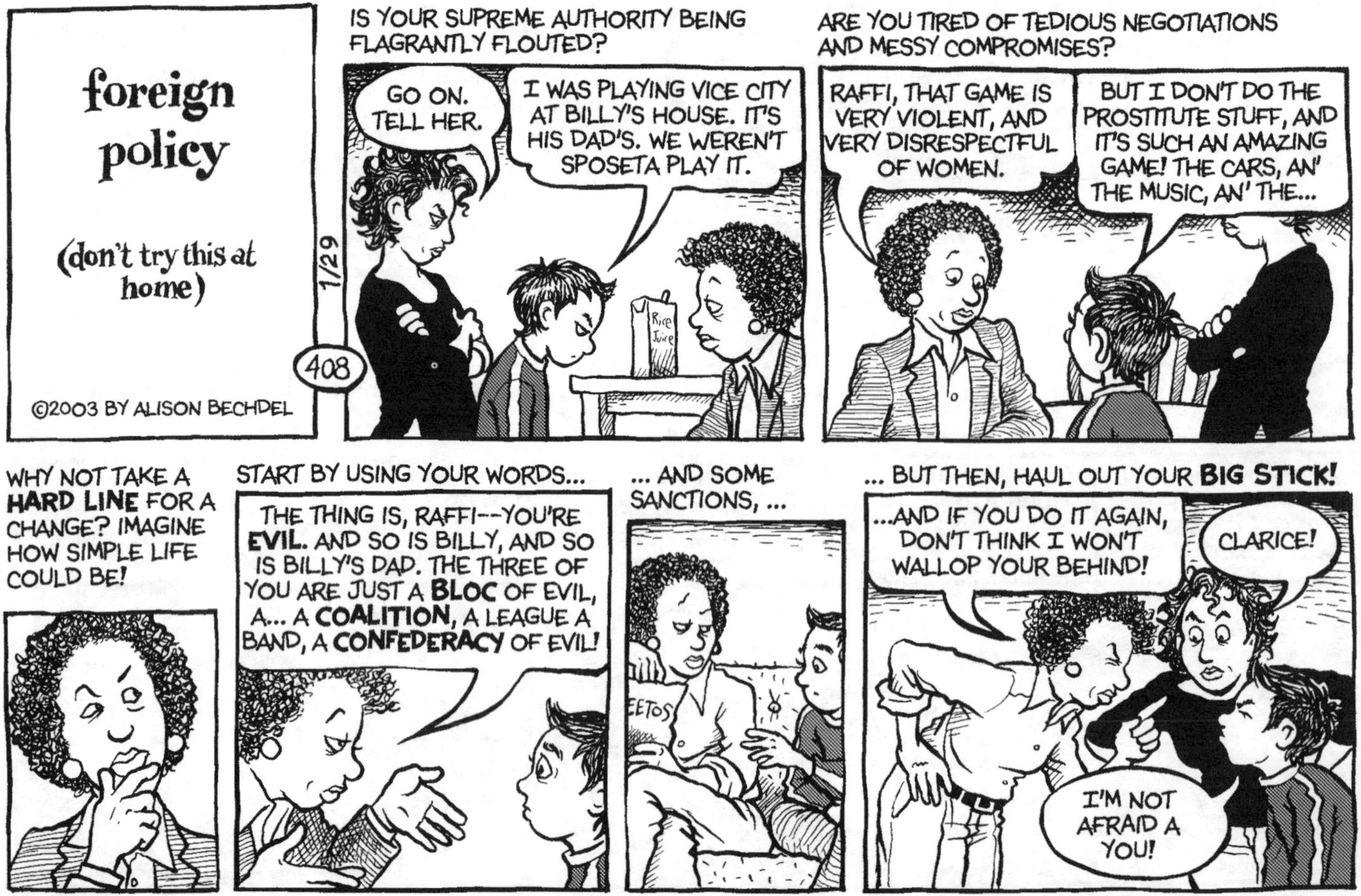
foreign policy
(don't try this at home)
©2003 BY ALISON BECHDEL
408
1/29
IS YOUR SUPREME AUTHORITY BEING FLAGRANTLY FLOUTED?
GO ON. TELL HER.
I WAS PLAYING VICE CITY AT BILLY'S HOUSE. IT'S HIS DAD'S. WE WEREN'T SPOSETA PLAY IT.
Rice Juice
ARE YOU TIRED OF TEDIOUS NEGOTIATIONS AND MESSY COMPROMISES?
RAFFI, THAT GAME IS VERY VIOLENT, AND VERY DISRESPECTFUL OF WOMEN.
BUT I DON'T DO THE PROSTITUTE STUFF, AND IT'S SUCH AN AMAZING GAME! THE CARS, AN' THE MUSIC, AN' THE...
WHY NOT TAKE A **HARD LINE** FOR A CHANGE? IMAGINE HOW SIMPLE LIFE COULD BE!
START BY USING YOUR WORDS...
THE THING IS, RAFFI--YOU'RE **EVIL.** AND SO IS BILLY, AND SO IS BILLY'S DAD. THE THREE OF YOU ARE JUST A **BLOC** OF EVIL, A... A **COALITION**, A LEAGUE A BAND, A **CONFEDERACY** OF EVIL!
... AND SOME SANCTIONS, ...
EETOS
... BUT THEN, HAUL OUT YOUR **BIG STICK!**
...AND IF YOU DO IT AGAIN, DON'T THINK I WON'T WALLOP YOUR BEHIND!
CLARICE!
I'M NOT AFRAID A YOU!

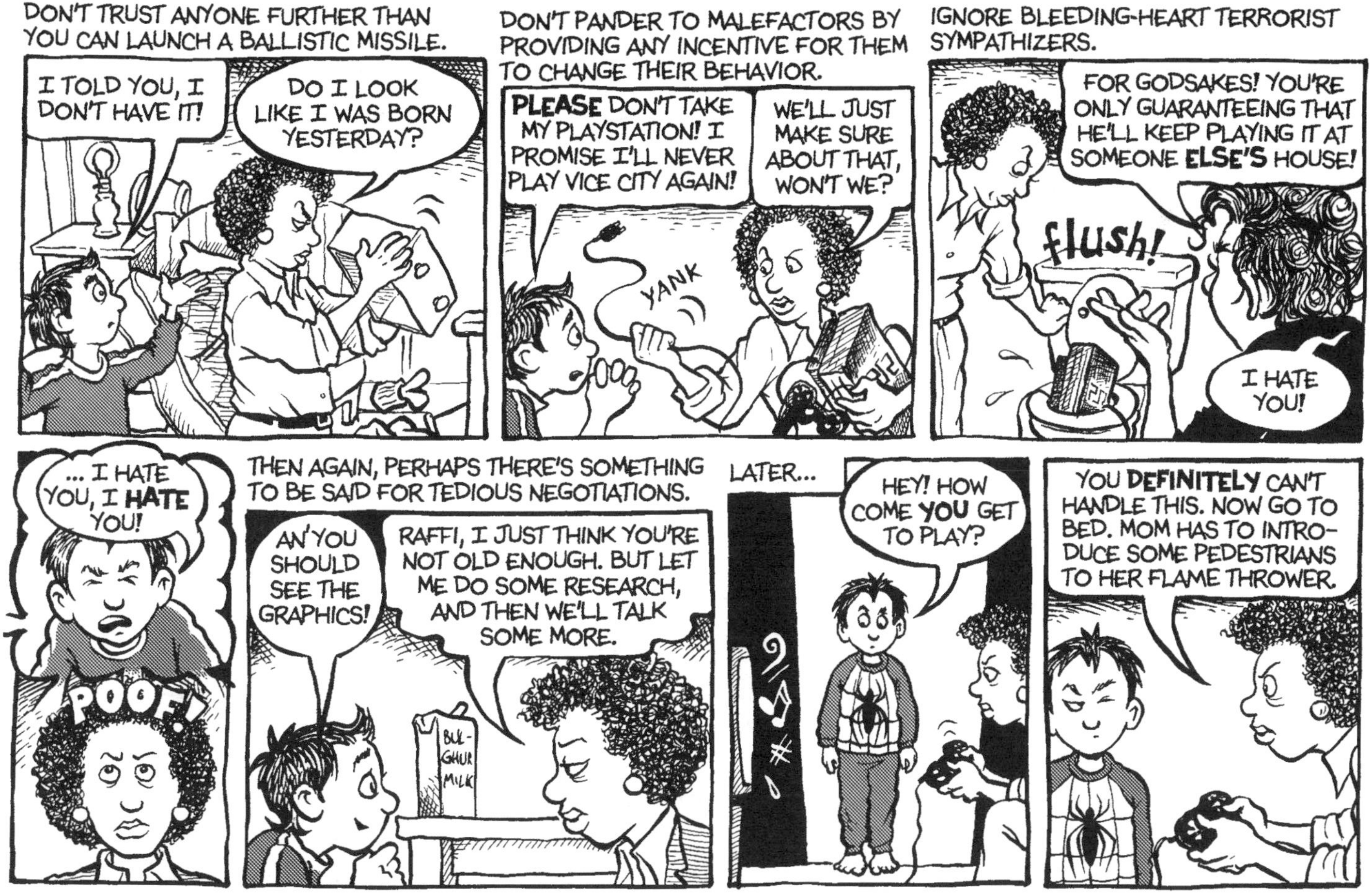

DON'T TRUST ANYONE FURTHER THAN YOU CAN LAUNCH A BALLISTIC MISSILE.
I TOLD YOU, I DON'T HAVE IT!
DO I LOOK LIKE I WAS BORN YESTERDAY?
DON'T PANDER TO MALEFACTORS BY PROVIDING ANY INCENTIVE FOR THEM TO CHANGE THEIR BEHAVIOR.
PLEASE DON'T TAKE MY PLAYSTATION! I PROMISE I'LL NEVER PLAY VICE CITY AGAIN!
WE'LL JUST MAKE SURE ABOUT THAT, WON'T WE?
YANK
IGNORE BLEEDING-HEART TERRORIST SYMPATHIZERS.
FOR GODSAKES! YOU'RE ONLY GUARANTEEING THAT HE'LL KEEP PLAYING IT AT SOMEONE ELSE'S HOUSE!
flush!
I HATE YOU!
... I HATE YOU, I HATE YOU!
POOF!
THEN AGAIN, PERHAPS THERE'S SOMETHING TO BE SAID FOR TEDIOUS NEGOTIATIONS.
AN' YOU SHOULD SEE THE GRAPHICS!
RAFFI, I JUST THINK YOU'RE NOT OLD ENOUGH. BUT LET ME DO SOME RESEARCH, AND THEN WE'LL TALK SOME MORE.
BUL-GHUR MILK
LATER...
HEY! HOW COME YOU GET TO PLAY?
YOU DEFINITELY CAN'T HANDLE THIS. NOW GO TO BED. MOM HAS TO INTRODUCE SOME PEDESTRIANS TO HER FLAME THROWER.

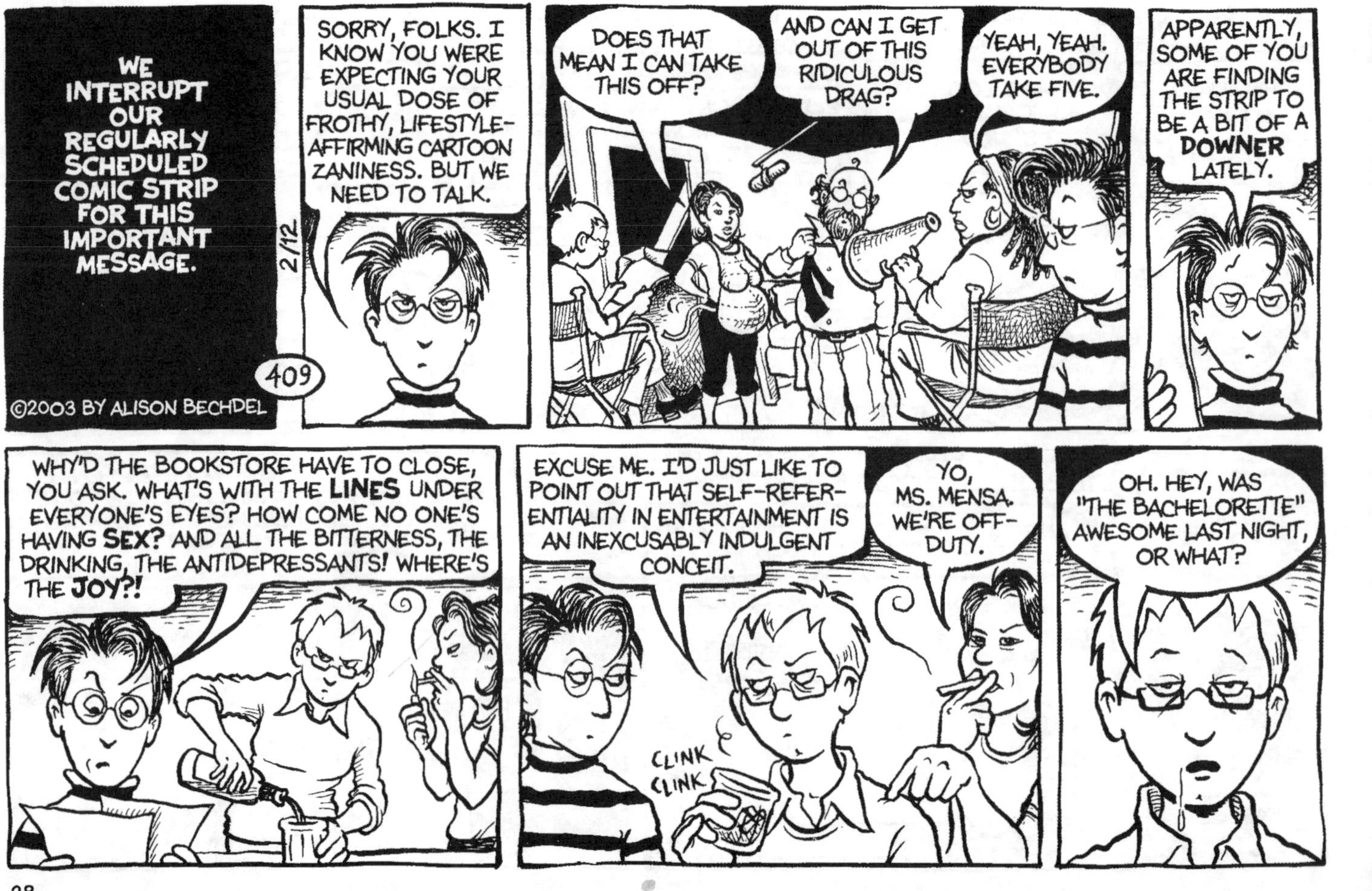
WE INTERRUPT OUR REGULARLY SCHEDULED COMIC STRIP FOR THIS IMPORTANT MESSAGE.
409
2/12
©2003 BY ALISON BECHDEL
SORRY, FOLKS. I KNOW YOU WERE EXPECTING YOUR USUAL DOSE OF FROTHY, LIFESTYLE-AFFIRMING CARTOON ZANINESS. BUT WE NEED TO TALK.
DOES THAT MEAN I CAN TAKE THIS OFF?
AND CAN I GET OUT OF THIS RIDICULOUS DRAG?
YEAH, YEAH. EVERYBODY TAKE FIVE.
APPARENTLY, SOME OF YOU ARE FINDING THE STRIP TO BE A BIT OF A **DOWNER** LATELY.
WHY'D THE BOOKSTORE HAVE TO CLOSE, YOU ASK. WHAT'S WITH THE **LINES** UNDER EVERYONE'S EYES? HOW COME NO ONE'S HAVING **SEX?** AND ALL THE BITTERNESS, THE DRINKING, THE ANTIDEPRESSANTS! WHERE'S THE **JOY?!**
EXCUSE ME. I'D JUST LIKE TO POINT OUT THAT SELF-REFERENTIALITY IN ENTERTAINMENT IS AN INEXCUSABLY INDULGENT CONCEIT.
YO, MS. MENSA. WE'RE OFF-DUTY.
CLINK CLINK
OH. HEY, WAS "THE BACHELORETTE" AWESOME LAST NIGHT, OR WHAT?

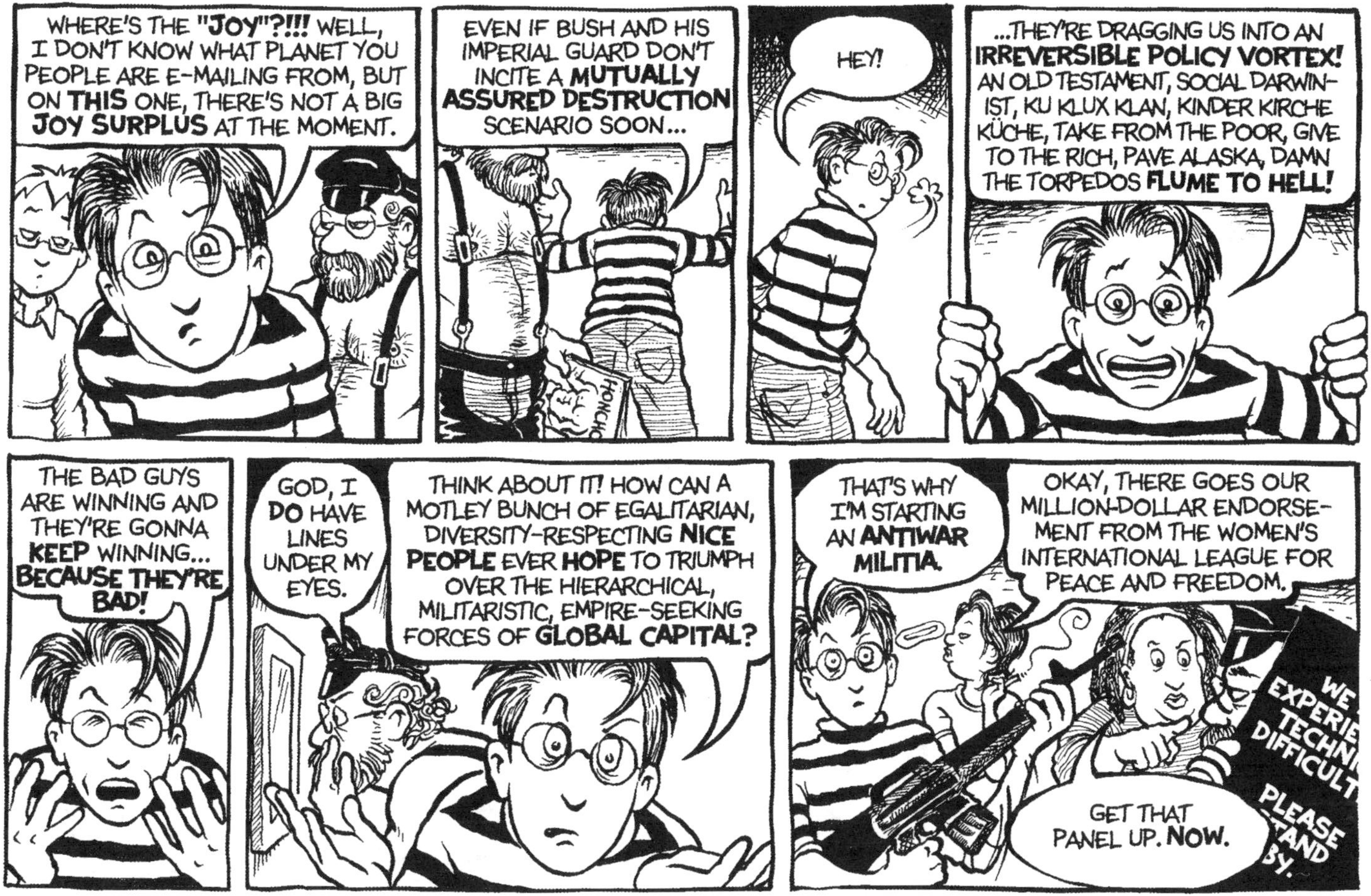

WHERE'S THE "JOY"?!!! WELL, I DON'T KNOW WHAT PLANET YOU PEOPLE ARE E-MAILING FROM, BUT ON THIS ONE, THERE'S NOT A BIG JOY SURPLUS AT THE MOMENT.
EVEN IF BUSH AND HIS IMPERIAL GUARD DON'T INCITE A MUTUALLY ASSURED DESTRUCTION SCENARIO SOON...
PONCHO
HEY!
...THEY'RE DRAGGING US INTO AN IRREVERSIBLE POLICY VORTEX! AN OLD TESTAMENT, SOCIAL DARWINIST, KU KLUX KLAN, KINDER KIRCHE KÜCHE, TAKE FROM THE POOR, GIVE TO THE RICH, PAVE ALASKA, DAMN THE TORPEDOS FLUME TO HELL!
THE BAD GUYS ARE WINNING AND THEY'RE GONNA KEEP WINNING... BECAUSE THEY'RE BAD!
GOD, I DO HAVE LINES UNDER MY EYES.
THINK ABOUT IT! HOW CAN A MOTLEY BUNCH OF EGALITARIAN, DIVERSITY-RESPECTING NICE PEOPLE EVER HOPE TO TRIUMPH OVER THE HIERARCHICAL, MILITARISTIC, EMPIRE-SEEKING FORCES OF GLOBAL CAPITAL?
THAT'S WHY I'M STARTING AN ANTIWAR MILITIA.
OKAY, THERE GOES OUR MILLION-DOLLAR ENDORSEMENT FROM THE WOMEN'S INTERNATIONAL LEAGUE FOR PEACE AND FREEDOM.
GET THAT PANEL UP. NOW.
WE EXPERIE TECHNI DIFFICULT PLEASE TAND BY.

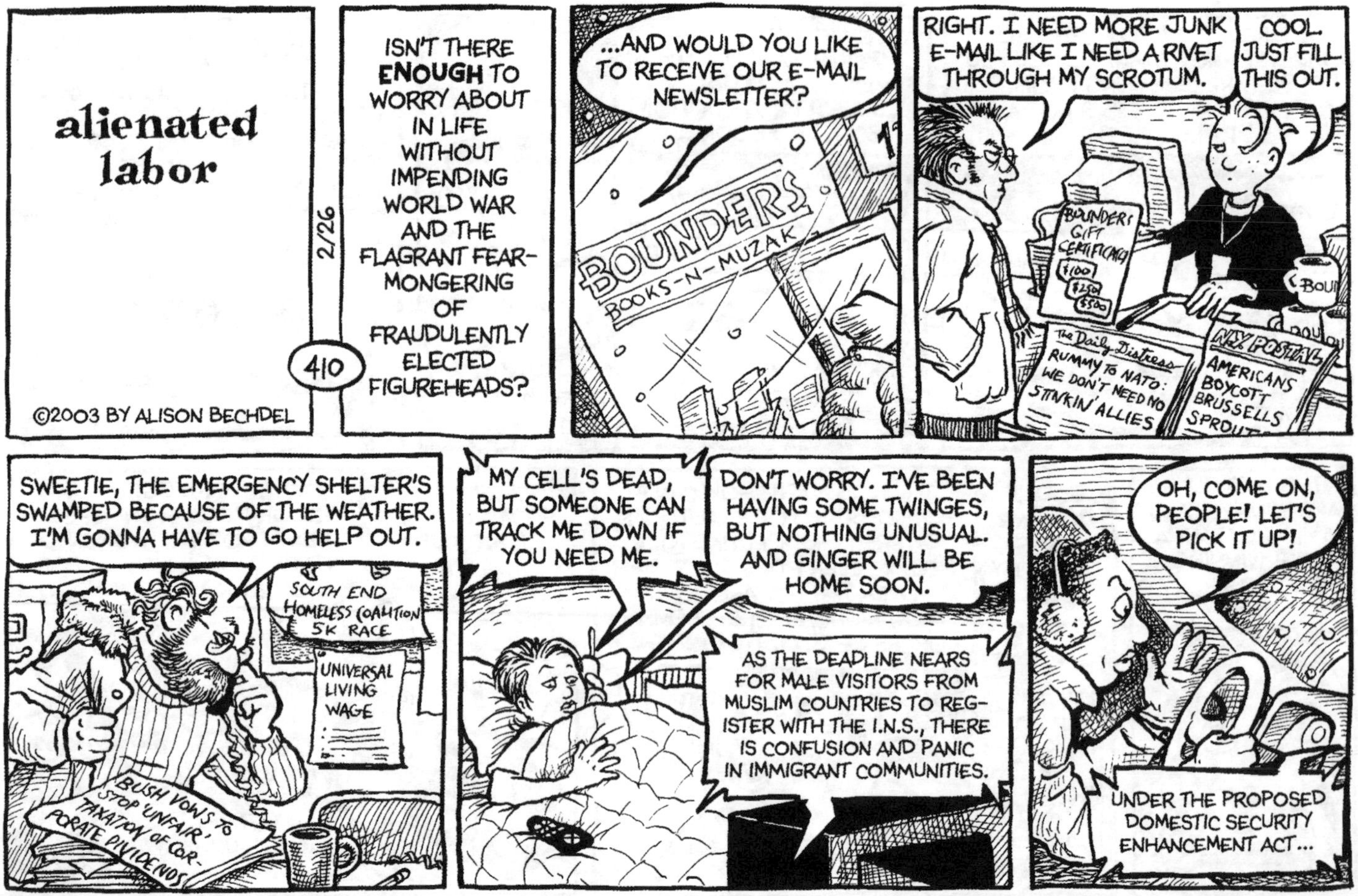
alienated labor
©2003 BY ALISON BECHDEL
410
2/26
ISN'T THERE **ENOUGH** TO WORRY ABOUT IN LIFE WITHOUT IMPENDING WORLD WAR AND THE FLAGRANT FEAR-MONGERING OF FRAUDULENTLY ELECTED FIGUREHEADS?
...AND WOULD YOU LIKE TO RECEIVE OUR E-MAIL NEWSLETTER?
BOUNDERS BOOKS-N-MUZAK
RIGHT. I NEED MORE JUNK E-MAIL LIKE I NEED A RIVET THROUGH MY SCROTUM.
COOL. JUST FILL THIS OUT.
BOUNDERS GIFT CERTIFICATES $100 $250 $500
The Daily Distress
RUMMY TO NATO: WE DON'T NEED NO STINKIN' ALLIES
NY POSTAL
AMERICANS BOYCOTT BRUSSELLS SPROUTS
SWEETIE, THE EMERGENCY SHELTER'S SWAMPED BECAUSE OF THE WEATHER. I'M GONNA HAVE TO GO HELP OUT.
SOUTH END HOMELESS COALITION 5K RACE
UNIVERSAL LIVING WAGE
BUSH VOWS TO STOP 'UNFAIR' TAXATION OF CORPORATE DIVIDENDS
MY CELL'S DEAD, BUT SOMEONE CAN TRACK ME DOWN IF YOU NEED ME.
DON'T WORRY. I'VE BEEN HAVING SOME TWINGES, BUT NOTHING UNUSUAL. AND GINGER WILL BE HOME SOON.
AS THE DEADLINE NEARS FOR MALE VISITORS FROM MUSLIM COUNTRIES TO REGISTER WITH THE I.N.S., THERE IS CONFUSION AND PANIC IN IMMIGRANT COMMUNITIES.
OH, COME ON, PEOPLE! LET'S PICK IT UP!
UNDER THE PROPOSED DOMESTIC SECURITY ENHANCEMENT ACT...

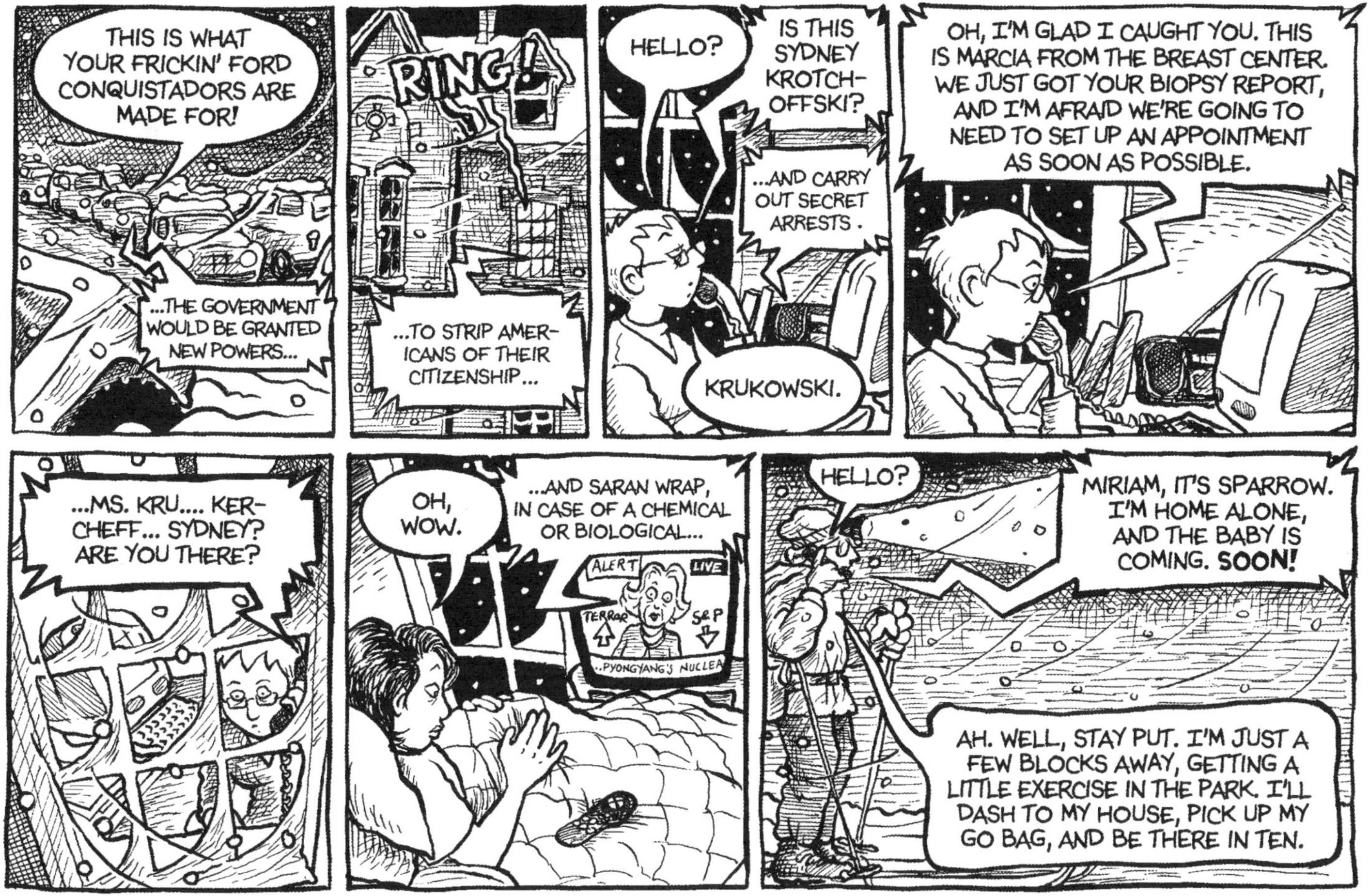

THIS IS WHAT YOUR FRICKIN' FORD CONQUISTADORS ARE MADE FOR!
...THE GOVERNMENT WOULD BE GRANTED NEW POWERS...
RING!
...TO STRIP AMER-ICANS OF THEIR CITIZENSHIP...
HELLO?
IS THIS SYDNEY KROTCH-OFFSKI?
...AND CARRY OUT SECRET ARRESTS.
KRUKOWSKI.
OH, I'M GLAD I CAUGHT YOU. THIS IS MARCIA FROM THE BREAST CENTER. WE JUST GOT YOUR BIOPSY REPORT, AND I'M AFRAID WE'RE GOING TO NEED TO SET UP AN APPOINTMENT AS SOON AS POSSIBLE.
...MS. KRU.... KER-CHEFF... SYDNEY? ARE YOU THERE?
OH, WOW.
...AND SARAN WRAP, IN CASE OF A CHEMICAL OR BIOLOGICAL...
ALERT
LIVE
TERROR
S&P
..PYONGYANG'S NUCLEA
HELLO?
MIRIAM, IT'S SPARROW. I'M HOME ALONE, AND THE BABY IS COMING. SOON!
AH. WELL, STAY PUT. I'M JUST A FEW BLOCKS AWAY, GETTING A LITTLE EXERCISE IN THE PARK. I'LL DASH TO MY HOUSE, PICK UP MY GO BAG, AND BE THERE IN TEN.

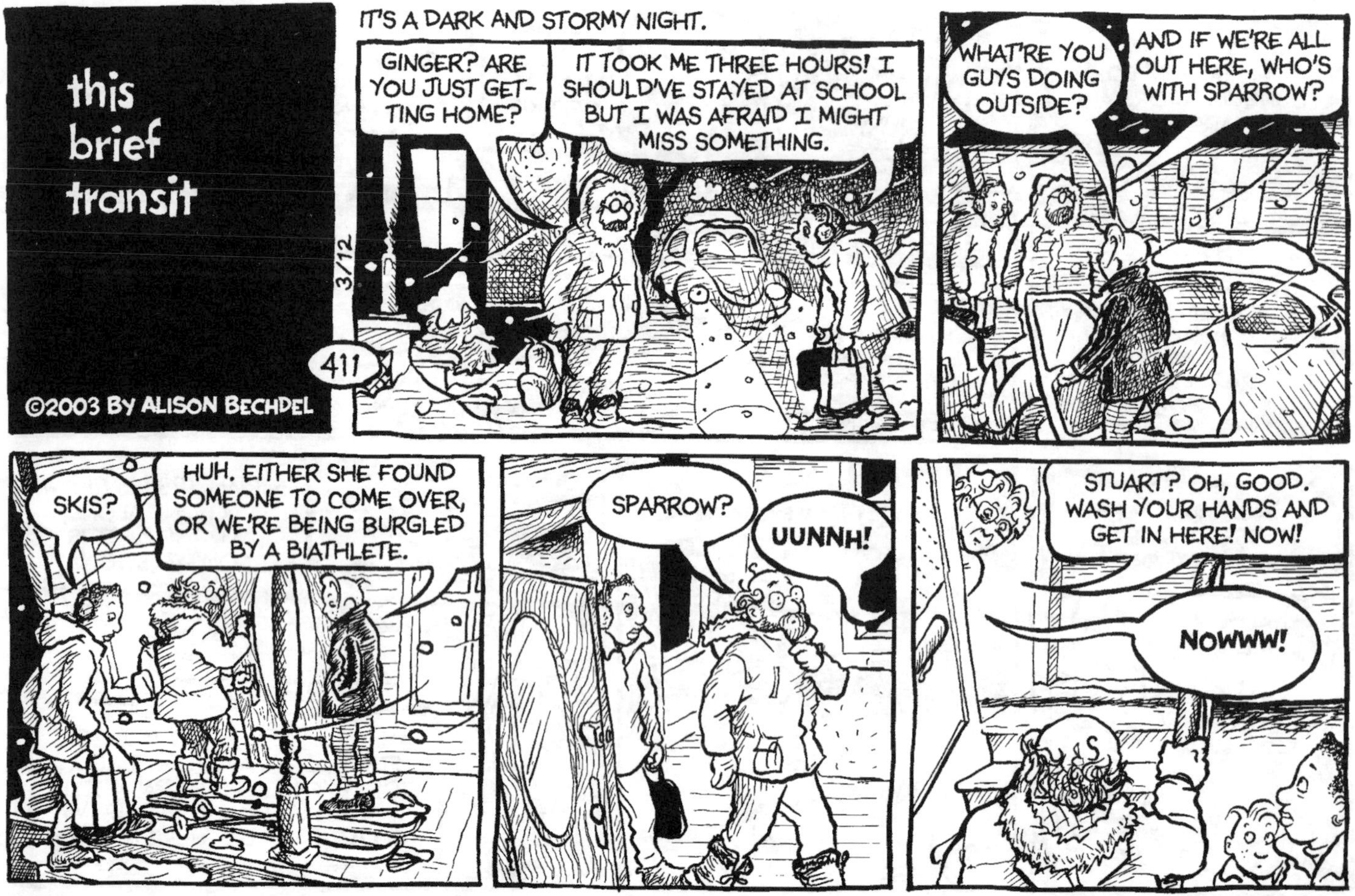
this brief transit
©2003 BY ALISON BECHDEL
411
3/12
IT'S A DARK AND STORMY NIGHT.
GINGER? ARE YOU JUST GETTING HOME?
IT TOOK ME THREE HOURS! I SHOULD'VE STAYED AT SCHOOL BUT I WAS AFRAID I MIGHT MISS SOMETHING.
WHAT'RE YOU GUYS DOING OUTSIDE?
AND IF WE'RE ALL OUT HERE, WHO'S WITH SPARROW?
SKIS?
HUH. EITHER SHE FOUND SOMEONE TO COME OVER, OR WE'RE BEING BURGLED BY A BIATHLETE.
SPARROW?
UUNNH!
STUART? OH, GOOD. WASH YOUR HANDS AND GET IN HERE! NOW!
NOWWW!

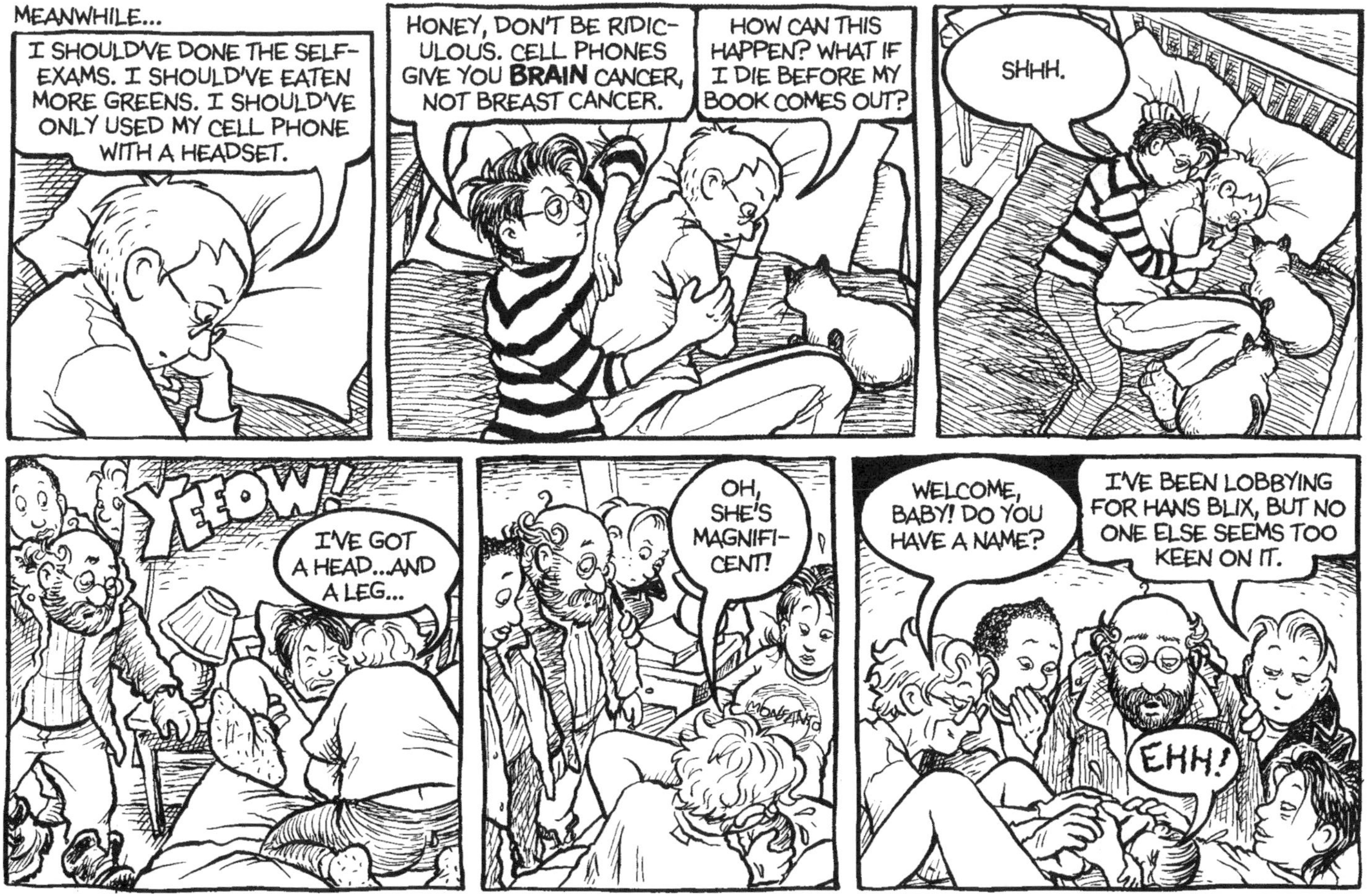
MEANWHILE...
I SHOULD'VE DONE THE SELF-EXAMS. I SHOULD'VE EATEN MORE GREENS. I SHOULD'VE ONLY USED MY CELL PHONE WITH A HEADSET.
HONEY, DON'T BE RIDICULOUS. CELL PHONES GIVE YOU **BRAIN** CANCER, NOT BREAST CANCER.
HOW CAN THIS HAPPEN? WHAT IF I DIE BEFORE MY BOOK COMES OUT?
SHHH.
YEEOW!
I'VE GOT A HEAD...AND A LEG...
OH, SHE'S MAGNIFICENT!
WELCOME, BABY! DO YOU HAVE A NAME?
I'VE BEEN LOBBYING FOR HANS BLIX, BUT NO ONE ELSE SEEMS TOO KEEN ON IT.
EHH!

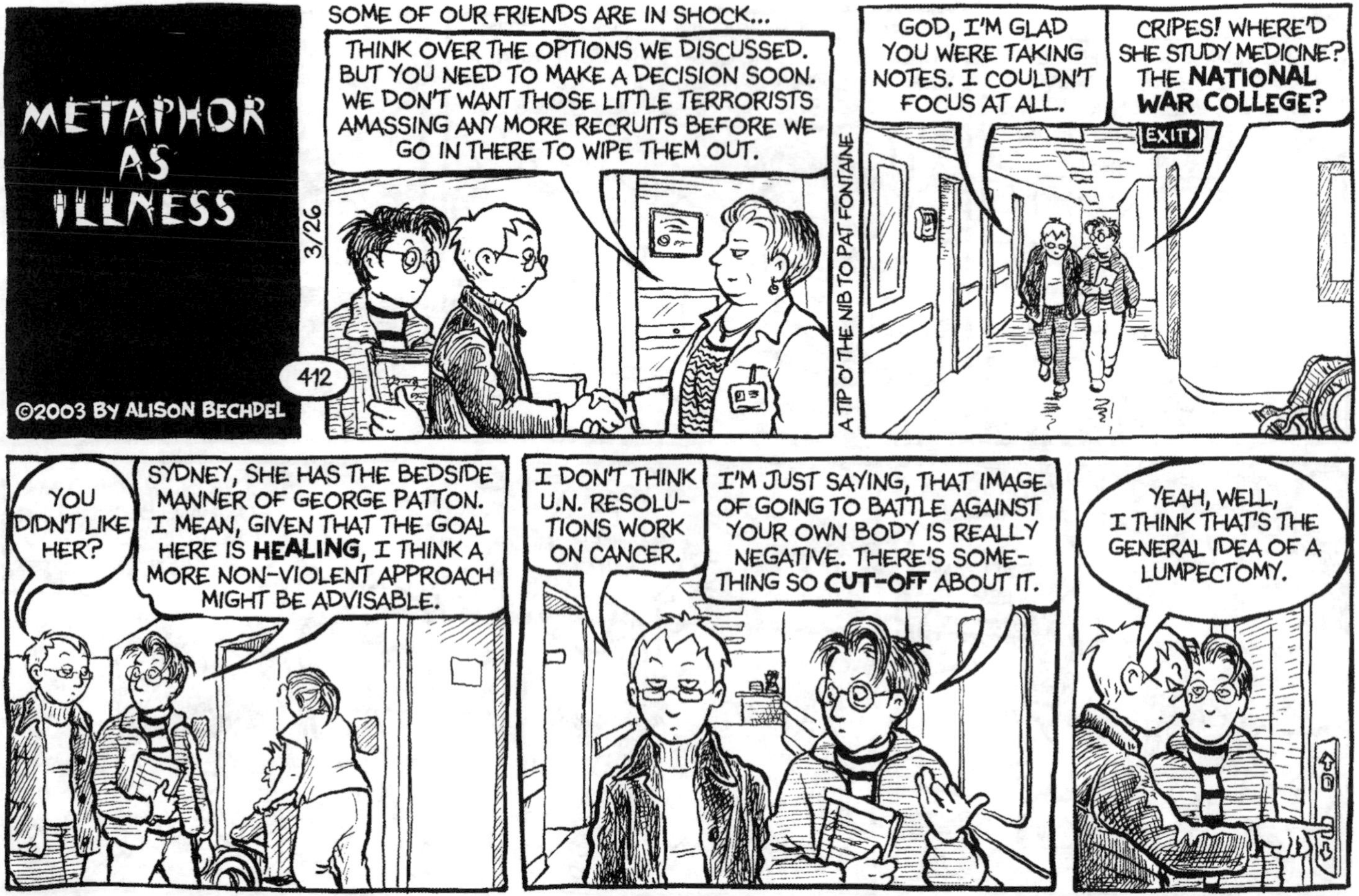

METAPHOR AS ILLNESS
3/26
412
©2003 BY ALISON BECHDEL
SOME OF OUR FRIENDS ARE IN SHOCK...
THINK OVER THE OPTIONS WE DISCUSSED. BUT YOU NEED TO MAKE A DECISION SOON. WE DON'T WANT THOSE LITTLE TERRORISTS AMASSING ANY MORE RECRUITS BEFORE WE GO IN THERE TO WIPE THEM OUT.
A TIP O' THE NIB TO PAT FONTAINE
GOD, I'M GLAD YOU WERE TAKING NOTES. I COULDN'T FOCUS AT ALL.
CRIPES! WHERE'D SHE STUDY MEDICINE? THE **NATIONAL WAR COLLEGE?**
EXIT
YOU DIDN'T LIKE HER?
SYDNEY, SHE HAS THE BEDSIDE MANNER OF GEORGE PATTON. I MEAN, GIVEN THAT THE GOAL HERE IS **HEALING**, I THINK A MORE NON-VIOLENT APPROACH MIGHT BE ADVISABLE.
I DON'T THINK U.N. RESOLUTIONS WORK ON CANCER.
I'M JUST SAYING, THAT IMAGE OF GOING TO BATTLE AGAINST YOUR OWN BODY IS REALLY NEGATIVE. THERE'S SOMETHING SO **CUT-OFF** ABOUT IT.
YEAH, WELL, I THINK THAT'S THE GENERAL IDEA OF A LUMPECTOMY.

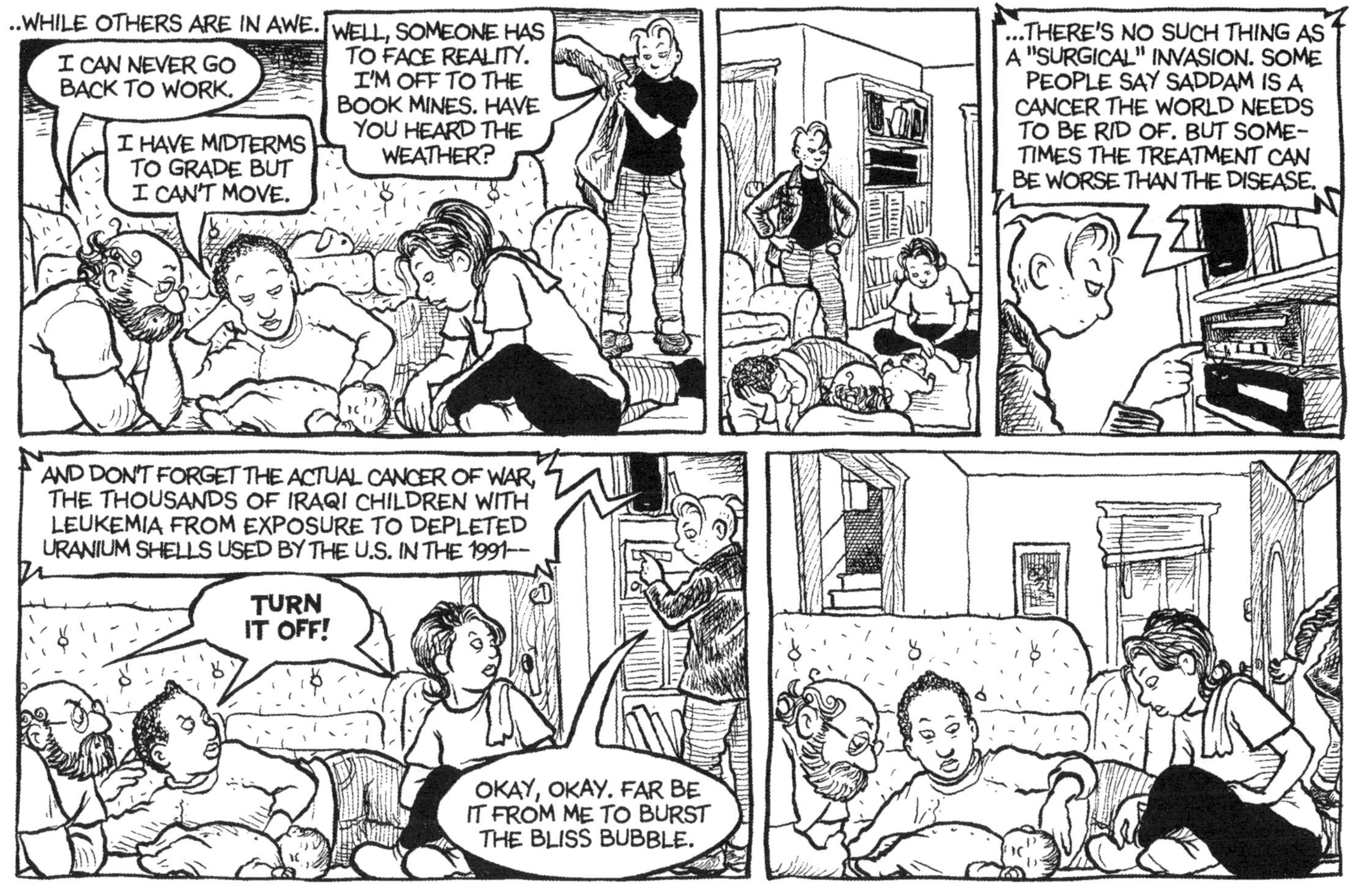
..WHILE OTHERS ARE IN AWE.
I CAN NEVER GO BACK TO WORK.
I HAVE MIDTERMS TO GRADE BUT I CAN'T MOVE.
WELL, SOMEONE HAS TO FACE REALITY. I'M OFF TO THE BOOK MINES. HAVE YOU HEARD THE WEATHER?
...THERE'S NO SUCH THING AS A "SURGICAL" INVASION. SOME PEOPLE SAY SADDAM IS A CANCER THE WORLD NEEDS TO BE RID OF. BUT SOMETIMES THE TREATMENT CAN BE WORSE THAN THE DISEASE.
AND DON'T FORGET THE ACTUAL CANCER OF WAR, THE THOUSANDS OF IRAQI CHILDREN WITH LEUKEMIA FROM EXPOSURE TO DEPLETED URANIUM SHELLS USED BY THE U.S. IN THE 1991--
TURN IT OFF!
OKAY, OKAY. FAR BE IT FROM ME TO BURST THE BLISS BUBBLE.

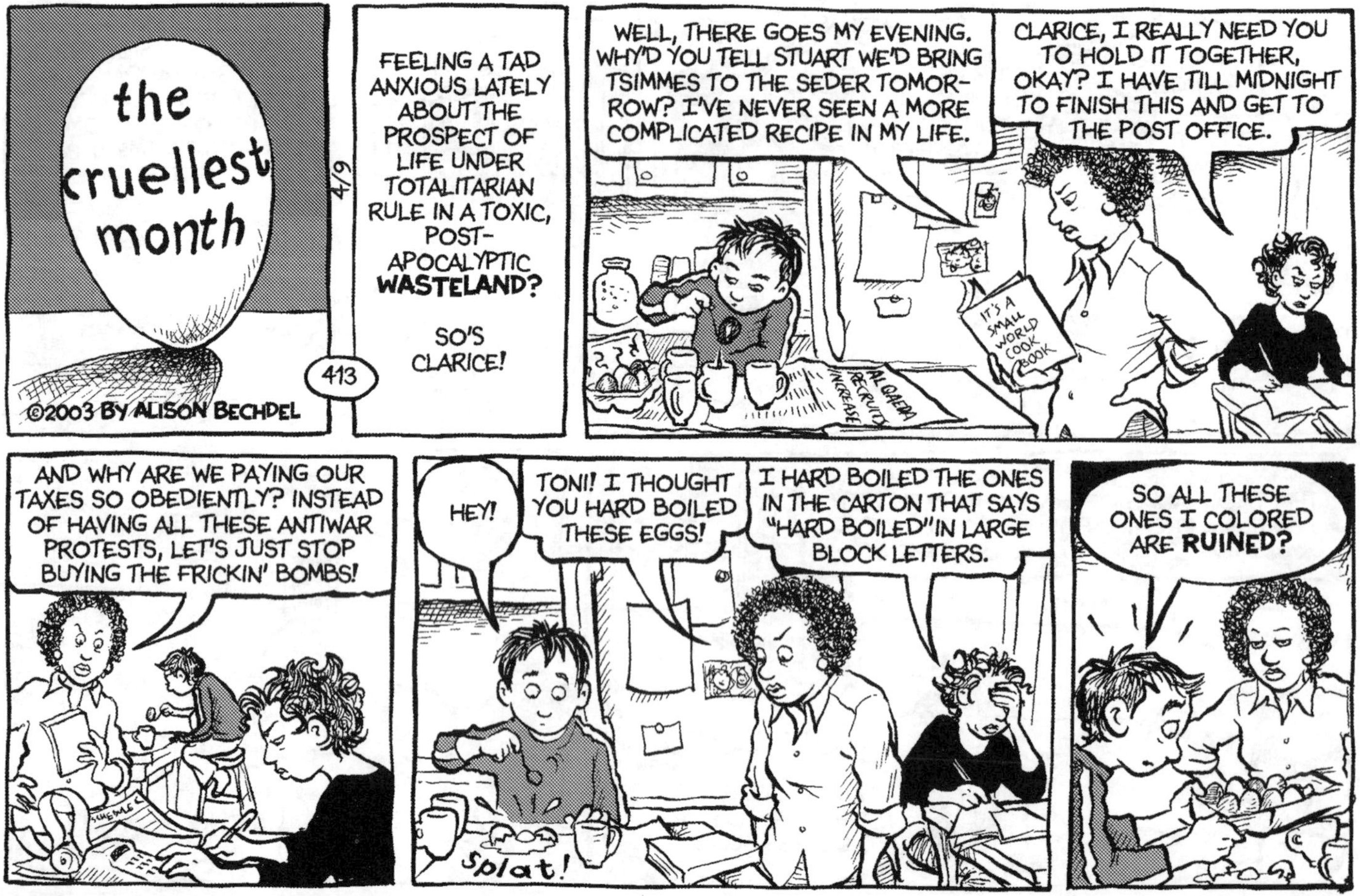
the cruellest month
©2003 BY ALISON BECHDEL
413
4/9
FEELING A TAD ANXIOUS LATELY ABOUT THE PROSPECT OF LIFE UNDER TOTALITARIAN RULE IN A TOXIC, POST-APOCALYPTIC **WASTELAND?**
SO'S CLARICE!
WELL, THERE GOES MY EVENING. WHY'D YOU TELL STUART WE'D BRING TSIMMES TO THE SEDER TOMORROW? I'VE NEVER SEEN A MORE COMPLICATED RECIPE IN MY LIFE.
IT'S A SMALL WORLD COOK BOOK
AL QAEDA RECRUITS INCREASE
CLARICE, I REALLY NEED YOU TO HOLD IT TOGETHER, OKAY? I HAVE TILL MIDNIGHT TO FINISH THIS AND GET TO THE POST OFFICE.
AND WHY ARE WE PAYING OUR TAXES SO OBEDIENTLY? INSTEAD OF HAVING ALL THESE ANTIWAR PROTESTS, LET'S JUST STOP BUYING THE FRICKIN' BOMBS!
HEY!
TONI! I THOUGHT YOU HARD BOILED THESE EGGS!
I HARD BOILED THE ONES IN THE CARTON THAT SAYS "HARD BOILED" IN LARGE BLOCK LETTERS.
Splat!
SO ALL THESE ONES I COLORED ARE **RUINED?**

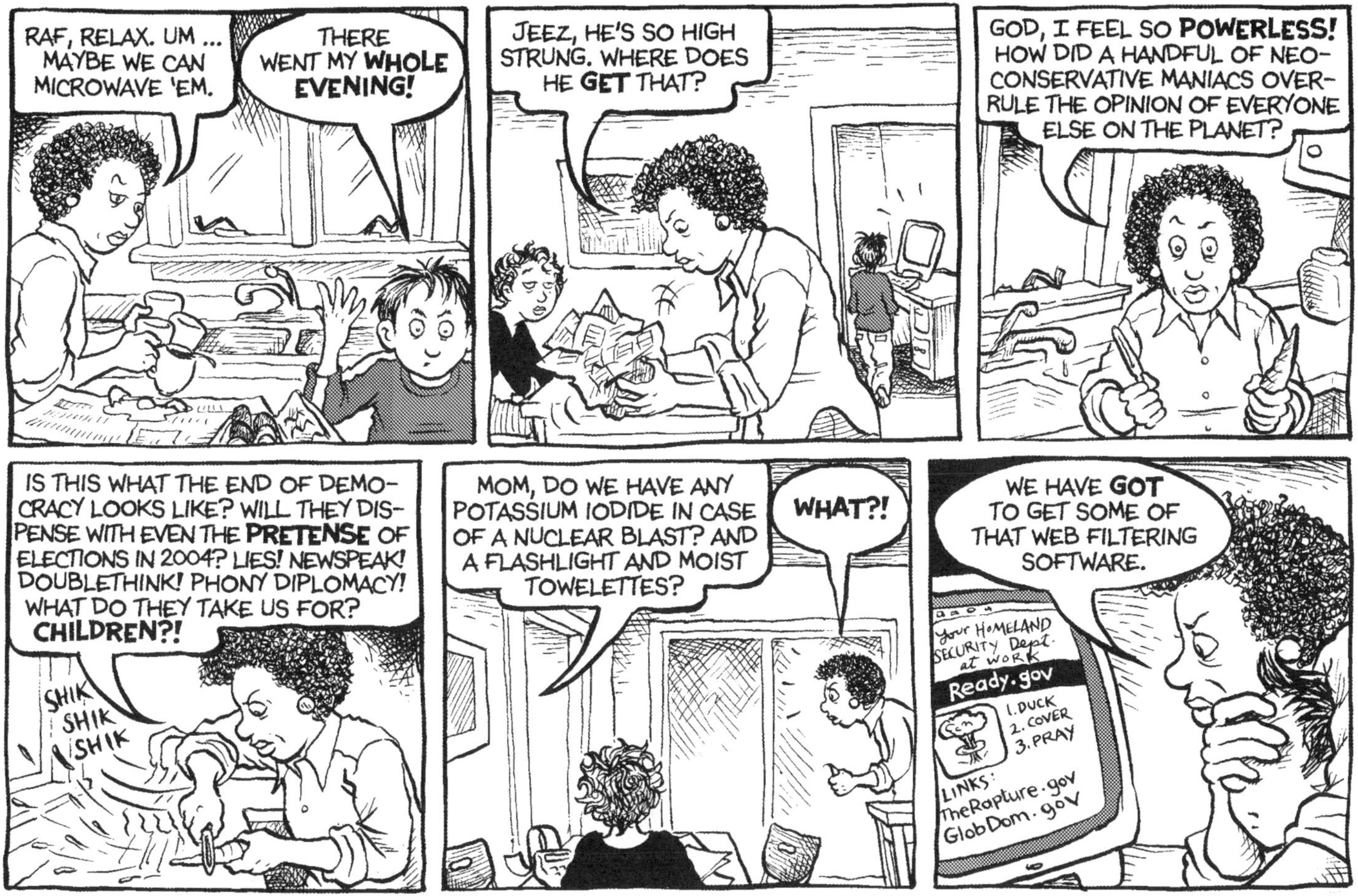
RAF, RELAX. UM ... MAYBE WE CAN MICROWAVE 'EM.
THERE WENT MY **WHOLE EVENING!**
JEEZ, HE'S SO HIGH STRUNG. WHERE DOES HE **GET** THAT?
GOD, I FEEL SO **POWERLESS!** HOW DID A HANDFUL OF NEO-CONSERVATIVE MANIACS OVER-RULE THE OPINION OF EVERYONE ELSE ON THE PLANET?
IS THIS WHAT THE END OF DEMOCRACY LOOKS LIKE? WILL THEY DISPENSE WITH EVEN THE **PRETENSE** OF ELECTIONS IN 2004? LIES! NEWSPEAK! DOUBLETHINK! PHONY DIPLOMACY! WHAT DO THEY TAKE US FOR? **CHILDREN?!**
SHIK SHIK SHIK
MOM, DO WE HAVE ANY POTASSIUM IODIDE IN CASE OF A NUCLEAR BLAST? AND A FLASHLIGHT AND MOIST TOWELETTES?
WHAT?!
WE HAVE **GOT** TO GET SOME OF THAT WEB FILTERING SOFTWARE.
Your HOMELAND SECURITY Dept. at WORK
Ready.gov
1. DUCK
2. COVER
3. PRAY
LINKS:
TheRapture.gov
GlobDom.gov

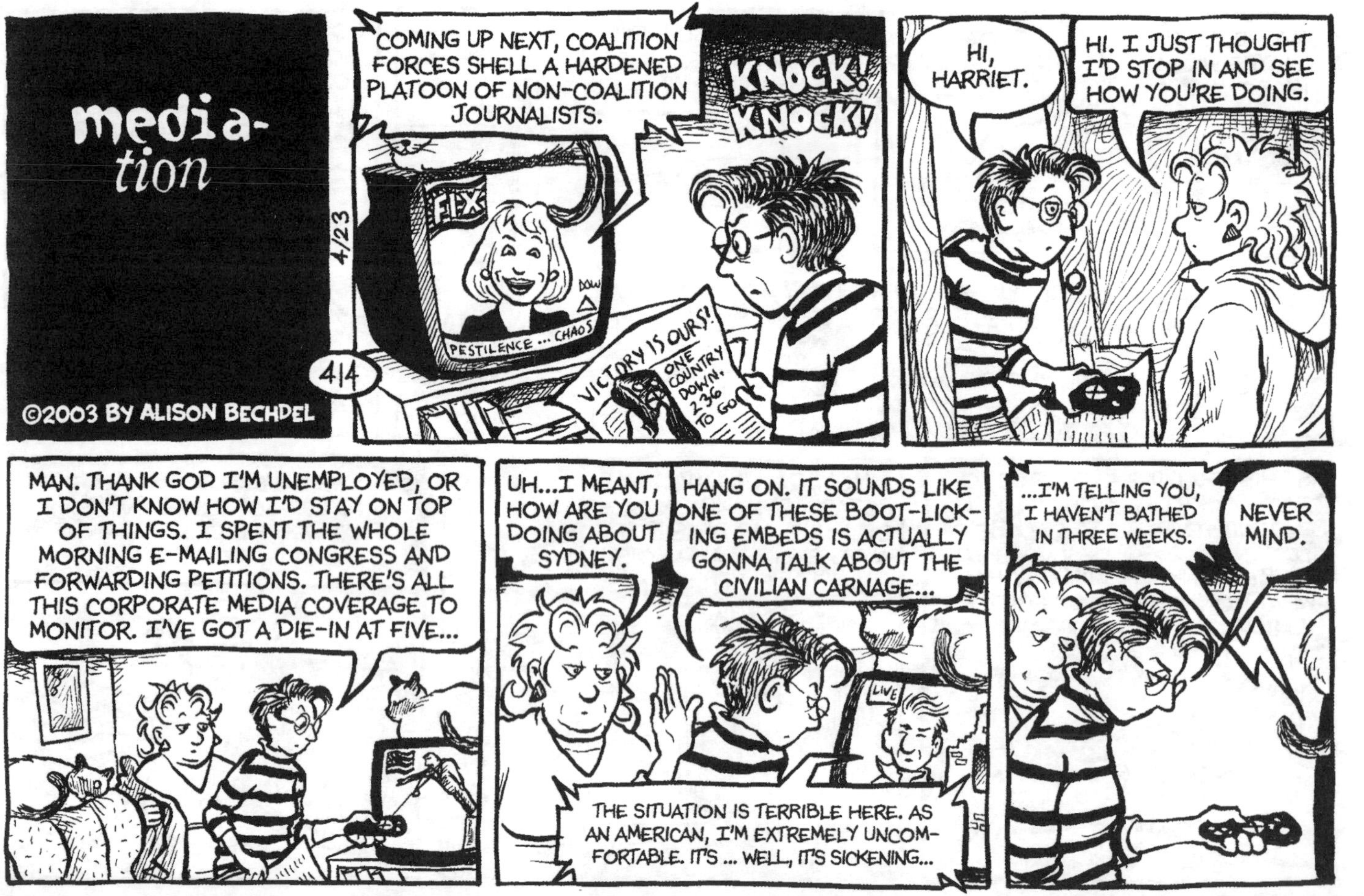
media-
tion
©2003 BY ALISON BECHDEL
4/23
414
COMING UP NEXT, COALITION FORCES SHELL A HARDENED PLATOON OF NON-COALITION JOURNALISTS.
KNOCK! KNOCK!
FIX
DOW
PESTILENCE ... CHAOS
VICTORY IS OURS!
ONE COUNTRY DOWN. 236 TO GO
HI, HARRIET.
HI. I JUST THOUGHT I'D STOP IN AND SEE HOW YOU'RE DOING.
MAN. THANK GOD I'M UNEMPLOYED, OR I DON'T KNOW HOW I'D STAY ON TOP OF THINGS. I SPENT THE WHOLE MORNING E-MAILING CONGRESS AND FORWARDING PETITIONS. THERE'S ALL THIS CORPORATE MEDIA COVERAGE TO MONITOR. I'VE GOT A DIE-IN AT FIVE...
UH...I MEANT, HOW ARE YOU DOING ABOUT SYDNEY.
HANG ON. IT SOUNDS LIKE ONE OF THESE BOOT-LICKING EMBEDS IS ACTUALLY GONNA TALK ABOUT THE CIVILIAN CARNAGE...
LIVE
THE SITUATION IS TERRIBLE HERE. AS AN AMERICAN, I'M EXTREMELY UNCOMFORTABLE. IT'S ... WELL, IT'S SICKENING...
...I'M TELLING YOU, I HAVEN'T BATHED IN THREE WEEKS.
NEVER MIND.

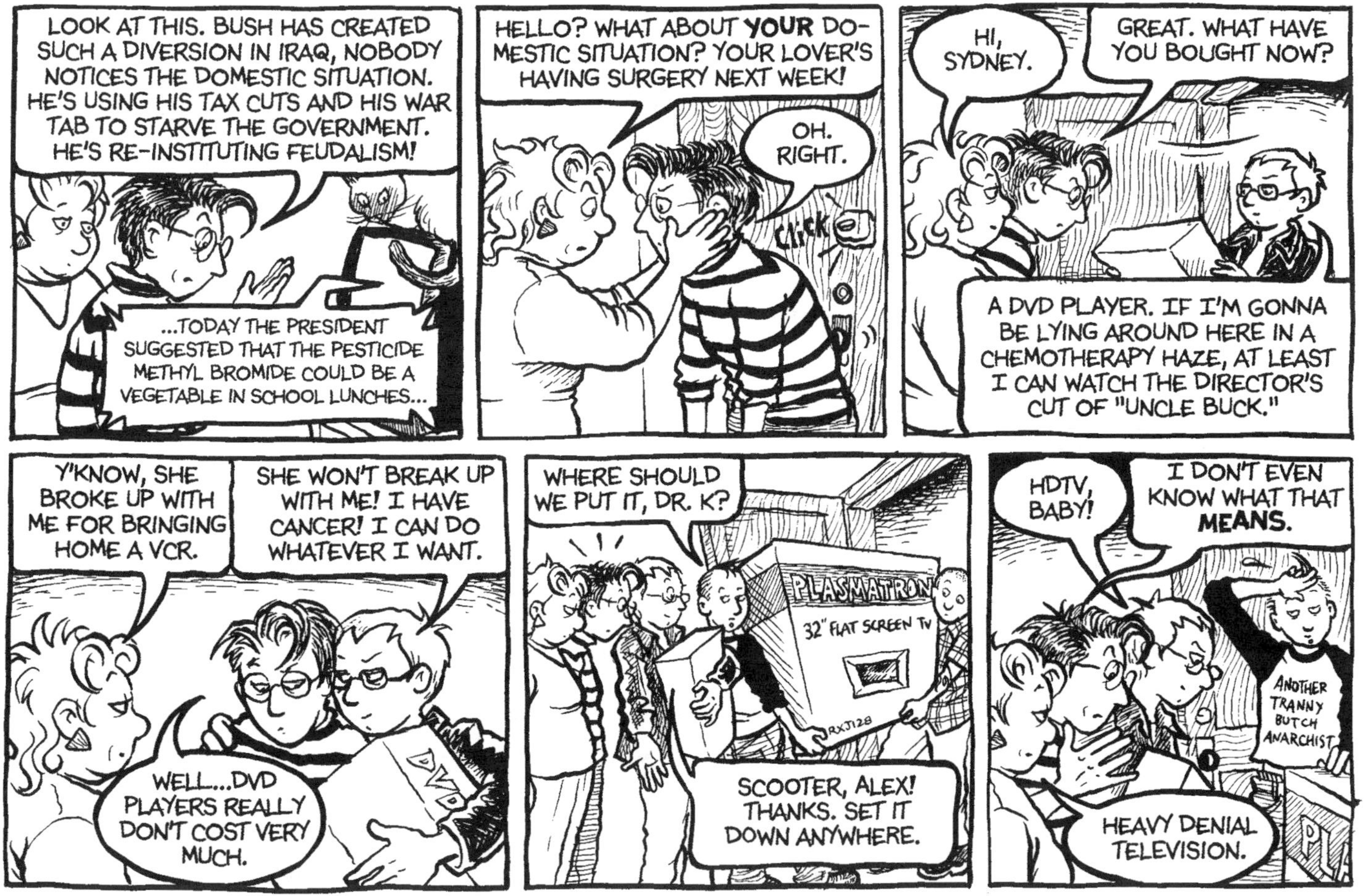

LOOK AT THIS. BUSH HAS CREATED SUCH A DIVERSION IN IRAQ, NOBODY NOTICES THE DOMESTIC SITUATION. HE'S USING HIS TAX CUTS AND HIS WAR TAB TO STARVE THE GOVERNMENT. HE'S RE-INSTITUTING FEUDALISM!
...TODAY THE PRESIDENT SUGGESTED THAT THE PESTICIDE METHYL BROMIDE COULD BE A VEGETABLE IN SCHOOL LUNCHES...
HELLO? WHAT ABOUT **YOUR** DOMESTIC SITUATION? YOUR LOVER'S HAVING SURGERY NEXT WEEK!
OH. RIGHT.
CLICK
HI, SYDNEY.
GREAT. WHAT HAVE YOU BOUGHT NOW?
A DVD PLAYER. IF I'M GONNA BE LYING AROUND HERE IN A CHEMOTHERAPY HAZE, AT LEAST I CAN WATCH THE DIRECTOR'S CUT OF "UNCLE BUCK."
Y'KNOW, SHE BROKE UP WITH ME FOR BRINGING HOME A VCR.
SHE WON'T BREAK UP WITH ME! I HAVE CANCER! I CAN DO WHATEVER I WANT.
WELL...DVD PLAYERS REALLY DON'T COST VERY MUCH.
DVD
WHERE SHOULD WE PUT IT, DR. K?
PLASMATRON
32" FLAT SCREEN TV
RXJ128
SCOOTER, ALEX! THANKS. SET IT DOWN ANYWHERE.
HDTV, BABY!
I DON'T EVEN KNOW WHAT THAT **MEANS.**
ANOTHER TRANNY BUTCH ANARCHIST
HEAVY DENIAL TELEVISION.

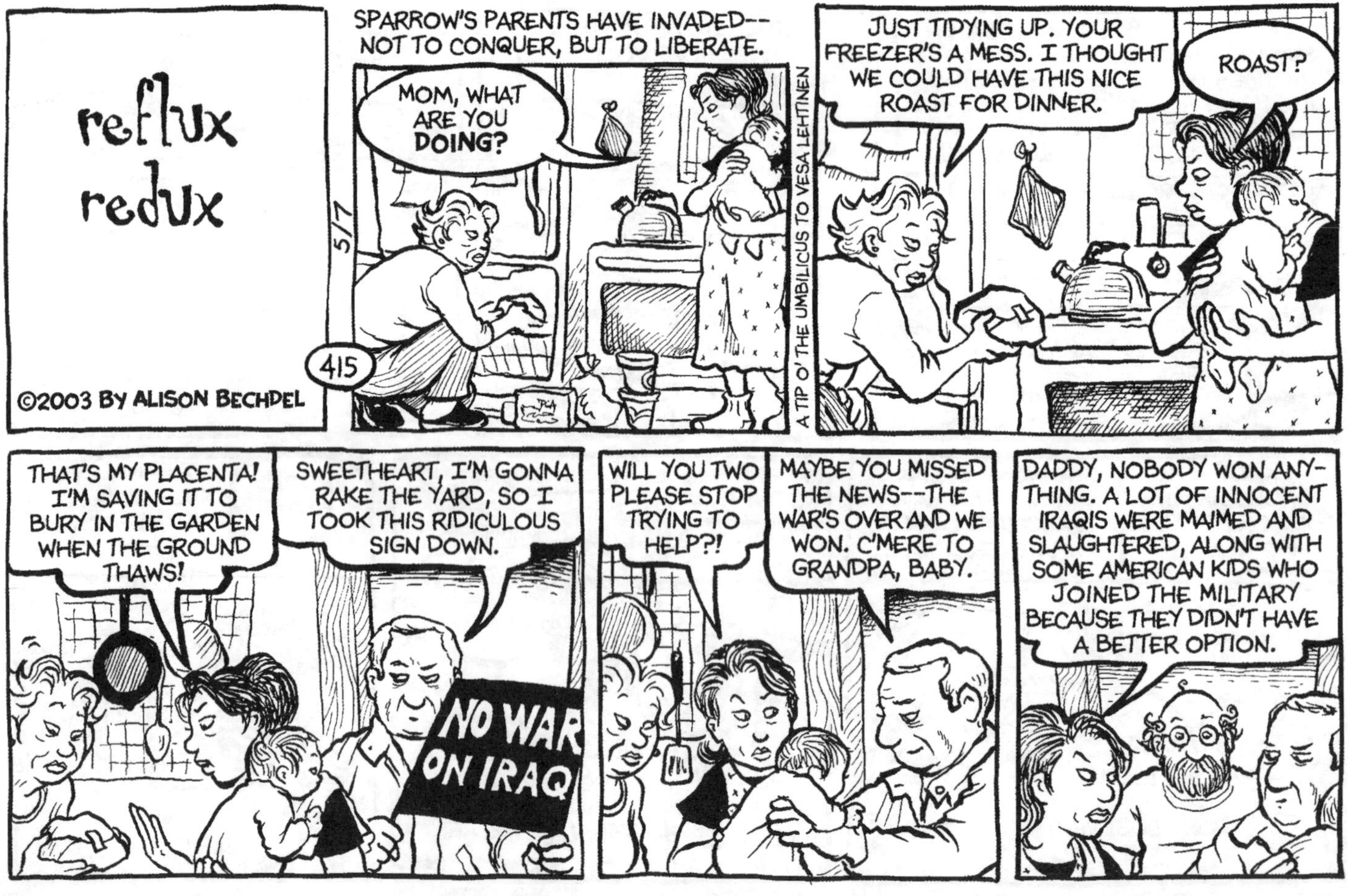
reflux redux
©2003 BY ALISON BECHDEL
415
5/7
SPARROW'S PARENTS HAVE INVADED-- NOT TO CONQUER, BUT TO LIBERATE.
MOM, WHAT ARE YOU DOING?
A TIP O' THE UMBILICUS TO VESA LEHTINEN
JUST TIDYING UP. YOUR FREEZER'S A MESS. I THOUGHT WE COULD HAVE THIS NICE ROAST FOR DINNER.
ROAST?
THAT'S MY PLACENTA! I'M SAVING IT TO BURY IN THE GARDEN WHEN THE GROUND THAWS!
SWEETHEART, I'M GONNA RAKE THE YARD, SO I TOOK THIS RIDICULOUS SIGN DOWN.
NO WAR ON IRAQ
WILL YOU TWO PLEASE STOP TRYING TO HELP?!
MAYBE YOU MISSED THE NEWS--THE WAR'S OVER AND WE WON. C'MERE TO GRANDPA, BABY.
DADDY, NOBODY WON ANYTHING. A LOT OF INNOCENT IRAQIS WERE MAIMED AND SLAUGHTERED, ALONG WITH SOME AMERICAN KIDS WHO JOINED THE MILITARY BECAUSE THEY DIDN'T HAVE A BETTER OPTION.

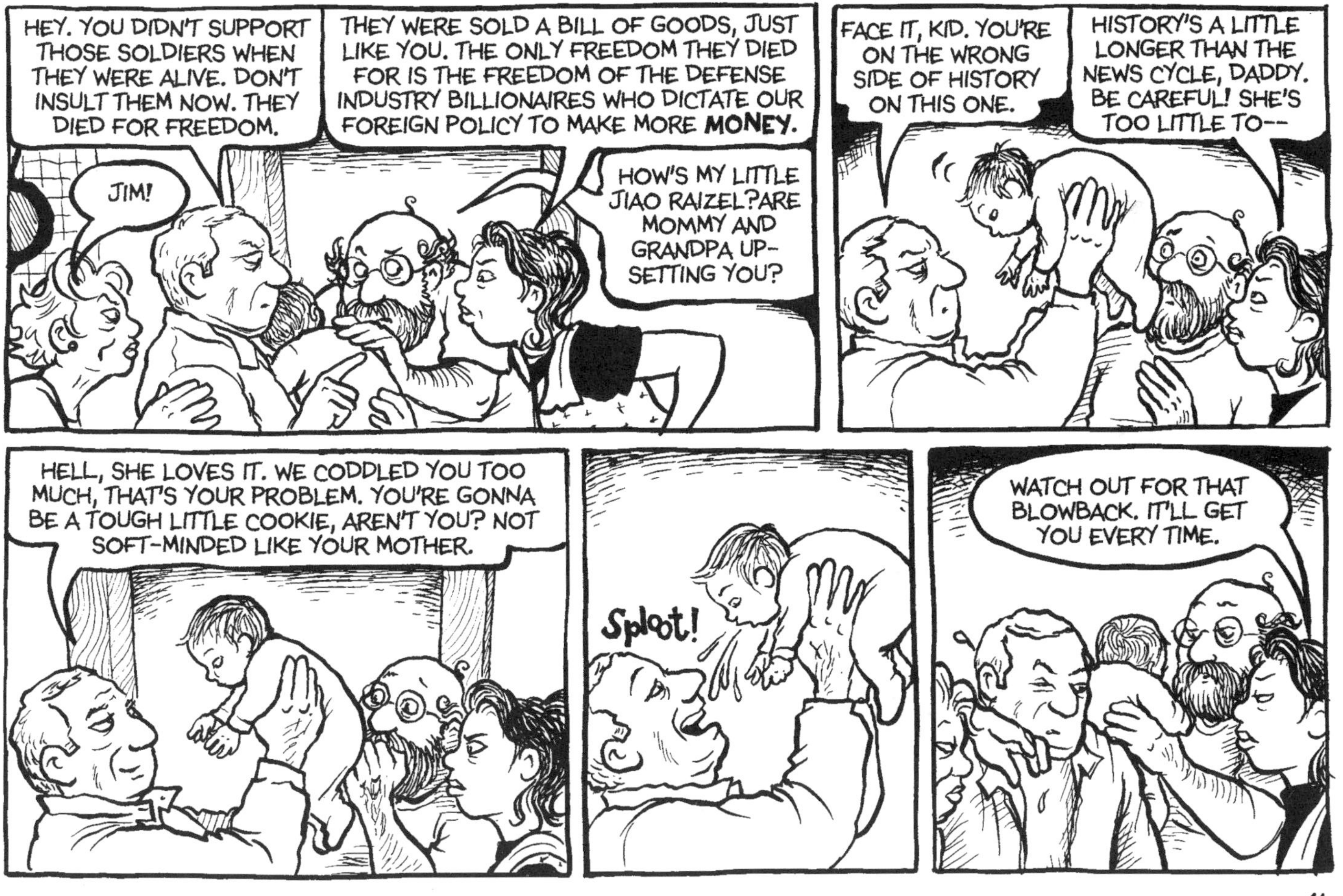
HEY. YOU DIDN'T SUPPORT THOSE SOLDIERS WHEN THEY WERE ALIVE. DON'T INSULT THEM NOW. THEY DIED FOR FREEDOM.
THEY WERE SOLD A BILL OF GOODS, JUST LIKE YOU. THE ONLY FREEDOM THEY DIED FOR IS THE FREEDOM OF THE DEFENSE INDUSTRY BILLIONAIRES WHO DICTATE OUR FOREIGN POLICY TO MAKE MORE **MONEY**.
JIM!
HOW'S MY LITTLE JIAO RAIZEL? ARE MOMMY AND GRANDPA UP-SETTING YOU?
FACE IT, KID. YOU'RE ON THE WRONG SIDE OF HISTORY ON THIS ONE.
HISTORY'S A LITTLE LONGER THAN THE NEWS CYCLE, DADDY. BE CAREFUL! SHE'S TOO LITTLE TO--
HELL, SHE LOVES IT. WE CODDLED YOU TOO MUCH, THAT'S YOUR PROBLEM. YOU'RE GONNA BE A TOUGH LITTLE COOKIE, AREN'T YOU? NOT SOFT-MINDED LIKE YOUR MOTHER.
Sploot!
WATCH OUT FOR THAT BLOWBACK. IT'LL GET YOU EVERY TIME.

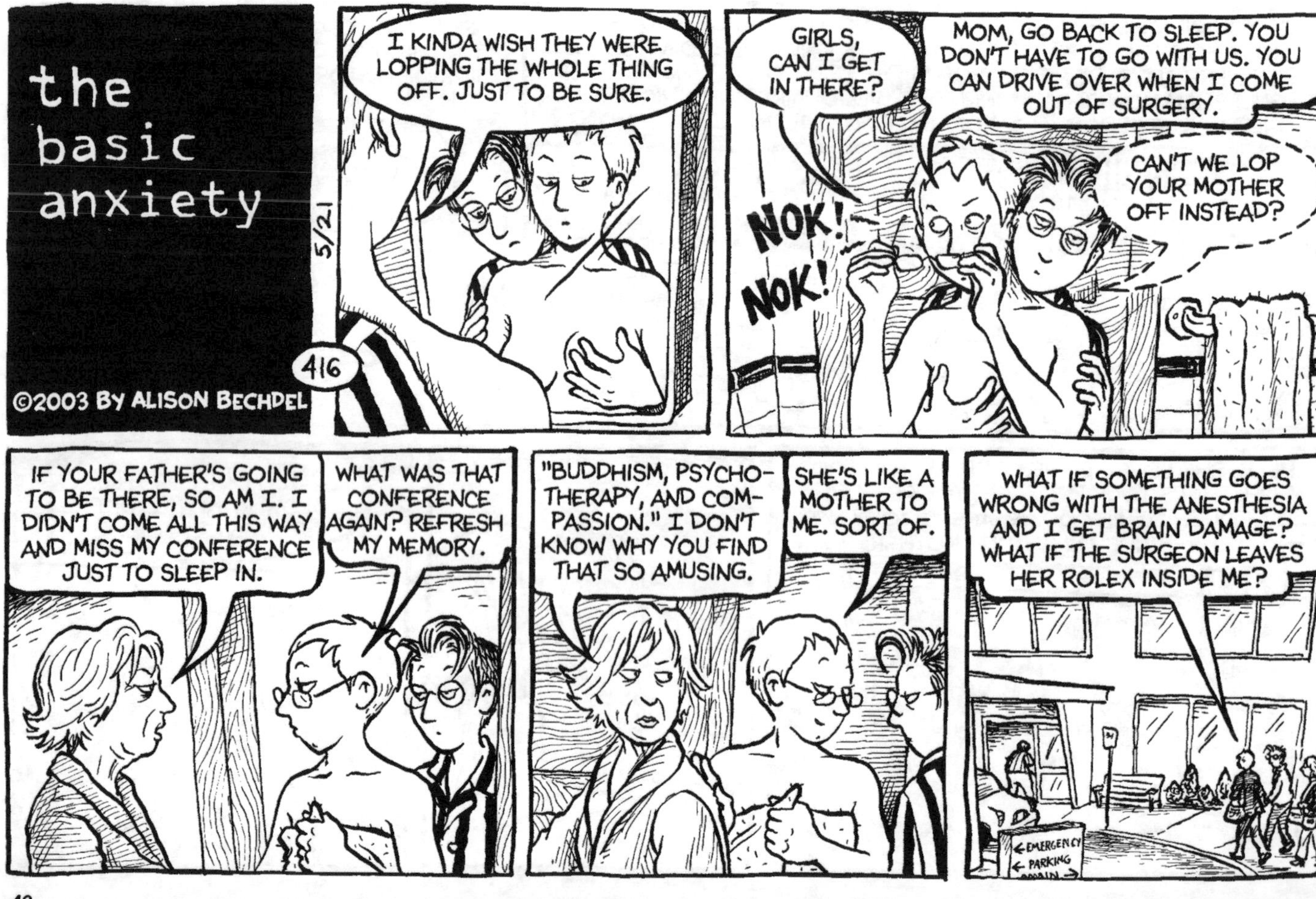
the basic anxiety
©2003 BY ALISON BECHDEL
416
5/21
I KINDA WISH THEY WERE LOPPING THE WHOLE THING OFF. JUST TO BE SURE.
GIRLS, CAN I GET IN THERE?
MOM, GO BACK TO SLEEP. YOU DON'T HAVE TO GO WITH US. YOU CAN DRIVE OVER WHEN I COME OUT OF SURGERY.
NOK! NOK!
CAN'T WE LOP YOUR MOTHER OFF INSTEAD?
IF YOUR FATHER'S GOING TO BE THERE, SO AM I. I DIDN'T COME ALL THIS WAY AND MISS MY CONFERENCE JUST TO SLEEP IN.
WHAT WAS THAT CONFERENCE AGAIN? REFRESH MY MEMORY.
"BUDDHISM, PSYCHO-THERAPY, AND COM-PASSION." I DON'T KNOW WHY YOU FIND THAT SO AMUSING.
SHE'S LIKE A MOTHER TO ME. SORT OF.
WHAT IF SOMETHING GOES WRONG WITH THE ANESTHESIA AND I GET BRAIN DAMAGE? WHAT IF THE SURGEON LEAVES HER ROLEX INSIDE ME?
← EMERGENCY
← PARKING

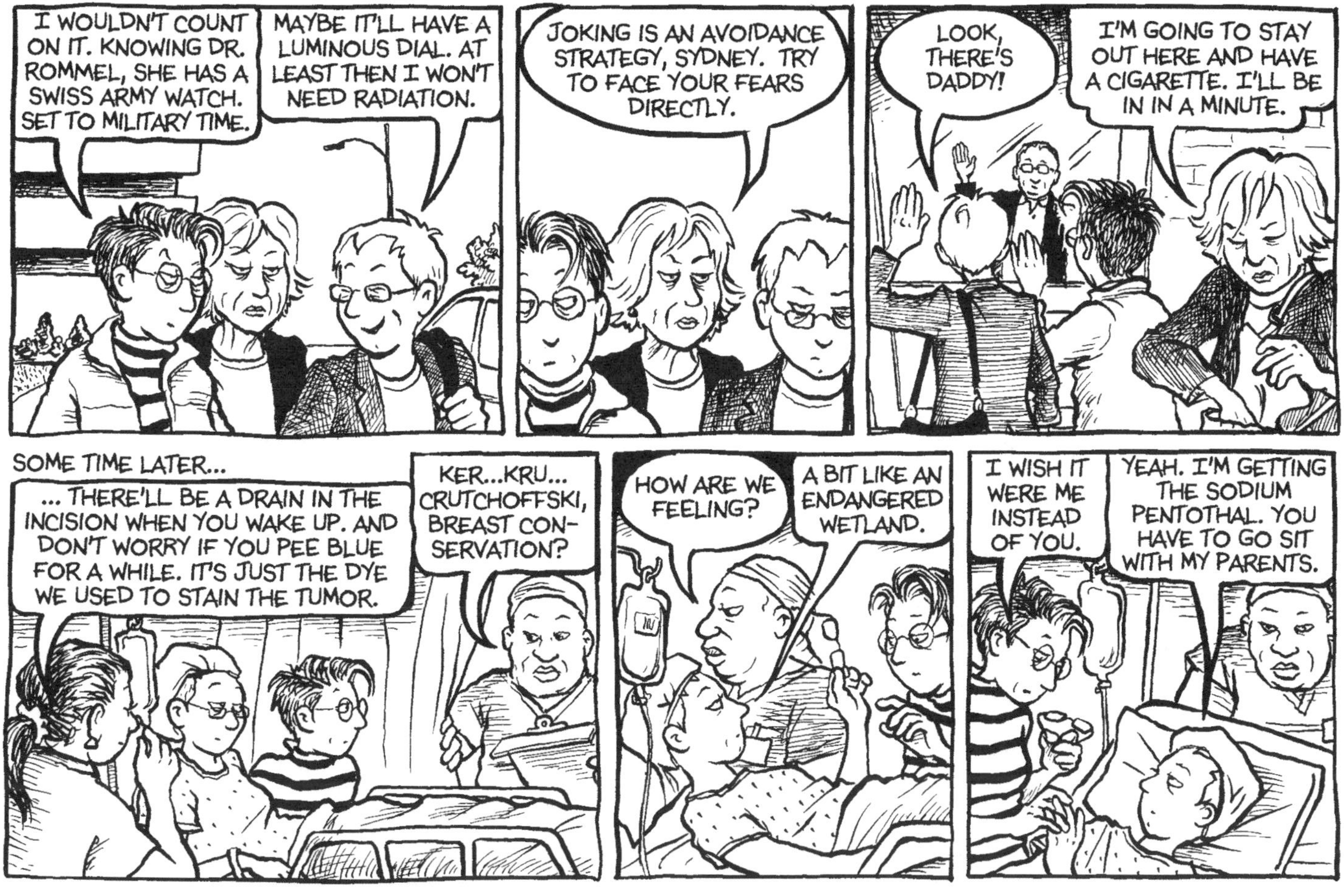
I WOULDN'T COUNT ON IT. KNOWING DR. ROMMEL, SHE HAS A SWISS ARMY WATCH. SET TO MILITARY TIME.
MAYBE IT'LL HAVE A LUMINOUS DIAL. AT LEAST THEN I WON'T NEED RADIATION.
JOKING IS AN AVOIDANCE STRATEGY, SYDNEY. TRY TO FACE YOUR FEARS DIRECTLY.
LOOK, THERE'S DADDY!
I'M GOING TO STAY OUT HERE AND HAVE A CIGARETTE. I'LL BE IN IN A MINUTE.
SOME TIME LATER...
... THERE'LL BE A DRAIN IN THE INCISION WHEN YOU WAKE UP. AND DON'T WORRY IF YOU PEE BLUE FOR A WHILE. IT'S JUST THE DYE WE USED TO STAIN THE TUMOR.
KER...KRU... CRUTCHOFFSKI, BREAST CON-SERVATION?
HOW ARE WE FEELING?
A BIT LIKE AN ENDANGERED WETLAND.
I WISH IT WERE ME INSTEAD OF YOU.
YEAH. I'M GETTING THE SODIUM PENTOTHAL. YOU HAVE TO GO SIT WITH MY PARENTS.

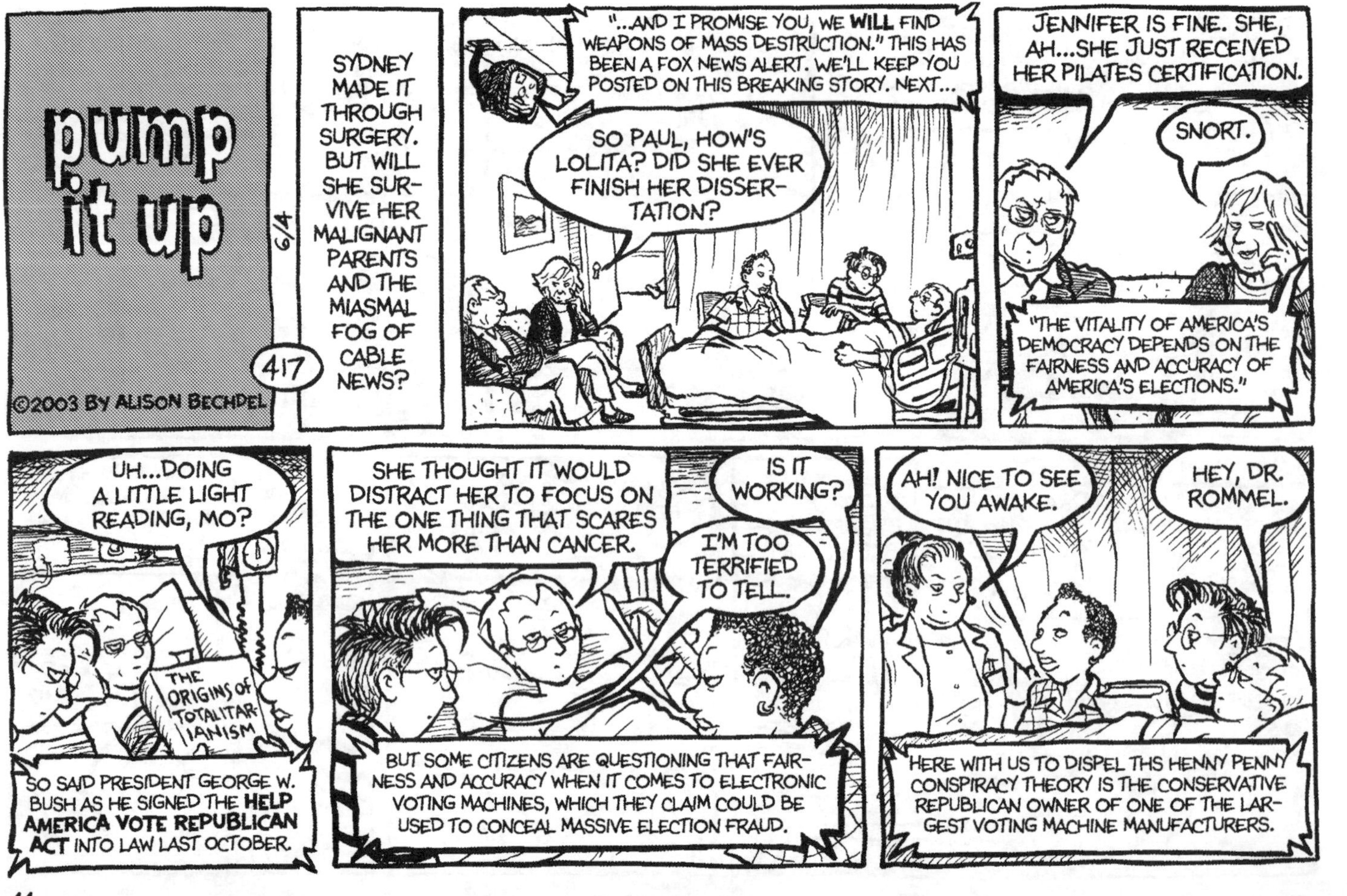
pump it up
©2003 BY ALISON BECHDEL
417
6/4
SYDNEY MADE IT THROUGH SURGERY. BUT WILL SHE SURVIVE HER MALIGNANT PARENTS AND THE MIASMAL FOG OF CABLE NEWS?
"...AND I PROMISE YOU, WE **WILL** FIND WEAPONS OF MASS DESTRUCTION." THIS HAS BEEN A FOX NEWS ALERT. WE'LL KEEP YOU POSTED ON THIS BREAKING STORY. NEXT...
SO PAUL, HOW'S LOLITA? DID SHE EVER FINISH HER DISSERTATION?
JENNIFER IS FINE. SHE, AH...SHE JUST RECEIVED HER PILATES CERTIFICATION.
SNORT.
"THE VITALITY OF AMERICA'S DEMOCRACY DEPENDS ON THE FAIRNESS AND ACCURACY OF AMERICA'S ELECTIONS."
UH...DOING A LITTLE LIGHT READING, MO?
THE ORIGINS OF TOTALITARIANISM
SO SAID PRESIDENT GEORGE W. BUSH AS HE SIGNED THE **HELP AMERICA VOTE REPUBLICAN ACT** INTO LAW LAST OCTOBER.
SHE THOUGHT IT WOULD DISTRACT HER TO FOCUS ON THE ONE THING THAT SCARES HER MORE THAN CANCER.
IS IT WORKING?
I'M TOO TERRIFIED TO TELL.
BUT SOME CITIZENS ARE QUESTIONING THAT FAIRNESS AND ACCURACY WHEN IT COMES TO ELECTRONIC VOTING MACHINES, WHICH THEY CLAIM COULD BE USED TO CONCEAL MASSIVE ELECTION FRAUD.
AH! NICE TO SEE YOU AWAKE.
HEY, DR. ROMMEL.
HERE WITH US TO DISPEL THS HENNY PENNY CONSPIRACY THEORY IS THE CONSERVATIVE REPUBLICAN OWNER OF ONE OF THE LARGEST VOTING MACHINE MANUFACTURERS.

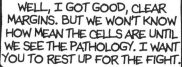

WELL, I GOT GOOD, CLEAR MARGINS. BUT WE WON'T KNOW HOW MEAN THE CELLS ARE UNTIL WE SEE THE PATHOLOGY. I WANT YOU TO REST UP FOR THE FIGHT.

GOD FOR HARRY, ENGLAND AND SAINT GEORGE! TO THE BREACH! TO THE **BREACH!**

UM...CHECK HER MORPHINE PUMP, NURSE.

SHE'S AS LUCID AS I AM. THAT'S "HENRY THE FIFTH."

THE PUMP'S FINE. GO AHEAD AND HIT IT AS SOON AS YOU FEEL ANY PAIN.

SO GINGER, YOU USED TO TEACH WITH SYDNEY AT THE UNIVERSITY?

YEAH. ENGLISH LIT. NOW I'M AT BUFFALO LAKE STATE.

THE STATE COLLEGES PRODUCE A FINE SCHOLAR NOW AND THEN. I DON'T KNOW IF SYD MENTIONED, I'M CHAIR OF THE ENGLISH DEPARTMENT AT CHICAGO UNIVERSITY.

SHE TOLD ME YOU JUST RETIRED.

AND SHE TOLD ME YOU'VE GOT YOUR SHOPLIFTING UNDER CONTROL. I'M GLAD TO HEAR IT.

THIS THING IS GREAT. TOO BAD I DIDN'T HAVE ONE WHEN I WAS GROWING UP.

BEEP

45

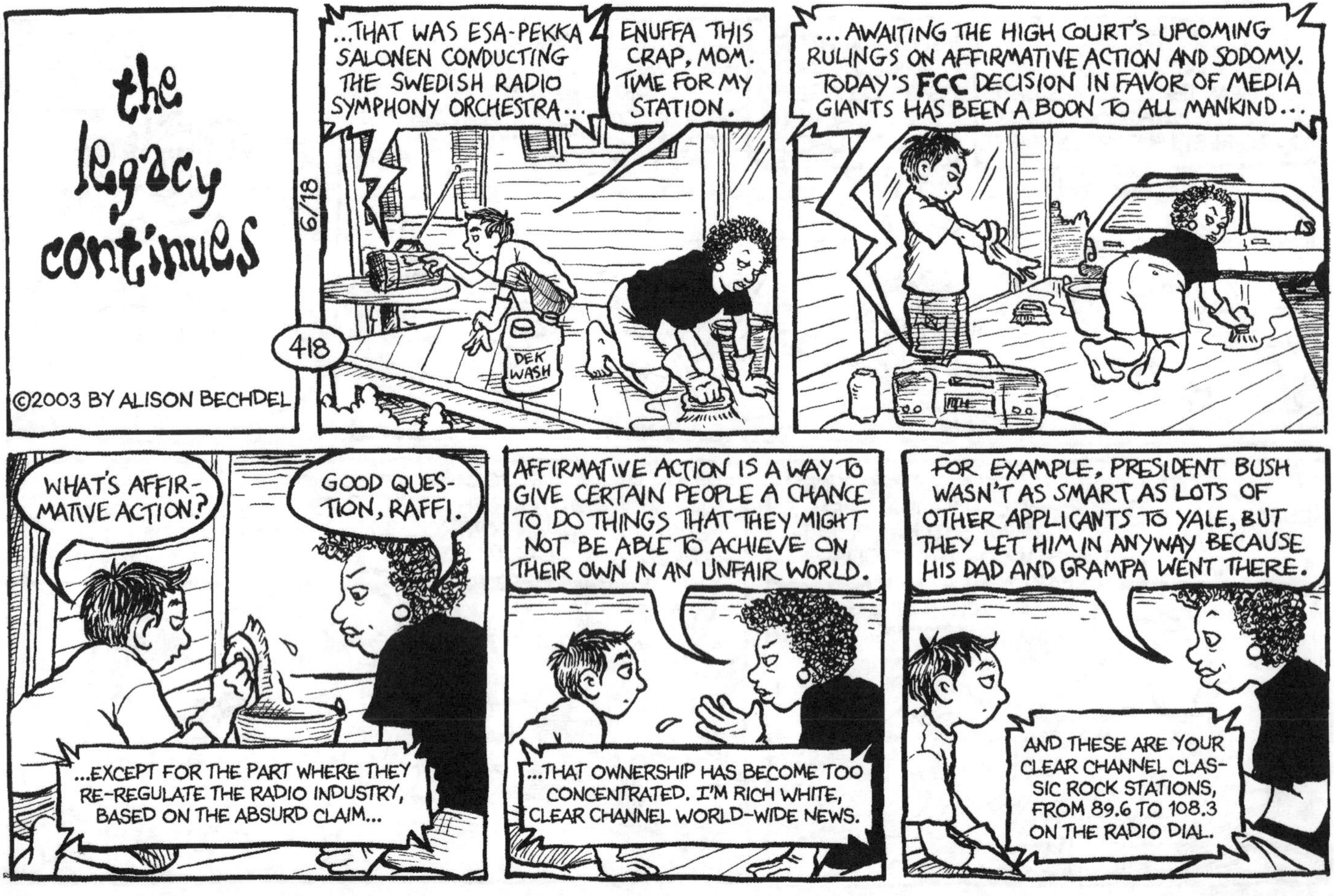
the legacy continues
©2003 BY ALISON BECHDEL
418
6/18
...THAT WAS ESA-PEKKA SALONEN CONDUCTING THE SWEDISH RADIO SYMPHONY ORCHESTRA...
ENUFFA THIS CRAP, MOM. TIME FOR MY STATION.
DEK WASH
...AWAITING THE HIGH COURT'S UPCOMING RULINGS ON AFFIRMATIVE ACTION AND SODOMY. TODAY'S FCC DECISION IN FAVOR OF MEDIA GIANTS HAS BEEN A BOON TO ALL MANKIND...
WHAT'S AFFIRMATIVE ACTION?
GOOD QUESTION, RAFFI.
...EXCEPT FOR THE PART WHERE THEY RE-REGULATE THE RADIO INDUSTRY, BASED ON THE ABSURD CLAIM...
AFFIRMATIVE ACTION IS A WAY TO GIVE CERTAIN PEOPLE A CHANCE TO DO THINGS THAT THEY MIGHT NOT BE ABLE TO ACHIEVE ON THEIR OWN IN AN UNFAIR WORLD.
...THAT OWNERSHIP HAS BECOME TOO CONCENTRATED. I'M RICH WHITE, CLEAR CHANNEL WORLD-WIDE NEWS.
FOR EXAMPLE, PRESIDENT BUSH WASN'T AS SMART AS LOTS OF OTHER APPLICANTS TO YALE, BUT THEY LET HIM IN ANYWAY BECAUSE HIS DAD AND GRAMPA WENT THERE.
AND THESE ARE YOUR CLEAR CHANNEL CLASSIC ROCK STATIONS, FROM 89.6 TO 108.3 ON THE RADIO DIAL.

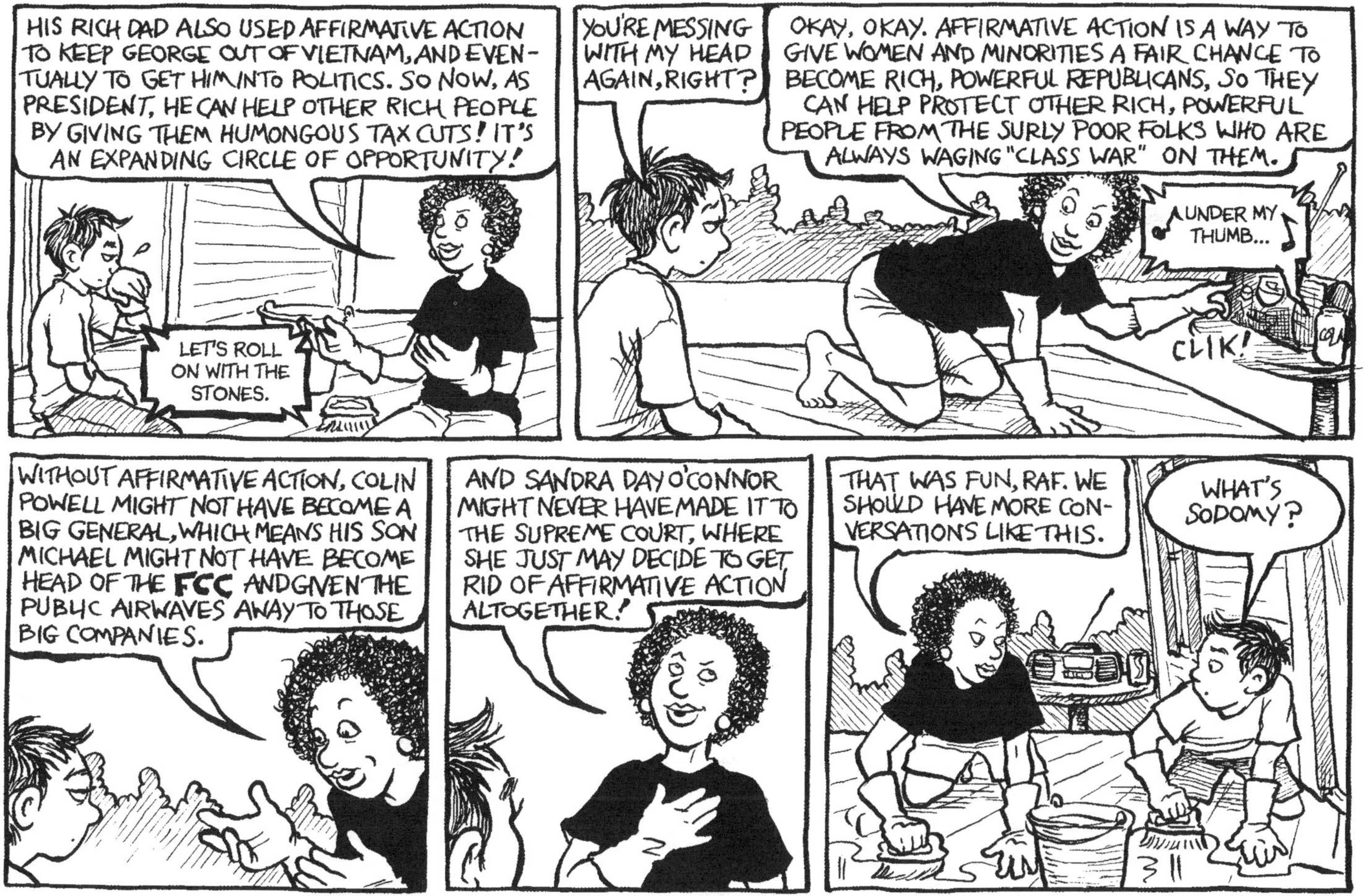
HIS RICH DAD ALSO USED AFFIRMATIVE ACTION TO KEEP GEORGE OUT OF VIETNAM, AND EVENTUALLY TO GET HIM INTO POLITICS. SO NOW, AS PRESIDENT, HE CAN HELP OTHER RICH PEOPLE BY GIVING THEM HUMONGOUS TAX CUTS! IT'S AN EXPANDING CIRCLE OF OPPORTUNITY!
LET'S ROLL ON WITH THE STONES.
YOU'RE MESSING WITH MY HEAD AGAIN, RIGHT?
OKAY, OKAY. AFFIRMATIVE ACTION IS A WAY TO GIVE WOMEN AND MINORITIES A FAIR CHANCE TO BECOME RICH, POWERFUL REPUBLICANS, SO THEY CAN HELP PROTECT OTHER RICH, POWERFUL PEOPLE FROM THE SURLY POOR FOLKS WHO ARE ALWAYS WAGING "CLASS WAR" ON THEM.
UNDER MY THUMB...
CLIK!
WITHOUT AFFIRMATIVE ACTION, COLIN POWELL MIGHT NOT HAVE BECOME A BIG GENERAL, WHICH MEANS HIS SON MICHAEL MIGHT NOT HAVE BECOME HEAD OF THE FCC AND GIVEN THE PUBLIC AIRWAVES AWAY TO THOSE BIG COMPANIES.
AND SANDRA DAY O'CONNOR MIGHT NEVER HAVE MADE IT TO THE SUPREME COURT, WHERE SHE JUST MAY DECIDE TO GET RID OF AFFIRMATIVE ACTION ALTOGETHER!
THAT WAS FUN, RAF. WE SHOULD HAVE MORE CONVERSATIONS LIKE THIS.
WHAT'S SODOMY?

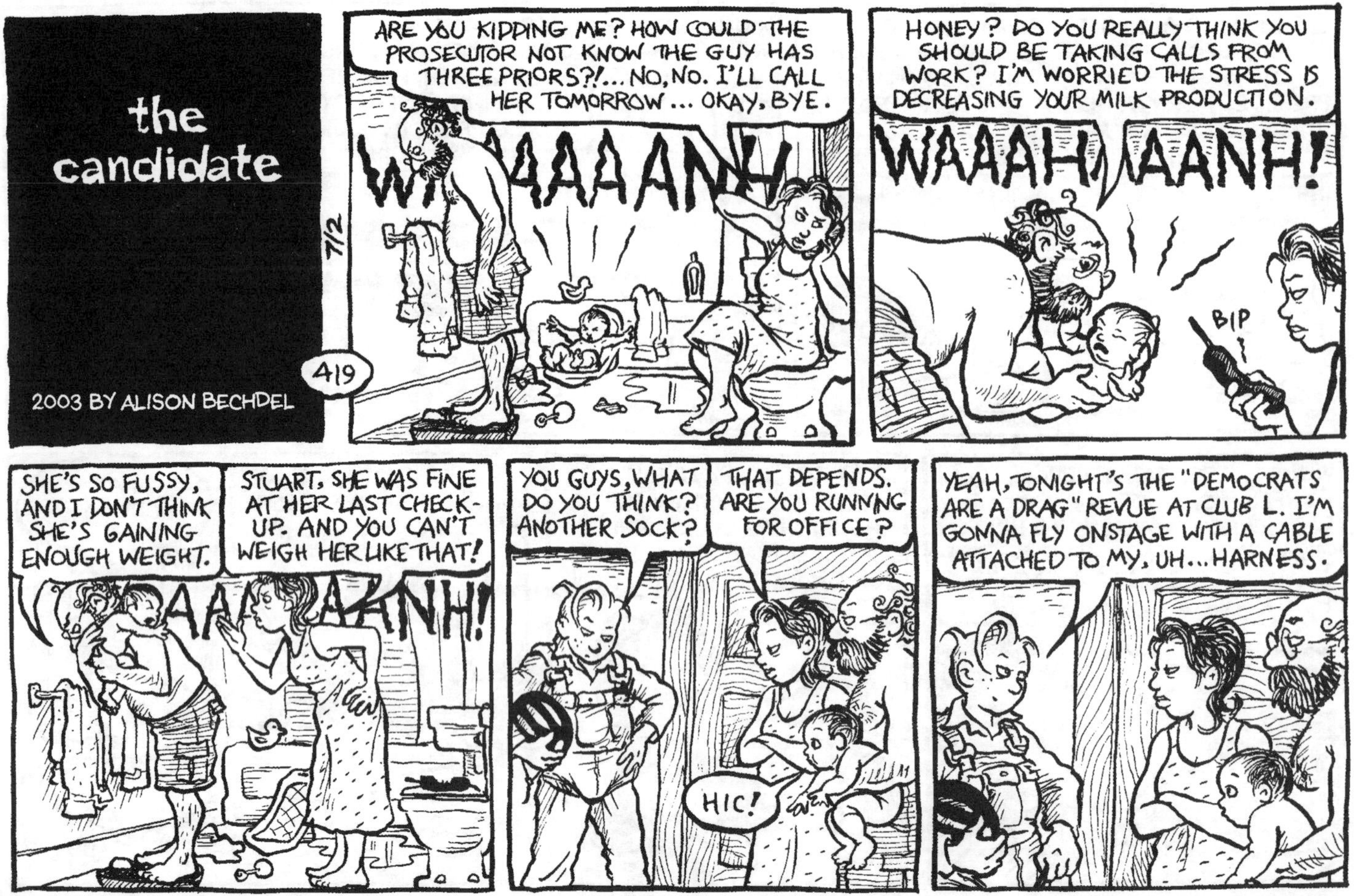
the candidate
2003 BY ALISON BECHDEL
7/2
419
ARE YOU KIDDING ME? HOW COULD THE PROSECUTOR NOT KNOW THE GUY HAS THREE PRIORS?!... NO, NO. I'LL CALL HER TOMORROW... OKAY, BYE.
AAAAANH
HONEY? DO YOU REALLY THINK YOU SHOULD BE TAKING CALLS FROM WORK? I'M WORRIED THE STRESS IS DECREASING YOUR MILK PRODUCTION.
WAAAH AANH!
BIP
SHE'S SO FUSSY, AND I DON'T THINK SHE'S GAINING ENOUGH WEIGHT.
STUART, SHE WAS FINE AT HER LAST CHECK-UP. AND YOU CAN'T WEIGH HER LIKE THAT!
AANH!
YOU GUYS, WHAT DO YOU THINK? ANOTHER SOCK?
THAT DEPENDS. ARE YOU RUNNING FOR OFFICE?
HIC!
YEAH, TONIGHT'S THE "DEMOCRATS ARE A DRAG" REVUE AT CLUB L. I'M GONNA FLY ONSTAGE WITH A CABLE ATTACHED TO MY, UH... HARNESS.

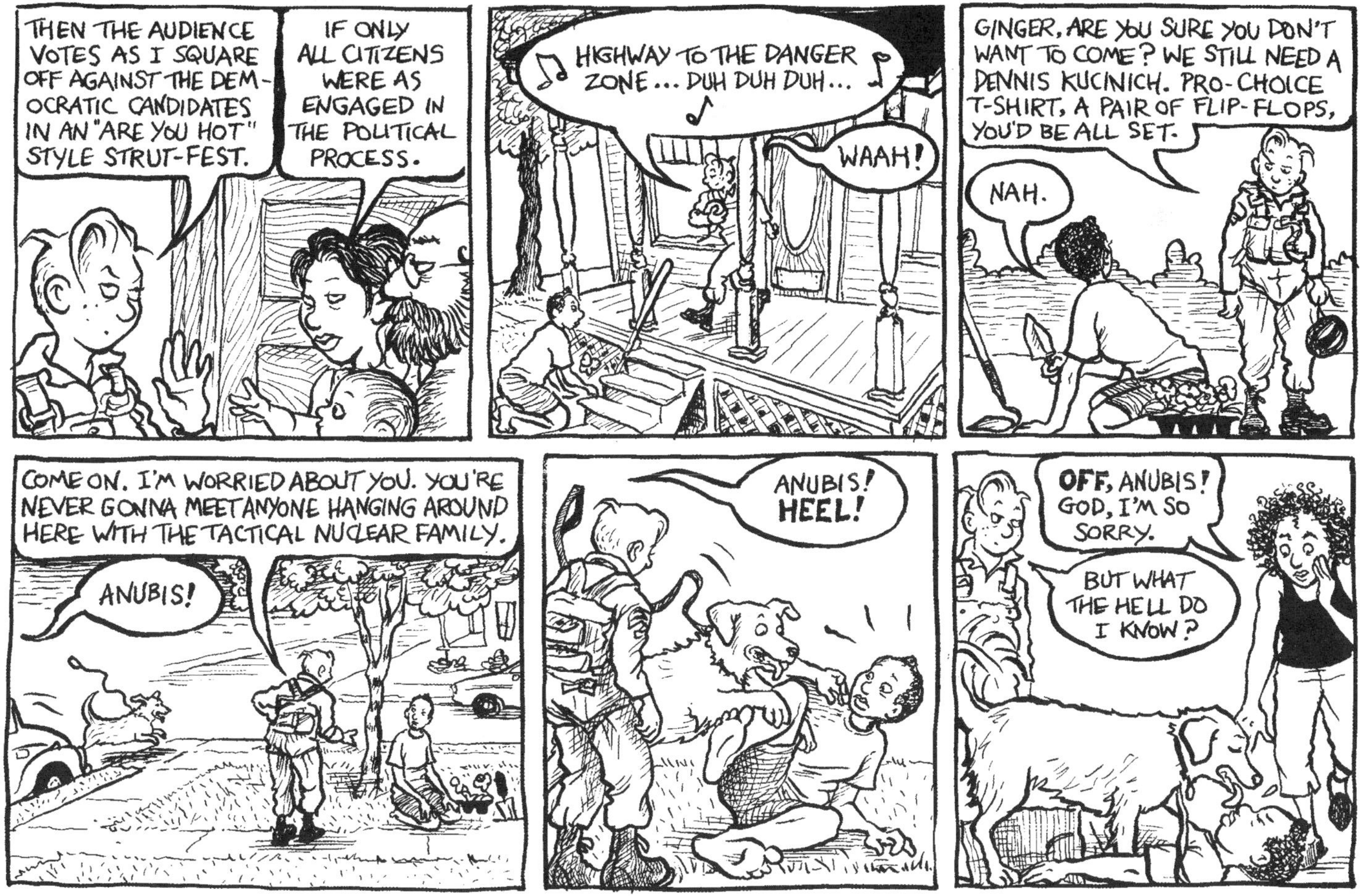
THEN THE AUDIENCE VOTES AS I SQUARE OFF AGAINST THE DEMOCRATIC CANDIDATES IN AN "ARE YOU HOT" STYLE STRUT-FEST.
IF ONLY ALL CITIZENS WERE AS ENGAGED IN THE POLITICAL PROCESS.
HIGHWAY TO THE DANGER ZONE... DUH DUH DUH...
WAAH!
GINGER, ARE YOU SURE YOU DON'T WANT TO COME? WE STILL NEED A DENNIS KUCINICH. PRO-CHOICE T-SHIRT, A PAIR OF FLIP-FLOPS, YOU'D BE ALL SET.
NAH.
COME ON. I'M WORRIED ABOUT YOU. YOU'RE NEVER GONNA MEET ANYONE HANGING AROUND HERE WITH THE TACTICAL NUCLEAR FAMILY.
ANUBIS!
ANUBIS! **HEEL!**
OFF, ANUBIS! GOD, I'M SO SORRY.
BUT WHAT THE HELL DO I KNOW?

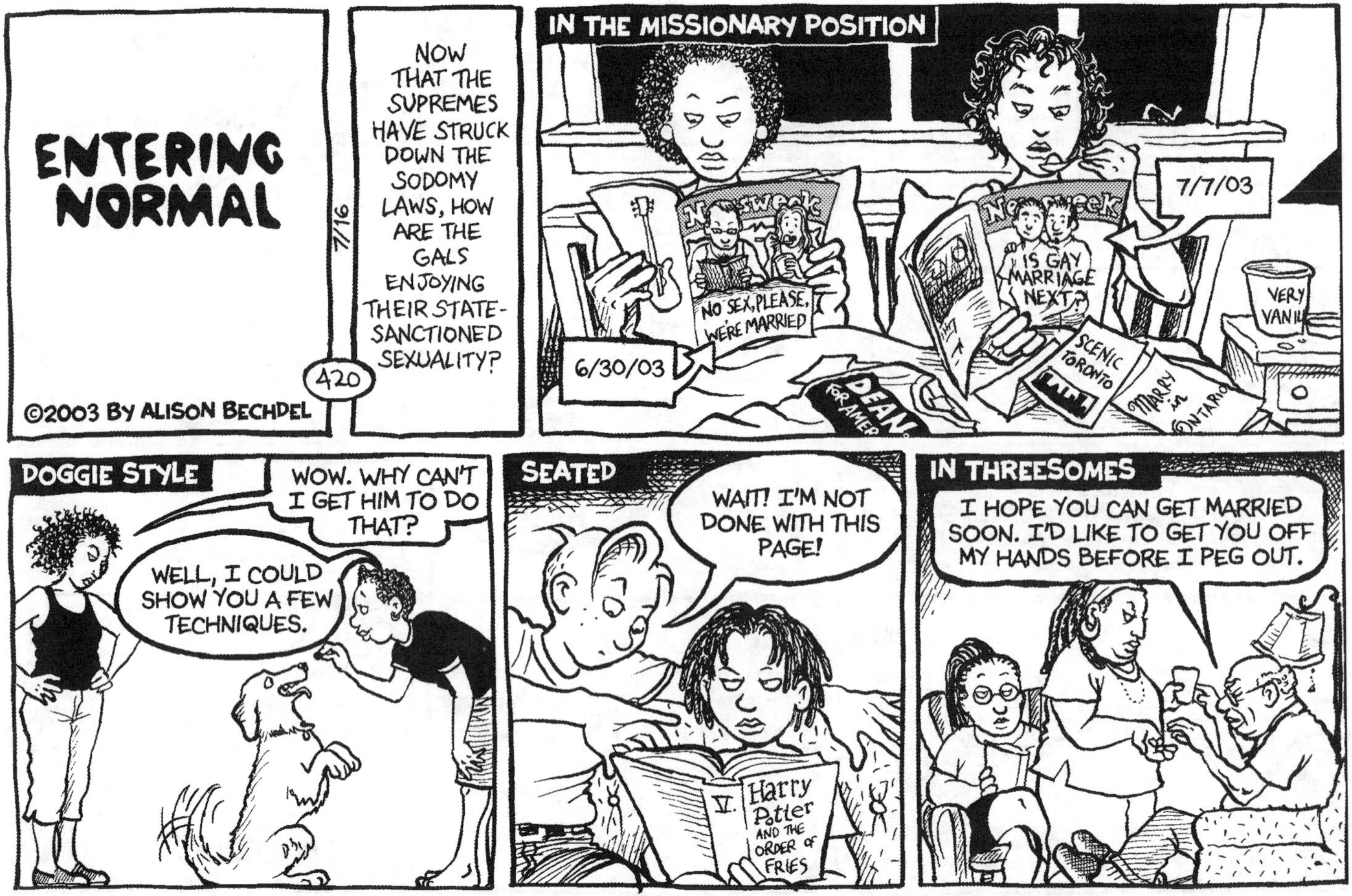

ENTERING NORMAL
©2003 BY ALISON BECHDEL
420
7/16
NOW THAT THE SUPREMES HAVE STRUCK DOWN THE SODOMY LAWS, HOW ARE THE GALS ENJOYING THEIR STATE-SANCTIONED SEXUALITY?
IN THE MISSIONARY POSITION
NO SEX, PLEASE, WE'RE MARRIED
6/30/03
IS GAY MARRIAGE NEXT?
7/7/03
SCENIC TORONTO
MARRY in ONTARIO
DOGGIE STYLE
WOW. WHY CAN'T I GET HIM TO DO THAT?
WELL, I COULD SHOW YOU A FEW TECHNIQUES.
SEATED
WAIT! I'M NOT DONE WITH THIS PAGE!
V. Harry Potter AND THE ORDER OF FRIES
IN THREESOMES
I HOPE YOU CAN GET MARRIED SOON. I'D LIKE TO GET YOU OFF MY HANDS BEFORE I PEG OUT.

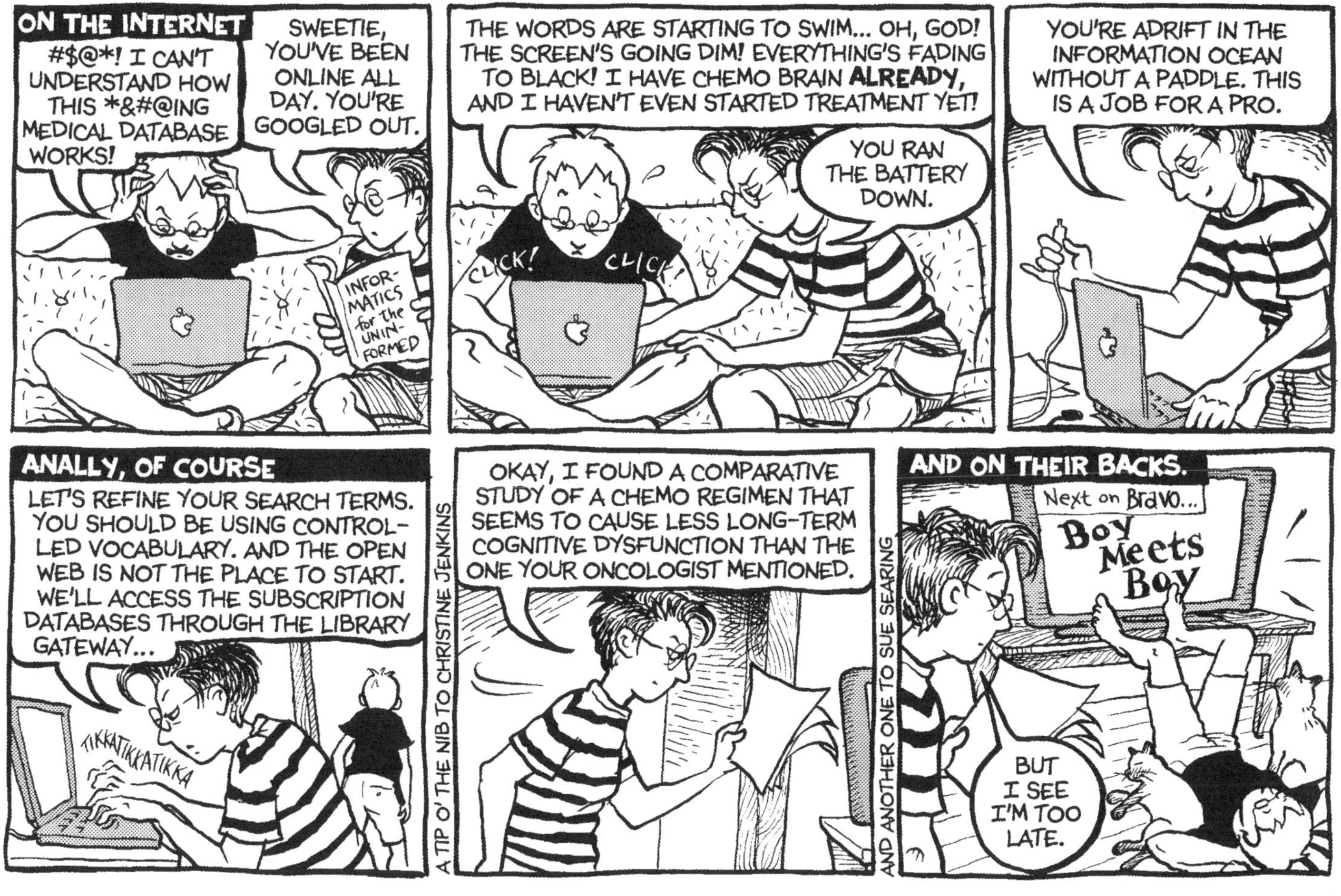
ON THE INTERNET
#$@*! I CAN'T UNDERSTAND HOW THIS *&#@ING MEDICAL DATABASE WORKS!
SWEETIE, YOU'VE BEEN ONLINE ALL DAY. YOU'RE GOOGLED OUT.
INFORMATICS for the UNINFORMED
THE WORDS ARE STARTING TO SWIM... OH, GOD! THE SCREEN'S GOING DIM! EVERYTHING'S FADING TO BLACK! I HAVE CHEMO BRAIN **ALREADY**, AND I HAVEN'T EVEN STARTED TREATMENT YET!
CLICK! CLICK
YOU RAN THE BATTERY DOWN.
YOU'RE ADRIFT IN THE INFORMATION OCEAN WITHOUT A PADDLE. THIS IS A JOB FOR A PRO.
ANALLY, OF COURSE
LET'S REFINE YOUR SEARCH TERMS. YOU SHOULD BE USING CONTROL-LED VOCABULARY. AND THE OPEN WEB IS NOT THE PLACE TO START. WE'LL ACCESS THE SUBSCRIPTION DATABASES THROUGH THE LIBRARY GATEWAY...
TIKKATIKKATIKKA
A TIP O' THE NIB TO CHRISTINE JENKINS
OKAY, I FOUND A COMPARATIVE STUDY OF A CHEMO REGIMEN THAT SEEMS TO CAUSE LESS LONG-TERM COGNITIVE DYSFUNCTION THAN THE ONE YOUR ONCOLOGIST MENTIONED.
AND ANOTHER ONE TO SUE SEARING
AND ON THEIR BACKS.
Next on Bravo...
Boy Meets Boy
BUT I SEE I'M TOO LATE.

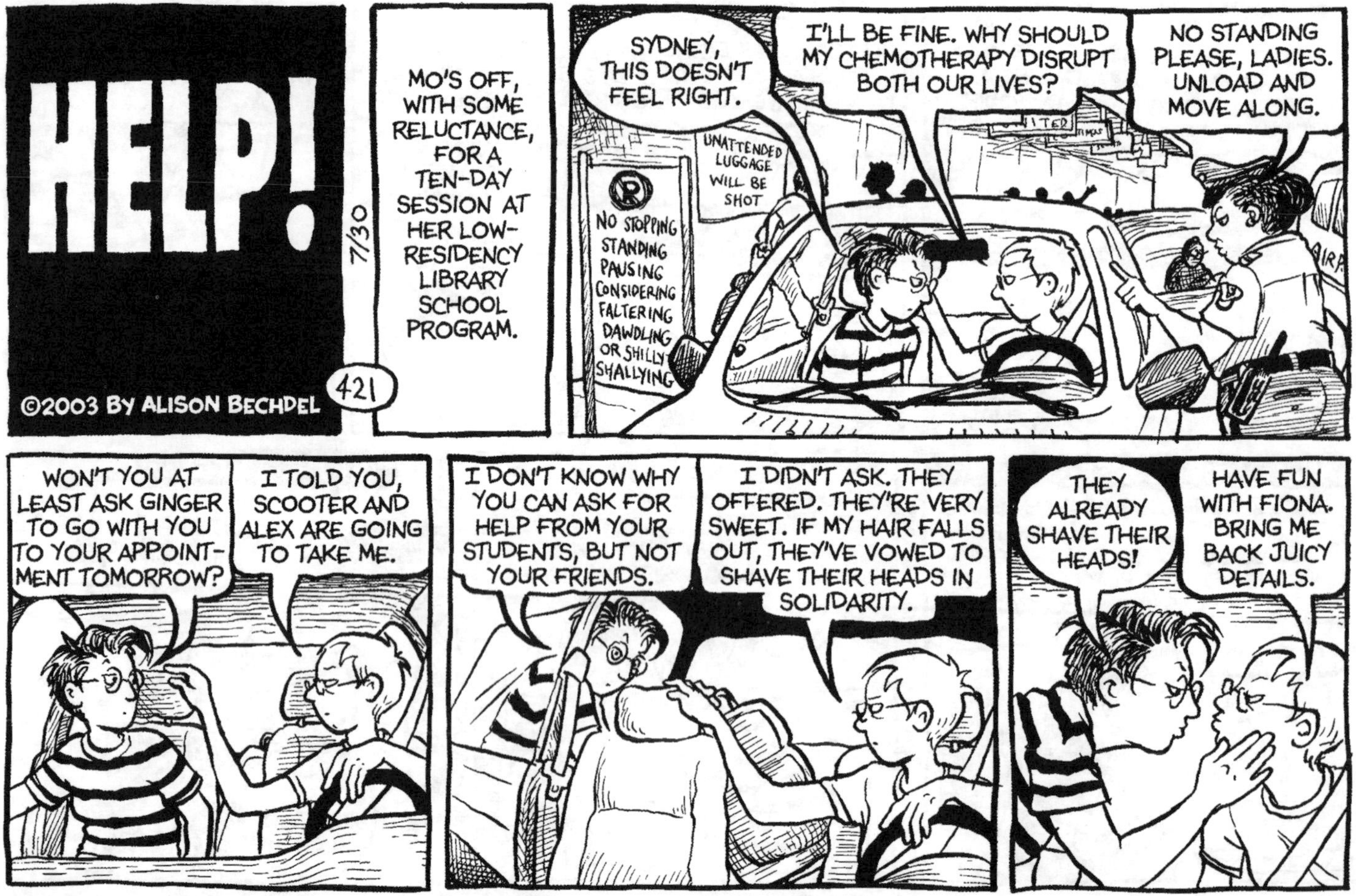
HELP!
©2003 BY ALISON BECHDEL
7/30
421
MO'S OFF, WITH SOME RELUCTANCE, FOR A TEN-DAY SESSION AT HER LOW-RESIDENCY LIBRARY SCHOOL PROGRAM.
SYDNEY, THIS DOESN'T FEEL RIGHT.
UNATTENDED LUGGAGE WILL BE SHOT
NO STOPPING STANDING PAUSING CONSIDERING FALTERING DAWDLING OR SHILLY SHALLYING
I'LL BE FINE. WHY SHOULD MY CHEMOTHERAPY DISRUPT BOTH OUR LIVES?
NO STANDING PLEASE, LADIES. UNLOAD AND MOVE ALONG.
WON'T YOU AT LEAST ASK GINGER TO GO WITH YOU TO YOUR APPOINTMENT TOMORROW?
I TOLD YOU, SCOOTER AND ALEX ARE GOING TO TAKE ME.
I DON'T KNOW WHY YOU CAN ASK FOR HELP FROM YOUR STUDENTS, BUT NOT YOUR FRIENDS.
I DIDN'T ASK. THEY OFFERED. THEY'RE VERY SWEET. IF MY HAIR FALLS OUT, THEY'VE VOWED TO SHAVE THEIR HEADS IN SOLIDARITY.
THEY ALREADY SHAVE THEIR HEADS!
HAVE FUN WITH FIONA. BRING ME BACK JUICY DETAILS.

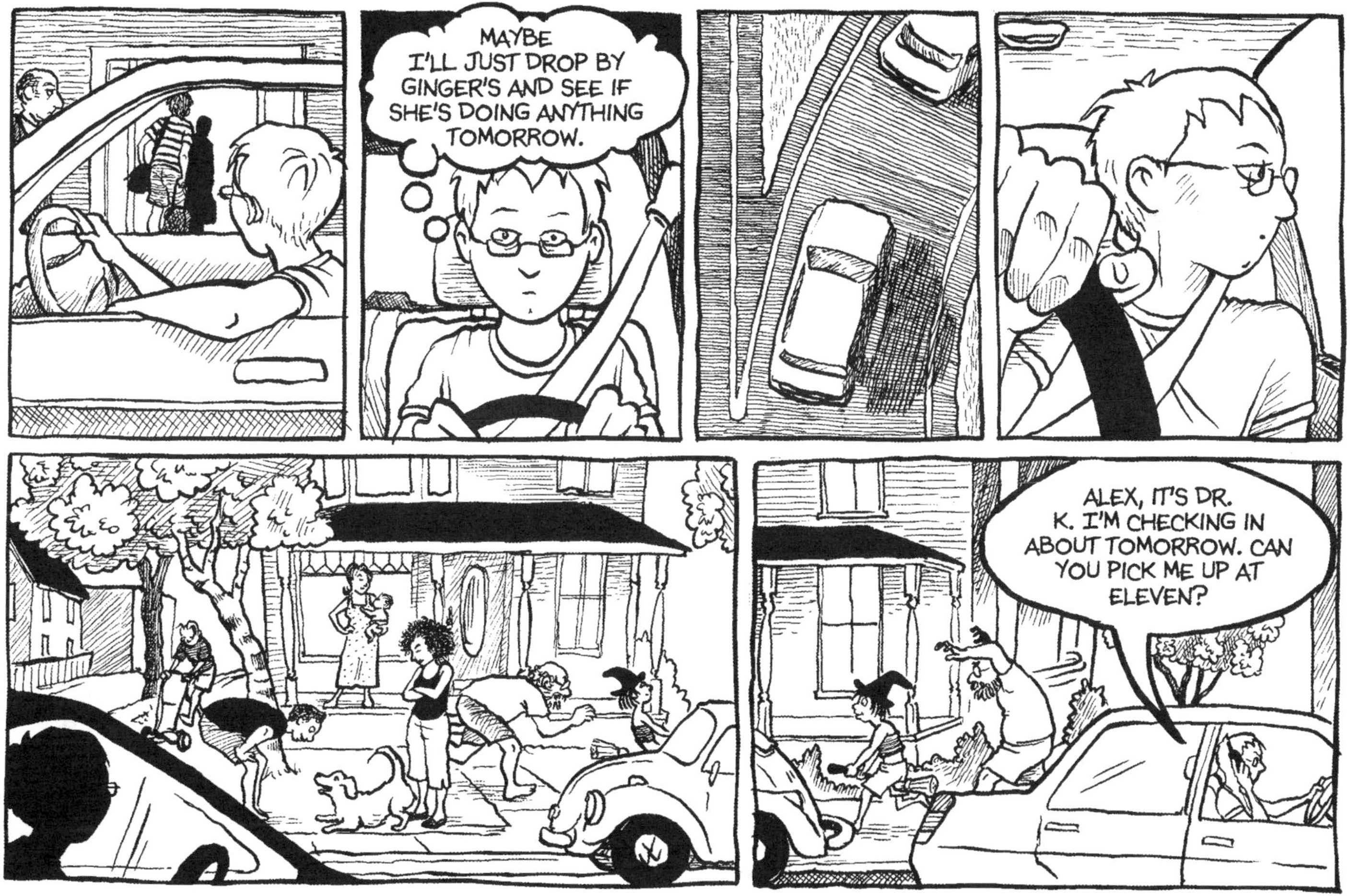
MAYBE I'LL JUST DROP BY GINGER'S AND SEE IF SHE'S DOING ANYTHING TOMORROW.
ALEX, IT'S DR. K. I'M CHECKING IN ABOUT TOMORROW. CAN YOU PICK ME UP AT ELEVEN?

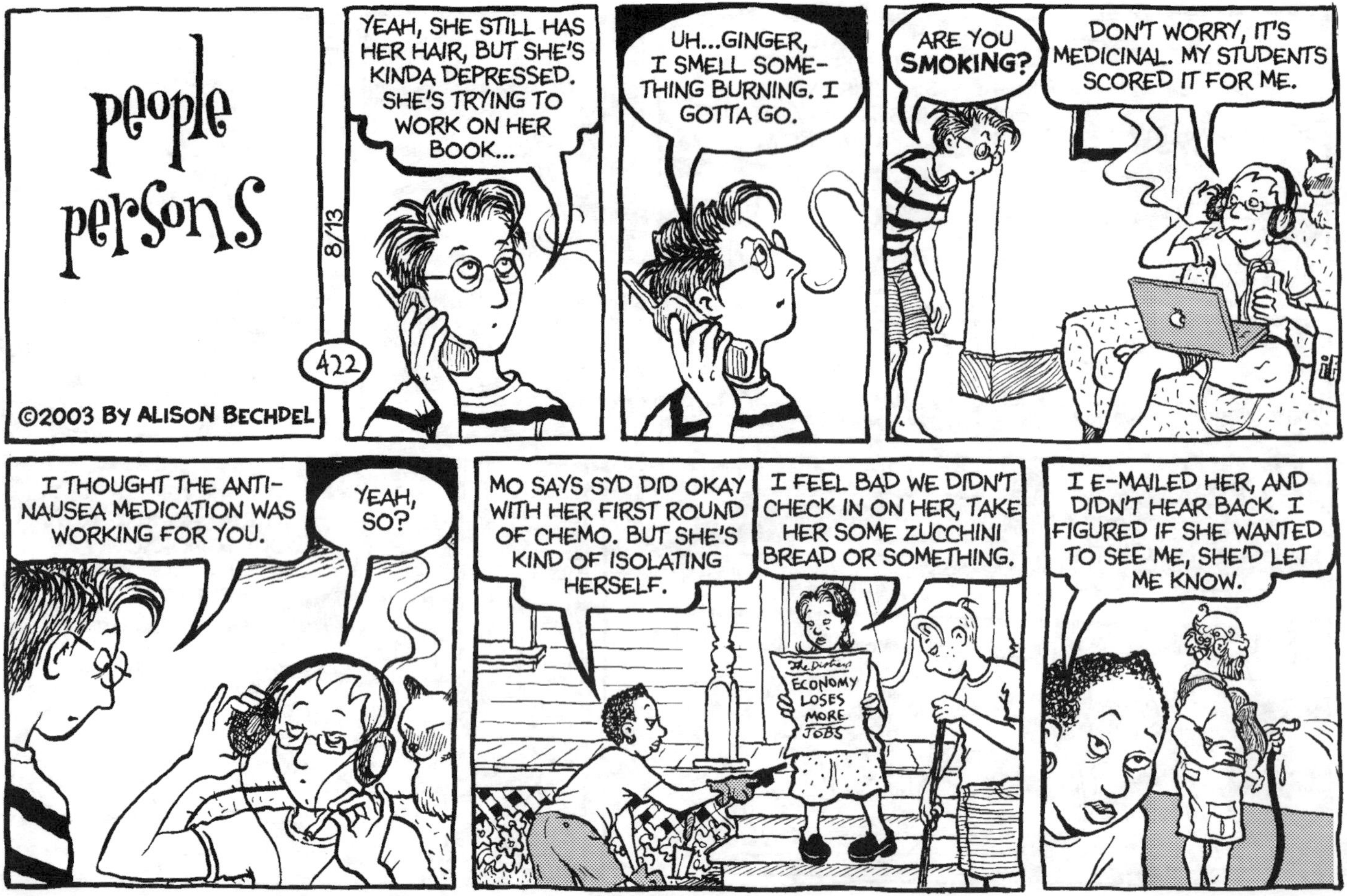
people persons
8/13
422
©2003 BY ALISON BECHDEL
YEAH, SHE STILL HAS HER HAIR, BUT SHE'S KINDA DEPRESSED. SHE'S TRYING TO WORK ON HER BOOK...
UH...GINGER, I SMELL SOMETHING BURNING. I GOTTA GO.
ARE YOU **SMOKING?**
DON'T WORRY, IT'S MEDICINAL. MY STUDENTS SCORED IT FOR ME.
I THOUGHT THE ANTI-NAUSEA MEDICATION WAS WORKING FOR YOU.
YEAH, SO?
MO SAYS SYD DID OKAY WITH HER FIRST ROUND OF CHEMO. BUT SHE'S KIND OF ISOLATING HERSELF.
I FEEL BAD WE DIDN'T CHECK IN ON HER, TAKE HER SOME ZUCCHINI BREAD OR SOMETHING.
The Dispatch
ECONOMY LOSES MORE JOBS
I E-MAILED HER, AND DIDN'T HEAR BACK. I FIGURED IF SHE WANTED TO SEE ME, SHE'D LET ME KNOW.

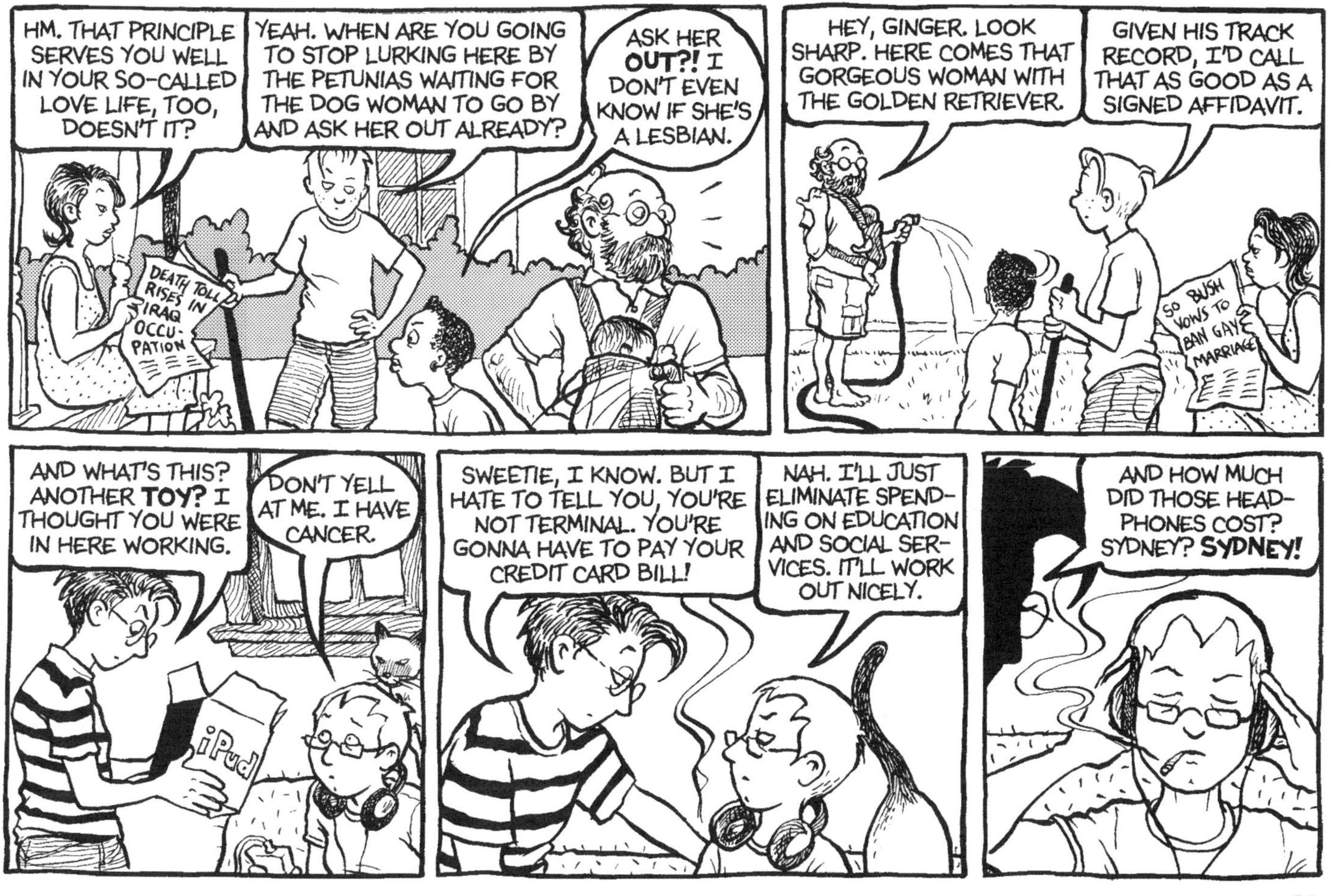
HM. THAT PRINCIPLE SERVES YOU WELL IN YOUR SO-CALLED LOVE LIFE, TOO, DOESN'T IT?
YEAH. WHEN ARE YOU GOING TO STOP LURKING HERE BY THE PETUNIAS WAITING FOR THE DOG WOMAN TO GO BY AND ASK HER OUT ALREADY?
ASK HER **OUT?!** I DON'T EVEN KNOW IF SHE'S A LESBIAN.
DEATH TOLL RISES IN IRAQ OCCUPATION
HEY, GINGER. LOOK SHARP. HERE COMES THAT GORGEOUS WOMAN WITH THE GOLDEN RETRIEVER.
GIVEN HIS TRACK RECORD, I'D CALL THAT AS GOOD AS A SIGNED AFFIDAVIT.
BUSH VOWS TO BAN GAY MARRIAGE
AND WHAT'S THIS? ANOTHER **TOY?** I THOUGHT YOU WERE IN HERE WORKING.
DON'T YELL AT ME. I HAVE CANCER.
iPud
SWEETIE, I KNOW. BUT I HATE TO TELL YOU, YOU'RE NOT TERMINAL. YOU'RE GONNA HAVE TO PAY YOUR CREDIT CARD BILL!
NAH. I'LL JUST ELIMINATE SPENDING ON EDUCATION AND SOCIAL SERVICES. IT'LL WORK OUT NICELY.
AND HOW MUCH DID THOSE HEADPHONES COST? SYDNEY? **SYDNEY!**

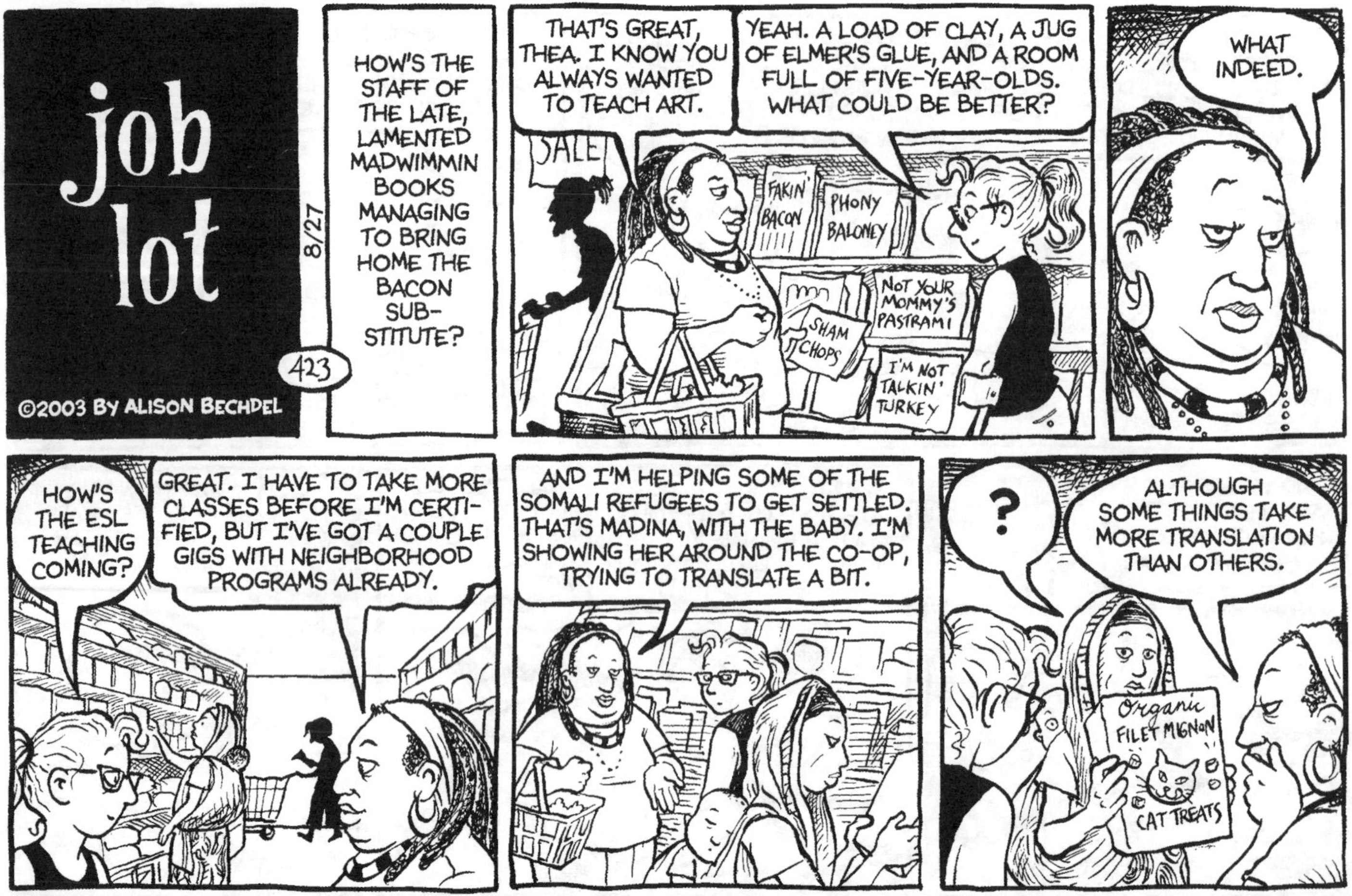
job lot
©2003 BY ALISON BECHDEL
423
8/27
HOW'S THE STAFF OF THE LATE, LAMENTED MADWIMMIN BOOKS MANAGING TO BRING HOME THE BACON SUB-STITUTE?
THAT'S GREAT, THEA. I KNOW YOU ALWAYS WANTED TO TEACH ART.
YEAH. A LOAD OF CLAY, A JUG OF ELMER'S GLUE, AND A ROOM FULL OF FIVE-YEAR-OLDS. WHAT COULD BE BETTER?
SALE
FAKIN' BACON
PHONY BALONEY
SHAM CHOPS
NOT YOUR MOMMY'S PASTRAMI
I'M NOT TALKIN' TURKEY
WHAT INDEED.
HOW'S THE ESL TEACHING COMING?
GREAT. I HAVE TO TAKE MORE CLASSES BEFORE I'M CERTI-FIED, BUT I'VE GOT A COUPLE GIGS WITH NEIGHBORHOOD PROGRAMS ALREADY.
AND I'M HELPING SOME OF THE SOMALI REFUGEES TO GET SETTLED. THAT'S MADINA, WITH THE BABY. I'M SHOWING HER AROUND THE CO-OP, TRYING TO TRANSLATE A BIT.
?
ALTHOUGH SOME THINGS TAKE MORE TRANSLATION THAN OTHERS.
Organic FILET MIGNON CAT TREATS

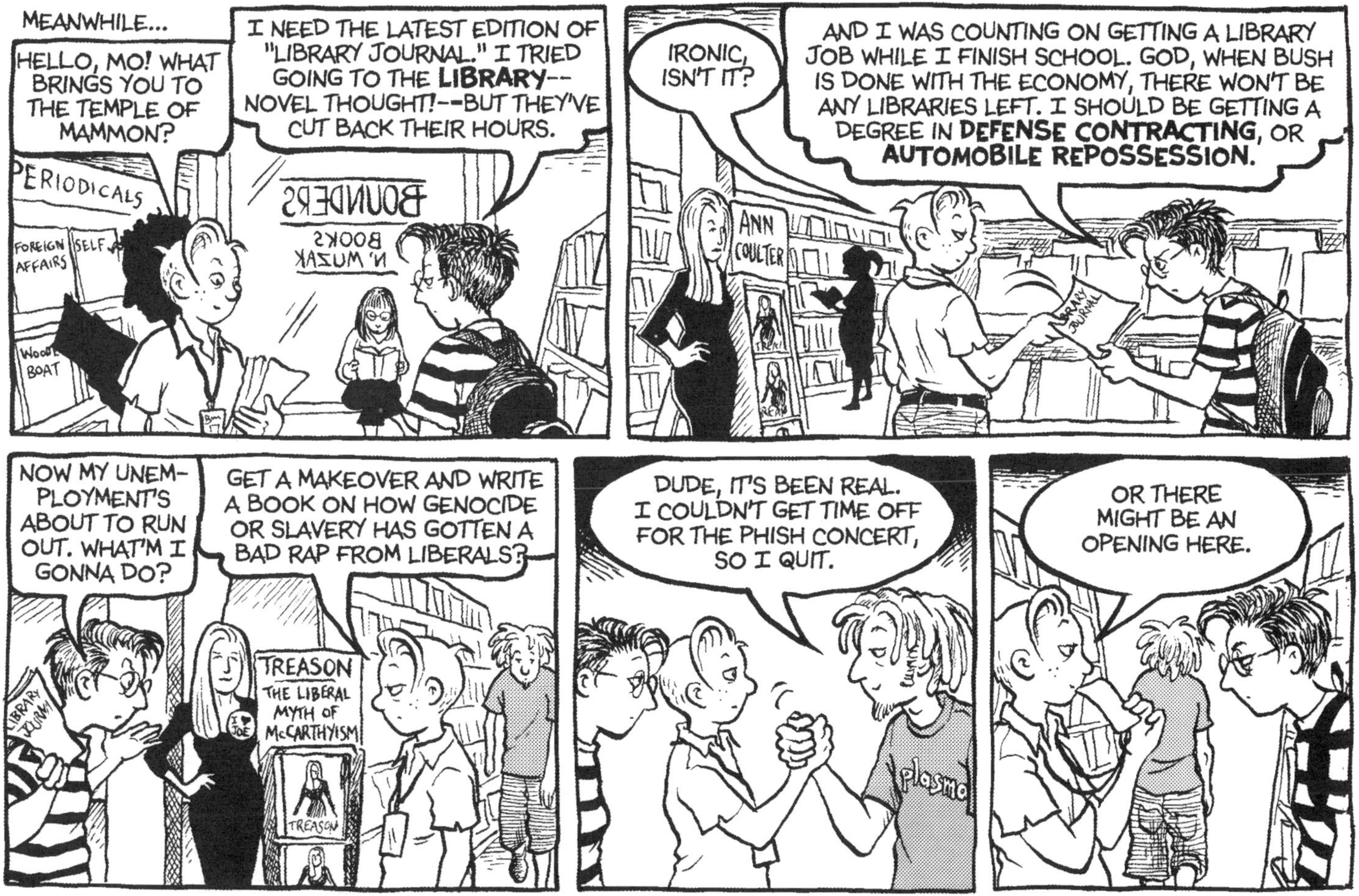
MEANWHILE...
HELLO, MO! WHAT BRINGS YOU TO THE TEMPLE OF MAMMON?
I NEED THE LATEST EDITION OF "LIBRARY JOURNAL." I TRIED GOING TO THE **LIBRARY**--NOVEL THOUGHT!--BUT THEY'VE CUT BACK THEIR HOURS.
PERIODICALS
FOREIGN AFFAIRS
SELF
BOAT
BOUNDERS
BOOKS N' MUZAK
IRONIC, ISN'T IT?
AND I WAS COUNTING ON GETTING A LIBRARY JOB WHILE I FINISH SCHOOL. GOD, WHEN BUSH IS DONE WITH THE ECONOMY, THERE WON'T BE ANY LIBRARIES LEFT. I SHOULD BE GETTING A DEGREE IN **DEFENSE CONTRACTING**, OR **AUTOMOBILE REPOSSESSION**.
ANN COULTER
NOW MY UNEMPLOYMENT'S ABOUT TO RUN OUT. WHAT'M I GONNA DO?
GET A MAKEOVER AND WRITE A BOOK ON HOW GENOCIDE OR SLAVERY HAS GOTTEN A BAD RAP FROM LIBERALS?
LIBRARY JOURNAL
I ♥ JOE
TREASON
THE LIBERAL MYTH OF McCARTHYISM
TREASON
DUDE, IT'S BEEN REAL. I COULDN'T GET TIME OFF FOR THE PHISH CONCERT, SO I QUIT.
plasma
OR THERE MIGHT BE AN OPENING HERE.

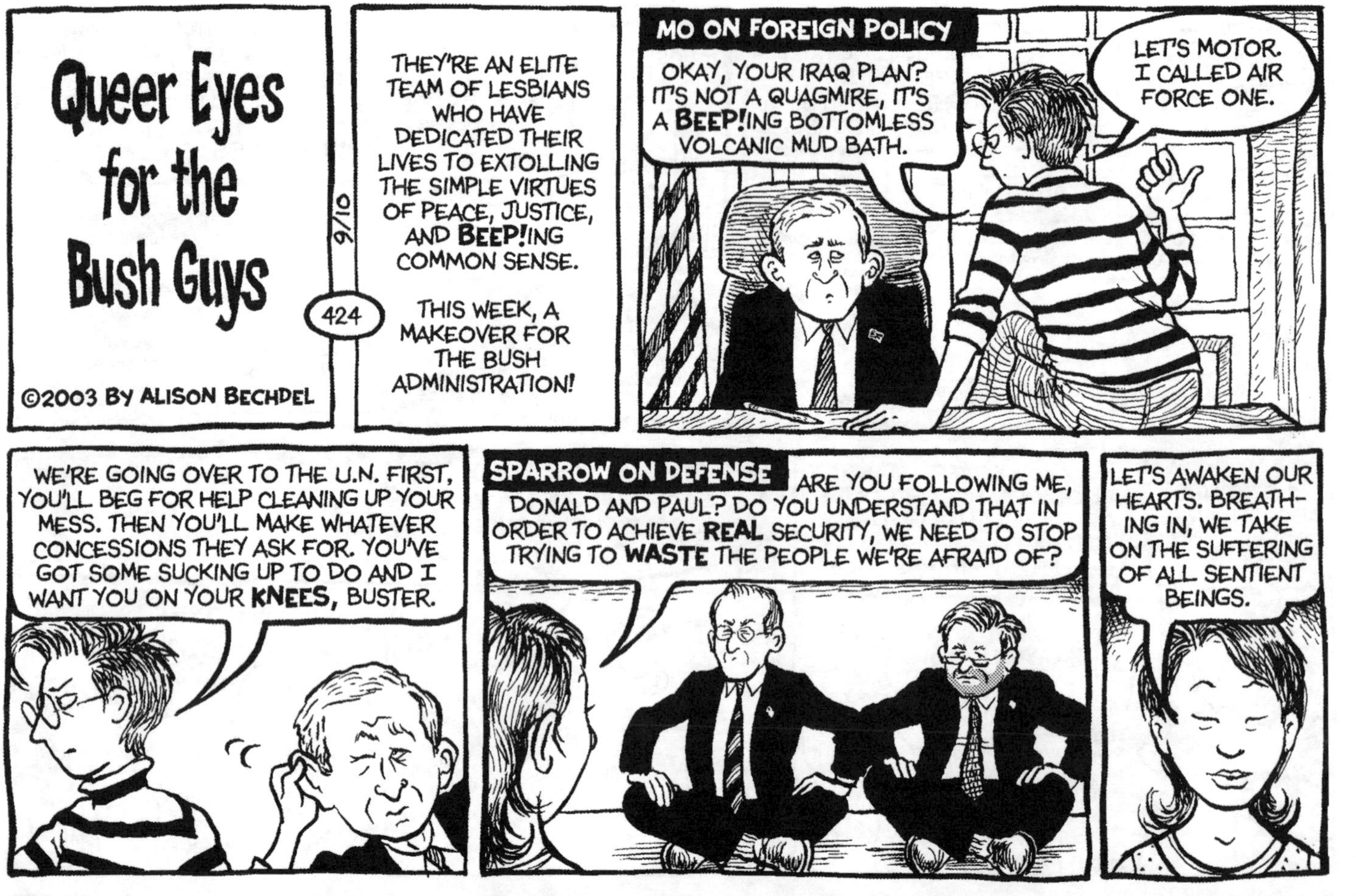

Queer Eyes for the Bush Guys
©2003 BY ALISON BECHDEL
424
9/10
THEY'RE AN ELITE TEAM OF LESBIANS WHO HAVE DEDICATED THEIR LIVES TO EXTOLLING THE SIMPLE VIRTUES OF PEACE, JUSTICE, AND BEEP!ING COMMON SENSE.
THIS WEEK, A MAKEOVER FOR THE BUSH ADMINISTRATION!
MO ON FOREIGN POLICY
OKAY, YOUR IRAQ PLAN? IT'S NOT A QUAGMIRE, IT'S A BEEP!ING BOTTOMLESS VOLCANIC MUD BATH.
LET'S MOTOR. I CALLED AIR FORCE ONE.
WE'RE GOING OVER TO THE U.N. FIRST, YOU'LL BEG FOR HELP CLEANING UP YOUR MESS. THEN YOU'LL MAKE WHATEVER CONCESSIONS THEY ASK FOR. YOU'VE GOT SOME SUCKING UP TO DO AND I WANT YOU ON YOUR KNEES, BUSTER.
SPARROW ON DEFENSE
ARE YOU FOLLOWING ME, DONALD AND PAUL? DO YOU UNDERSTAND THAT IN ORDER TO ACHIEVE REAL SECURITY, WE NEED TO STOP TRYING TO WASTE THE PEOPLE WE'RE AFRAID OF?
LET'S AWAKEN OUR HEARTS. BREATHING IN, WE TAKE ON THE SUFFERING OF ALL SENTIENT BEINGS.

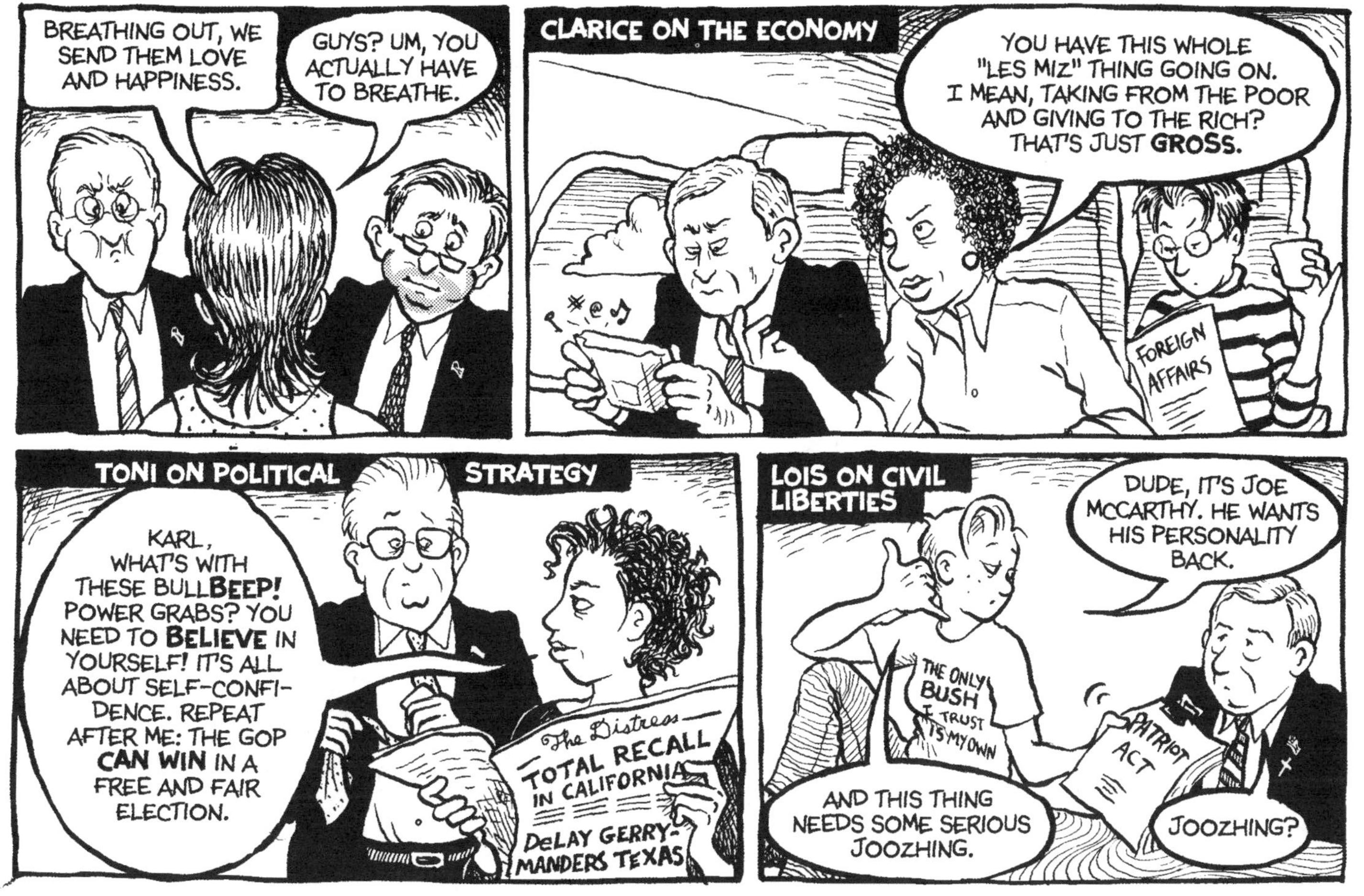

BREATHING OUT, WE SEND THEM LOVE AND HAPPINESS.
GUYS? UM, YOU ACTUALLY HAVE TO BREATHE.
CLARICE ON THE ECONOMY
YOU HAVE THIS WHOLE "LES MIZ" THING GOING ON. I MEAN, TAKING FROM THE POOR AND GIVING TO THE RICH? THAT'S JUST GROSS.
FOREIGN AFFAIRS
TONI ON POLITICAL STRATEGY
KARL, WHAT'S WITH THESE BULLBEEP! POWER GRABS? YOU NEED TO BELIEVE IN YOURSELF! IT'S ALL ABOUT SELF-CONFIDENCE. REPEAT AFTER ME: THE GOP CAN WIN IN A FREE AND FAIR ELECTION.
The Distress
TOTAL RECALL IN CALIFORNIA
DeLAY GERRYMANDERS TEXAS
LOIS ON CIVIL LIBERTIES
DUDE, IT'S JOE MCCARTHY. HE WANTS HIS PERSONALITY BACK.
THE ONLY BUSH I TRUST IS MY OWN
PATRIOT ACT
AND THIS THING NEEDS SOME SERIOUS JOOZHING.
JOOZHING?

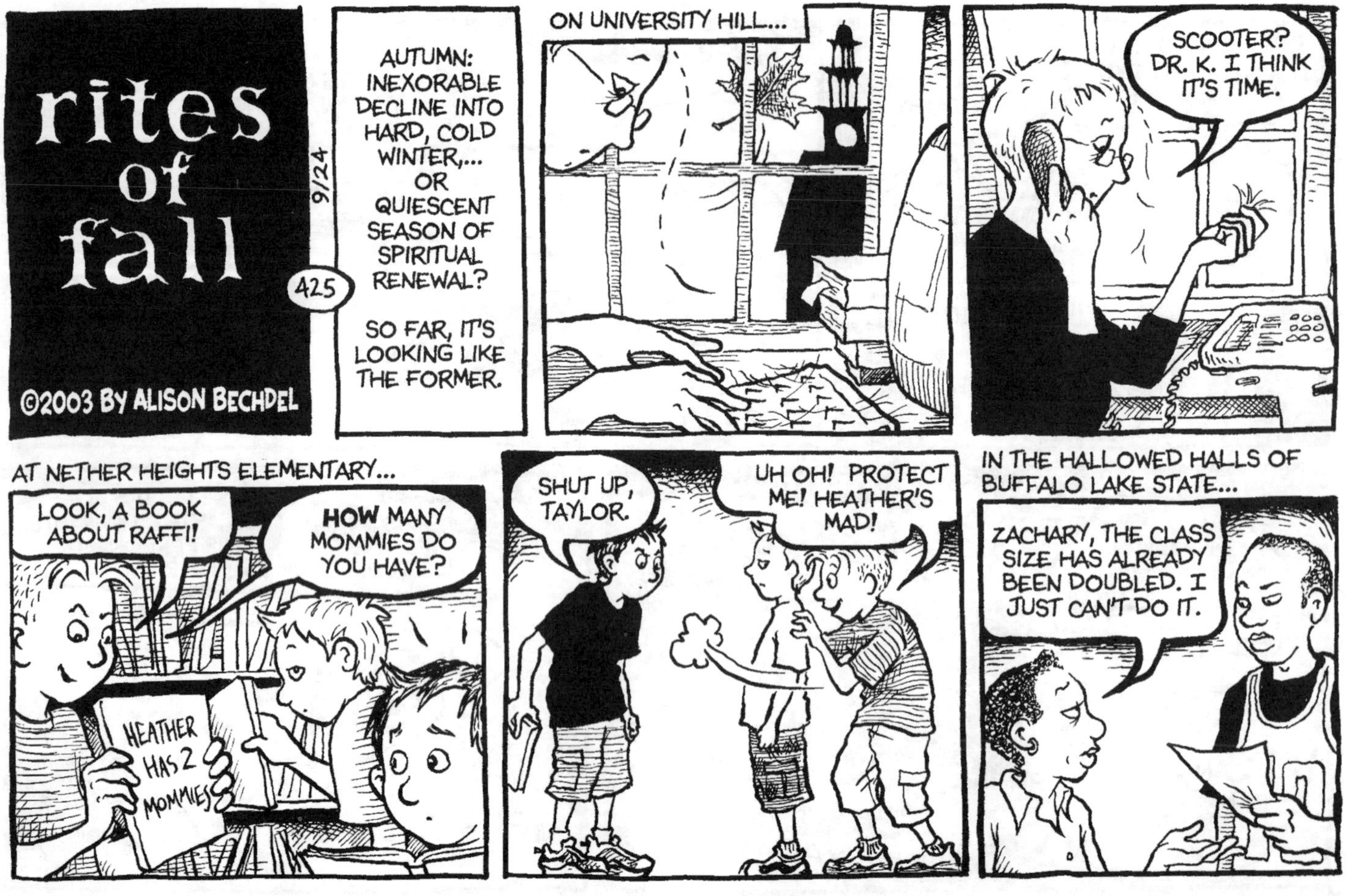
rites of fall
425
9/24
©2003 BY ALISON BECHDEL
AUTUMN: INEXORABLE DECLINE INTO HARD, COLD WINTER,... OR QUIESCENT SEASON OF SPIRITUAL RENEWAL?
SO FAR, IT'S LOOKING LIKE THE FORMER.
ON UNIVERSITY HILL...
SCOOTER? DR. K. I THINK IT'S TIME.
AT NETHER HEIGHTS ELEMENTARY...
LOOK, A BOOK ABOUT RAFFI!
HOW MANY MOMMIES DO YOU HAVE?
HEATHER HAS 2 MOMMIES
SHUT UP, TAYLOR.
UH OH! PROTECT ME! HEATHER'S MAD!
IN THE HALLOWED HALLS OF BUFFALO LAKE STATE...
ZACHARY, THE CLASS SIZE HAS ALREADY BEEN DOUBLED. I JUST CAN'T DO IT.

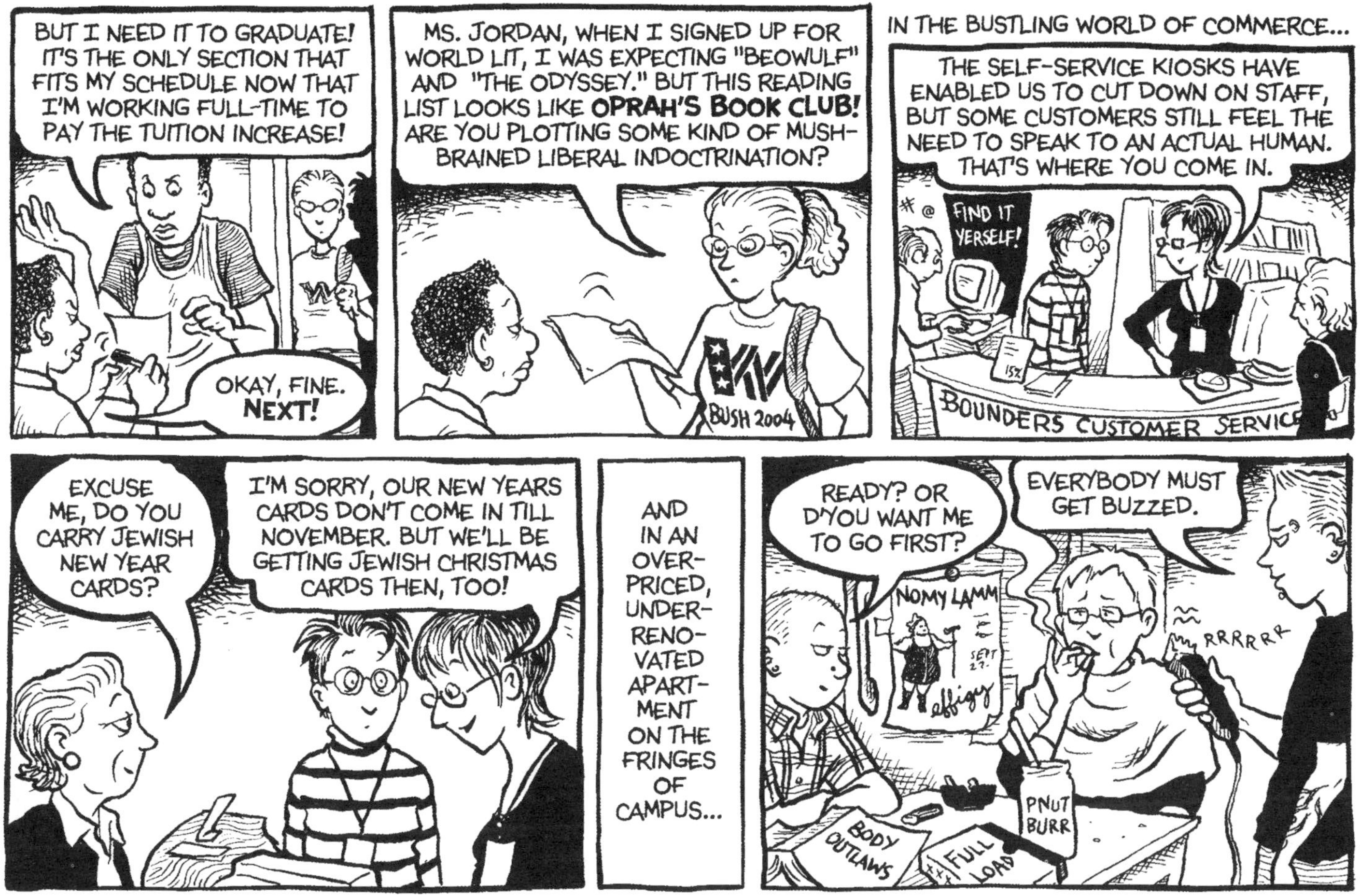
BUT I NEED IT TO GRADUATE! IT'S THE ONLY SECTION THAT FITS MY SCHEDULE NOW THAT I'M WORKING FULL-TIME TO PAY THE TUITION INCREASE!
OKAY, FINE. NEXT!
MS. JORDAN, WHEN I SIGNED UP FOR WORLD LIT, I WAS EXPECTING "BEOWULF" AND "THE ODYSSEY." BUT THIS READING LIST LOOKS LIKE OPRAH'S BOOK CLUB! ARE YOU PLOTTING SOME KIND OF MUSH-BRAINED LIBERAL INDOCTRINATION?
BUSH 2004
IN THE BUSTLING WORLD OF COMMERCE...
THE SELF-SERVICE KIOSKS HAVE ENABLED US TO CUT DOWN ON STAFF, BUT SOME CUSTOMERS STILL FEEL THE NEED TO SPEAK TO AN ACTUAL HUMAN. THAT'S WHERE YOU COME IN.
FIND IT YERSELF!
BOUNDERS CUSTOMER SERVICE
EXCUSE ME, DO YOU CARRY JEWISH NEW YEAR CARDS?
I'M SORRY, OUR NEW YEARS CARDS DON'T COME IN TILL NOVEMBER. BUT WE'LL BE GETTING JEWISH CHRISTMAS CARDS THEN, TOO!
AND IN AN OVER-PRICED, UNDER-RENO-VATED APART-MENT ON THE FRINGES OF CAMPUS...
READY? OR D'YOU WANT ME TO GO FIRST?
EVERYBODY MUST GET BUZZED.
NOMY LAMM
effigy
RRRRRR
PNUT BURR
BODY OUTLAWS
FULL LOAD

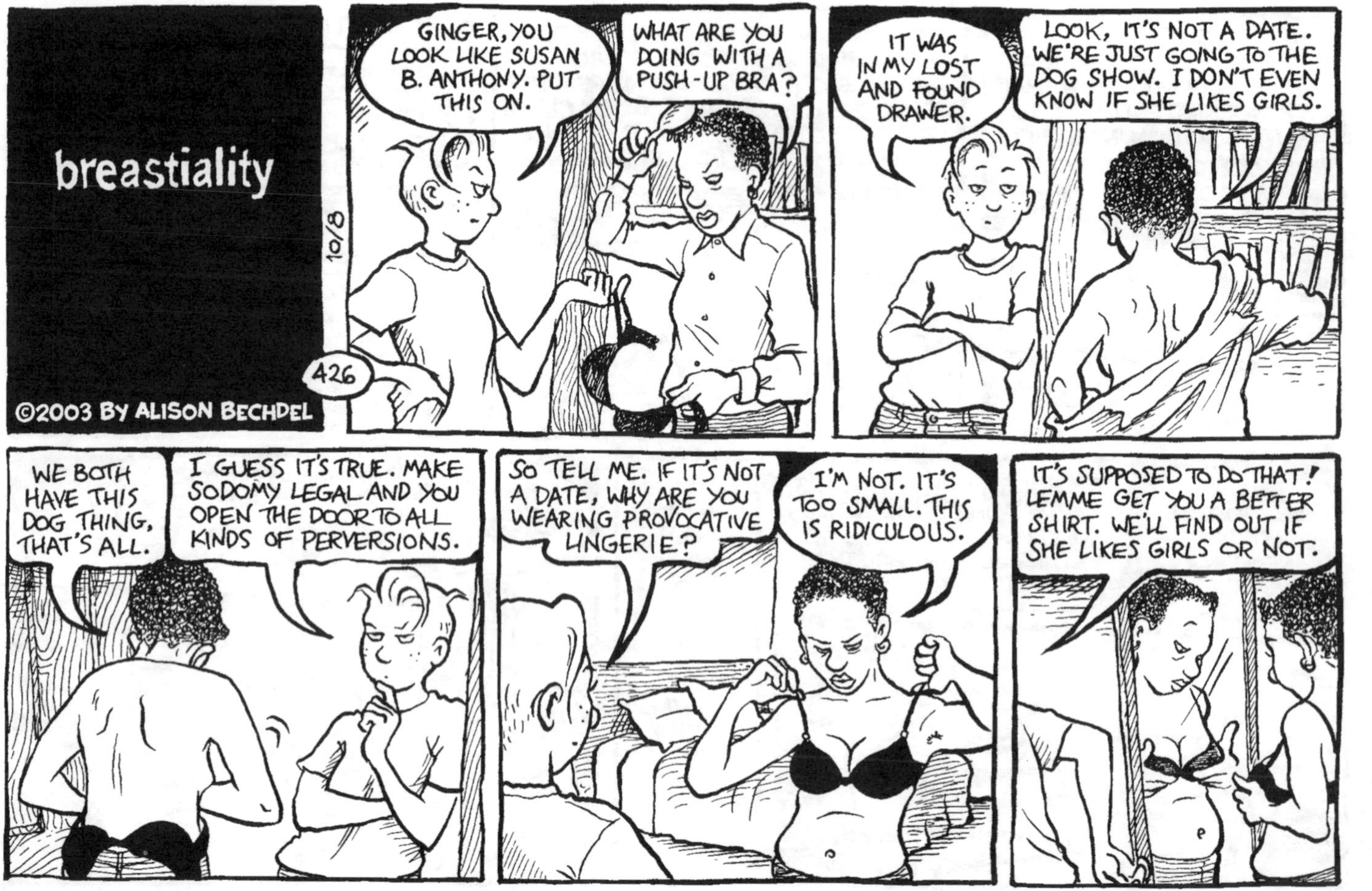
breastiality
10/8
426
©2003 BY ALISON BECHDEL
GINGER, YOU LOOK LIKE SUSAN B. ANTHONY. PUT THIS ON.
WHAT ARE YOU DOING WITH A PUSH-UP BRA?
IT WAS IN MY LOST AND FOUND DRAWER.
LOOK, IT'S NOT A DATE. WE'RE JUST GOING TO THE DOG SHOW. I DON'T EVEN KNOW IF SHE LIKES GIRLS.
WE BOTH HAVE THIS DOG THING, THAT'S ALL.
I GUESS IT'S TRUE. MAKE SODOMY LEGAL AND YOU OPEN THE DOOR TO ALL KINDS OF PERVERSIONS.
SO TELL ME. IF IT'S NOT A DATE, WHY ARE YOU WEARING PROVOCATIVE LINGERIE?
I'M NOT. IT'S TOO SMALL. THIS IS RIDICULOUS.
IT'S SUPPOSED TO DO THAT! LEMME GET YOU A BETTER SHIRT. WE'LL FIND OUT IF SHE LIKES GIRLS OR NOT.

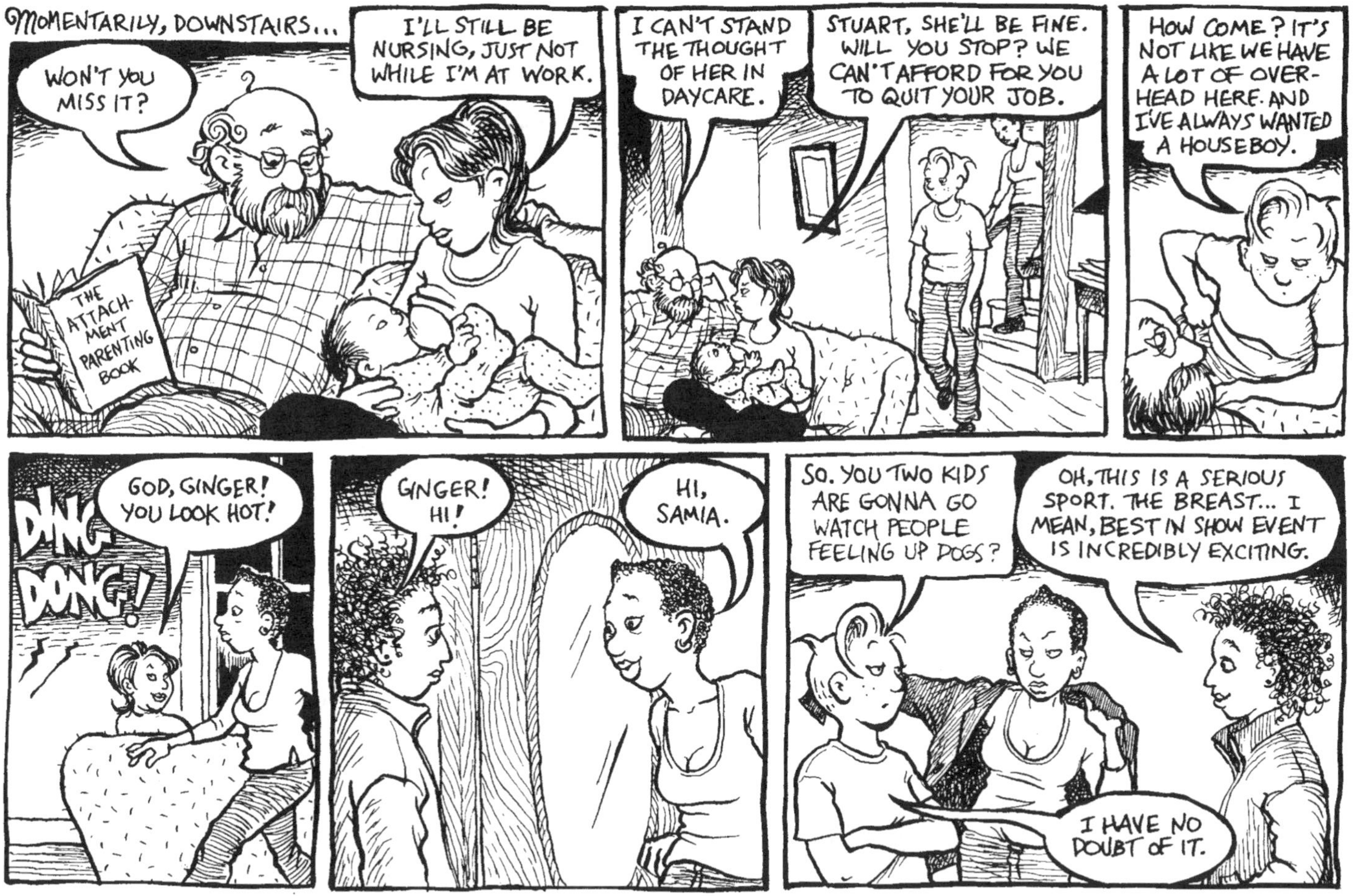
MOMENTARILY, DOWNSTAIRS...
WON'T YOU MISS IT?
I'LL STILL BE NURSING, JUST NOT WHILE I'M AT WORK.
THE ATTACHMENT PARENTING BOOK
I CAN'T STAND THE THOUGHT OF HER IN DAYCARE.
STUART, SHE'LL BE FINE. WILL YOU STOP? WE CAN'T AFFORD FOR YOU TO QUIT YOUR JOB.
HOW COME? IT'S NOT LIKE WE HAVE A LOT OF OVERHEAD HERE. AND I'VE ALWAYS WANTED A HOUSEBOY.
DING DONG!
GOD, GINGER! YOU LOOK HOT!
GINGER! HI!
HI, SAMIA.
SO. YOU TWO KIDS ARE GONNA GO WATCH PEOPLE FEELING UP DOGS?
OH, THIS IS A SERIOUS SPORT. THE BREAST... I MEAN, BEST IN SHOW EVENT IS INCREDIBLY EXCITING.
I HAVE NO DOUBT OF IT.

how quickly they grow
©2003 BY ALISON BECHDEL
427
10/22
I'M SO RELIEVED HIS POLL NUMBERS ARE DOWN, I COULD WEEP.
I JUST WONDER WHAT FRESH HELL THEY'RE PLOTTING TO GET THEM BACK UP AGAIN.
I'M WITH YOU. BUT SYDNEY THINKS WE'RE CYNICAL CASSANDRAS.
YES, I DO. BUT I'M GRIMACING BECAUSE EVERYTHING TASTES SO WEIRD AFTER A TREATMENT. THIS IS LIKE MOLYBDENUM VINAIGRETTE.
SYDNEY, LET ME SEE YOUR HEAD AGAIN.
COOL.
RAFFI, WHY DON'T YOU GO DOWNLOAD SOME BEYONCÉ OR SOMETHING?
NO, STAY, RAF. TELL ME HOW FIFTH GRADE'S GOING.
IT'S OKAY. EXCEPT FOR TAYLOR MAKING FUN OF ME FOR HAVING TWO MOTHERS. I'M GONNA KICK HIS @$$.
RAFFI, LANGUAGE. I KNOW TAYLOR'S A PROBLEM, BUT VIOLENCE ISN'T THE SOLUTION.

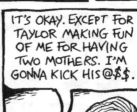

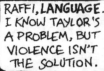

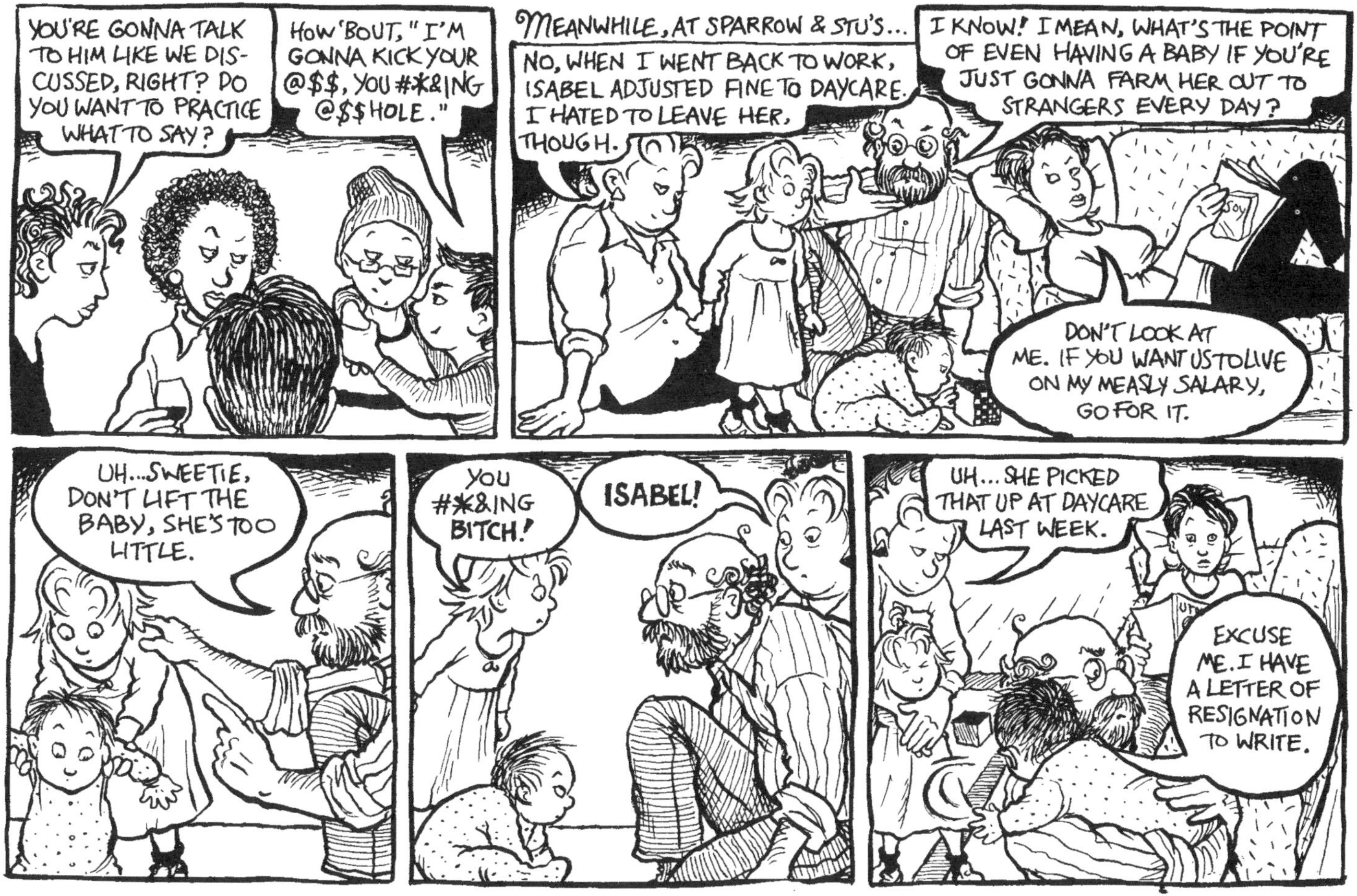

YOU'RE GONNA TALK TO HIM LIKE WE DISCUSSED, RIGHT? DO YOU WANT TO PRACTICE WHAT TO SAY?
HOW 'BOUT, "I'M GONNA KICK YOUR @$$, YOU #*&ING @$$HOLE."
MEANWHILE, AT SPARROW & STU'S...
NO, WHEN I WENT BACK TO WORK, ISABEL ADJUSTED FINE TO DAYCARE. I HATED TO LEAVE HER, THOUGH.
I KNOW! I MEAN, WHAT'S THE POINT OF EVEN HAVING A BABY IF YOU'RE JUST GONNA FARM HER OUT TO STRANGERS EVERY DAY?
DON'T LOOK AT ME. IF YOU WANT US TO LIVE ON MY MEASLY SALARY, GO FOR IT.
UH...SWEETIE, DON'T LIFT THE BABY, SHE'S TOO LITTLE.
YOU #*&ING BITCH!
ISABEL!
UH... SHE PICKED THAT UP AT DAYCARE LAST WEEK.
EXCUSE ME. I HAVE A LETTER OF RESIGNATION TO WRITE.

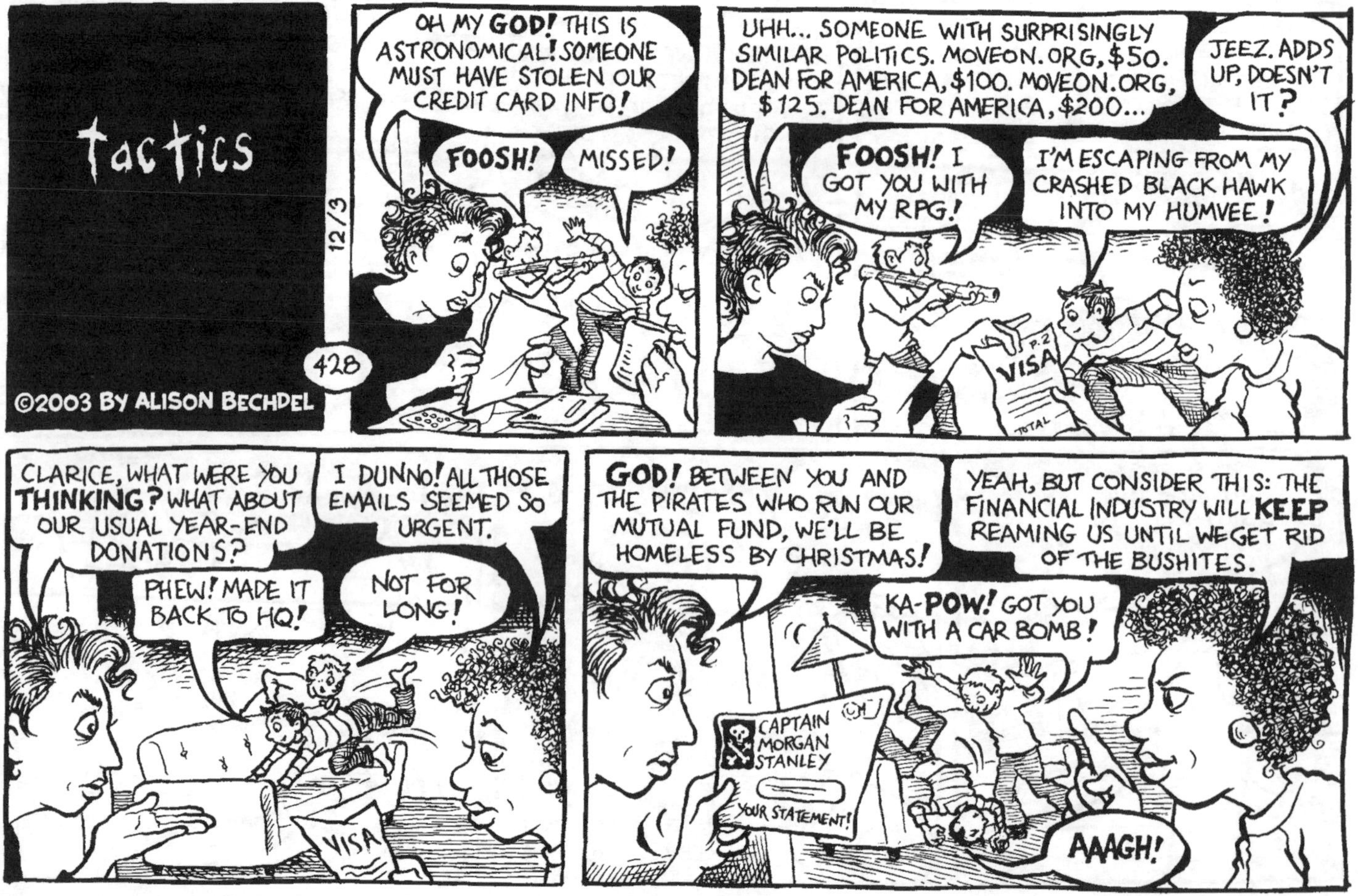
tactics
©2003 BY ALISON BECHDEL
428
12/3
OH MY **GOD!** THIS IS ASTRONOMICAL! SOMEONE MUST HAVE STOLEN OUR CREDIT CARD INFO!
FOOSH!
MISSED!
UHH... SOMEONE WITH SURPRISINGLY SIMILAR POLITICS. MOVEON.ORG, $50. DEAN FOR AMERICA, $100. MOVEON.ORG, $125. DEAN FOR AMERICA, $200...
JEEZ. ADDS UP, DOESN'T IT?
FOOSH! I GOT YOU WITH MY RPG!
I'M ESCAPING FROM MY CRASHED BLACK HAWK INTO MY HUMVEE!
P. 2
VISA
TOTAL
CLARICE, WHAT WERE YOU **THINKING?** WHAT ABOUT OUR USUAL YEAR-END DONATIONS?
I DUNNO! ALL THOSE EMAILS SEEMED SO URGENT.
PHEW! MADE IT BACK TO HQ!
NOT FOR LONG!
VISA
GOD! BETWEEN YOU AND THE PIRATES WHO RUN OUR MUTUAL FUND, WE'LL BE HOMELESS BY CHRISTMAS!
YEAH, BUT CONSIDER THIS: THE FINANCIAL INDUSTRY WILL **KEEP** REAMING US UNTIL WE GET RID OF THE BUSHITES.
KA-**POW!** GOT YOU WITH A CAR BOMB!
CAPTAIN MORGAN STANLEY
YOUR STATEMENT!
AAAGH!

MAYBE THE BEST THING WE CAN DO FOR THE CAUSES WE CARE ABOUT IS TO FUNNEL AS MUCH MONEY AS POSSIBLE INTO THE ELECTION!

I'M TAKING YOUR HUMVEE!

HEY!

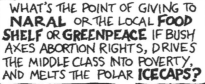

WHAT'S THE POINT OF GIVING TO **NARAL** OR THE LOCAL **FOOD SHELF** OR **GREENPEACE** IF BUSH AXES ABORTION RIGHTS, DRIVES THE MIDDLE CLASS INTO POVERTY, AND MELTS THE POLAR **ICECAPS**?

CLARICE, THAT HAS TO BE THE MOST IRRESPONSIBLE THING YOU'VE EV—

BOYS! WHAT ARE YOU **DOING?**

CRASH!

OW!

BILLY MADE A SUICIDE ATTACK ON ME BUT HE WON'T DIE!

I ONLY GOT MAIMED, YOU **WUSSPANTS!**

TOO BAD THERE'S A $2,000 CAMPAIGN LIMIT. MAYBE WE COULD TAKE OUT A SECOND MORTGAGE AND WORK THE SOFT-MONEY ANGLE.

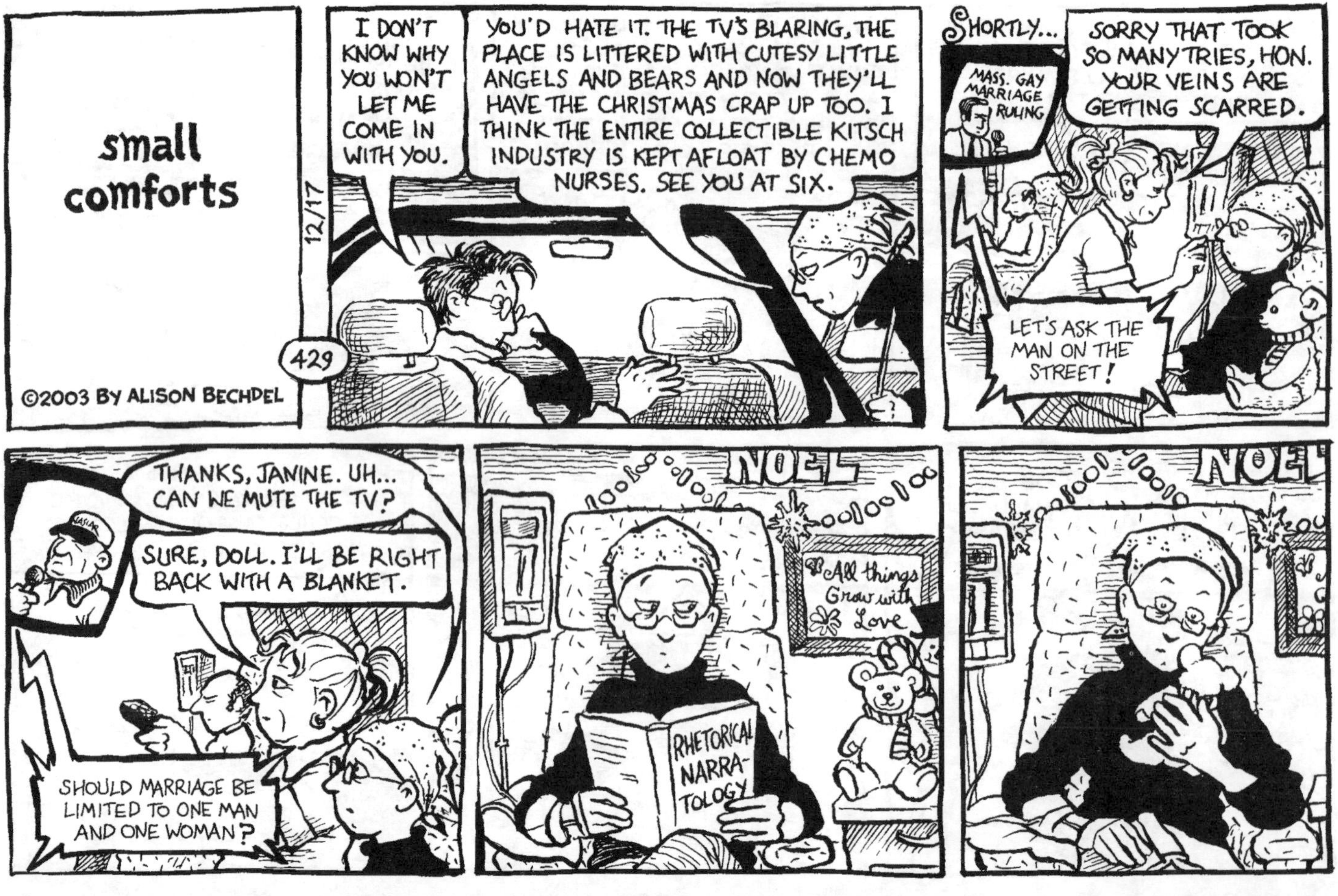
small comforts
©2003 BY ALISON BECHDEL
12/17
429
I DON'T KNOW WHY YOU WON'T LET ME COME IN WITH YOU.
YOU'D HATE IT. THE TV'S BLARING, THE PLACE IS LITTERED WITH CUTESY LITTLE ANGELS AND BEARS AND NOW THEY'LL HAVE THE CHRISTMAS CRAP UP TOO. I THINK THE ENTIRE COLLECTIBLE KITSCH INDUSTRY IS KEPT AFLOAT BY CHEMO NURSES. SEE YOU AT SIX.
SHORTLY...
MASS. GAY MARRIAGE RULING
SORRY THAT TOOK SO MANY TRIES, HON. YOUR VEINS ARE GETTING SCARRED.
LET'S ASK THE MAN ON THE STREET!
NASCAR
THANKS, JANINE. UH... CAN WE MUTE THE TV?
SURE, DOLL. I'LL BE RIGHT BACK WITH A BLANKET.
SHOULD MARRIAGE BE LIMITED TO ONE MAN AND ONE WOMAN?
NOEL
All things Grow with Love
RHETORICAL NARRATOLOGY
NOEL

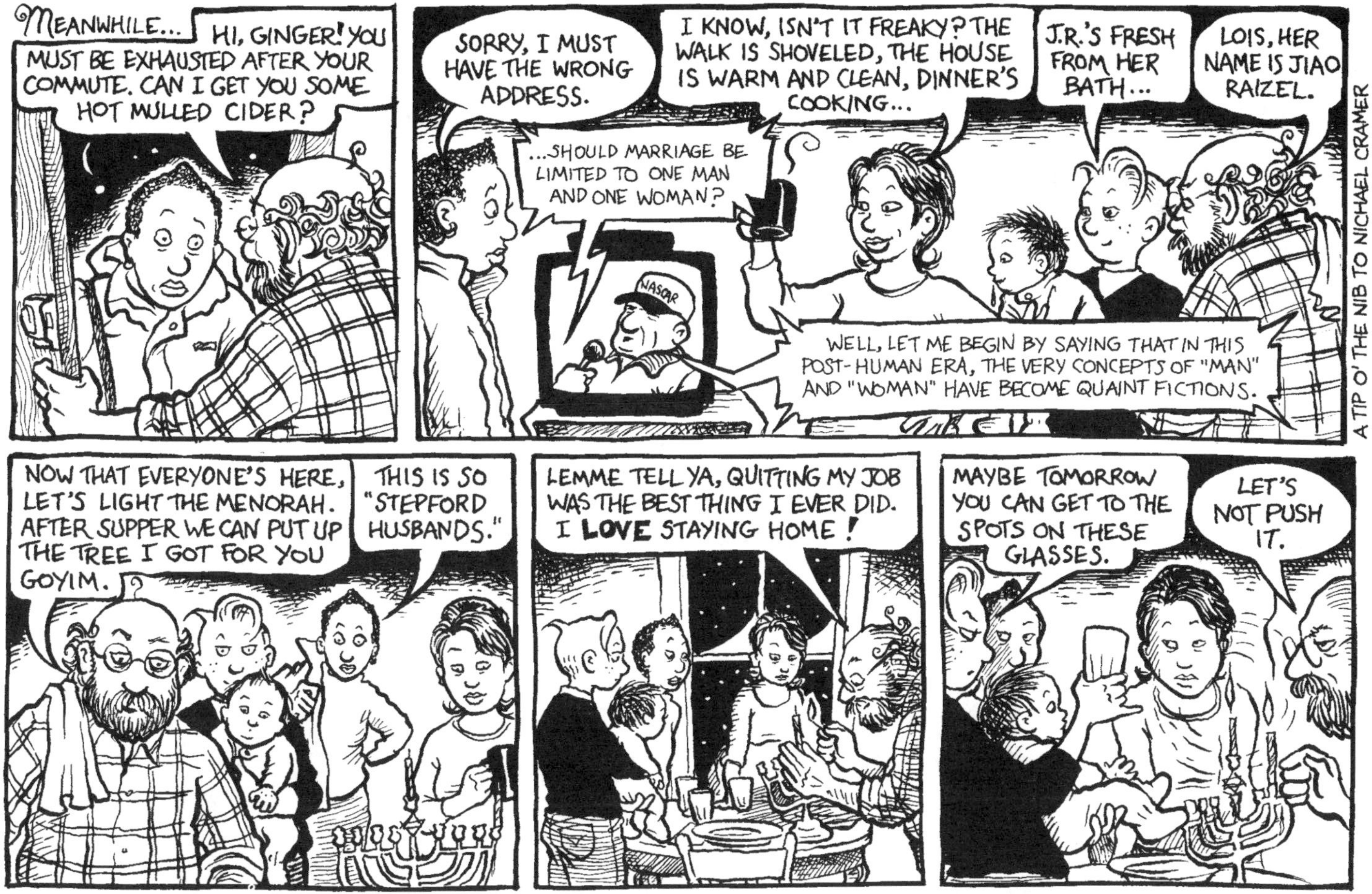
MEANWHILE...
HI, GINGER! YOU MUST BE EXHAUSTED AFTER YOUR COMMUTE. CAN I GET YOU SOME HOT MULLED CIDER?
SORRY, I MUST HAVE THE WRONG ADDRESS.
...SHOULD MARRIAGE BE LIMITED TO ONE MAN AND ONE WOMAN?
NASCAR
I KNOW, ISN'T IT FREAKY? THE WALK IS SHOVELED, THE HOUSE IS WARM AND CLEAN, DINNER'S COOKING...
J.R.'S FRESH FROM HER BATH...
LOIS, HER NAME IS JIAO RAIZEL.
WELL, LET ME BEGIN BY SAYING THAT IN THIS POST-HUMAN ERA, THE VERY CONCEPTS OF "MAN" AND "WOMAN" HAVE BECOME QUAINT FICTIONS.
A TIP O' THE NIB TO MICHAEL CRAMER
NOW THAT EVERYONE'S HERE, LET'S LIGHT THE MENORAH. AFTER SUPPER WE CAN PUT UP THE TREE I GOT FOR YOU GOYIM.
THIS IS SO "STEPFORD HUSBANDS."
LEMME TELL YA, QUITTING MY JOB WAS THE BEST THING I EVER DID. I LOVE STAYING HOME!
MAYBE TOMORROW YOU CAN GET TO THE SPOTS ON THESE GLASSES.
LET'S NOT PUSH IT.

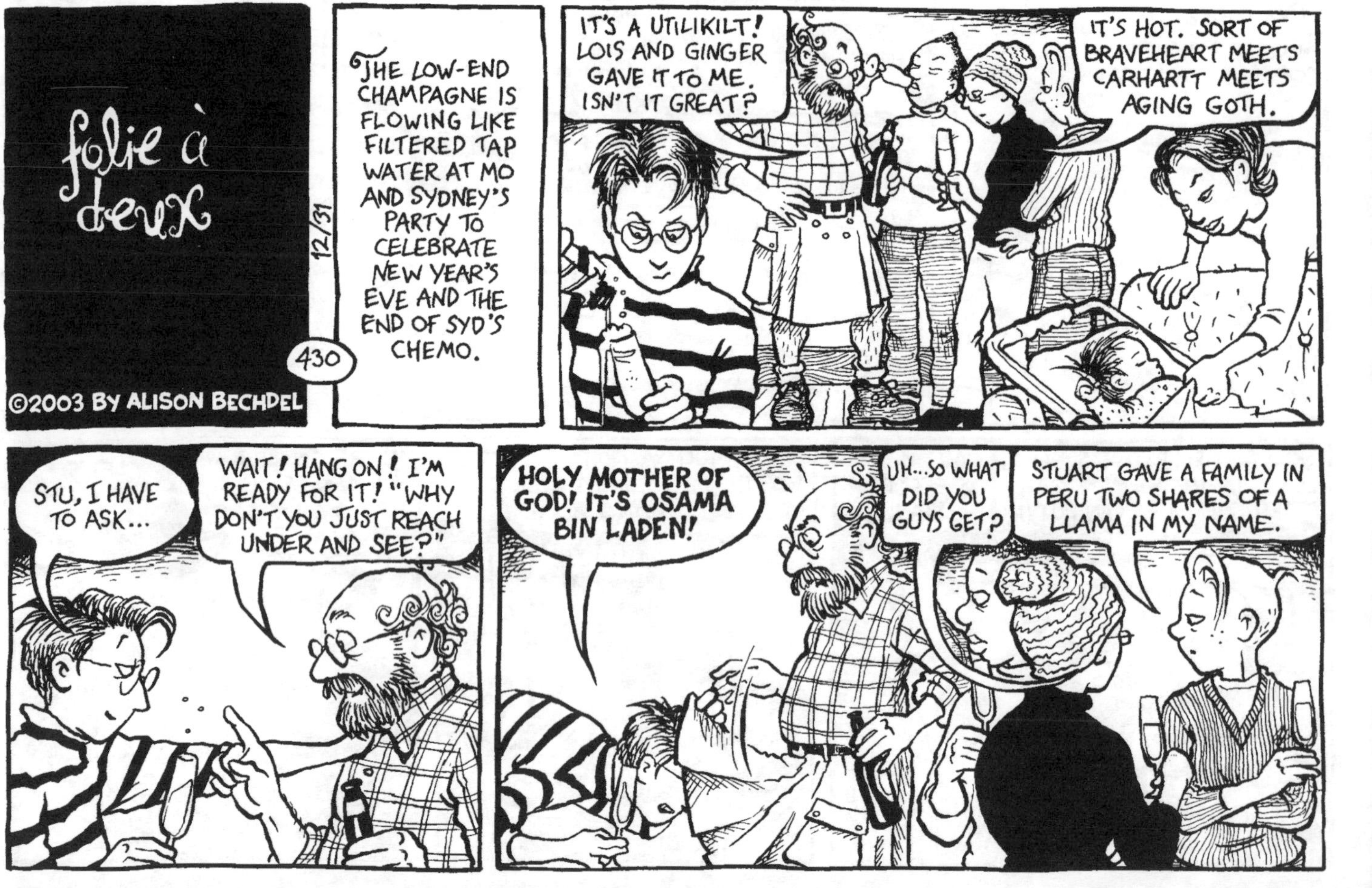
folie à deux
12/31
430
©2003 BY ALISON BECHDEL
THE LOW-END CHAMPAGNE IS FLOWING LIKE FILTERED TAP WATER AT MO AND SYDNEY'S PARTY TO CELEBRATE NEW YEAR'S EVE AND THE END OF SYD'S CHEMO.
IT'S A UTILIKILT! LOIS AND GINGER GAVE IT TO ME. ISN'T IT GREAT?
IT'S HOT. SORT OF BRAVEHEART MEETS CARHARTT MEETS AGING GOTH.
STU, I HAVE TO ASK...
WAIT! HANG ON! I'M READY FOR IT! "WHY DON'T YOU JUST REACH UNDER AND SEE?"
HOLY MOTHER OF GOD! IT'S OSAMA BIN LADEN!
UH...SO WHAT DID YOU GUYS GET?
STUART GAVE A FAMILY IN PERU TWO SHARES OF A LLAMA IN MY NAME.

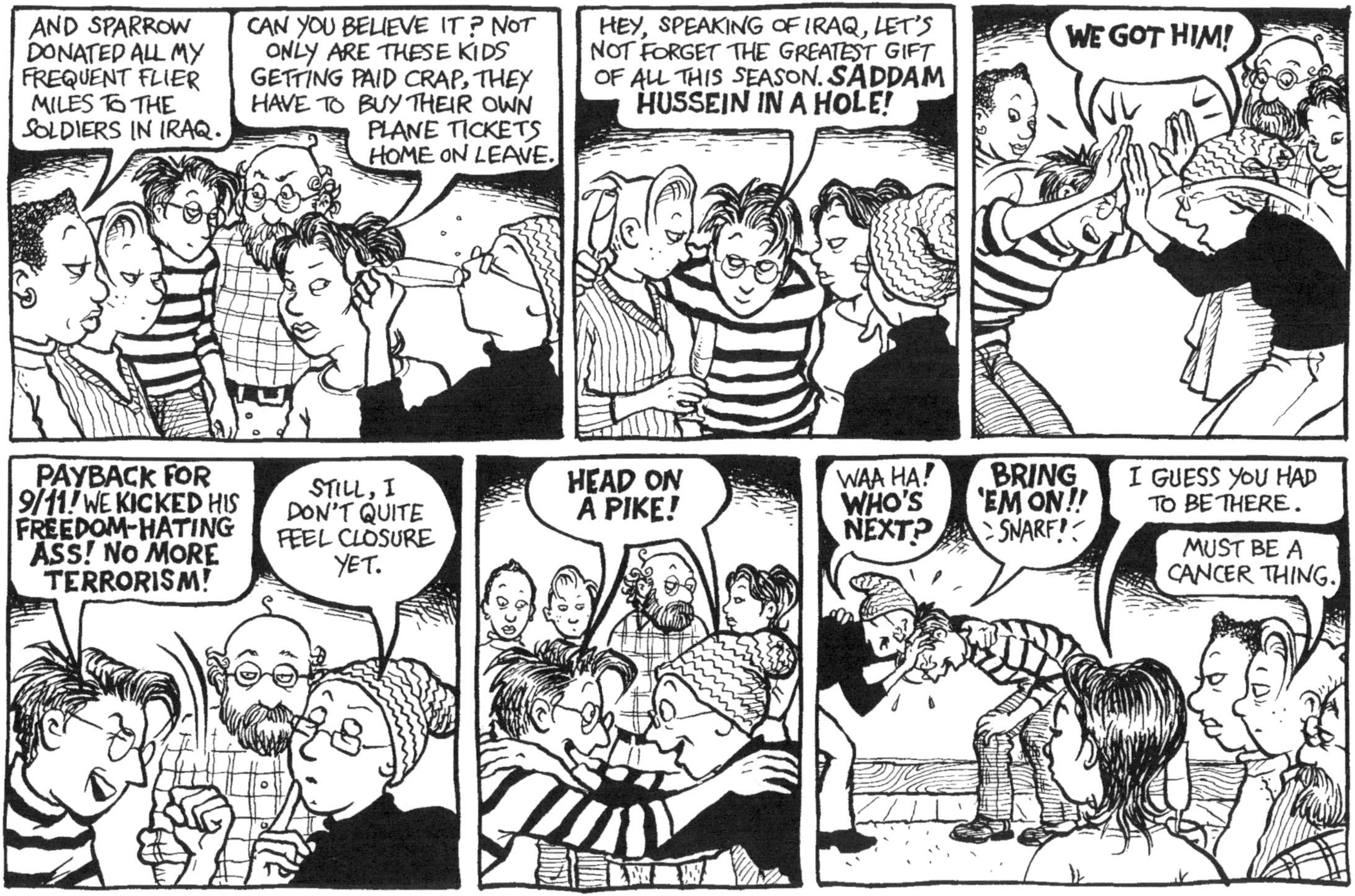

AND SPARROW DONATED ALL MY FREQUENT FLIER MILES TO THE SOLDIERS IN IRAQ.
CAN YOU BELIEVE IT? NOT ONLY ARE THESE KIDS GETTING PAID CRAP, THEY HAVE TO BUY THEIR OWN PLANE TICKETS HOME ON LEAVE.
HEY, SPEAKING OF IRAQ, LET'S NOT FORGET THE GREATEST GIFT OF ALL THIS SEASON. SADDAM HUSSEIN IN A HOLE!
WE GOT HIM!
PAYBACK FOR 9/11! WE KICKED HIS FREEDOM-HATING ASS! NO MORE TERRORISM!
STILL, I DON'T QUITE FEEL CLOSURE YET.
HEAD ON A PIKE!
WAA HA! WHO'S NEXT?
BRING 'EM ON!! SNARF!
I GUESS YOU HAD TO BE THERE.
MUST BE A CANCER THING.

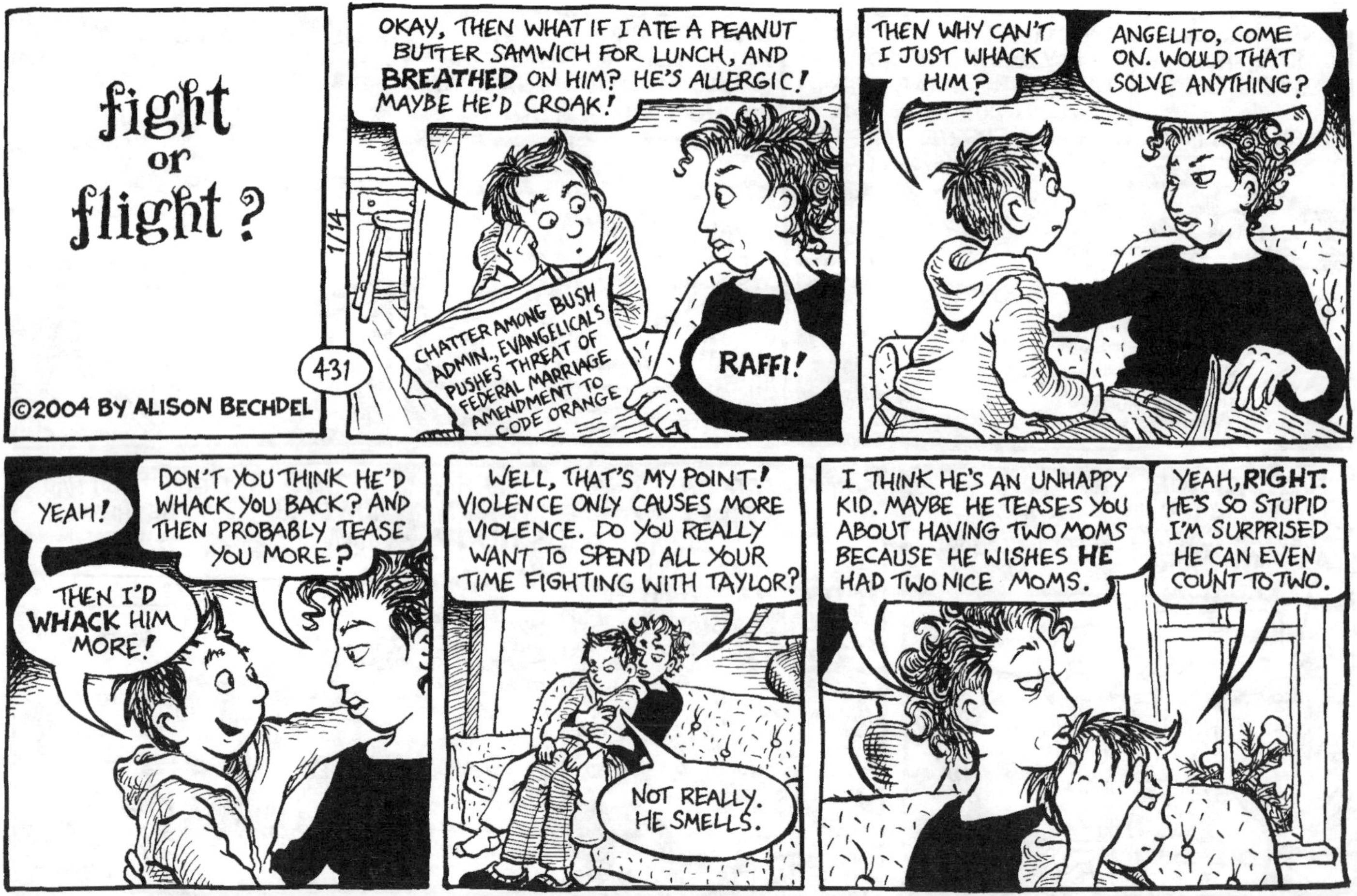

fight or flight?
©2004 BY ALISON BECHDEL
431
1/14
OKAY, THEN WHAT IF I ATE A PEANUT BUTTER SAMWICH FOR LUNCH, AND **BREATHED** ON HIM? HE'S ALLERGIC! MAYBE HE'D CROAK!
CHATTER AMONG BUSH ADMIN., EVANGELICALS PUSHES THREAT OF FEDERAL MARRIAGE AMENDMENT TO CODE ORANGE
RAFFI!
THEN WHY CAN'T I JUST WHACK HIM?
ANGELITO, COME ON. WOULD THAT SOLVE ANYTHING?
DON'T YOU THINK HE'D WHACK YOU BACK? AND THEN PROBABLY TEASE YOU MORE?
YEAH!
THEN I'D **WHACK** HIM MORE!
WELL, THAT'S MY POINT! VIOLENCE ONLY CAUSES MORE VIOLENCE. DO YOU REALLY WANT TO SPEND ALL YOUR TIME FIGHTING WITH TAYLOR?
NOT REALLY. HE SMELLS.
I THINK HE'S AN UNHAPPY KID. MAYBE HE TEASES YOU ABOUT HAVING TWO MOMS BECAUSE HE WISHES **HE** HAD TWO NICE MOMS.
YEAH, **RIGHT**. HE'S SO STUPID I'M SURPRISED HE CAN EVEN COUNT TO TWO.

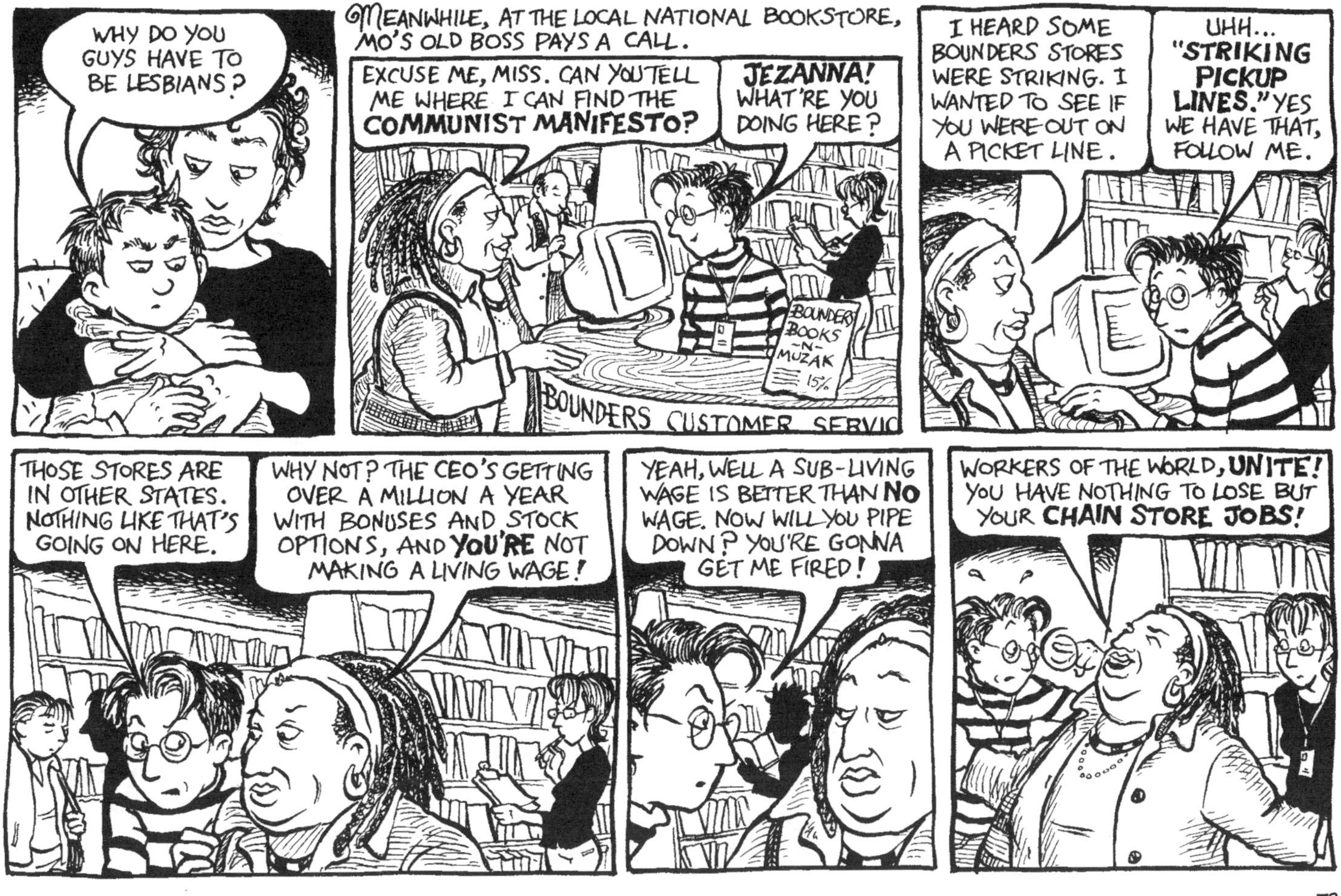
WHY DO YOU GUYS HAVE TO BE LESBIANS?
MEANWHILE, AT THE LOCAL NATIONAL BOOKSTORE, MO'S OLD BOSS PAYS A CALL.
EXCUSE ME, MISS. CAN YOU TELL ME WHERE I CAN FIND THE **COMMUNIST MANIFESTO?**
JEZANNA! WHAT'RE YOU DOING HERE?
BOUNDERS BOOKS -N- MUZAK 15%
BOUNDERS CUSTOMER SERVIC
I HEARD SOME BOUNDERS STORES WERE STRIKING. I WANTED TO SEE IF YOU WERE OUT ON A PICKET LINE.
UHH... **"STRIKING PICKUP LINES."** YES WE HAVE THAT, FOLLOW ME.
THOSE STORES ARE IN OTHER STATES. NOTHING LIKE THAT'S GOING ON HERE.
WHY NOT? THE CEO'S GETTING OVER A MILLION A YEAR WITH BONUSES AND STOCK OPTIONS, AND **YOU'RE** NOT MAKING A LIVING WAGE!
YEAH, WELL A SUB-LIVING WAGE IS BETTER THAN **NO** WAGE. NOW WILL YOU PIPE DOWN? YOU'RE GONNA GET ME FIRED!
WORKERS OF THE WORLD, **UNITE!** YOU HAVE NOTHING TO LOSE BUT YOUR **CHAIN STORE JOBS!**

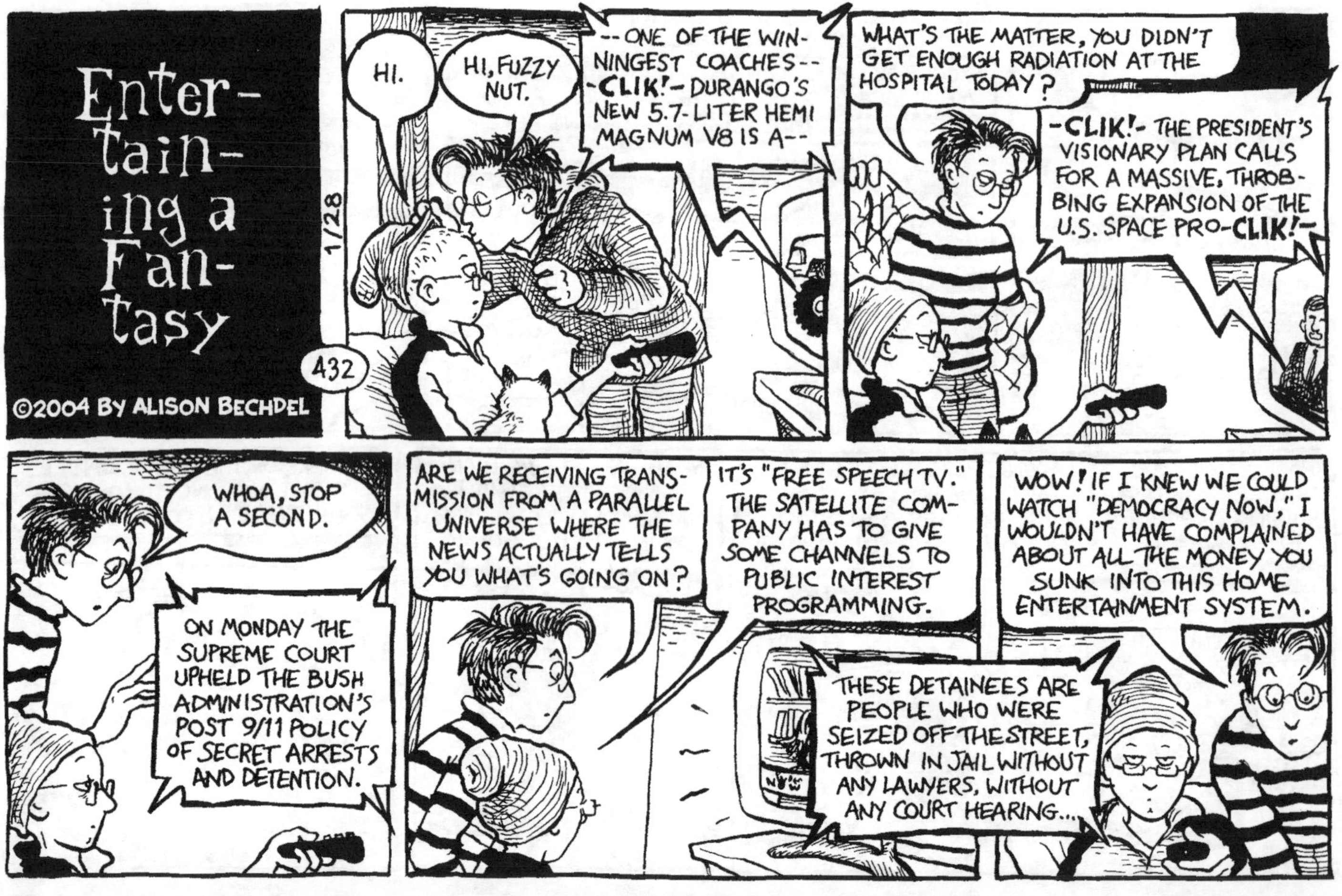
Enter-taining a Fantasy
©2004 BY ALISON BECHDEL
432
1/28
HI.
HI, FUZZY NUT.
--ONE OF THE WINNINGEST COACHES-- -CLIK!- DURANGO'S NEW 5.7-LITER HEMI MAGNUM V8 IS A--
WHAT'S THE MATTER, YOU DIDN'T GET ENOUGH RADIATION AT THE HOSPITAL TODAY?
-CLIK!- THE PRESIDENT'S VISIONARY PLAN CALLS FOR A MASSIVE, THROBBING EXPANSION OF THE U.S. SPACE PRO-CLIK!-
WHOA, STOP A SECOND.
ON MONDAY THE SUPREME COURT UPHELD THE BUSH ADMINISTRATION'S POST 9/11 POLICY OF SECRET ARRESTS AND DETENTION.
ARE WE RECEIVING TRANSMISSION FROM A PARALLEL UNIVERSE WHERE THE NEWS ACTUALLY TELLS YOU WHAT'S GOING ON?
IT'S "FREE SPEECH TV." THE SATELLITE COMPANY HAS TO GIVE SOME CHANNELS TO PUBLIC INTEREST PROGRAMMING.
THESE DETAINEES ARE PEOPLE WHO WERE SEIZED OFF THE STREET, THROWN IN JAIL WITHOUT ANY LAWYERS, WITHOUT ANY COURT HEARING...
WOW! IF I KNEW WE COULD WATCH "DEMOCRACY NOW," I WOULDN'T HAVE COMPLAINED ABOUT ALL THE MONEY YOU SUNK INTO THIS HOME ENTERTAINMENT SYSTEM.

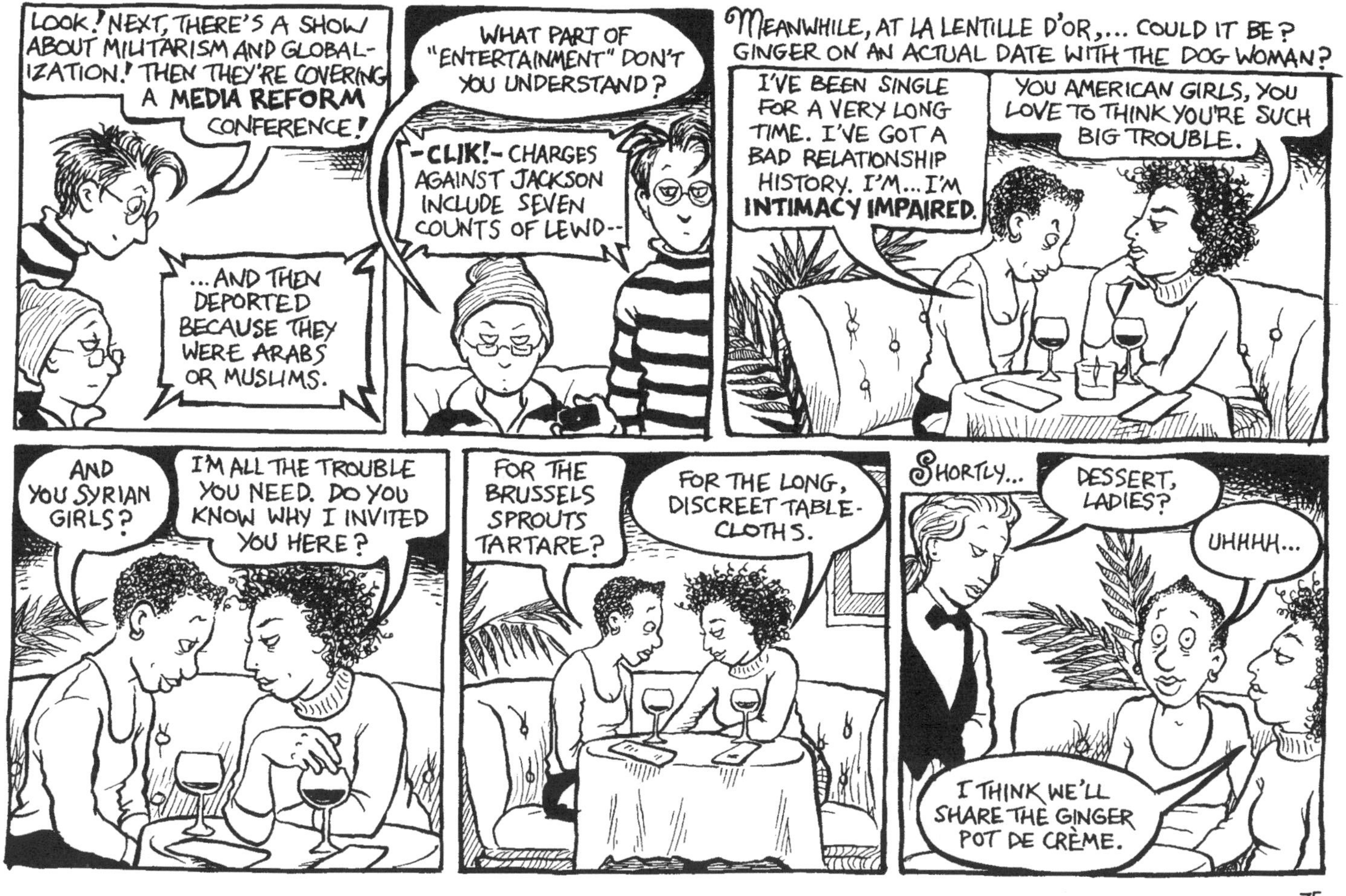

LOOK! NEXT, THERE'S A SHOW ABOUT MILITARISM AND GLOBALIZATION! THEN THEY'RE COVERING A **MEDIA REFORM** CONFERENCE!
...AND THEN DEPORTED BECAUSE THEY WERE ARABS OR MUSLIMS.
WHAT PART OF "ENTERTAINMENT" DON'T YOU UNDERSTAND?
-CLIK!- CHARGES AGAINST JACKSON INCLUDE SEVEN COUNTS OF LEWD--
MEANWHILE, AT LA LENTILLE D'OR,... COULD IT BE? GINGER ON AN ACTUAL DATE WITH THE DOG WOMAN?
I'VE BEEN SINGLE FOR A VERY LONG TIME. I'VE GOT A BAD RELATIONSHIP HISTORY. I'M... I'M **INTIMACY IMPAIRED.**
YOU AMERICAN GIRLS, YOU LOVE TO THINK YOU'RE SUCH BIG TROUBLE.
AND YOU SYRIAN GIRLS?
I'M ALL THE TROUBLE YOU NEED. DO YOU KNOW WHY I INVITED YOU HERE?
FOR THE BRUSSELS SPROUTS TARTARE?
FOR THE LONG, DISCREET TABLECLOTHS.
SHORTLY...
DESSERT, LADIES?
UHHHH...
I THINK WE'LL SHARE THE GINGER POT DE CRÈME.

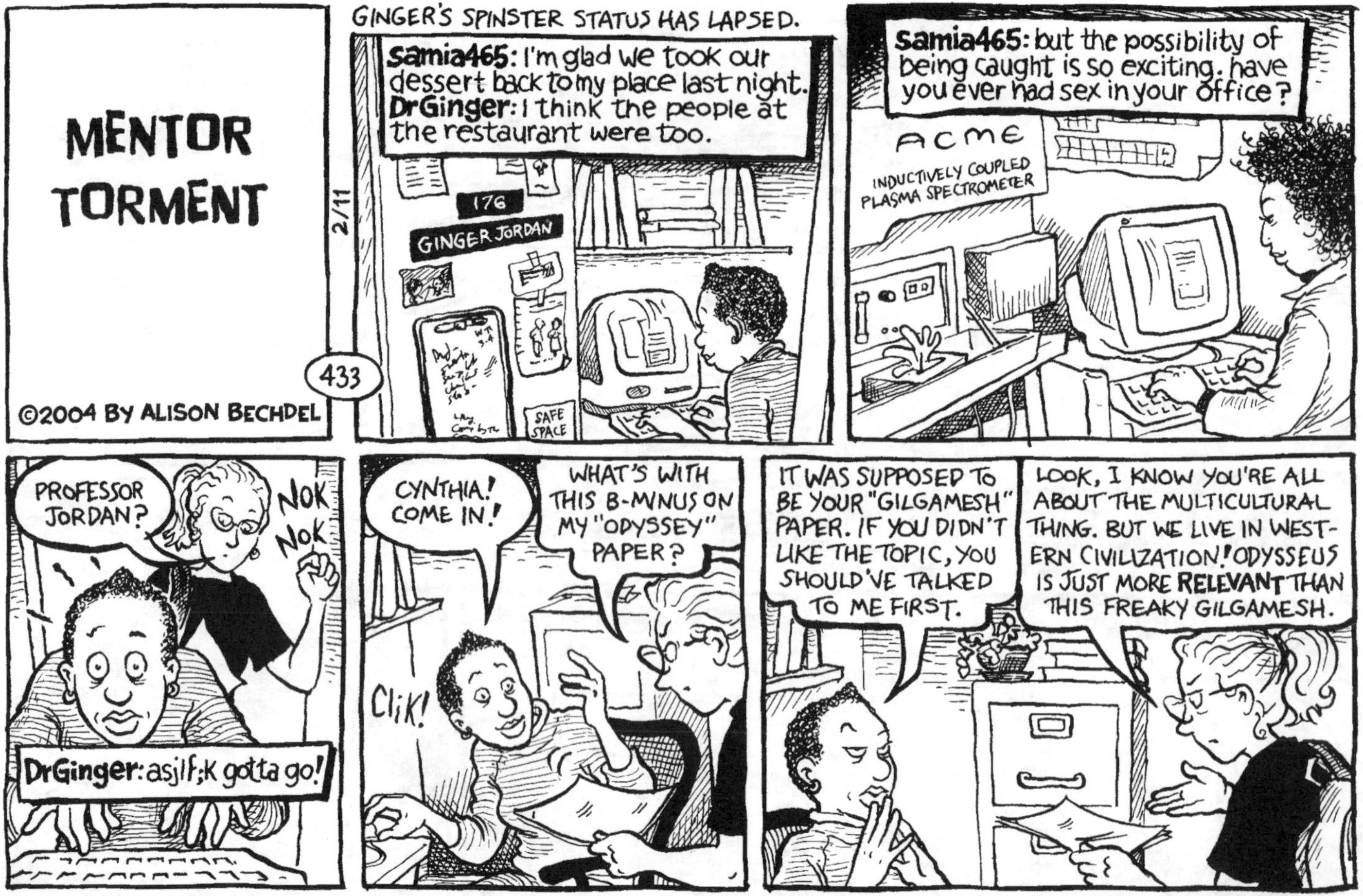
MENTOR TORMENT
©2004 BY ALISON BECHDEL
433
2/11
GINGER'S SPINSTER STATUS HAS LAPSED.
Samia465: I'm glad we took our dessert back to my place last night.
DrGinger: I think the people at the restaurant were too.
176
GINGER JORDAN
SAFE SPACE
Samia465: but the possibility of being caught is so exciting. have you ever had sex in your office?
ACME
INDUCTIVELY COUPLED PLASMA SPECTROMETER
PROFESSOR JORDAN?
NOK NOK
DrGinger: asjlf;k gotta go!
CYNTHIA! COME IN!
CLIK!
WHAT'S WITH THIS B-MINUS ON MY "ODYSSEY" PAPER?
IT WAS SUPPOSED TO BE YOUR "GILGAMESH" PAPER. IF YOU DIDN'T LIKE THE TOPIC, YOU SHOULD'VE TALKED TO ME FIRST.
LOOK, I KNOW YOU'RE ALL ABOUT THE MULTICULTURAL THING. BUT WE LIVE IN WESTERN CIVILIZATION! ODYSSEUS IS JUST MORE RELEVANT THAN THIS FREAKY GILGAMESH.

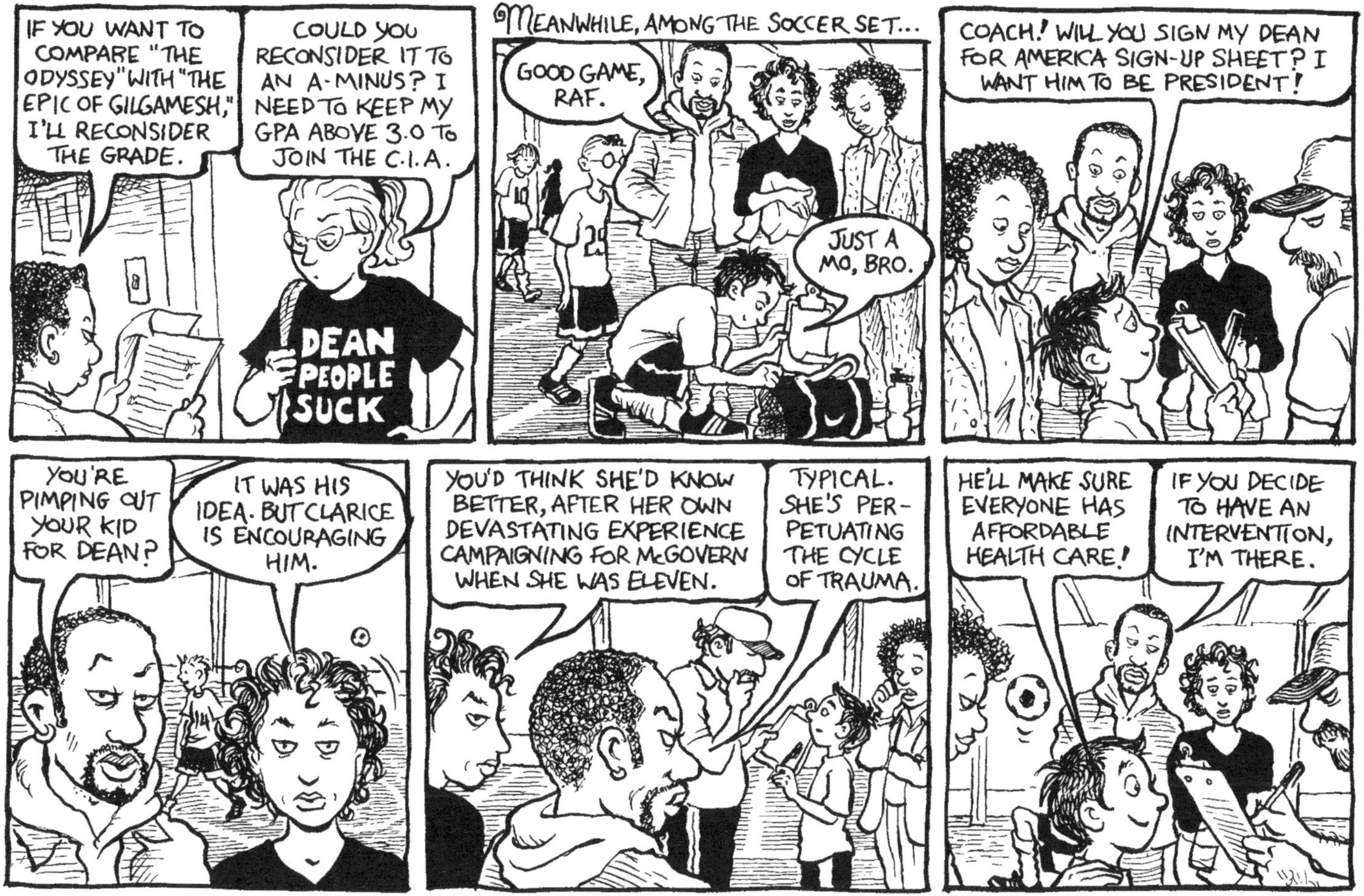
IF YOU WANT TO COMPARE "THE ODYSSEY" WITH "THE EPIC OF GILGAMESH," I'LL RECONSIDER THE GRADE.
COULD YOU RECONSIDER IT TO AN A-MINUS? I NEED TO KEEP MY GPA ABOVE 3.0 TO JOIN THE C.I.A.
DEAN PEOPLE SUCK
MEANWHILE, AMONG THE SOCCER SET...
GOOD GAME, RAF.
JUST A MO, BRO.
COACH! WILL YOU SIGN MY DEAN FOR AMERICA SIGN-UP SHEET? I WANT HIM TO BE PRESIDENT!
YOU'RE PIMPING OUT YOUR KID FOR DEAN?
IT WAS HIS IDEA. BUT CLARICE IS ENCOURAGING HIM.
YOU'D THINK SHE'D KNOW BETTER, AFTER HER OWN DEVASTATING EXPERIENCE CAMPAIGNING FOR McGOVERN WHEN SHE WAS ELEVEN.
TYPICAL. SHE'S PERPETUATING THE CYCLE OF TRAUMA.
HE'LL MAKE SURE EVERYONE HAS AFFORDABLE HEALTH CARE!
IF YOU DECIDE TO HAVE AN INTERVENTION, I'M THERE.

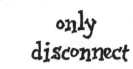

only
disconnect

2/25

434

©2004 BY ALISON BECHDEL

HELLO, SHABOOK-ADOOK!

UH... HI! WHAT PUT YOU IN SUCH A GOOD MOOD?

CHECK IT OUT! I GOT THIS FANCY CD PLAYER AND HOOKED THE TV UP TO IT.

OH.

HOSE

I CAN CONNECT IT TO MY LAPTOP TOO. AND MY IPUD, BUT I NEED TO GET A SPECIAL CABLE. GREAT SOUND, HUH?

OKAY! **THAT'S** IT! I'VE KEPT MY MOUTH SHUT ABOUT ALL THE CRAP YOU'VE BOUGHT SINCE YOU GOT SICK, BECAUSE IT SEEMED TO MAKE YOU FEEL BETTER, IF ONLY FOR A NANOSECOND.

IT IS ESSENTIAL THAT WHEN WE SEE A THREAT, WE DEAL WITH THOSE THREATS BEFORE THEY BECOME IMMINENT. IT'S TOO LATE IF THEY BECOME IMMINENT.

BUT YOU HAVE TO **STOP!** I DON'T EVEN WANT TO **THINK** ABOUT HOW MUCH DEBT YOU'RE IN!

Kerry '04

MASS. COURT RULES GAYS CAN MARRY

THAT'S WHY I'M LAUNCHING A GROUND OFFENSIVE ON MASSACHUSETTS.

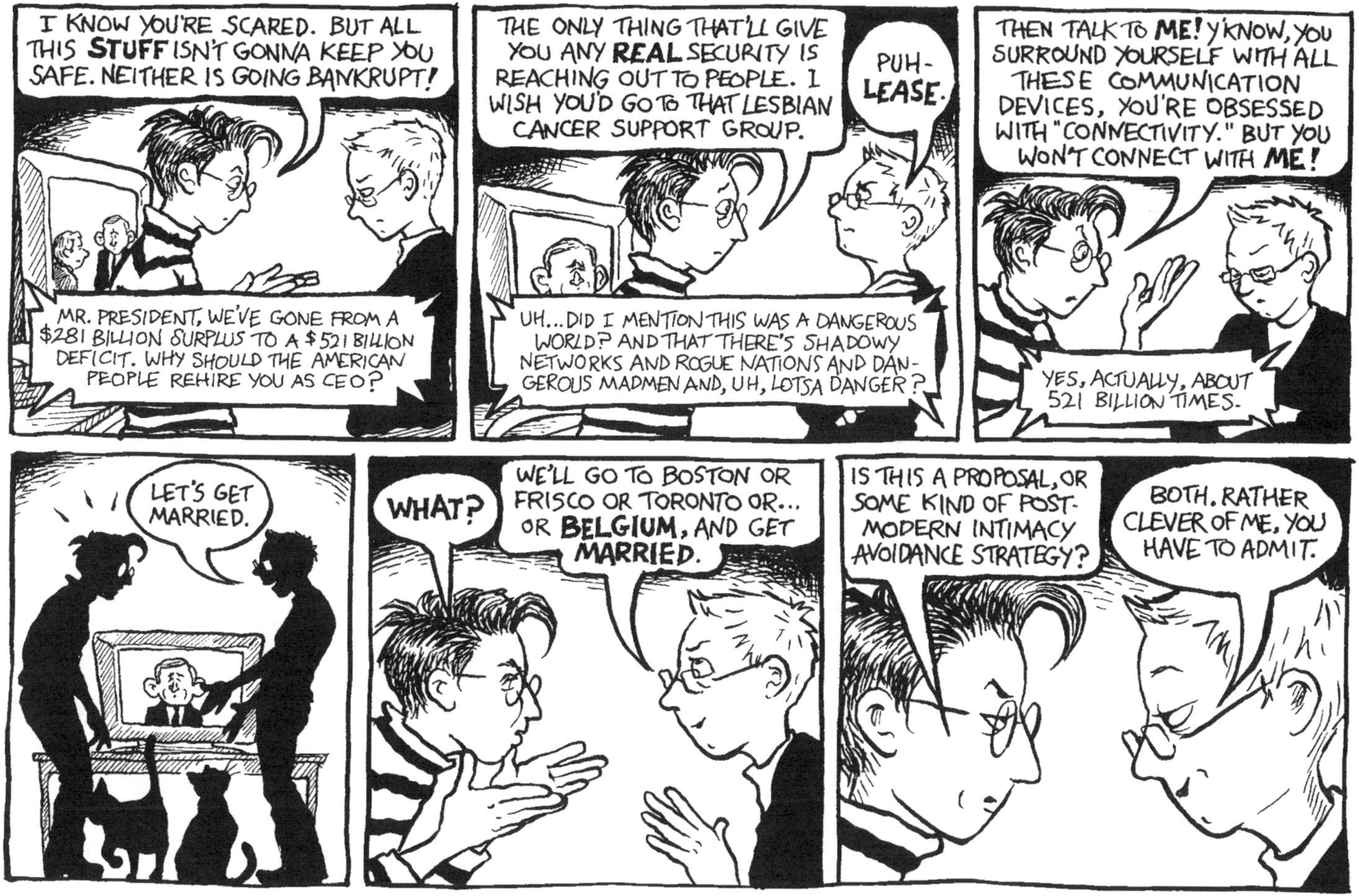
I KNOW YOU'RE SCARED. BUT ALL THIS **STUFF** ISN'T GONNA KEEP YOU SAFE. NEITHER IS GOING BANKRUPT!
MR. PRESIDENT, WE'VE GONE FROM A $281 BILLION SURPLUS TO A $521 BILLION DEFICIT. WHY SHOULD THE AMERICAN PEOPLE REHIRE YOU AS CEO?
THE ONLY THING THAT'LL GIVE YOU ANY **REAL** SECURITY IS REACHING OUT TO PEOPLE. I WISH YOU'D GO TO THAT LESBIAN CANCER SUPPORT GROUP.
PUH-**LEASE**.
UH...DID I MENTION THIS WAS A DANGEROUS WORLD? AND THAT THERE'S SHADOWY NETWORKS AND ROGUE NATIONS AND DANGEROUS MADMEN AND, UH, LOTSA DANGER?
THEN TALK TO **ME!** Y'KNOW, YOU SURROUND YOURSELF WITH ALL THESE COMMUNICATION DEVICES, YOU'RE OBSESSED WITH "CONNECTIVITY." BUT YOU WON'T CONNECT WITH **ME!**
YES, ACTUALLY, ABOUT 521 BILLION TIMES.
LET'S GET MARRIED.
WHAT?
WE'LL GO TO BOSTON OR FRISCO OR TORONTO OR... OR **BELGIUM**, AND GET **MARRIED**.
IS THIS A PROPOSAL, OR SOME KIND OF POST-MODERN INTIMACY AVOIDANCE STRATEGY?
BOTH. RATHER CLEVER OF ME, YOU HAVE TO ADMIT.

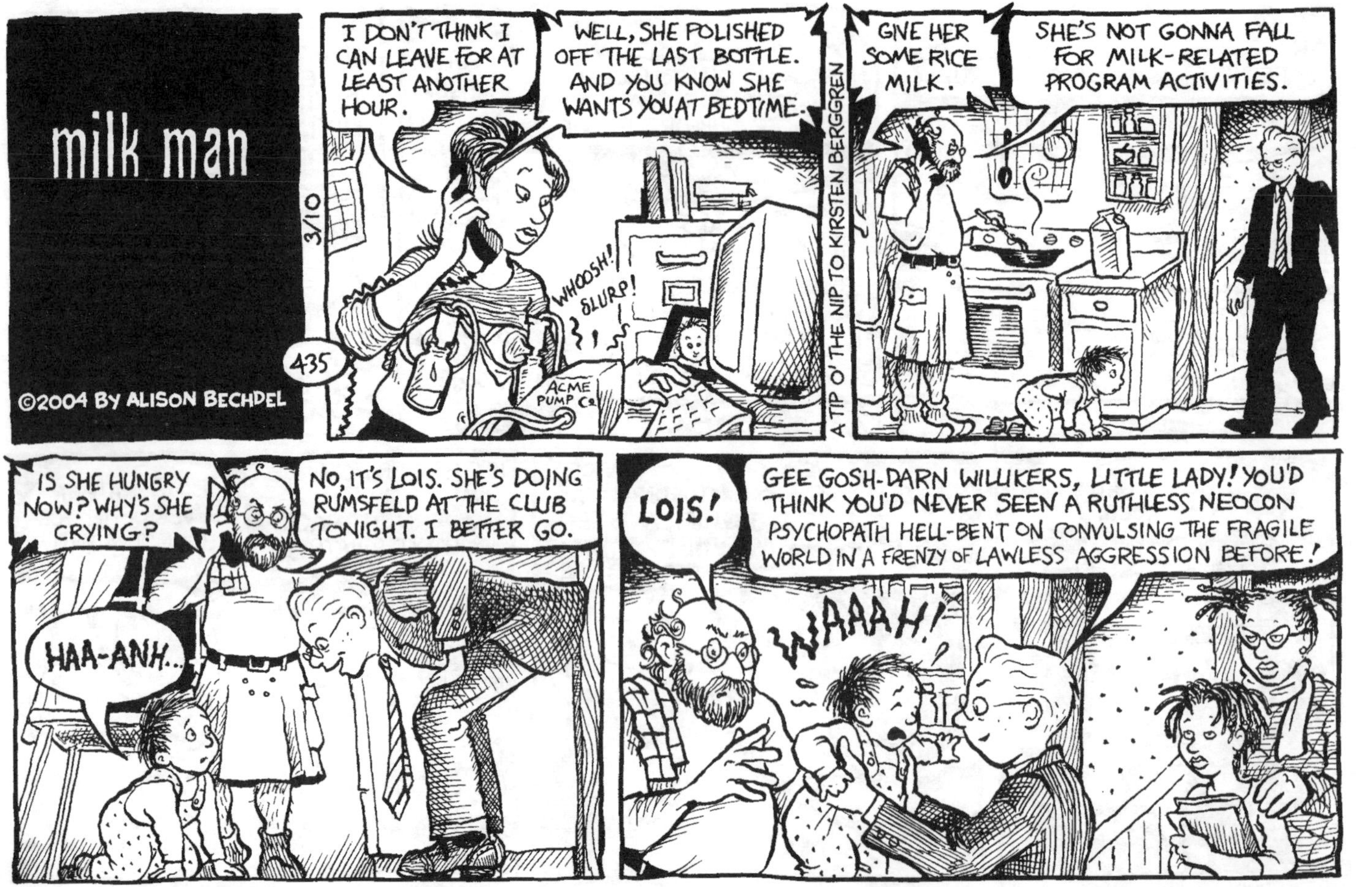
milk man
©2004 BY ALISON BECHDEL
435
3/10
I DON'T THINK I CAN LEAVE FOR AT LEAST ANOTHER HOUR.
WELL, SHE POLISHED OFF THE LAST BOTTLE. AND YOU KNOW SHE WANTS YOU AT BEDTIME.
WHOOSH!
SLURP!
ACME PUMP CO.
A TIP O' THE NIP TO KIRSTEN BERGGREN
GIVE HER SOME RICE MILK.
SHE'S NOT GONNA FALL FOR MILK-RELATED PROGRAM ACTIVITIES.
IS SHE HUNGRY NOW? WHY'S SHE CRYING?
NO, IT'S LOIS. SHE'S DOING RUMSFELD AT THE CLUB TONIGHT. I BETTER GO.
HAA-ANH...
LOIS!
GEE GOSH-DARN WILLIKERS, LITTLE LADY! YOU'D THINK YOU'D NEVER SEEN A RUTHLESS NEOCON PSYCHOPATH HELL-BENT ON CONVULSING THE FRAGILE WORLD IN A FRENZY OF LAWLESS AGGRESSION BEFORE!
WAAAH!

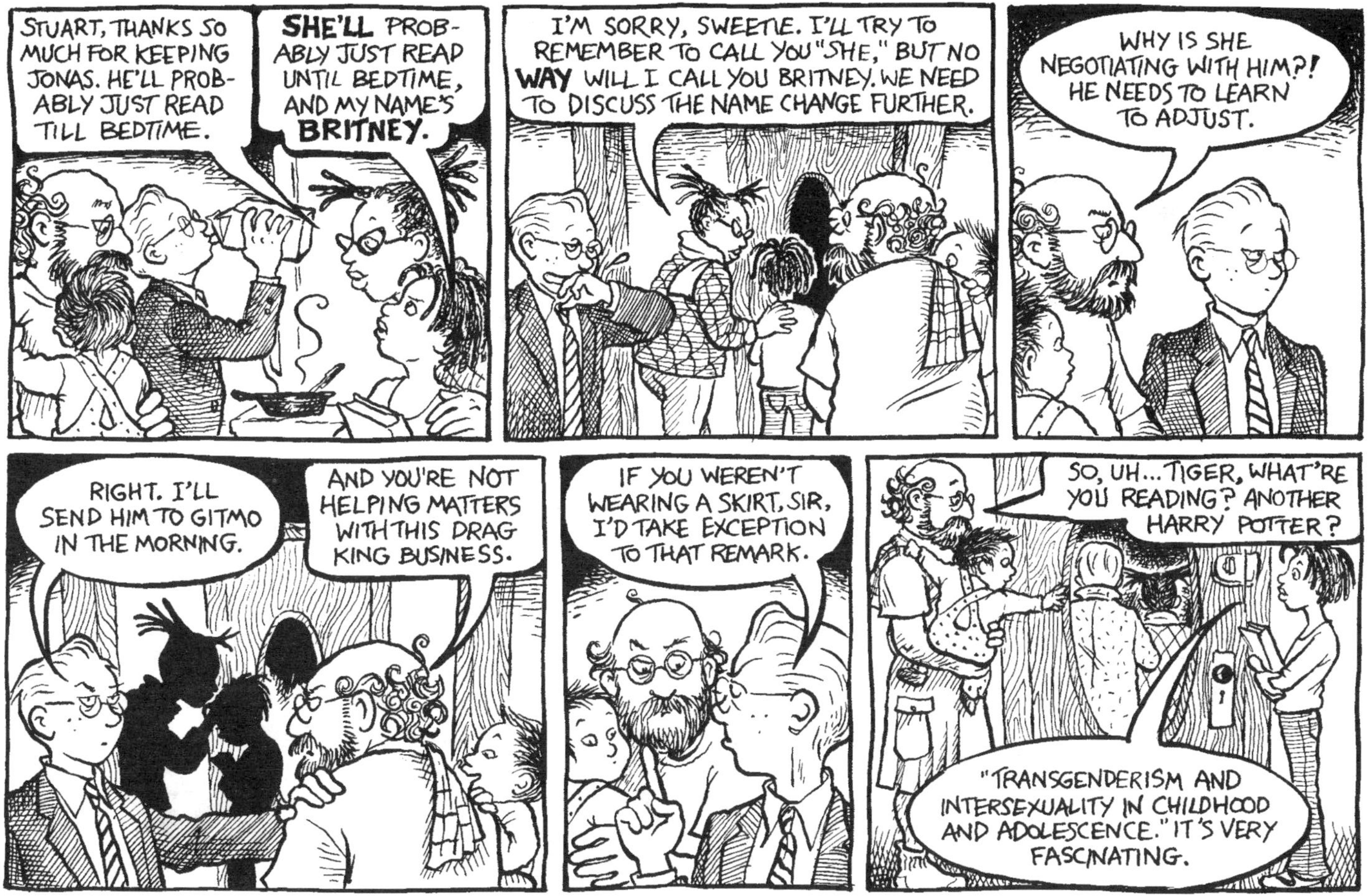
STUART, THANKS SO MUCH FOR KEEPING JONAS. HE'LL PROBABLY JUST READ TILL BEDTIME.
SHE'LL PROBABLY JUST READ UNTIL BEDTIME, AND MY NAME'S BRITNEY.
I'M SORRY, SWEETIE. I'LL TRY TO REMEMBER TO CALL YOU "SHE," BUT NO WAY WILL I CALL YOU BRITNEY. WE NEED TO DISCUSS THE NAME CHANGE FURTHER.
WHY IS SHE NEGOTIATING WITH HIM?! HE NEEDS TO LEARN TO ADJUST.
RIGHT. I'LL SEND HIM TO GITMO IN THE MORNING.
AND YOU'RE NOT HELPING MATTERS WITH THIS DRAG KING BUSINESS.
IF YOU WEREN'T WEARING A SKIRT, SIR, I'D TAKE EXCEPTION TO THAT REMARK.
SO, UH... TIGER, WHAT'RE YOU READING? ANOTHER HARRY POTTER?
"TRANSGENDERISM AND INTERSEXUALITY IN CHILDHOOD AND ADOLESCENCE." IT'S VERY FASCINATING.

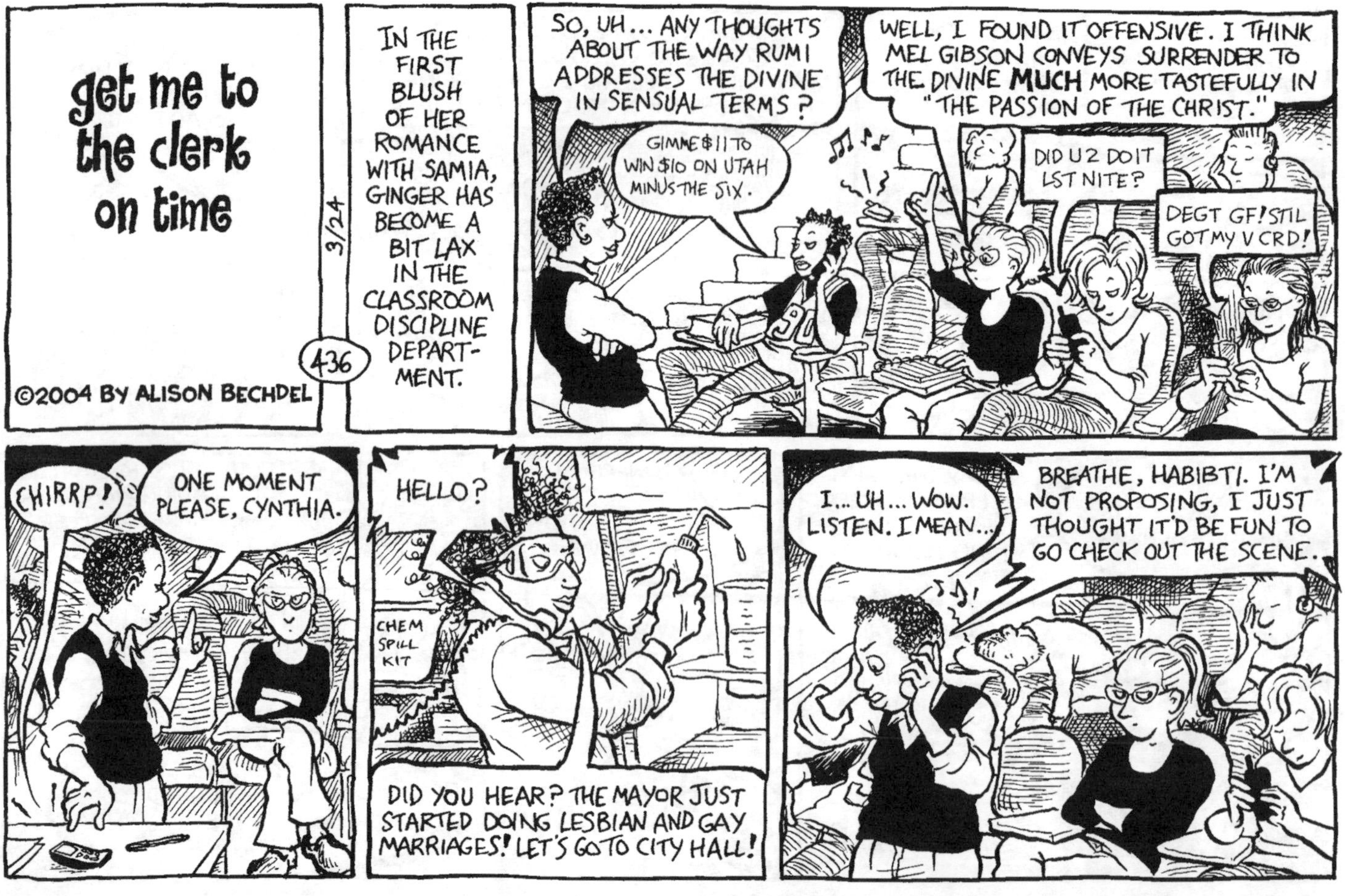
get me to the clerk on time
©2004 BY ALISON BECHDEL
436
3/24
IN THE FIRST BLUSH OF HER ROMANCE WITH SAMIA, GINGER HAS BECOME A BIT LAX IN THE CLASSROOM DISCIPLINE DEPARTMENT.
SO, UH... ANY THOUGHTS ABOUT THE WAY RUMI ADDRESSES THE DIVINE IN SENSUAL TERMS?
GIMME $11 TO WIN $10 ON UTAH MINUS THE SIX.
WELL, I FOUND IT OFFENSIVE. I THINK MEL GIBSON CONVEYS SURRENDER TO THE DIVINE **MUCH** MORE TASTEFULLY IN "THE PASSION OF THE CHRIST."
DID U 2 DO IT LST NITE?
DEGT GF! STIL GOT MY V CRD!
CHIRRP!
ONE MOMENT PLEASE, CYNTHIA.
HELLO?
CHEM SPILL KIT
DID YOU HEAR? THE MAYOR JUST STARTED DOING LESBIAN AND GAY MARRIAGES! LET'S GO TO CITY HALL!
I... UH... WOW. LISTEN. I MEAN...
BREATHE, HABIBTI. I'M NOT PROPOSING, I JUST THOUGHT IT'D BE FUN TO GO CHECK OUT THE SCENE.

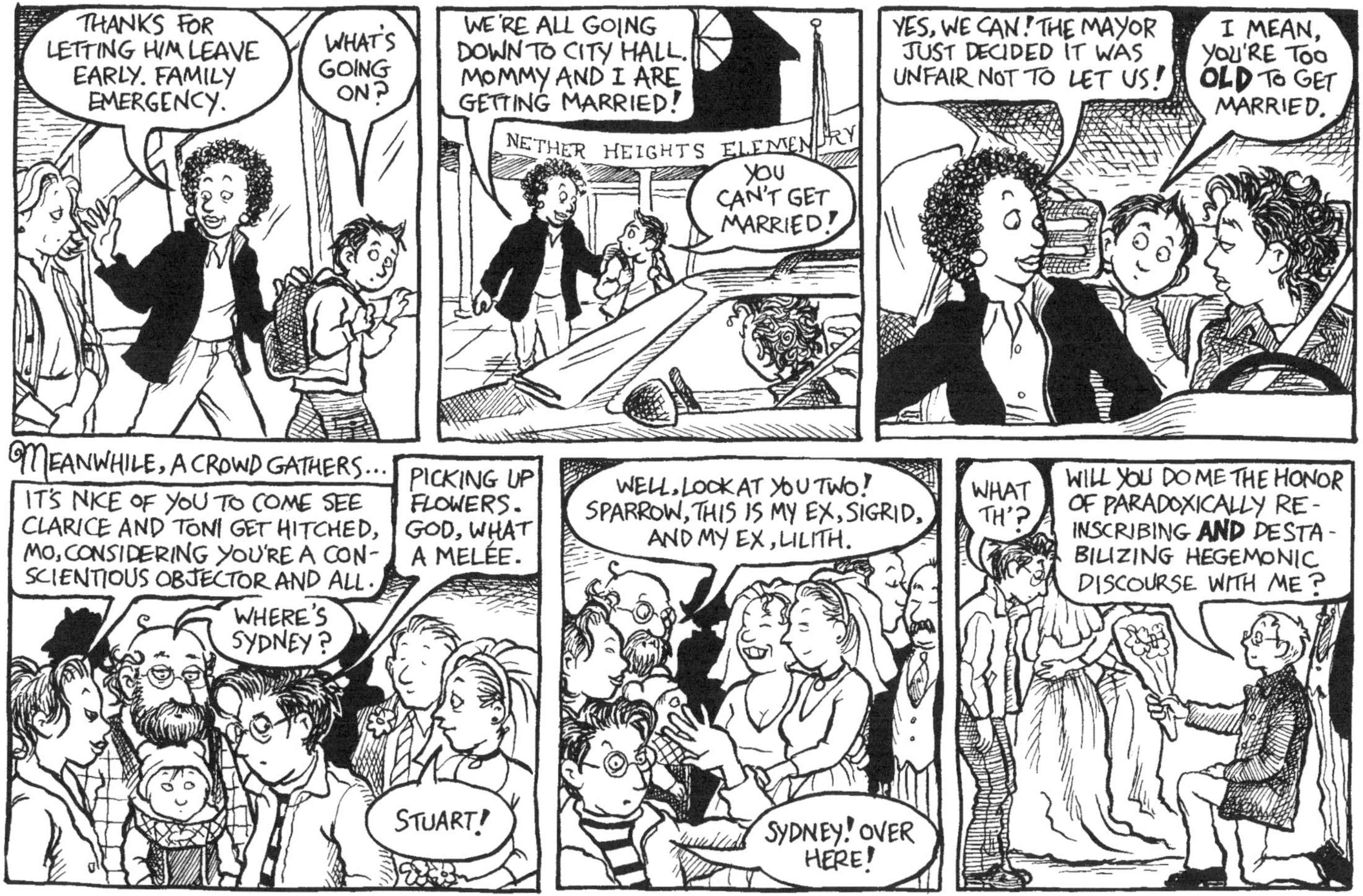
THANKS FOR LETTING HIM LEAVE EARLY. FAMILY EMERGENCY.
WHAT'S GOING ON?
WE'RE ALL GOING DOWN TO CITY HALL. MOMMY AND I ARE GETTING MARRIED!
NETHER HEIGHTS ELEMENTARY
YOU CAN'T GET MARRIED!
YES, WE CAN! THE MAYOR JUST DECIDED IT WAS UNFAIR NOT TO LET US!
I MEAN, YOU'RE TOO **OLD** TO GET MARRIED.
MEANWHILE, A CROWD GATHERS...
IT'S NICE OF YOU TO COME SEE CLARICE AND TONI GET HITCHED, MO, CONSIDERING YOU'RE A CONSCIENTIOUS OBJECTOR AND ALL.
PICKING UP FLOWERS. GOD, WHAT A MELÉE.
WHERE'S SYDNEY?
STUART!
WELL, LOOK AT YOU TWO! SPARROW, THIS IS MY EX, SIGRID, AND MY EX, LILITH.
SYDNEY! OVER HERE!
WHAT TH'?
WILL YOU DO ME THE HONOR OF PARADOXICALLY RE-INSCRIBING **AND** DESTABILIZING HEGEMONIC DISCOURSE WITH ME?

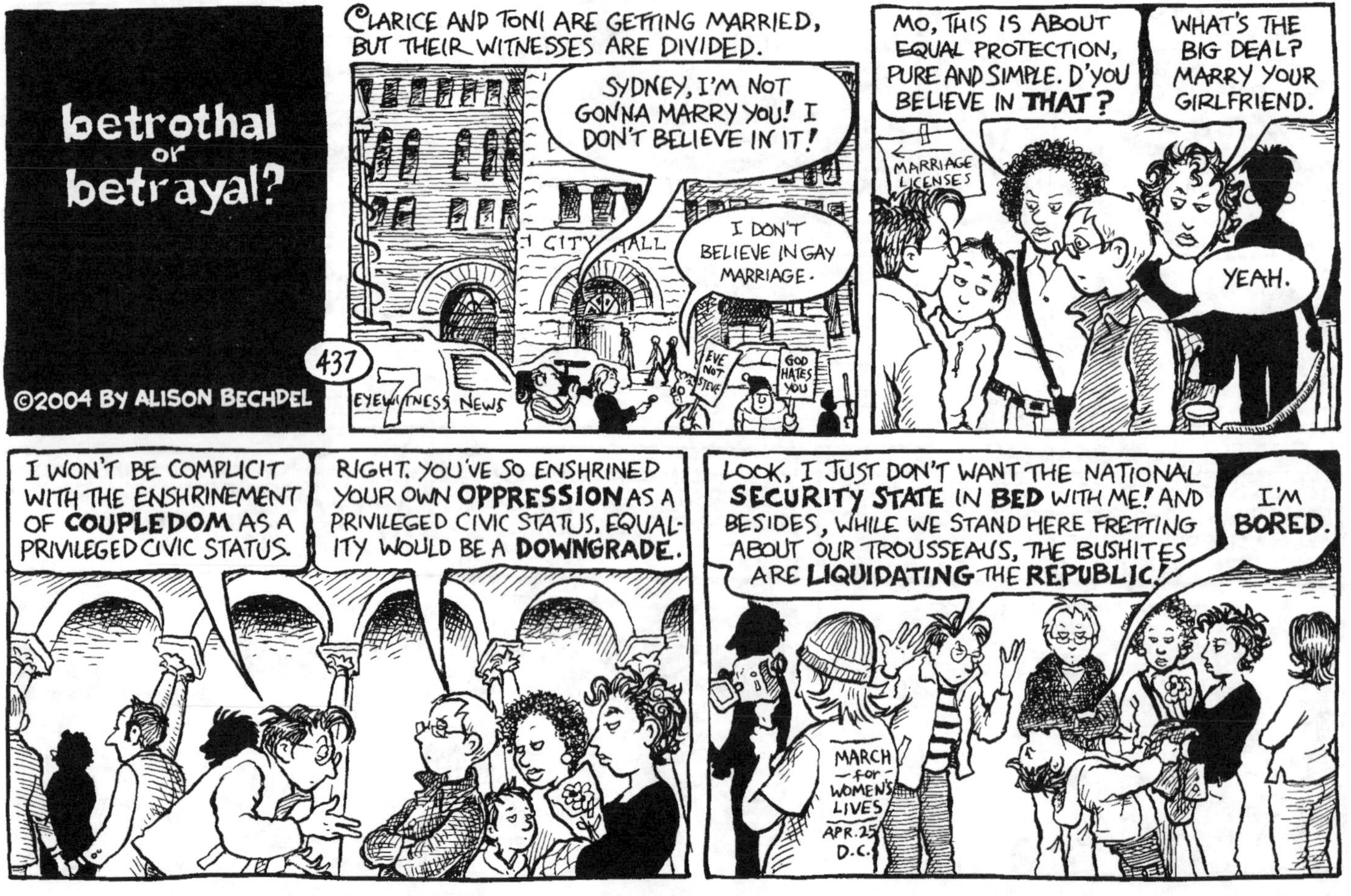

betrothal or betrayal?
437
©2004 BY ALISON BECHDEL
CLARICE AND TONI ARE GETTING MARRIED, BUT THEIR WITNESSES ARE DIVIDED.
SYDNEY, I'M NOT GONNA MARRY YOU! I DON'T BELIEVE IN IT!
I DON'T BELIEVE IN GAY MARRIAGE.
CITY HALL
EYE NOT STEVE
GOD HATES YOU
7 EYEWITNESS NEWS
MARRIAGE LICENSES
MO, THIS IS ABOUT EQUAL PROTECTION, PURE AND SIMPLE. D'YOU BELIEVE IN **THAT**?
WHAT'S THE BIG DEAL? MARRY YOUR GIRLFRIEND.
YEAH.
I WON'T BE COMPLICIT WITH THE ENSHRINEMENT OF **COUPLEDOM** AS A PRIVILEGED CIVIC STATUS.
RIGHT. YOU'VE SO ENSHRINED YOUR OWN **OPPRESSION** AS A PRIVILEGED CIVIC STATUS, EQUALITY WOULD BE A **DOWNGRADE**.
LOOK, I JUST DON'T WANT THE NATIONAL **SECURITY STATE** IN **BED** WITH ME! AND BESIDES, WHILE WE STAND HERE FRETTING ABOUT OUR TROUSSEAUS, THE BUSHITES ARE **LIQUIDATING** THE **REPUBLIC**!
I'M **BORED**.
MARCH for WOMEN'S LIVES APR. 25 D.C.

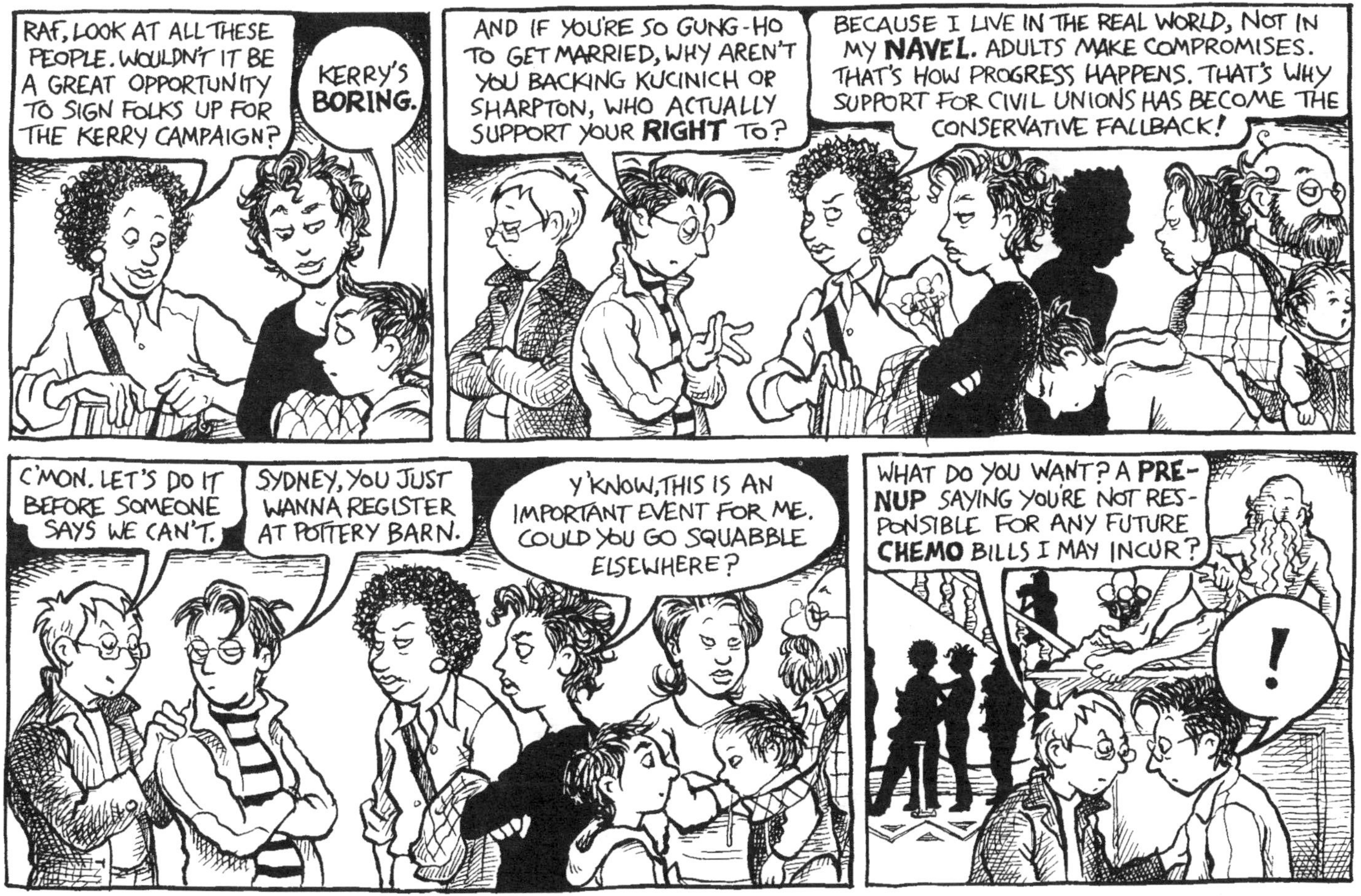

RAF, LOOK AT ALL THESE PEOPLE. WOULDN'T IT BE A GREAT OPPORTUNITY TO SIGN FOLKS UP FOR THE KERRY CAMPAIGN?
KERRY'S **BORING.**
AND IF YOU'RE SO GUNG-HO TO GET MARRIED, WHY AREN'T YOU BACKING KUCINICH OR SHARPTON, WHO ACTUALLY SUPPORT YOUR **RIGHT** TO?
BECAUSE I LIVE IN THE REAL WORLD, NOT IN MY **NAVEL**. ADULTS MAKE COMPROMISES. THAT'S HOW PROGRESS HAPPENS. THAT'S WHY SUPPORT FOR CIVIL UNIONS HAS BECOME THE CONSERVATIVE FALLBACK!
C'MON. LET'S DO IT BEFORE SOMEONE SAYS WE CAN'T.
SYDNEY, YOU JUST WANNA REGISTER AT POTTERY BARN.
Y'KNOW, THIS IS AN IMPORTANT EVENT FOR ME. COULD YOU GO SQUABBLE ELSEWHERE?
WHAT DO YOU WANT? A **PRE-NUP** SAYING YOU'RE NOT RES-PONSIBLE FOR ANY FUTURE **CHEMO** BILLS I MAY INCUR?
!

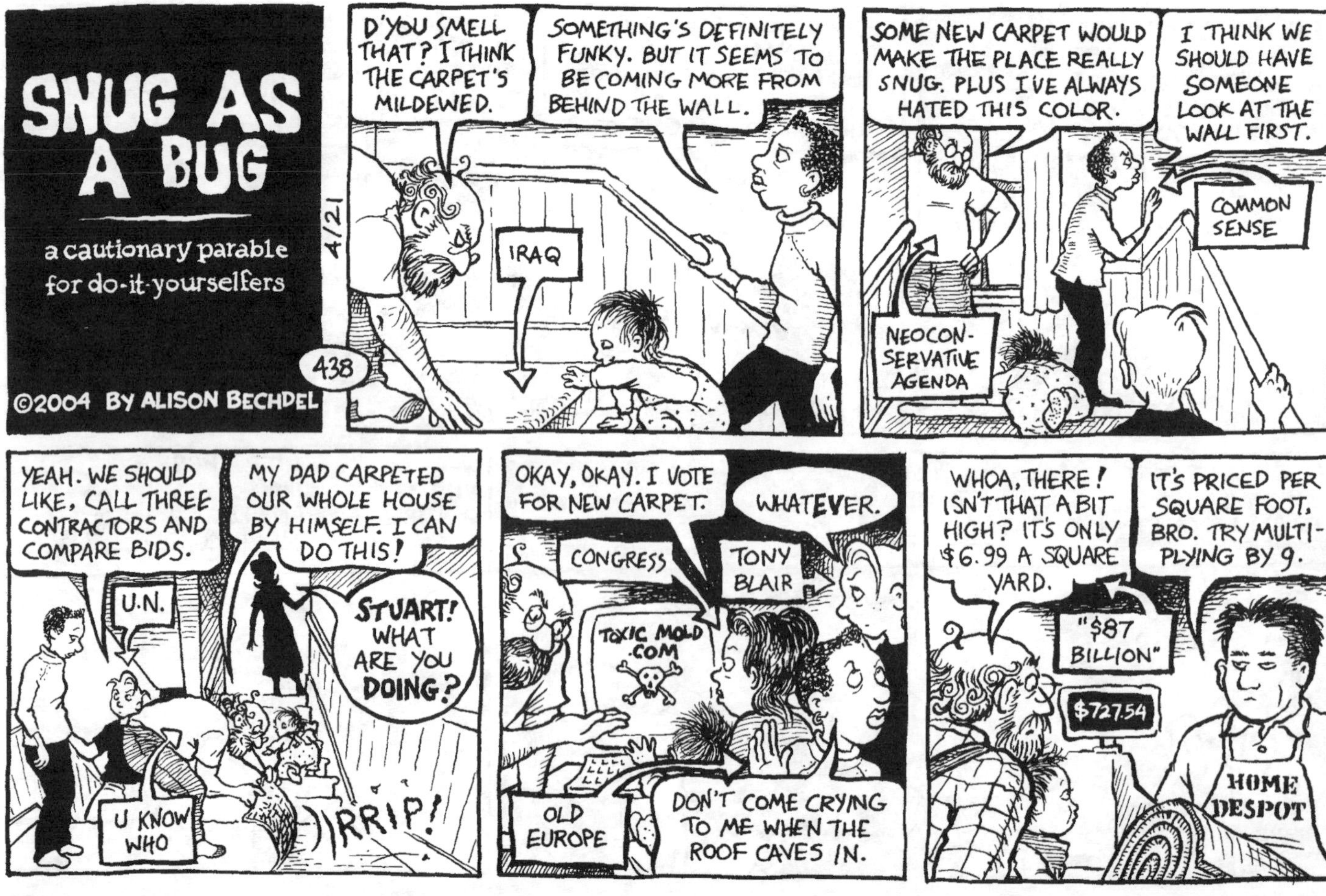

SNUG AS A BUG
a cautionary parable for do-it-yourselfers
©2004 BY ALISON BECHDEL
438
4/21
D'YOU SMELL THAT? I THINK THE CARPET'S MILDEWED.
SOMETHING'S DEFINITELY FUNKY. BUT IT SEEMS TO BE COMING MORE FROM BEHIND THE WALL.
IRAQ
SOME NEW CARPET WOULD MAKE THE PLACE REALLY SNUG. PLUS I'VE ALWAYS HATED THIS COLOR.
I THINK WE SHOULD HAVE SOMEONE LOOK AT THE WALL FIRST.
COMMON SENSE
NEOCON-SERVATIVE AGENDA
YEAH. WE SHOULD LIKE, CALL THREE CONTRACTORS AND COMPARE BIDS.
MY DAD CARPETED OUR WHOLE HOUSE BY HIMSELF. I CAN DO THIS!
U.N.
STUART! WHAT ARE YOU DOING?
U KNOW WHO
RRRIP!
OKAY, OKAY. I VOTE FOR NEW CARPET.
WHATEVER.
CONGRESS
TONY BLAIR
TOXIC MOLD .COM
OLD EUROPE
DON'T COME CRYING TO ME WHEN THE ROOF CAVES IN.
WHOA, THERE! ISN'T THAT A BIT HIGH? IT'S ONLY $6.99 A SQUARE YARD.
IT'S PRICED PER SQUARE FOOT, BRO. TRY MULTI-PLYING BY 9.
"$87 BILLION"
$727.54
HOME DESPOT

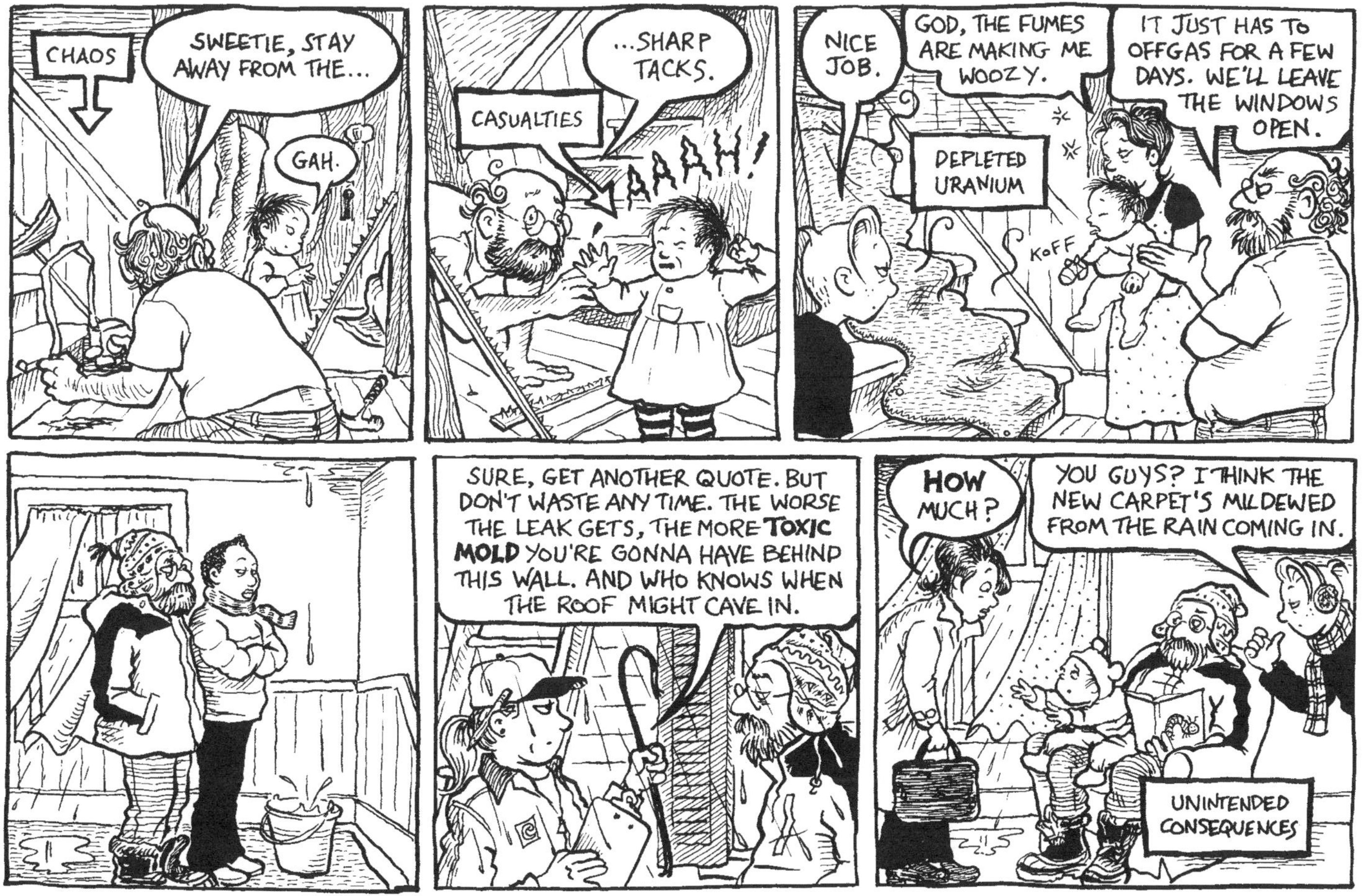

CHAOS
SWEETIE, STAY AWAY FROM THE...
GAH.
...SHARP TACKS.
CASUALTIES
AAAH!
NICE JOB.
GOD, THE FUMES ARE MAKING ME WOOZY.
IT JUST HAS TO OFFGAS FOR A FEW DAYS. WE'LL LEAVE THE WINDOWS OPEN.
DEPLETED URANIUM
KOFF
SURE, GET ANOTHER QUOTE. BUT DON'T WASTE ANY TIME. THE WORSE THE LEAK GETS, THE MORE **TOXIC MOLD** YOU'RE GONNA HAVE BEHIND THIS WALL. AND WHO KNOWS WHEN THE ROOF MIGHT CAVE IN.
HOW MUCH?
YOU GUYS? I THINK THE NEW CARPET'S MILDEWED FROM THE RAIN COMING IN.
UNINTENDED CONSEQUENCES

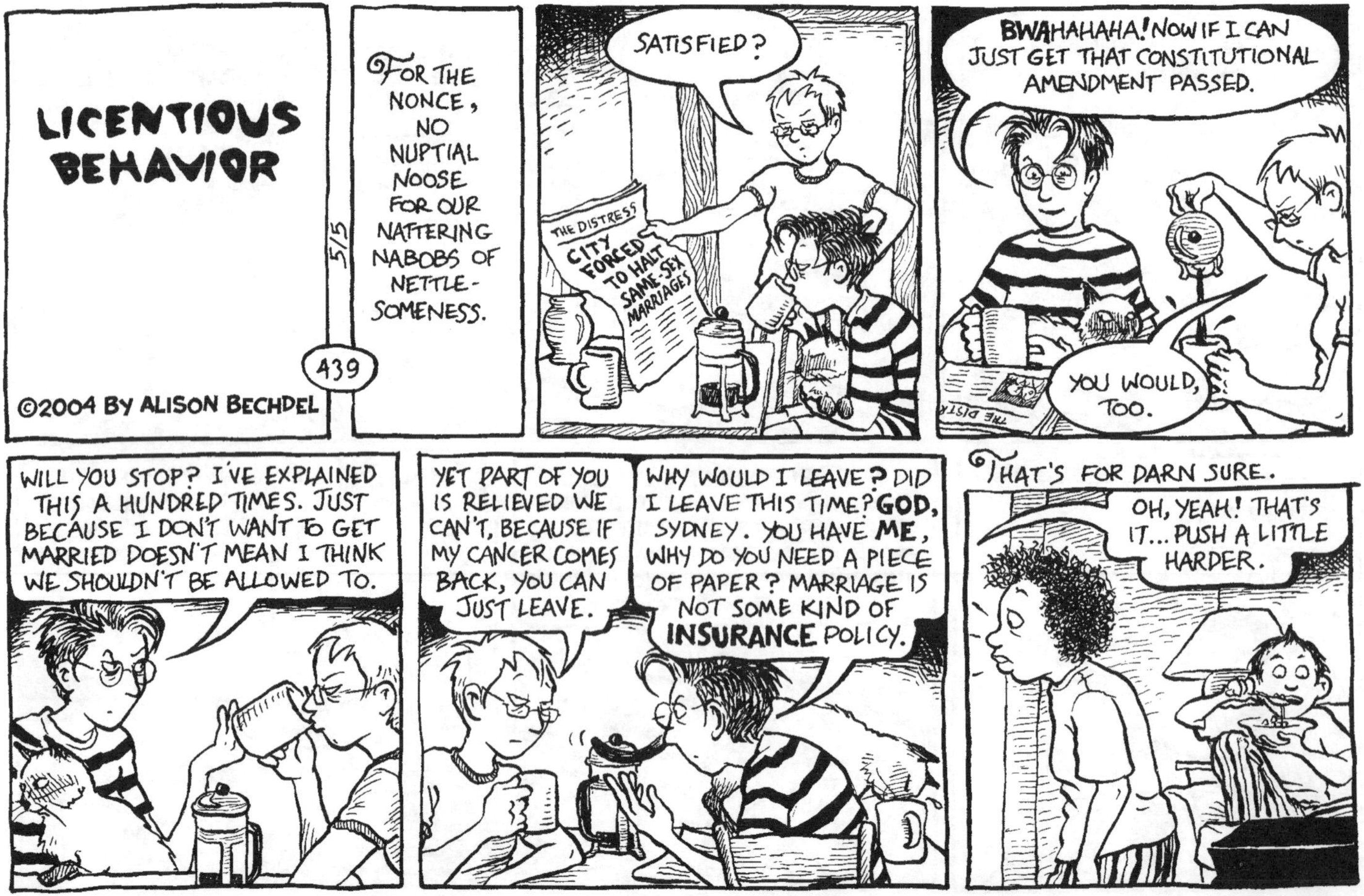

LICENTIOUS BEHAVIOR
©2004 BY ALISON BECHDEL
439
5/5
FOR THE NONCE, NO NUPTIAL NOOSE FOR OUR NATTERING NABOBS OF NETTLESOMENESS.
SATISFIED?
THE DISTRESS
CITY FORCED TO HALT SAME-SEX MARRIAGES
BWAHAHAHA! NOW IF I CAN JUST GET THAT CONSTITUTIONAL AMENDMENT PASSED.
YOU WOULD, TOO.
THE DISTR
WILL YOU STOP? I'VE EXPLAINED THIS A HUNDRED TIMES. JUST BECAUSE I DON'T WANT TO GET MARRIED DOESN'T MEAN I THINK WE SHOULDN'T BE ALLOWED TO.
YET PART OF YOU IS RELIEVED WE CAN'T, BECAUSE IF MY CANCER COMES BACK, YOU CAN JUST LEAVE.
WHY WOULD I LEAVE? DID I LEAVE THIS TIME? GOD, SYDNEY. YOU HAVE ME, WHY DO YOU NEED A PIECE OF PAPER? MARRIAGE IS NOT SOME KIND OF INSURANCE POLICY.
THAT'S FOR DARN SURE.
OH, YEAH! THAT'S IT... PUSH A LITTLE HARDER.

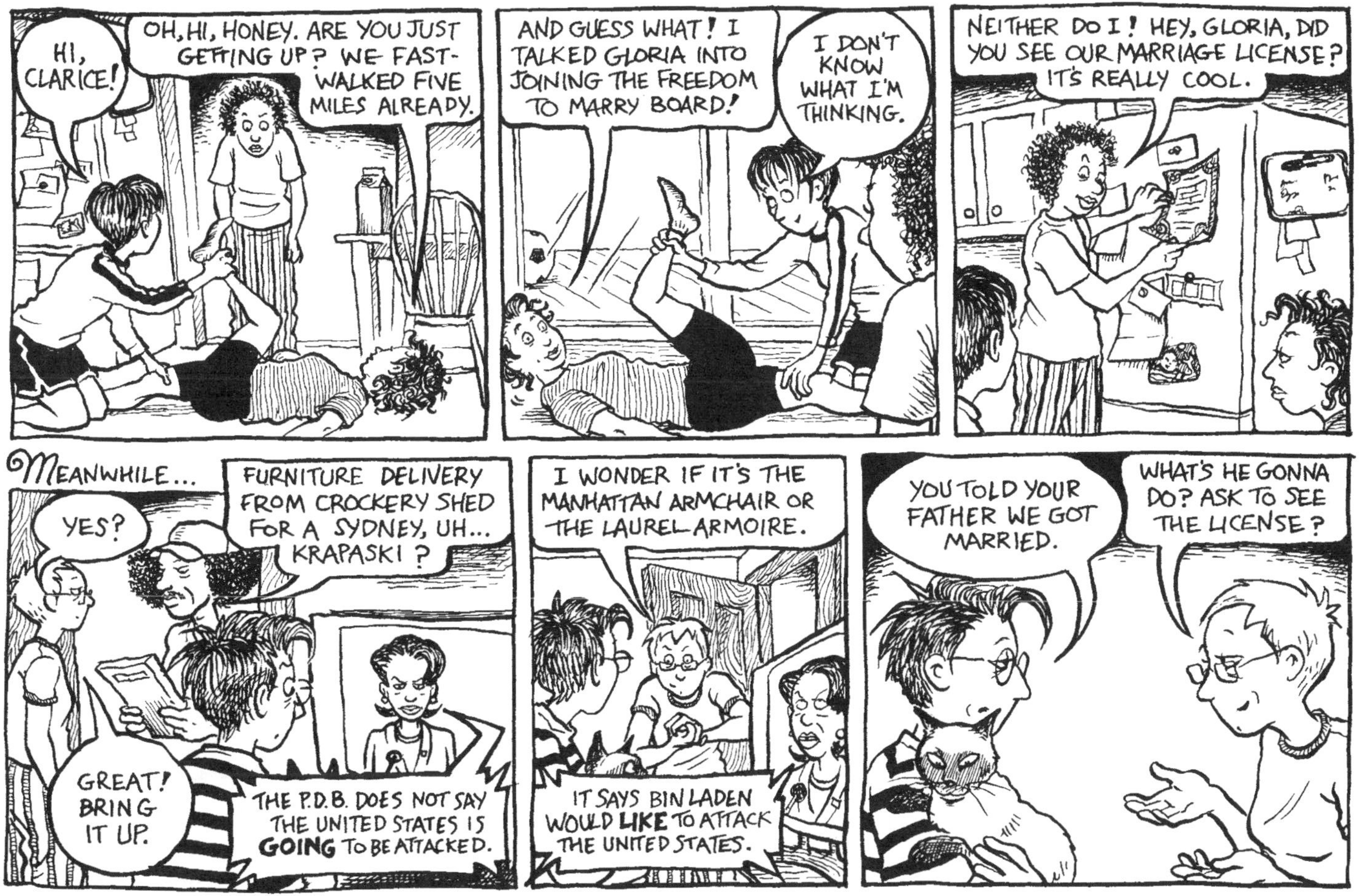
HI, CLARICE!
OH, HI, HONEY. ARE YOU JUST GETTING UP? WE FAST-WALKED FIVE MILES ALREADY.
AND GUESS WHAT! I TALKED GLORIA INTO JOINING THE FREEDOM TO MARRY BOARD!
I DON'T KNOW WHAT I'M THINKING.
NEITHER DO I! HEY, GLORIA, DID YOU SEE OUR MARRIAGE LICENSE? IT'S REALLY COOL.
MEANWHILE...
YES?
FURNITURE DELIVERY FROM CROCKERY SHED FOR A SYDNEY, UH... KRAPASKI?
GREAT! BRING IT UP.
THE P.D.B. DOES NOT SAY THE UNITED STATES IS **GOING** TO BE ATTACKED.
I WONDER IF IT'S THE MANHATTAN ARMCHAIR OR THE LAUREL ARMOIRE.
IT SAYS BIN LADEN WOULD **LIKE** TO ATTACK THE UNITED STATES.
YOU TOLD YOUR FATHER WE GOT MARRIED.
WHAT'S HE GONNA DO? ASK TO SEE THE LICENSE?

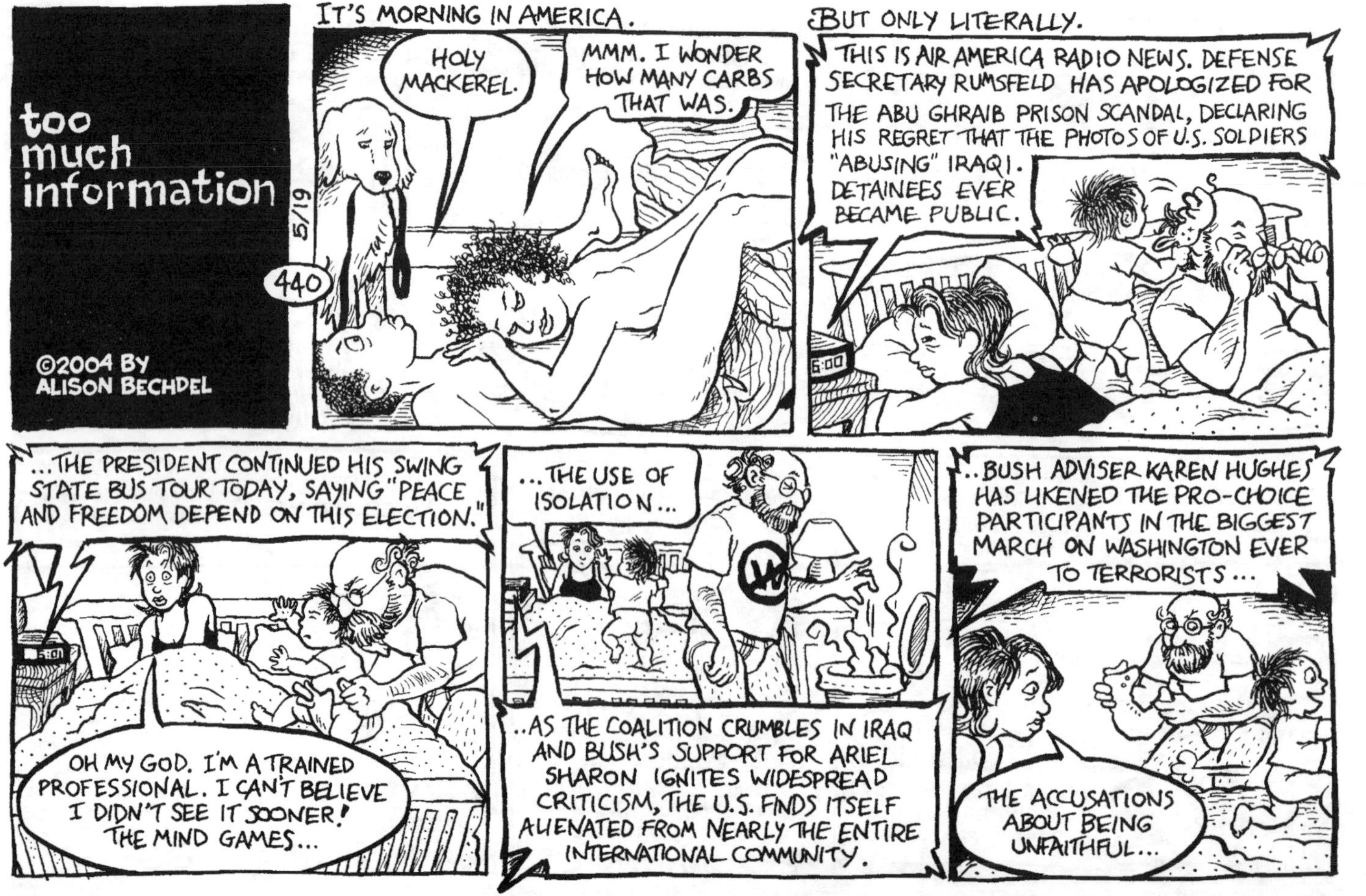
too much information
5/19
440
©2004 BY ALISON BECHDEL
IT'S MORNING IN AMERICA.
HOLY MACKEREL.
MMM. I WONDER HOW MANY CARBS THAT WAS.
BUT ONLY LITERALLY.
THIS IS AIR AMERICA RADIO NEWS. DEFENSE SECRETARY RUMSFELD HAS APOLOGIZED FOR THE ABU GHRAIB PRISON SCANDAL, DECLARING HIS REGRET THAT THE PHOTOS OF U.S. SOLDIERS "ABUSING" IRAQI DETAINEES EVER BECAME PUBLIC.
6:00
...THE PRESIDENT CONTINUED HIS SWING STATE BUS TOUR TODAY, SAYING "PEACE AND FREEDOM DEPEND ON THIS ELECTION."
OH MY GOD. I'M A TRAINED PROFESSIONAL. I CAN'T BELIEVE I DIDN'T SEE IT SOONER! THE MIND GAMES...
...THE USE OF ISOLATION...
..AS THE COALITION CRUMBLES IN IRAQ AND BUSH'S SUPPORT FOR ARIEL SHARON IGNITES WIDESPREAD CRITICISM, THE U.S. FINDS ITSELF ALIENATED FROM NEARLY THE ENTIRE INTERNATIONAL COMMUNITY.
..BUSH ADVISER KAREN HUGHES HAS LIKENED THE PRO-CHOICE PARTICIPANTS IN THE BIGGEST MARCH ON WASHINGTON EVER TO TERRORISTS...
THE ACCUSATIONS ABOUT BEING UNFAITHFUL...

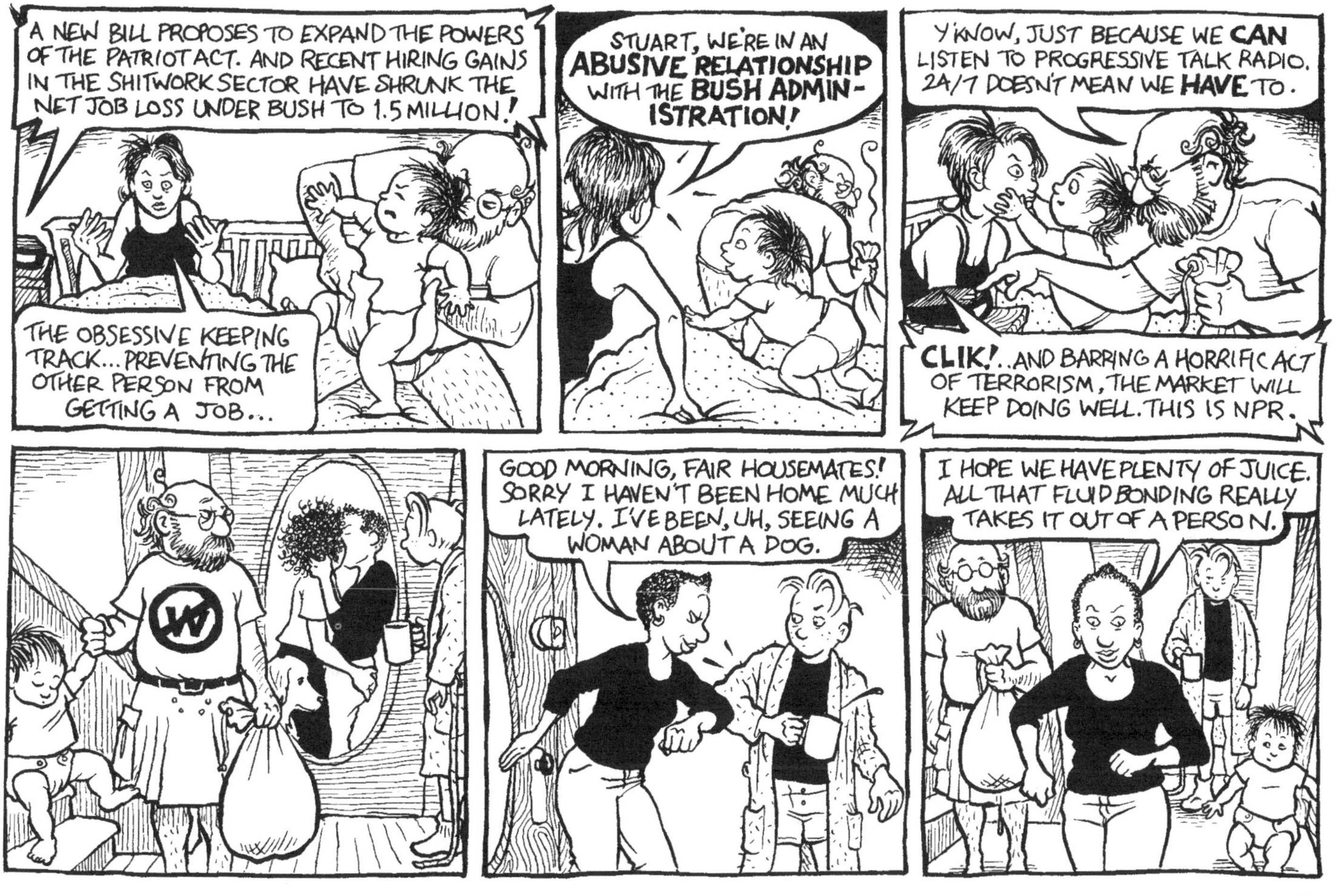

A NEW BILL PROPOSES TO EXPAND THE POWERS OF THE PATRIOT ACT. AND RECENT HIRING GAINS IN THE SHITWORK SECTOR HAVE SHRUNK THE NET JOB LOSS UNDER BUSH TO 1.5 MILLION!
THE OBSESSIVE KEEPING TRACK... PREVENTING THE OTHER PERSON FROM GETTING A JOB...
STUART, WE'RE IN AN ABUSIVE RELATIONSHIP WITH THE BUSH ADMINISTRATION!
Y'KNOW, JUST BECAUSE WE CAN LISTEN TO PROGRESSIVE TALK RADIO 24/7 DOESN'T MEAN WE HAVE TO.
CLIK! ..AND BARRING A HORRIFIC ACT OF TERRORISM, THE MARKET WILL KEEP DOING WELL. THIS IS NPR.
GOOD MORNING, FAIR HOUSEMATES! SORRY I HAVEN'T BEEN HOME MUCH LATELY. I'VE BEEN, UH, SEEING A WOMAN ABOUT A DOG.
I HOPE WE HAVE PLENTY OF JUICE. ALL THAT FLUID BONDING REALLY TAKES IT OUT OF A PERSON.

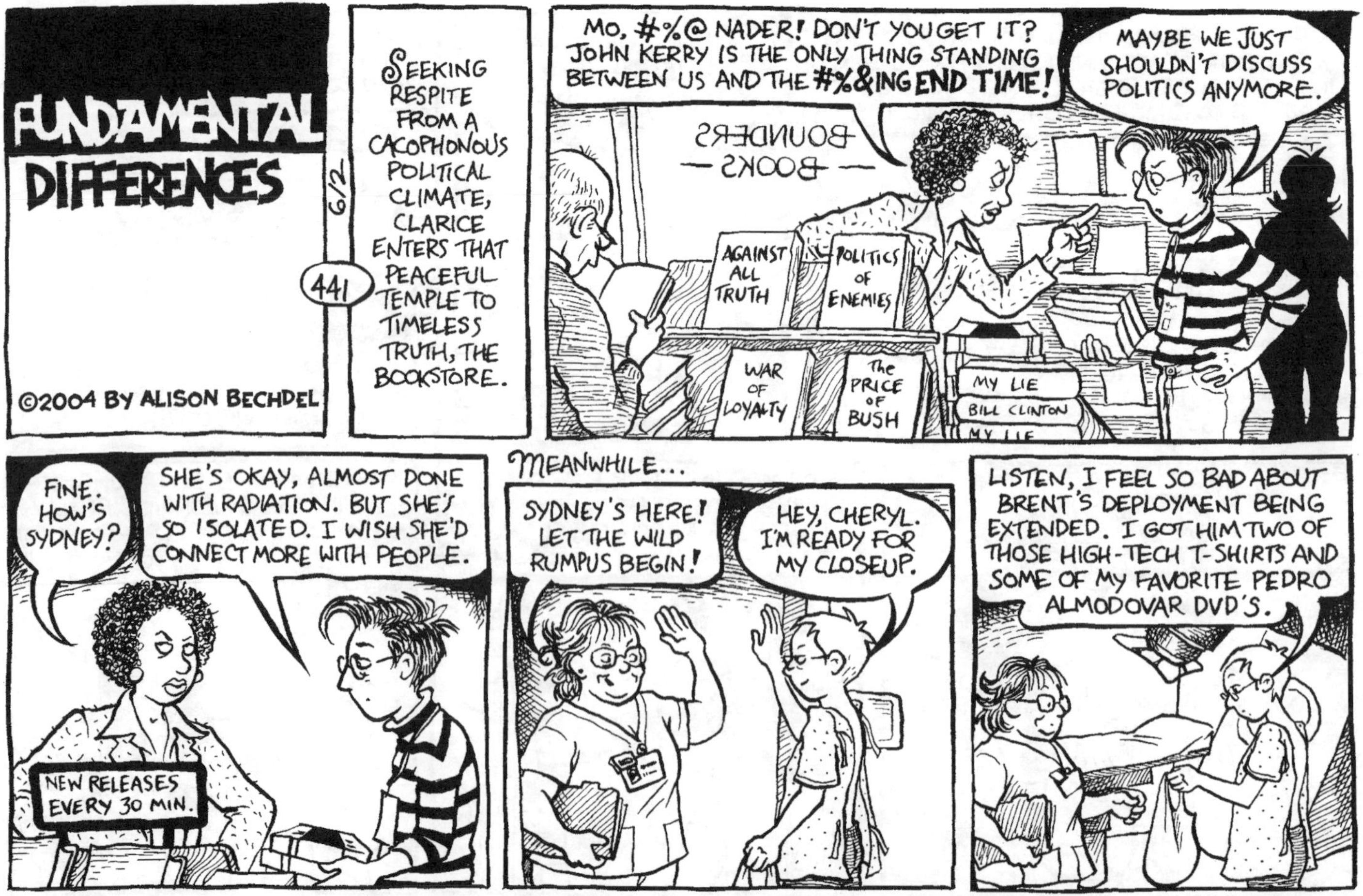
FUNDAMENTAL DIFFERENCES
441
6/2
©2004 BY ALISON BECHDEL
SEEKING RESPITE FROM A CACOPHONOUS POLITICAL CLIMATE, CLARICE ENTERS THAT PEACEFUL TEMPLE TO TIMELESS TRUTH, THE BOOKSTORE.
MO, #%@ NADER! DON'T YOU GET IT? JOHN KERRY IS THE ONLY THING STANDING BETWEEN US AND THE #%&ING END TIME!
MAYBE WE JUST SHOULDN'T DISCUSS POLITICS ANYMORE.
BOUNDERS BOOKS
AGAINST ALL TRUTH
POLITICS OF ENEMIES
WAR OF LOYALTY
The PRICE OF BUSH
MY LIE
BILL CLINTON
MY LIE
FINE. HOW'S SYDNEY?
SHE'S OKAY, ALMOST DONE WITH RADIATION. BUT SHE'S SO ISOLATED. I WISH SHE'D CONNECT MORE WITH PEOPLE.
NEW RELEASES EVERY 30 MIN.
MEANWHILE...
SYDNEY'S HERE! LET THE WILD RUMPUS BEGIN!
HEY, CHERYL. I'M READY FOR MY CLOSEUP.
LISTEN, I FEEL SO BAD ABOUT BRENT'S DEPLOYMENT BEING EXTENDED. I GOT HIM TWO OF THOSE HIGH-TECH T-SHIRTS AND SOME OF MY FAVORITE PEDRO ALMODOVAR DVD'S.

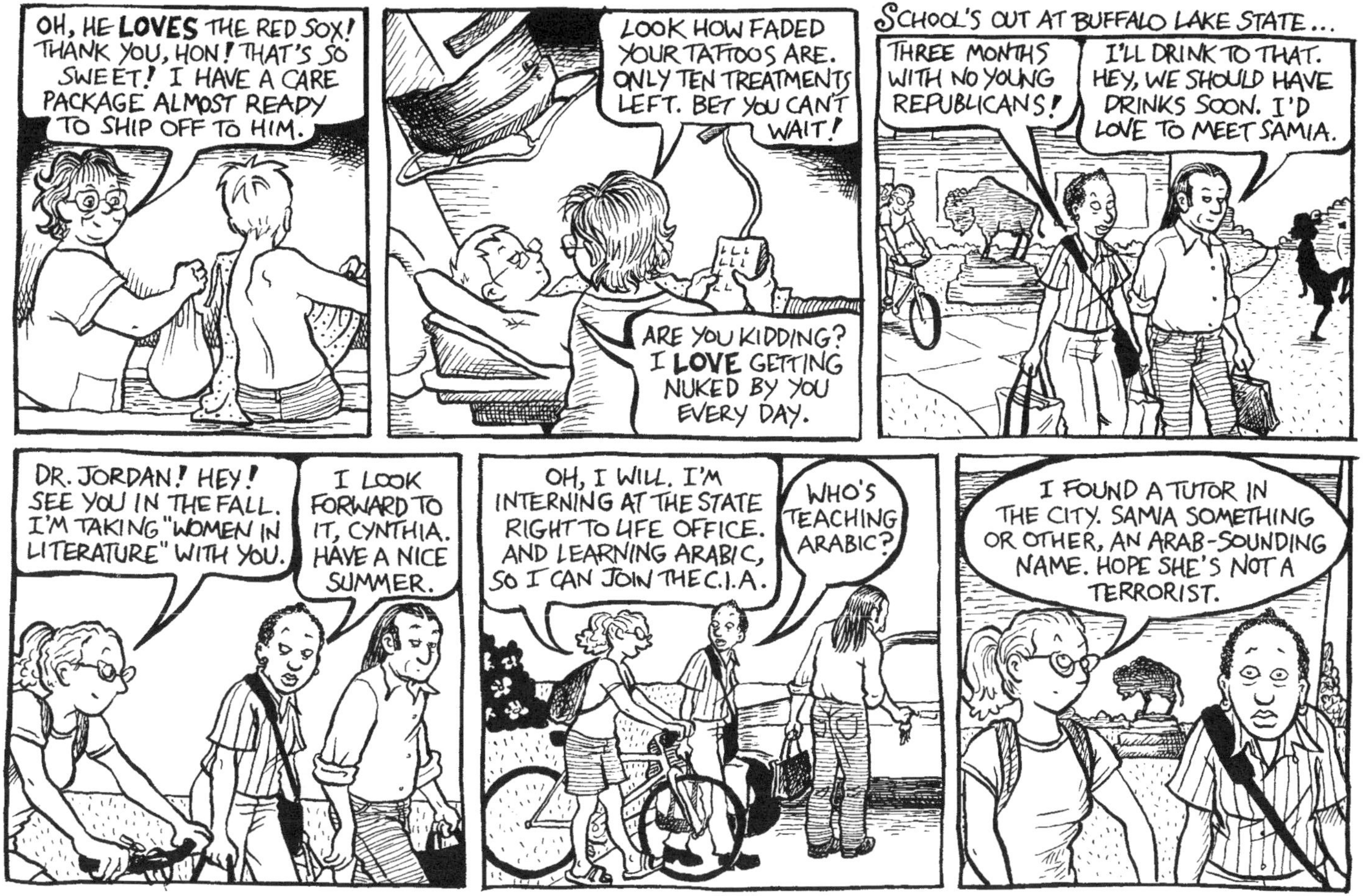

OH, HE **LOVES** THE RED SOX! THANK YOU, HON! THAT'S SO SWEET! I HAVE A CARE PACKAGE ALMOST READY TO SHIP OFF TO HIM.
LOOK HOW FADED YOUR TATTOOS ARE. ONLY TEN TREATMENTS LEFT. BET YOU CAN'T WAIT!
ARE YOU KIDDING? I **LOVE** GETTING NUKED BY YOU EVERY DAY.
SCHOOL'S OUT AT BUFFALO LAKE STATE...
THREE MONTHS WITH NO YOUNG REPUBLICANS!
I'LL DRINK TO THAT. HEY, WE SHOULD HAVE DRINKS SOON. I'D LOVE TO MEET SAMIA.
DR. JORDAN! HEY! SEE YOU IN THE FALL. I'M TAKING "WOMEN IN LITERATURE" WITH YOU.
I LOOK FORWARD TO IT, CYNTHIA. HAVE A NICE SUMMER.
OH, I WILL. I'M INTERNING AT THE STATE RIGHT TO LIFE OFFICE. AND LEARNING ARABIC, SO I CAN JOIN THE C.I.A.
WHO'S TEACHING ARABIC?
I FOUND A TUTOR IN THE CITY. SAMIA SOMETHING OR OTHER, AN ARAB-SOUNDING NAME. HOPE SHE'S NOT A TERRORIST.

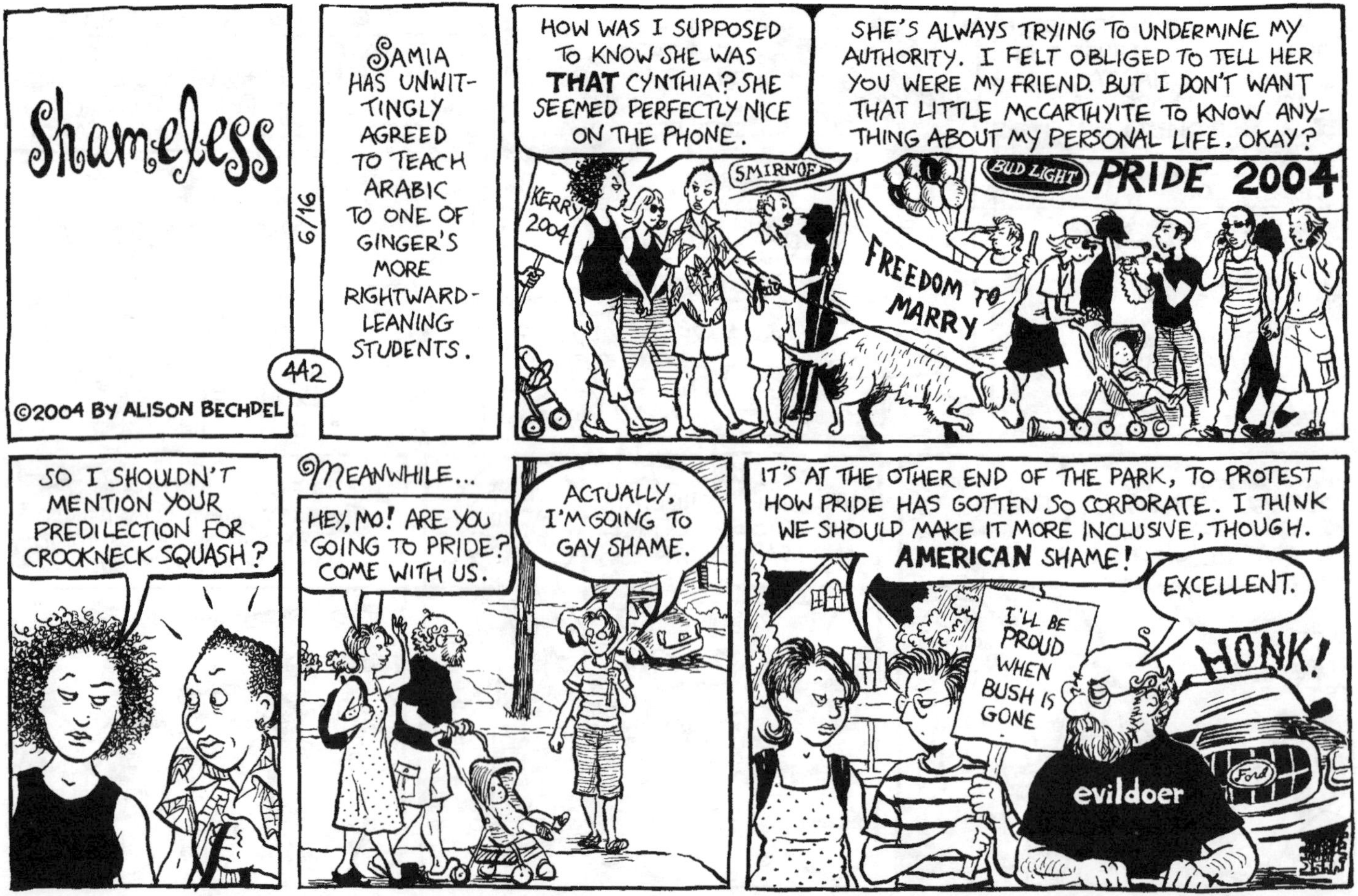
Shameless
©2004 BY ALISON BECHDEL
442
6/16
SAMIA HAS UNWITTINGLY AGREED TO TEACH ARABIC TO ONE OF GINGER'S MORE RIGHTWARD-LEANING STUDENTS.
HOW WAS I SUPPOSED TO KNOW SHE WAS **THAT** CYNTHIA? SHE SEEMED PERFECTLY NICE ON THE PHONE.
SHE'S ALWAYS TRYING TO UNDERMINE MY AUTHORITY. I FELT OBLIGED TO TELL HER YOU WERE MY FRIEND. BUT I DON'T WANT THAT LITTLE McCARTHYITE TO KNOW ANYTHING ABOUT MY PERSONAL LIFE, OKAY?
KERRY 2004
SMIRNOFF
BUD LIGHT
PRIDE 2004
FREEDOM TO MARRY
SO I SHOULDN'T MENTION YOUR PREDILECTION FOR CROOKNECK SQUASH?
MEANWHILE...
HEY, MO! ARE YOU GOING TO PRIDE? COME WITH US.
ACTUALLY, I'M GOING TO GAY SHAME.
IT'S AT THE OTHER END OF THE PARK, TO PROTEST HOW PRIDE HAS GOTTEN SO CORPORATE. I THINK WE SHOULD MAKE IT MORE INCLUSIVE, THOUGH. **AMERICAN** SHAME!
EXCELLENT.
I'LL BE PROUD WHEN BUSH IS GONE
HONK!
evildoer
Ford

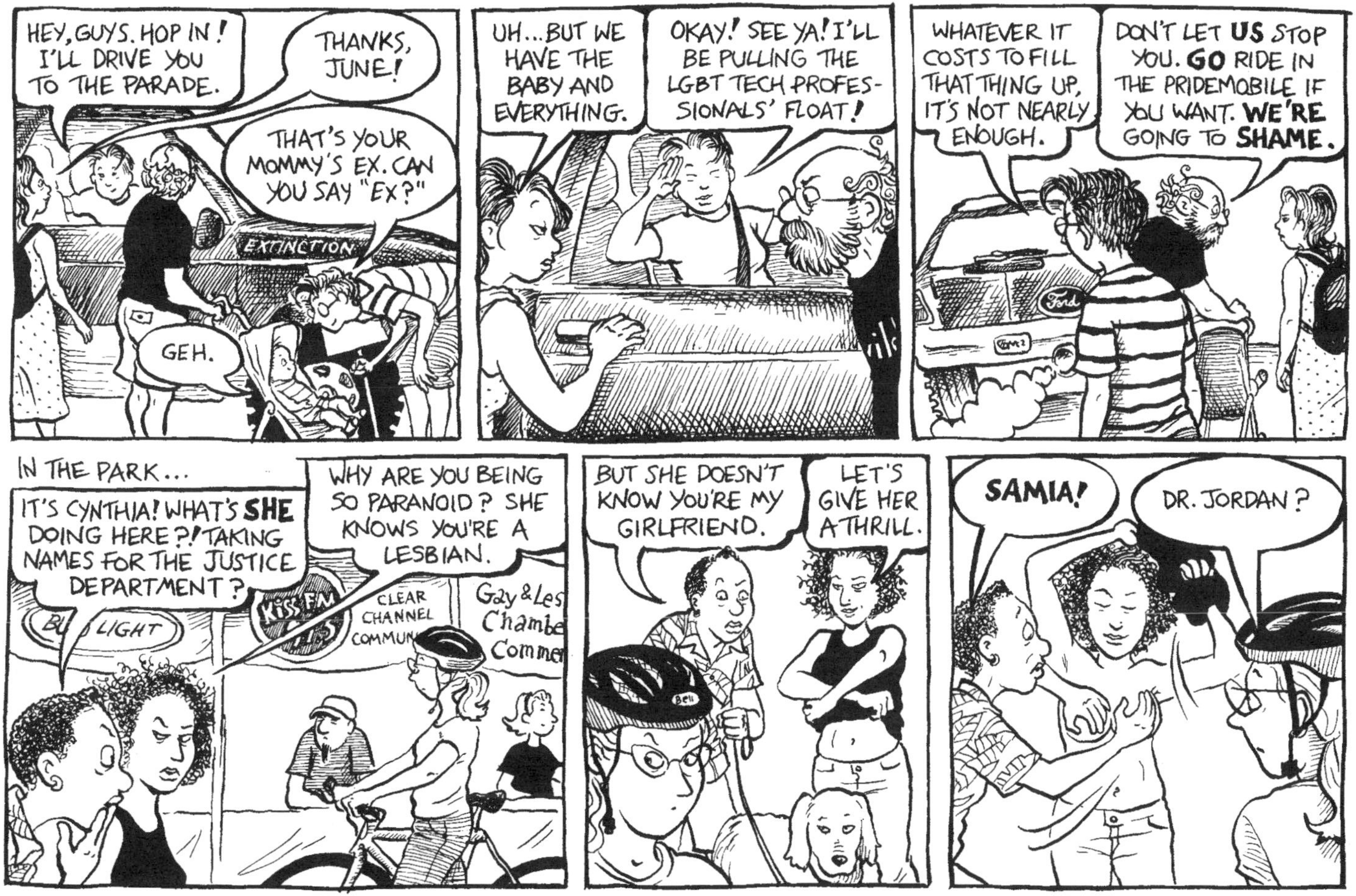
HEY, GUYS. HOP IN! I'LL DRIVE YOU TO THE PARADE.
THANKS, JUNE!
THAT'S YOUR MOMMY'S EX. CAN YOU SAY "EX?"
EXTINCTION
GEH.
UH...BUT WE HAVE THE BABY AND EVERYTHING.
OKAY! SEE YA! I'LL BE PULLING THE LGBT TECH PROFES-SIONALS' FLOAT!
WHATEVER IT COSTS TO FILL THAT THING UP, IT'S NOT NEARLY ENOUGH.
DON'T LET **US** STOP YOU. **GO** RIDE IN THE PRIDEMOBILE IF YOU WANT. **WE'RE** GOING TO **SHAME**.
IN THE PARK...
IT'S CYNTHIA! WHAT'S **SHE** DOING HERE?! TAKING NAMES FOR THE JUSTICE DEPARTMENT?
WHY ARE YOU BEING SO PARANOID? SHE KNOWS YOU'RE A LESBIAN.
CLEAR CHANNEL
BUT SHE DOESN'T KNOW YOU'RE MY GIRLFRIEND.
LET'S GIVE HER A THRILL.
SAMIA!
DR. JORDAN?

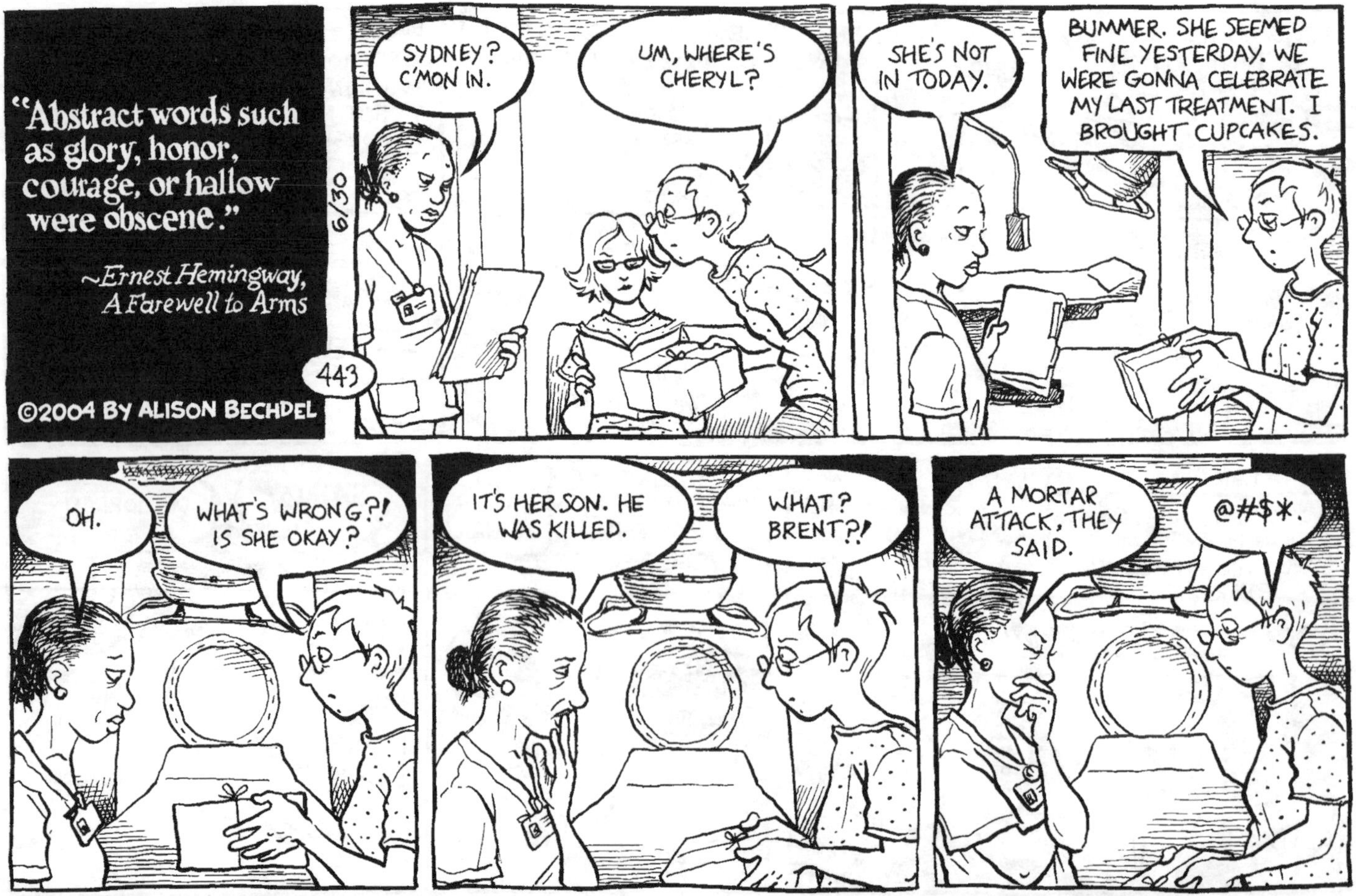
"Abstract words such as glory, honor, courage, or hallow were obscene."
~Ernest Hemingway, A Farewell to Arms
©2004 BY ALISON BECHDEL
443
6/30
SYDNEY? C'MON IN.
UM, WHERE'S CHERYL?
SHE'S NOT IN TODAY.
BUMMER. SHE SEEMED FINE YESTERDAY. WE WERE GONNA CELEBRATE MY LAST TREATMENT. I BROUGHT CUPCAKES.
OH.
WHAT'S WRONG?! IS SHE OKAY?
IT'S HER SON. HE WAS KILLED.
WHAT? BRENT?!
A MORTAR ATTACK, THEY SAID.
@#$*.

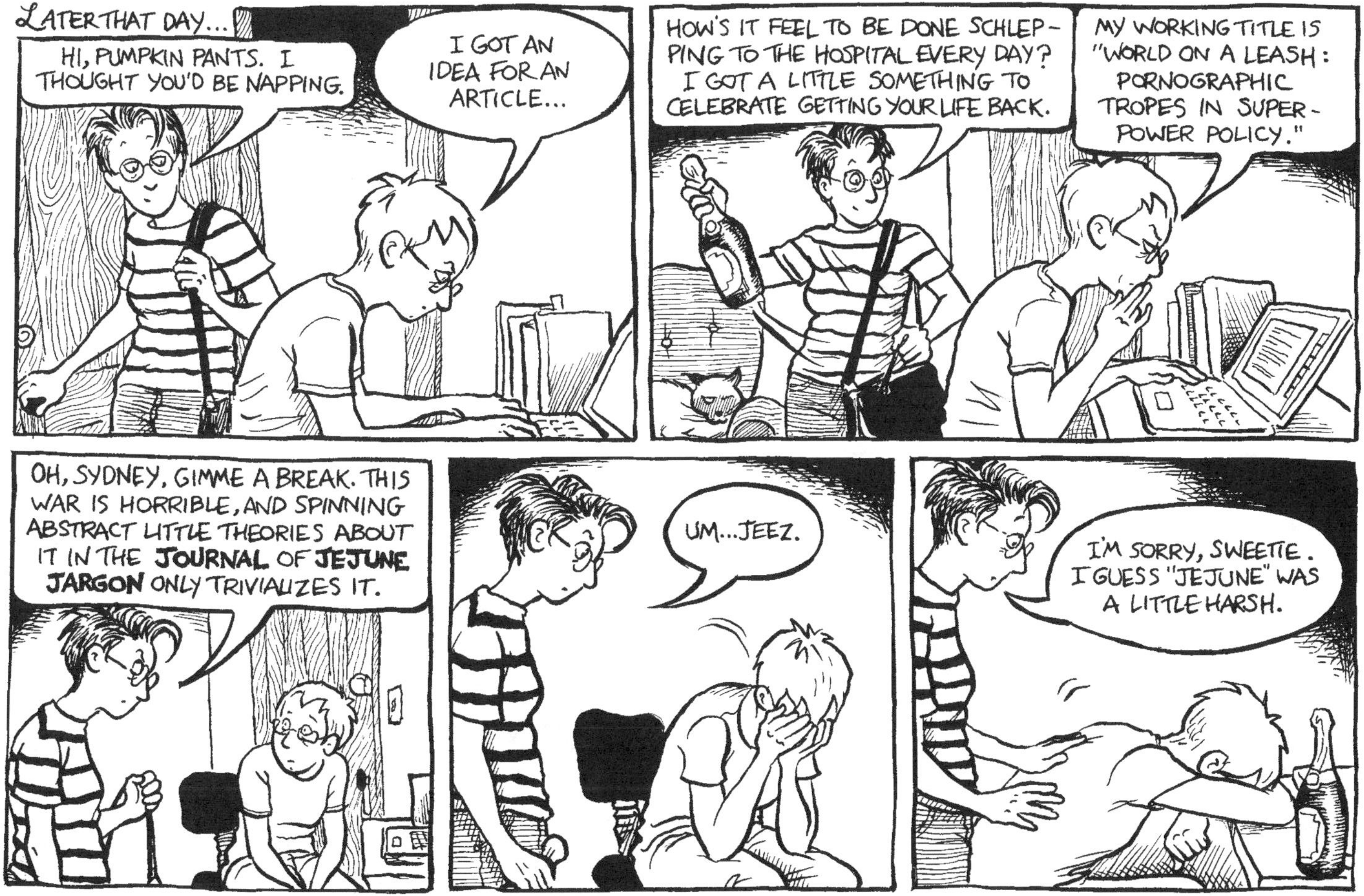
LATER THAT DAY...
HI, PUMPKIN PANTS. I THOUGHT YOU'D BE NAPPING.
I GOT AN IDEA FOR AN ARTICLE...
HOW'S IT FEEL TO BE DONE SCHLEP-PING TO THE HOSPITAL EVERY DAY? I GOT A LITTLE SOMETHING TO CELEBRATE GETTING YOUR LIFE BACK.
MY WORKING TITLE IS "WORLD ON A LEASH: PORNOGRAPHIC TROPES IN SUPER-POWER POLICY."
OH, SYDNEY, GIMME A BREAK. THIS WAR IS HORRIBLE, AND SPINNING ABSTRACT LITTLE THEORIES ABOUT IT IN THE **JOURNAL** OF **JEJUNE JARGON** ONLY TRIVIALIZES IT.
UM...JEEZ.
I'M SORRY, SWEETIE. I GUESS "JEJUNE" WAS A LITTLE HARSH.

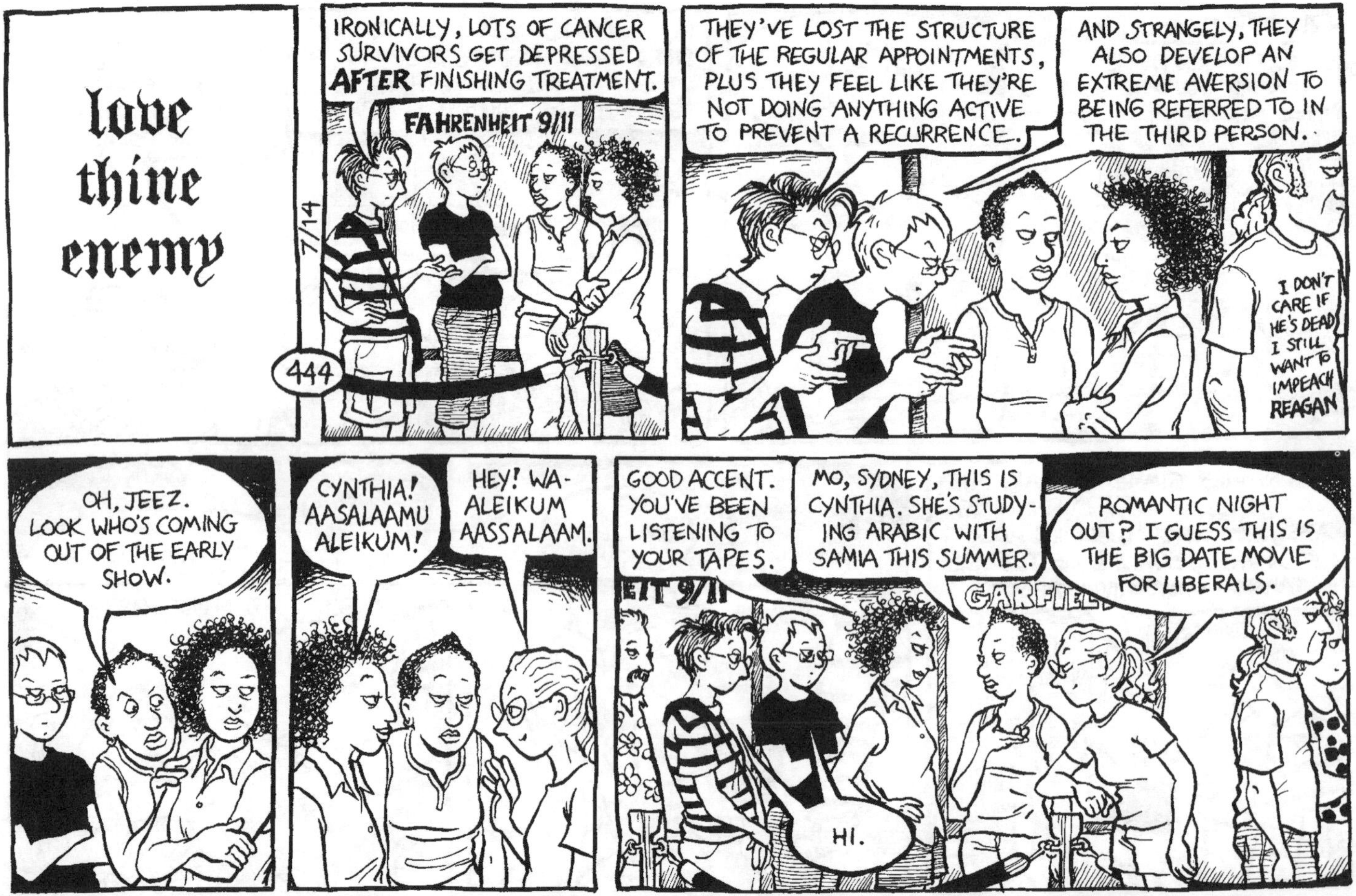

love thine enemy
7/14
444
IRONICALLY, LOTS OF CANCER SURVIVORS GET DEPRESSED **AFTER** FINISHING TREATMENT.
FAHRENHEIT 9/11
THEY'VE LOST THE STRUCTURE OF THE REGULAR APPOINTMENTS, PLUS THEY FEEL LIKE THEY'RE NOT DOING ANYTHING ACTIVE TO PREVENT A RECURRENCE.
AND STRANGELY, THEY ALSO DEVELOP AN EXTREME AVERSION TO BEING REFERRED TO IN THE THIRD PERSON.
I DON'T CARE IF HE'S DEAD I STILL WANT TO IMPEACH REAGAN
OH, JEEZ. LOOK WHO'S COMING OUT OF THE EARLY SHOW.
CYNTHIA! AASALAAMU ALEIKUM!
HEY! WA-ALEIKUM AASSALAAM.
GOOD ACCENT. YOU'VE BEEN LISTENING TO YOUR TAPES.
MO, SYDNEY, THIS IS CYNTHIA. SHE'S STUDYING ARABIC WITH SAMIA THIS SUMMER.
HI.
ROMANTIC NIGHT OUT? I GUESS THIS IS THE BIG DATE MOVIE FOR LIBERALS.

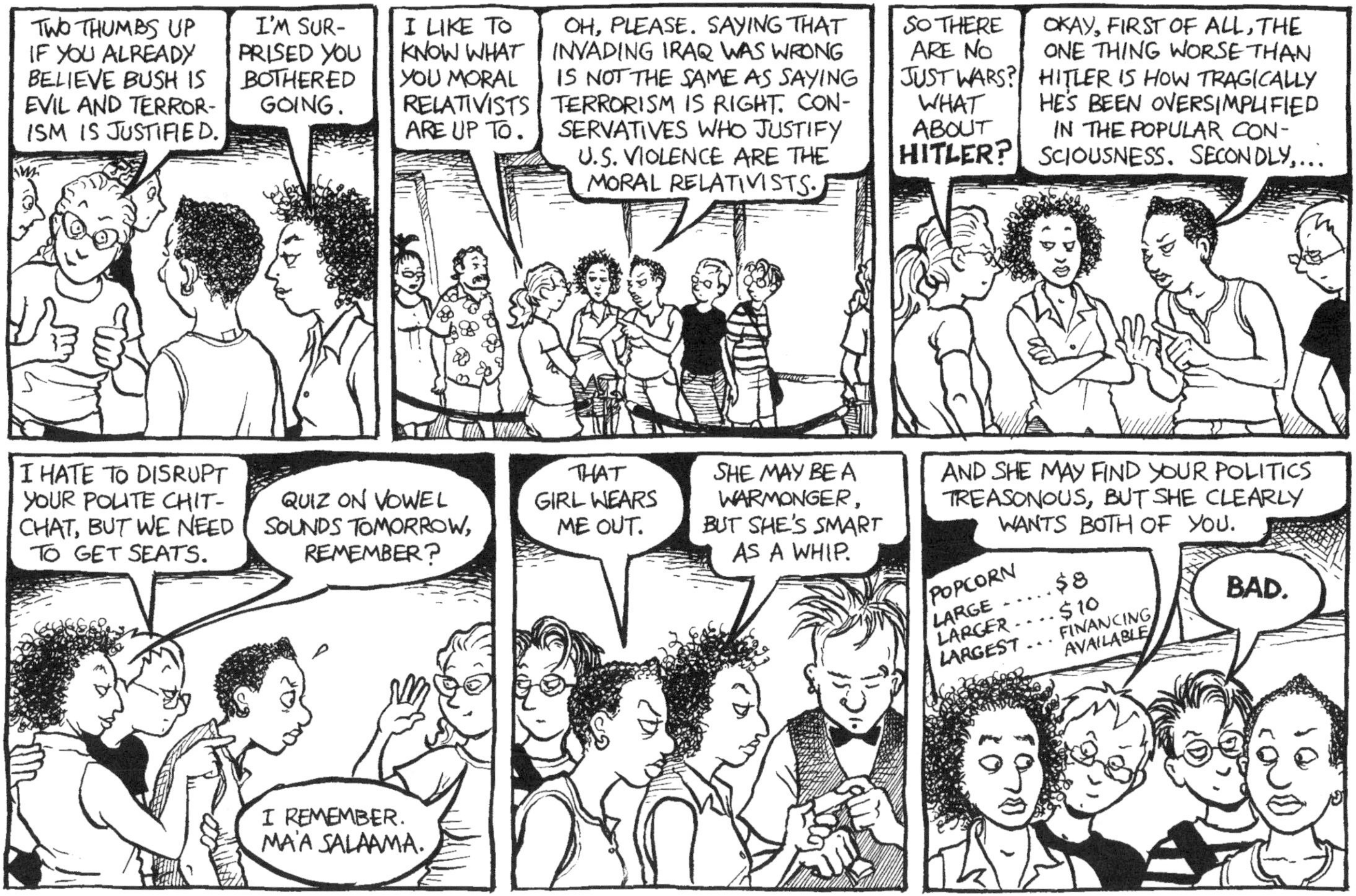
TWO THUMBS UP IF YOU ALREADY BELIEVE BUSH IS EVIL AND TERRORISM IS JUSTIFIED.
I'M SURPRISED YOU BOTHERED GOING.
I LIKE TO KNOW WHAT YOU MORAL RELATIVISTS ARE UP TO.
OH, PLEASE. SAYING THAT INVADING IRAQ WAS WRONG IS NOT THE SAME AS SAYING TERRORISM IS RIGHT. CONSERVATIVES WHO JUSTIFY U.S. VIOLENCE ARE THE MORAL RELATIVISTS.
SO THERE ARE NO JUST WARS? WHAT ABOUT **HITLER?**
OKAY, FIRST OF ALL, THE ONE THING WORSE THAN HITLER IS HOW TRAGICALLY HE'S BEEN OVERSIMPLIFIED IN THE POPULAR CONSCIOUSNESS. SECONDLY,...
I HATE TO DISRUPT YOUR POLITE CHIT-CHAT, BUT WE NEED TO GET SEATS.
QUIZ ON VOWEL SOUNDS TOMORROW, REMEMBER?
I REMEMBER. MA'A SALAAMA.
THAT GIRL WEARS ME OUT.
SHE MAY BE A WARMONGER, BUT SHE'S SMART AS A WHIP.
AND SHE MAY FIND YOUR POLITICS TREASONOUS, BUT SHE CLEARLY WANTS BOTH OF YOU.
POPCORN
LARGE $8
LARGER $10
LARGEST . . . FINANCING AVAILABLE
BAD.

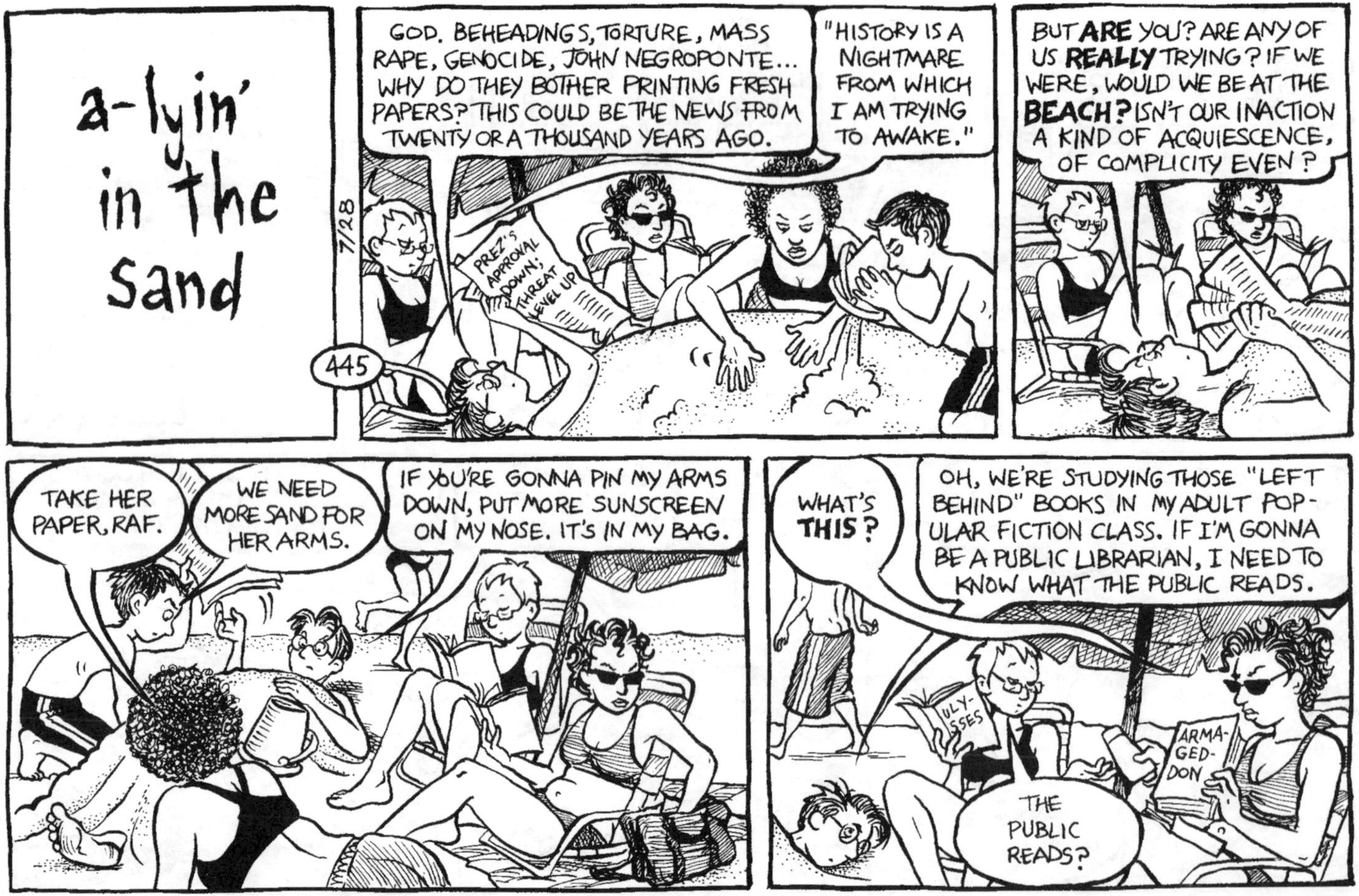
a-lyin' in the sand
7/28
445
GOD. BEHEADINGS, TORTURE, MASS RAPE, GENOCIDE, JOHN NEGROPONTE... WHY DO THEY BOTHER PRINTING FRESH PAPERS? THIS COULD BE THE NEWS FROM TWENTY OR A THOUSAND YEARS AGO.
PREZ'S APPROVAL DOWN; THREAT LEVEL UP
"HISTORY IS A NIGHTMARE FROM WHICH I AM TRYING TO AWAKE."
BUT **ARE** YOU? ARE ANY OF US **REALLY** TRYING? IF WE WERE, WOULD WE BE AT THE **BEACH?** ISN'T OUR INACTION A KIND OF ACQUIESCENCE, OF COMPLICITY EVEN?
TAKE HER PAPER, RAF.
WE NEED MORE SAND FOR HER ARMS.
IF YOU'RE GONNA PIN MY ARMS DOWN, PUT MORE SUNSCREEN ON MY NOSE. IT'S IN MY BAG.
WHAT'S **THIS**?
OH, WE'RE STUDYING THOSE "LEFT BEHIND" BOOKS IN MY ADULT POPULAR FICTION CLASS. IF I'M GONNA BE A PUBLIC LIBRARIAN, I NEED TO KNOW WHAT THE PUBLIC READS.
ULYSSES
ARMAGEDDON
THE PUBLIC READS?

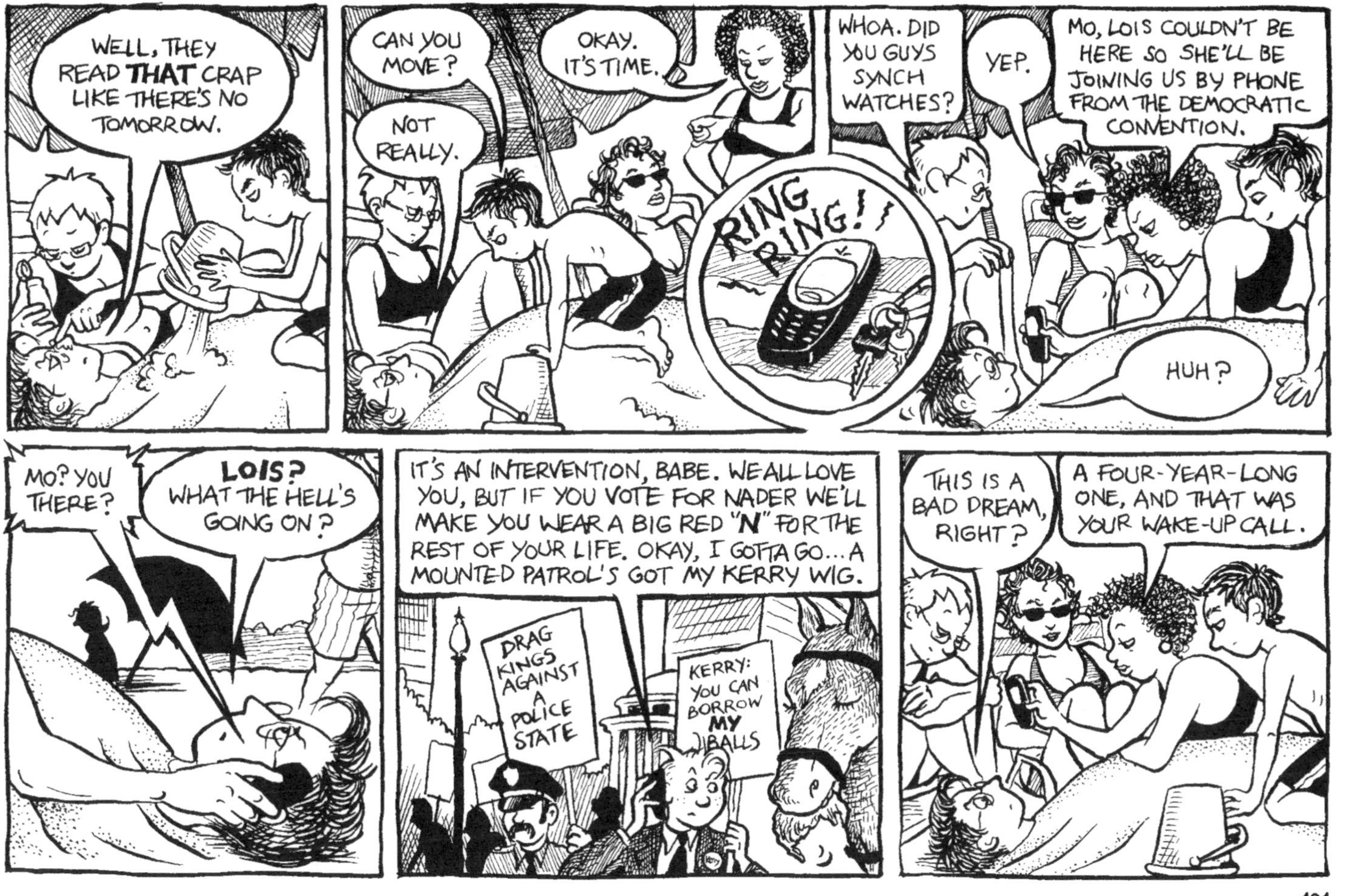

WELL, THEY READ **THAT** CRAP LIKE THERE'S NO TOMORROW.
CAN YOU MOVE?
NOT REALLY.
OKAY. IT'S TIME.
RING RING!!
WHOA. DID YOU GUYS SYNCH WATCHES?
YEP.
MO, LOIS COULDN'T BE HERE SO SHE'LL BE JOINING US BY PHONE FROM THE DEMOCRATIC CONVENTION.
HUH?
MO? YOU THERE?
LOIS? WHAT THE HELL'S GOING ON?
IT'S AN INTERVENTION, BABE. WE ALL LOVE YOU, BUT IF YOU VOTE FOR NADER WE'LL MAKE YOU WEAR A BIG RED "**N**" FOR THE REST OF YOUR LIFE. OKAY, I GOTTA GO... A MOUNTED PATROL'S GOT MY KERRY WIG.
DRAG KINGS AGAINST A POLICE STATE
KERRY: YOU CAN BORROW **MY** BALLS
THIS IS A BAD DREAM, RIGHT?
A FOUR-YEAR-LONG ONE, AND THAT WAS YOUR WAKE-UP CALL.

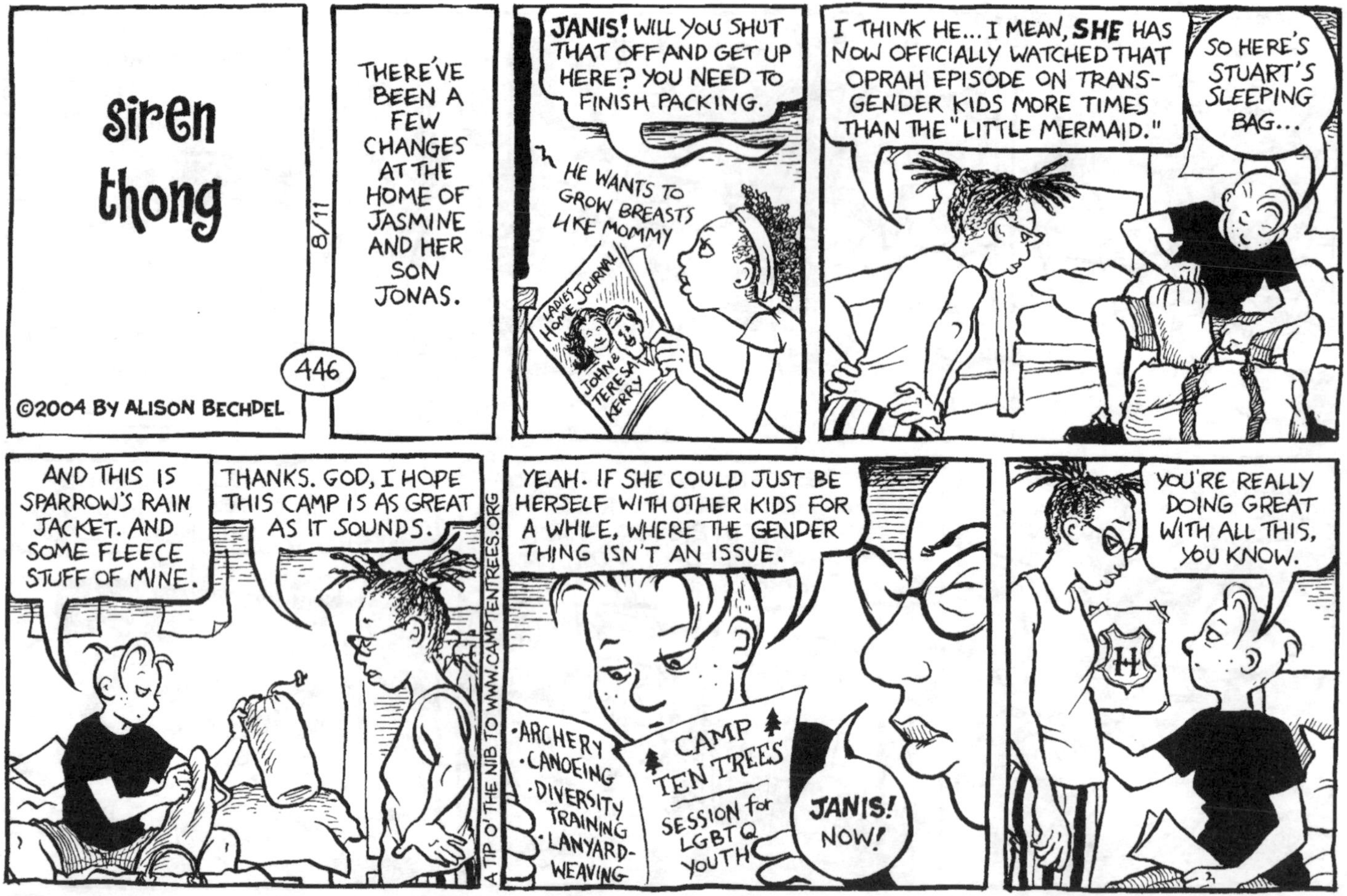
siren thong
©2004 BY ALISON BECHDEL
446
8/11
THERE'VE BEEN A FEW CHANGES AT THE HOME OF JASMINE AND HER SON JONAS.
JANIS! WILL YOU SHUT THAT OFF AND GET UP HERE? YOU NEED TO FINISH PACKING.
HE WANTS TO GROW BREASTS LIKE MOMMY
LADIES HOME JOURNAL
JOHN & TERESA KERRY
I THINK HE... I MEAN, SHE HAS NOW OFFICIALLY WATCHED THAT OPRAH EPISODE ON TRANS-GENDER KIDS MORE TIMES THAN THE "LITTLE MERMAID."
SO HERE'S STUART'S SLEEPING BAG...
AND THIS IS SPARROW'S RAIN JACKET. AND SOME FLEECE STUFF OF MINE.
THANKS. GOD, I HOPE THIS CAMP IS AS GREAT AS IT SOUNDS.
A TIP O' THE NIB TO WWW.CAMPTENTREES.ORG
YEAH. IF SHE COULD JUST BE HERSELF WITH OTHER KIDS FOR A WHILE, WHERE THE GENDER THING ISN'T AN ISSUE.
CAMP TEN TREES
SESSION for LGBTQ YOUTH
·ARCHERY
·CANOEING
·DIVERSITY TRAINING
·LANYARD-WEAVING
JANIS! NOW!
YOU'RE REALLY DOING GREAT WITH ALL THIS, YOU KNOW.

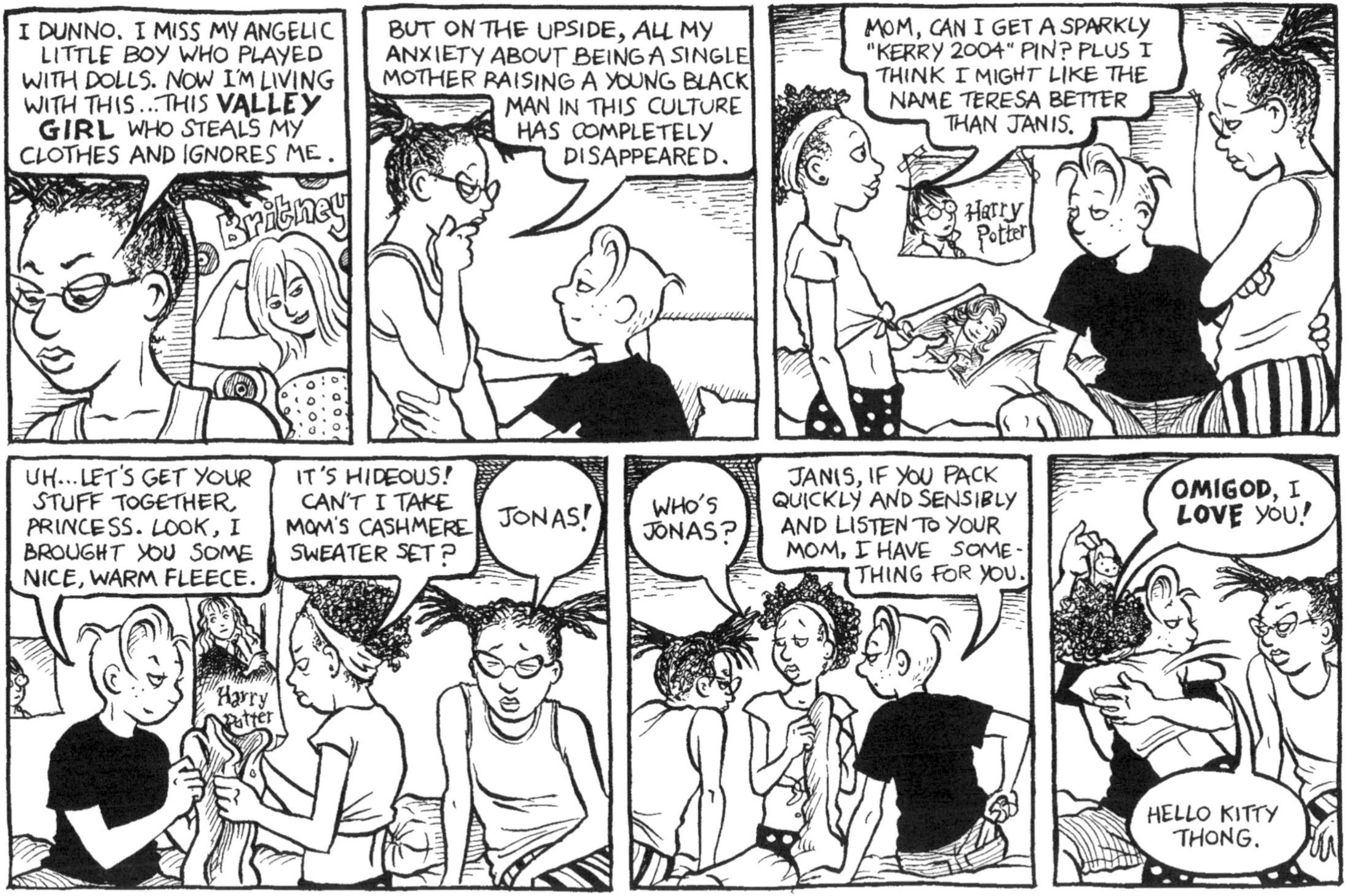

I DUNNO. I MISS MY ANGELIC LITTLE BOY WHO PLAYED WITH DOLLS. NOW I'M LIVING WITH THIS...THIS **VALLEY GIRL** WHO STEALS MY CLOTHES AND IGNORES ME.
Britney
BUT ON THE UPSIDE, ALL MY ANXIETY ABOUT BEING A SINGLE MOTHER RAISING A YOUNG BLACK MAN IN THIS CULTURE HAS COMPLETELY DISAPPEARED.
MOM, CAN I GET A SPARKLY "KERRY 2004" PIN? PLUS I THINK I MIGHT LIKE THE NAME TERESA BETTER THAN JANIS.
Harry Potter
UH...LET'S GET YOUR STUFF TOGETHER, PRINCESS. LOOK, I BROUGHT YOU SOME NICE, WARM FLEECE.
IT'S HIDEOUS! CAN'T I TAKE MOM'S CASHMERE SWEATER SET?
JONAS!
Harry Potter
WHO'S JONAS?
JANIS, IF YOU PACK QUICKLY AND SENSIBLY AND LISTEN TO YOUR MOM, I HAVE SOMETHING FOR YOU.
OMIGOD, I **LOVE** YOU!
HELLO KITTY THONG.

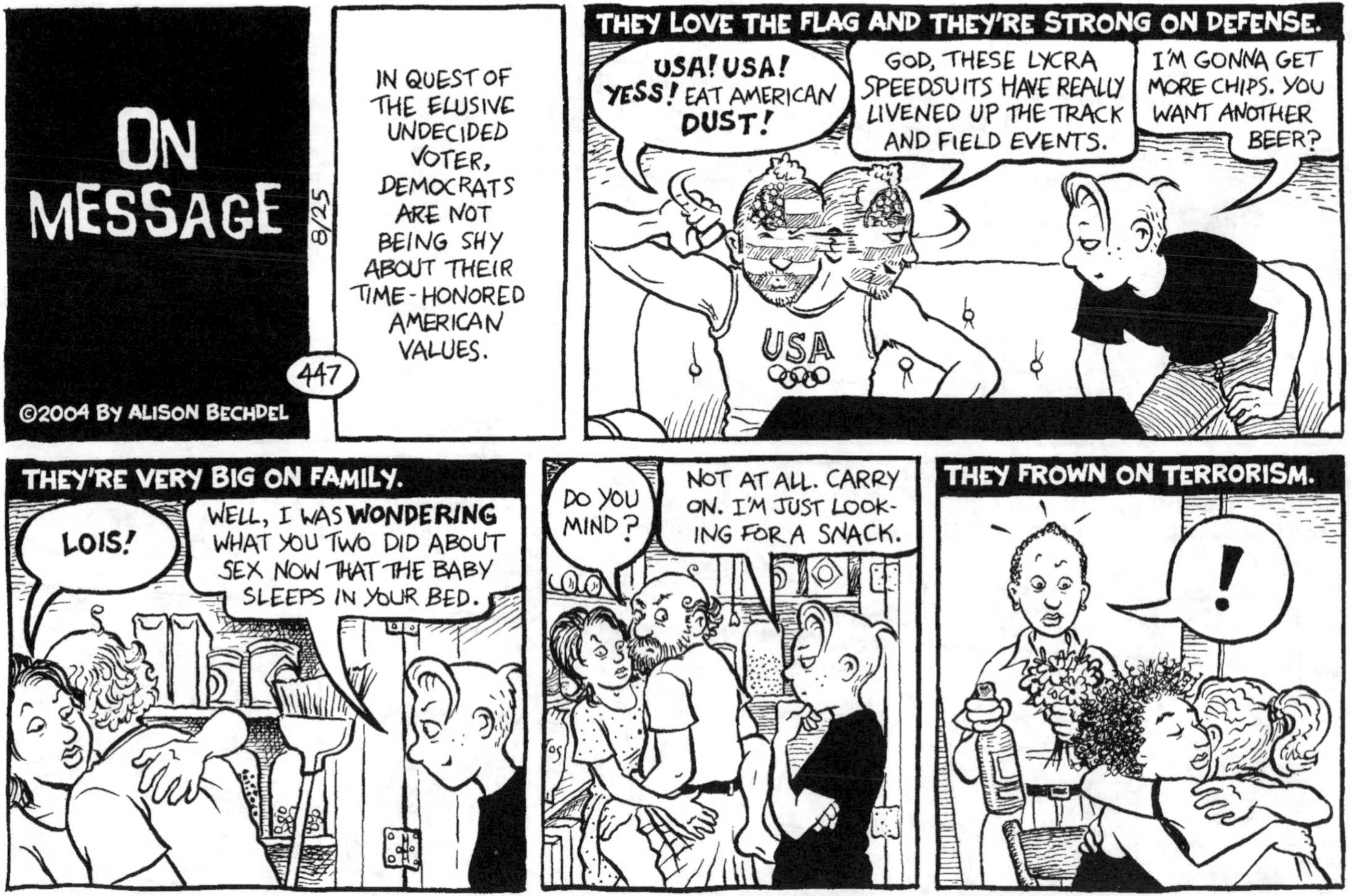
ON MESSAGE
©2004 BY ALISON BECHDEL
8/25
447
IN QUEST OF THE ELUSIVE UNDECIDED VOTER, DEMOCRATS ARE NOT BEING SHY ABOUT THEIR TIME-HONORED AMERICAN VALUES.
THEY LOVE THE FLAG AND THEY'RE STRONG ON DEFENSE.
USA! USA! YESS! EAT AMERICAN DUST!
GOD, THESE LYCRA SPEEDSUITS HAVE REALLY LIVENED UP THE TRACK AND FIELD EVENTS.
I'M GONNA GET MORE CHIPS. YOU WANT ANOTHER BEER?
USA
THEY'RE VERY BIG ON FAMILY.
LOIS!
WELL, I WAS WONDERING WHAT YOU TWO DID ABOUT SEX NOW THAT THE BABY SLEEPS IN YOUR BED.
DO YOU MIND?
NOT AT ALL. CARRY ON. I'M JUST LOOKING FOR A SNACK.
THEY FROWN ON TERRORISM.
!

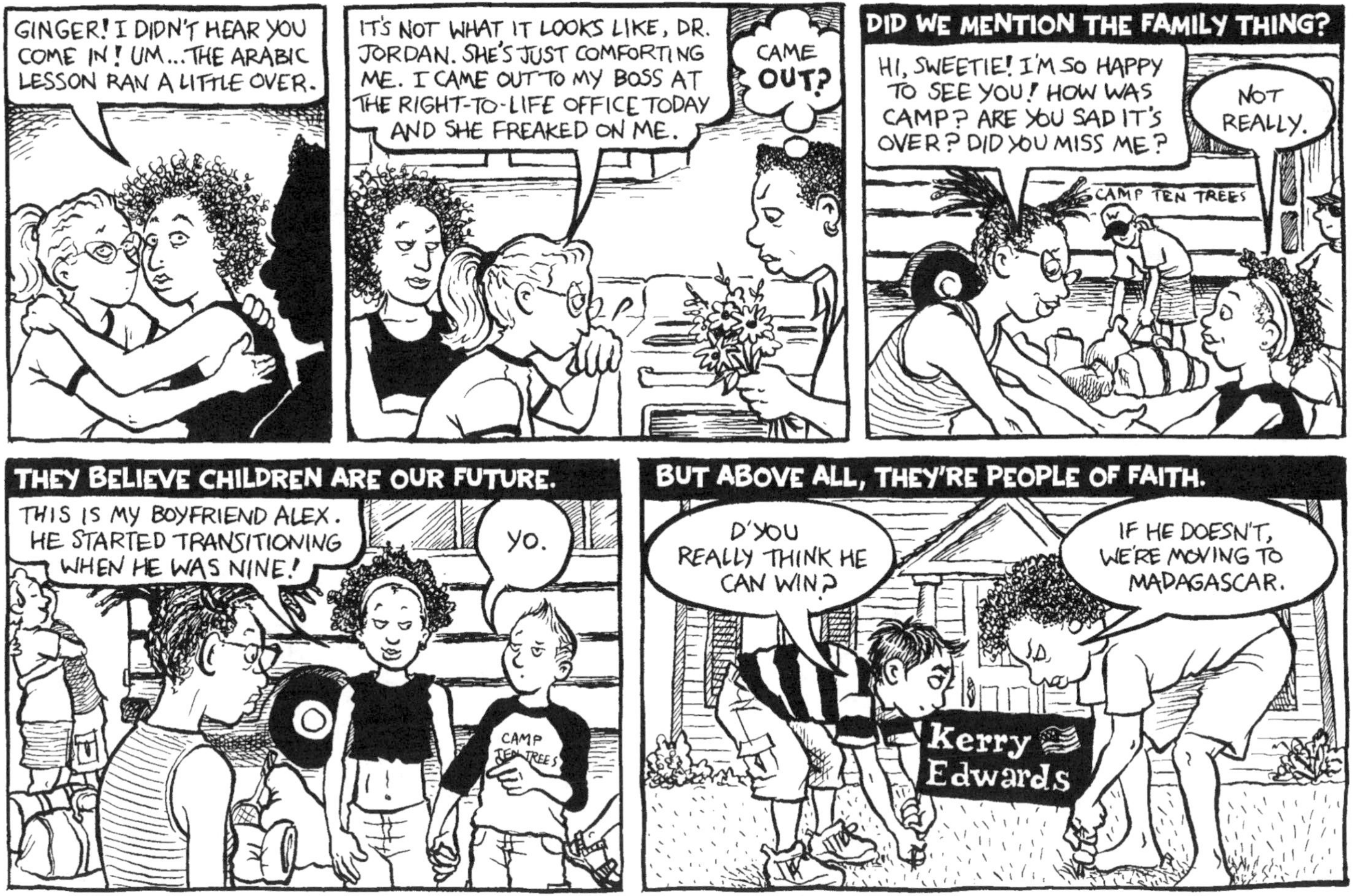
GINGER! I DIDN'T HEAR YOU COME IN! UM... THE ARABIC LESSON RAN A LITTLE OVER.
IT'S NOT WHAT IT LOOKS LIKE, DR. JORDAN. SHE'S JUST COMFORTING ME. I CAME OUT TO MY BOSS AT THE RIGHT-TO-LIFE OFFICE TODAY AND SHE FREAKED ON ME.
CAME OUT?
DID WE MENTION THE FAMILY THING?
HI, SWEETIE! I'M SO HAPPY TO SEE YOU! HOW WAS CAMP? ARE YOU SAD IT'S OVER? DID YOU MISS ME?
NOT REALLY.
CAMP TEN TREES
THEY BELIEVE CHILDREN ARE OUR FUTURE.
THIS IS MY BOYFRIEND ALEX. HE STARTED TRANSITIONING WHEN HE WAS NINE!
YO.
CAMP TEN TREES
BUT ABOVE ALL, THEY'RE PEOPLE OF FAITH.
D'YOU REALLY THINK HE CAN WIN?
IF HE DOESN'T, WE'RE MOVING TO MADAGASCAR.
Kerry Edwards

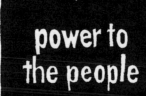

power to the people

9/8

448

©2004 BY ALISON BECHDEL

subversive parenting
notes from a stay-at-home dad

About Me

Name: Stuart
Goodman
Location:

8.29.04
virtually active

Jiao Raizel and I are canning tomato sauce and watching the RNC protest on C-SPAN, listening to the rally on streaming radio, and monitoring the indymedia site for breaking news. Wish I was there with my housemate Lois, but this is almost better because I'm getting my canning done at the same time.

SEE DADDY'S LATEST POST? ARE WE WIRED, OR WHAT?

PWEE.

MILK

LET'S CALL LOIS FOR A MARCH UPDATE!

NYC

HELLO?

LOIS! ME AGAIN. HOW'S IT GOING?

THANKS NEW YORK
www.Ropconvent

BUSH

POVERTY IS A WEAPON OF MASS DESTRUCTION

NO WAR

GOD, IT'S *#@ING INCREDIBLE!

FUSH

NY

GOOD BUSH

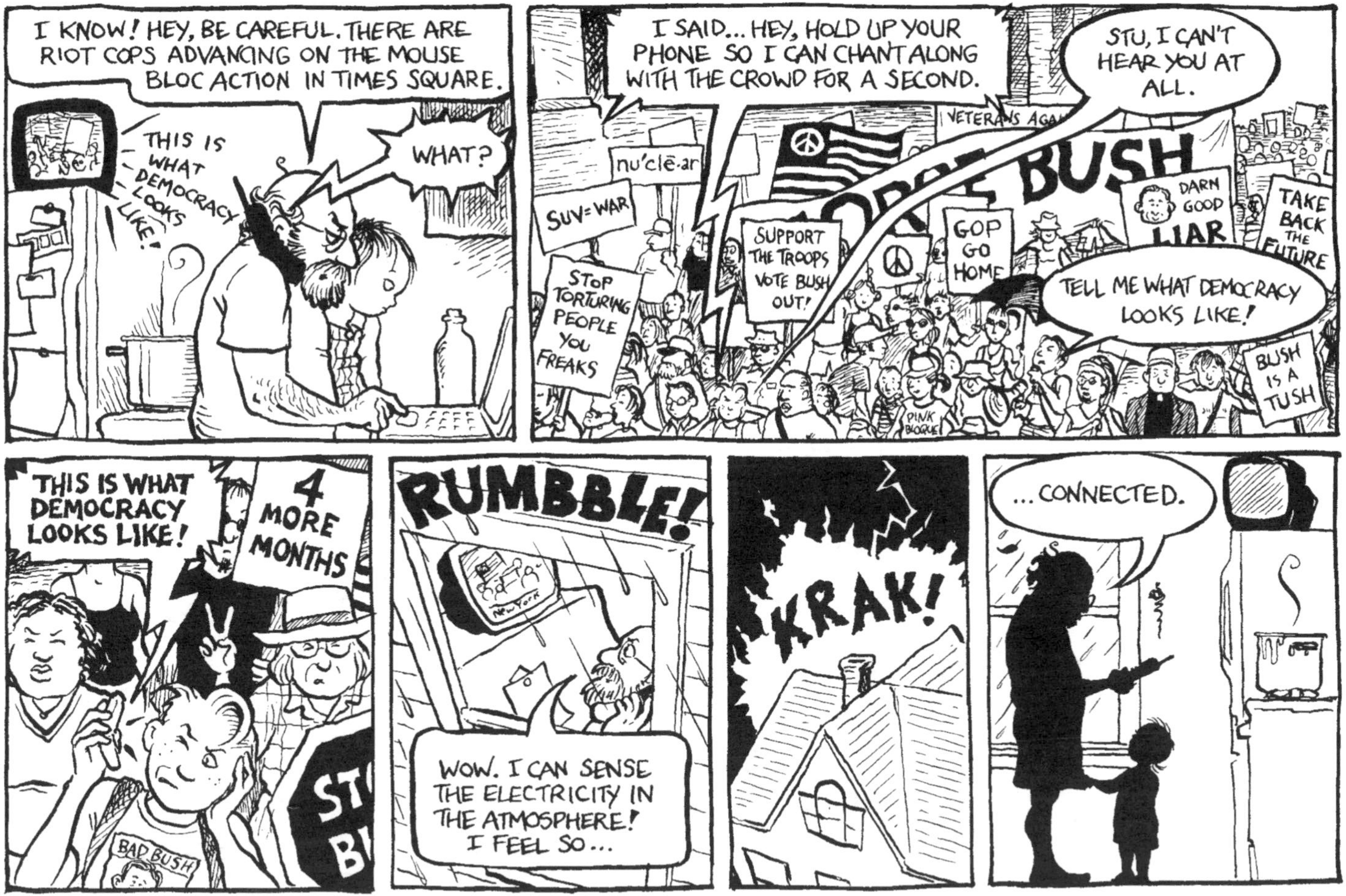
I KNOW! HEY, BE CAREFUL. THERE ARE RIOT COPS ADVANCING ON THE MOUSE BLOC ACTION IN TIMES SQUARE.
THIS IS WHAT DEMOCRACY LOOKS LIKE!
WHAT?
I SAID... HEY, HOLD UP YOUR PHONE SO I CAN CHANT ALONG WITH THE CROWD FOR A SECOND.
STU, I CAN'T HEAR YOU AT ALL.
nu'clē·ar
SUV=WAR
VETERANS AGA
BUSH
DARN GOOD LIAR
TAKE BACK THE FUTURE
SUPPORT THE TROOPS VOTE BUSH OUT!
GOP GO HOME
STOP TORTURING PEOPLE YOU FREAKS
TELL ME WHAT DEMOCRACY LOOKS LIKE!
BUSH IS A TUSH
PINK BLOQUE
THIS IS WHAT DEMOCRACY LOOKS LIKE!
4 MORE MONTHS
BAD BUSH
RUMBBLE!
NEW YORK
WOW. I CAN SENSE THE ELECTRICITY IN THE ATMOSPHERE! I FEEL SO...
KRAK!
...CONNECTED.

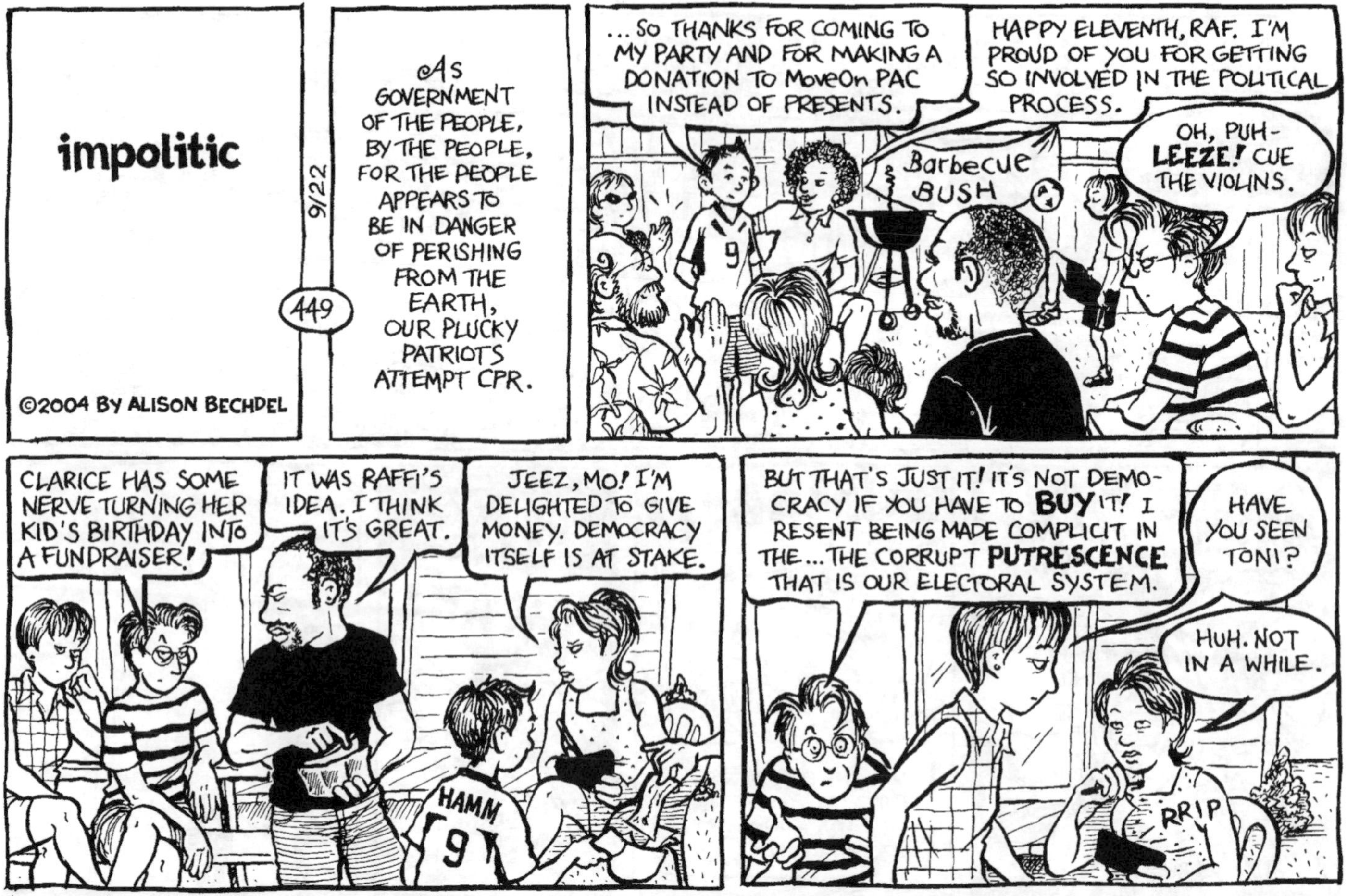
impolitic
©2004 BY ALISON BECHDEL
9/22
449
AS GOVERNMENT OF THE PEOPLE, BY THE PEOPLE, FOR THE PEOPLE APPEARS TO BE IN DANGER OF PERISHING FROM THE EARTH, OUR PLUCKY PATRIOTS ATTEMPT CPR.
...SO THANKS FOR COMING TO MY PARTY AND FOR MAKING A DONATION TO MoveOn PAC INSTEAD OF PRESENTS.
HAPPY ELEVENTH, RAF. I'M PROUD OF YOU FOR GETTING SO INVOLVED IN THE POLITICAL PROCESS.
Barbecue BUSH
OH, PUH-LEEZE! CUE THE VIOLINS.
CLARICE HAS SOME NERVE TURNING HER KID'S BIRTHDAY INTO A FUNDRAISER!
IT WAS RAFFI'S IDEA. I THINK IT'S GREAT.
JEEZ, MO! I'M DELIGHTED TO GIVE MONEY. DEMOCRACY ITSELF IS AT STAKE.
HAMM 9
BUT THAT'S JUST IT! IT'S NOT DEMOCRACY IF YOU HAVE TO BUY IT! I RESENT BEING MADE COMPLICIT IN THE...THE CORRUPT PUTRESCENCE THAT IS OUR ELECTORAL SYSTEM.
HAVE YOU SEEN TONI?
HUH. NOT IN A WHILE.
RRIP

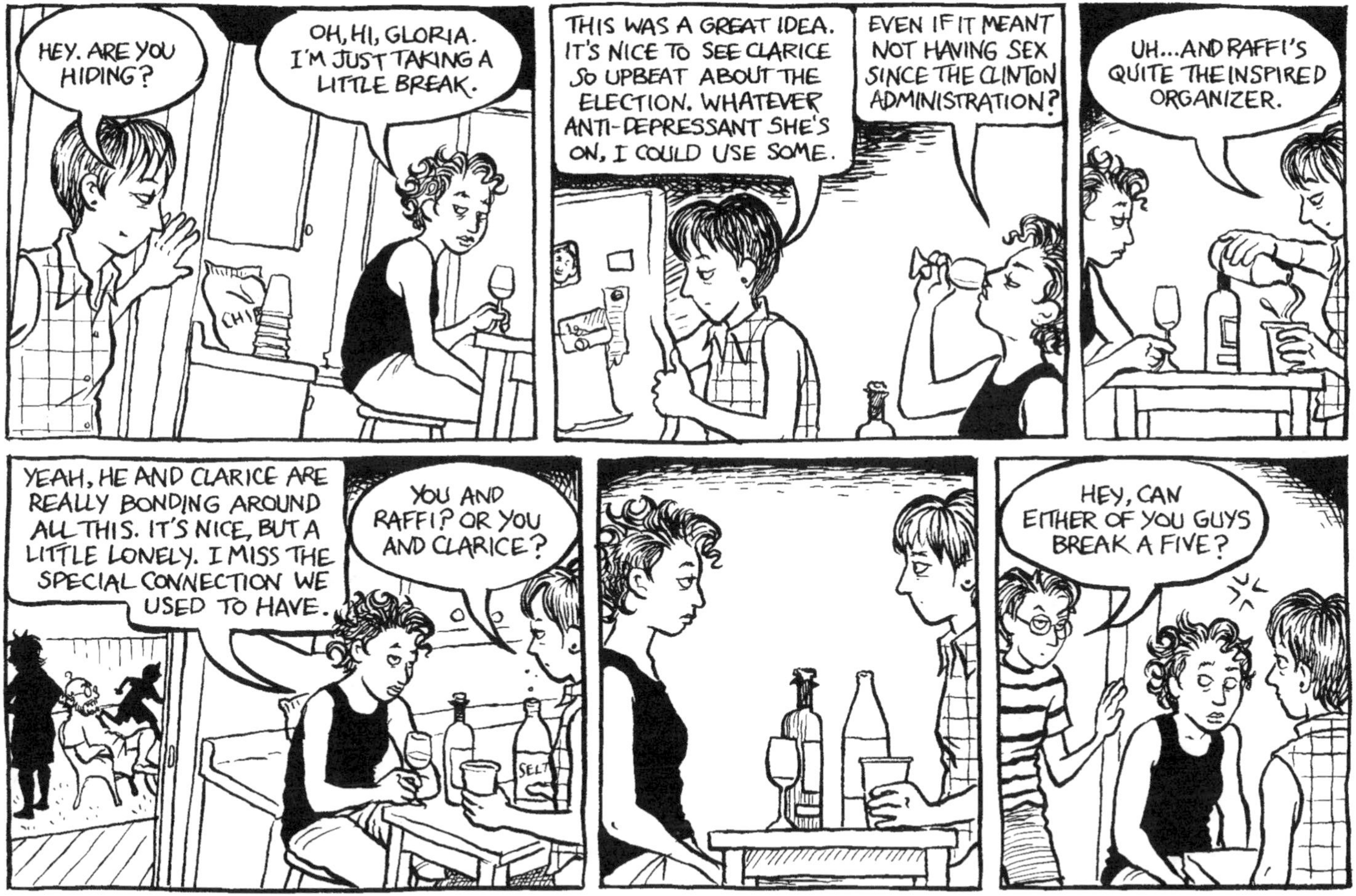
HEY. ARE YOU HIDING?
OH, HI, GLORIA. I'M JUST TAKING A LITTLE BREAK.
CHI
THIS WAS A GREAT IDEA. IT'S NICE TO SEE CLARICE SO UPBEAT ABOUT THE ELECTION. WHATEVER ANTI-DEPRESSANT SHE'S ON, I COULD USE SOME.
EVEN IF IT MEANT NOT HAVING SEX SINCE THE CLINTON ADMINISTRATION?
UH... AND RAFFI'S QUITE THE INSPIRED ORGANIZER.
YEAH, HE AND CLARICE ARE REALLY BONDING AROUND ALL THIS. IT'S NICE, BUT A LITTLE LONELY. I MISS THE SPECIAL CONNECTION WE USED TO HAVE.
YOU AND RAFFI? OR YOU AND CLARICE?
SELT
HEY, CAN EITHER OF YOU GUYS BREAK A FIVE?

"*What is the first part of politics? education. The second? education. And the third? education.*"
~Michelet

©2004 BY ALISON BECHDEL

SCHOOL'S BACK IN SESSION, AND NOT A MOMENT TOO SOON CONSIDERING IT'S THE EVE OF AN ELECTION IN WHICH A MINUTE TIP OF THE IDEOLOGICAL BALANCE COULD USHER IN A RIGHT-WING ICE AGE.

SO, DID ANYONE NOTICE ANYTHING FAMILIAR ABOUT THE WORLD OF ORWELL'S "1984"?

1984 + 20
War is peace.
Freedom is slavery
Ignorance is Strength

1984 +
War is
Freedom
Ignorance

NOTHING RANG A BELL FOR ANY OF YOU? LIKE, SAY, THE DECEPTIVE AND EUPHEMISTIC USE OF LANGUAGE? THE SURVEILLANCE? THE TORTURE? THE ONGOING WAR? THE ERASURE OF HISTORY AND MEMORY?!

1984

ASHLEY! THANK YOU!

UM, THOSE FLAT-SCREEN TV'S?

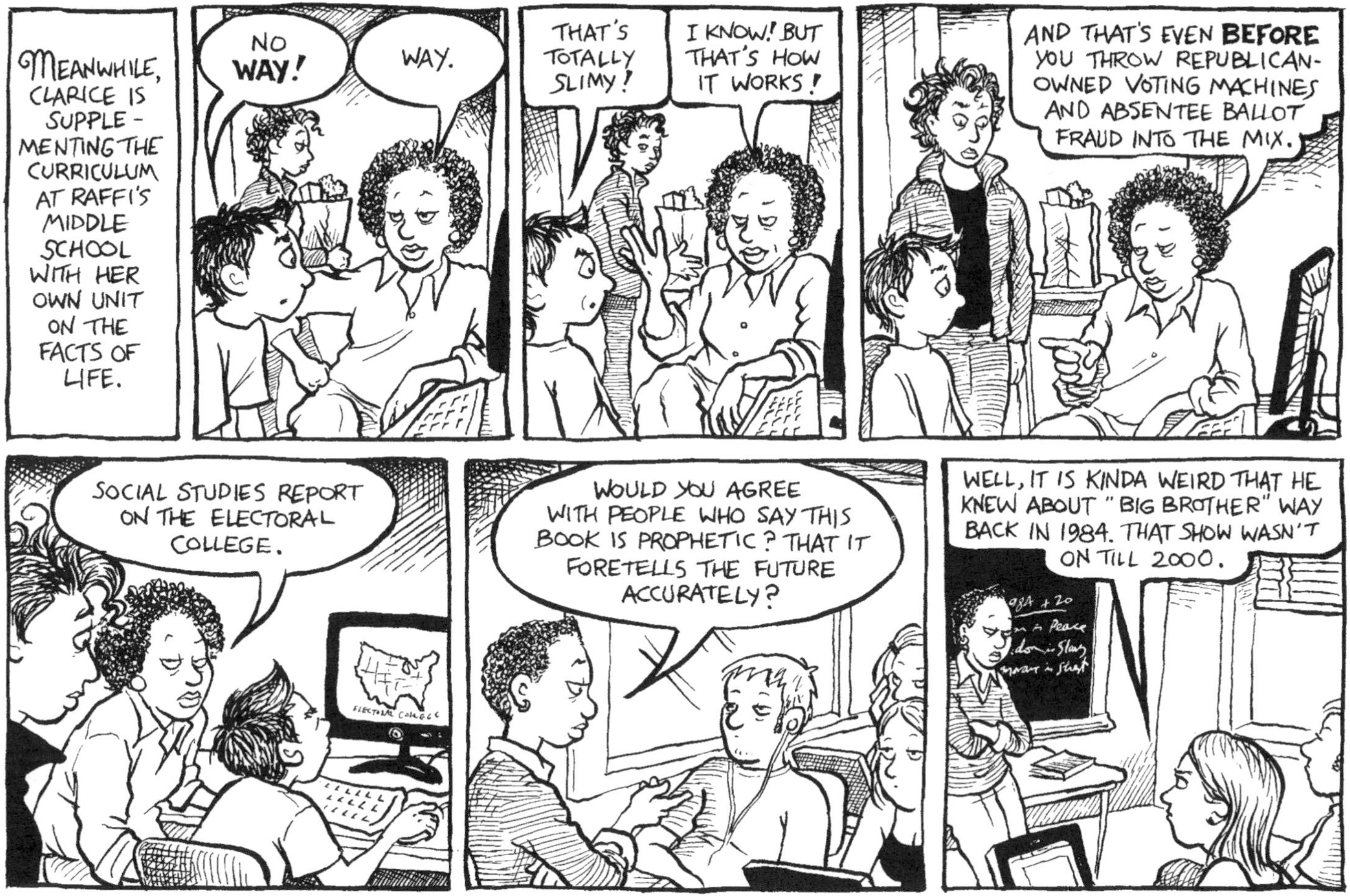
MEANWHILE, CLARICE IS SUPPLE-MENTING THE CURRICULUM AT RAFFI'S MIDDLE SCHOOL WITH HER OWN UNIT ON THE FACTS OF LIFE.
NO **WAY**!
WAY.
THAT'S TOTALLY SLIMY!
I KNOW! BUT THAT'S HOW IT WORKS!
AND THAT'S EVEN **BEFORE** YOU THROW REPUBLICAN-OWNED VOTING MACHINES AND ABSENTEE BALLOT FRAUD INTO THE MIX.
SOCIAL STUDIES REPORT ON THE ELECTORAL COLLEGE.
WOULD YOU AGREE WITH PEOPLE WHO SAY THIS BOOK IS PROPHETIC? THAT IT FORETELLS THE FUTURE ACCURATELY?
WELL, IT IS KINDA WEIRD THAT HE KNEW ABOUT "BIG BROTHER" WAY BACK IN 1984. THAT SHOW WASN'T ON TILL 2000.

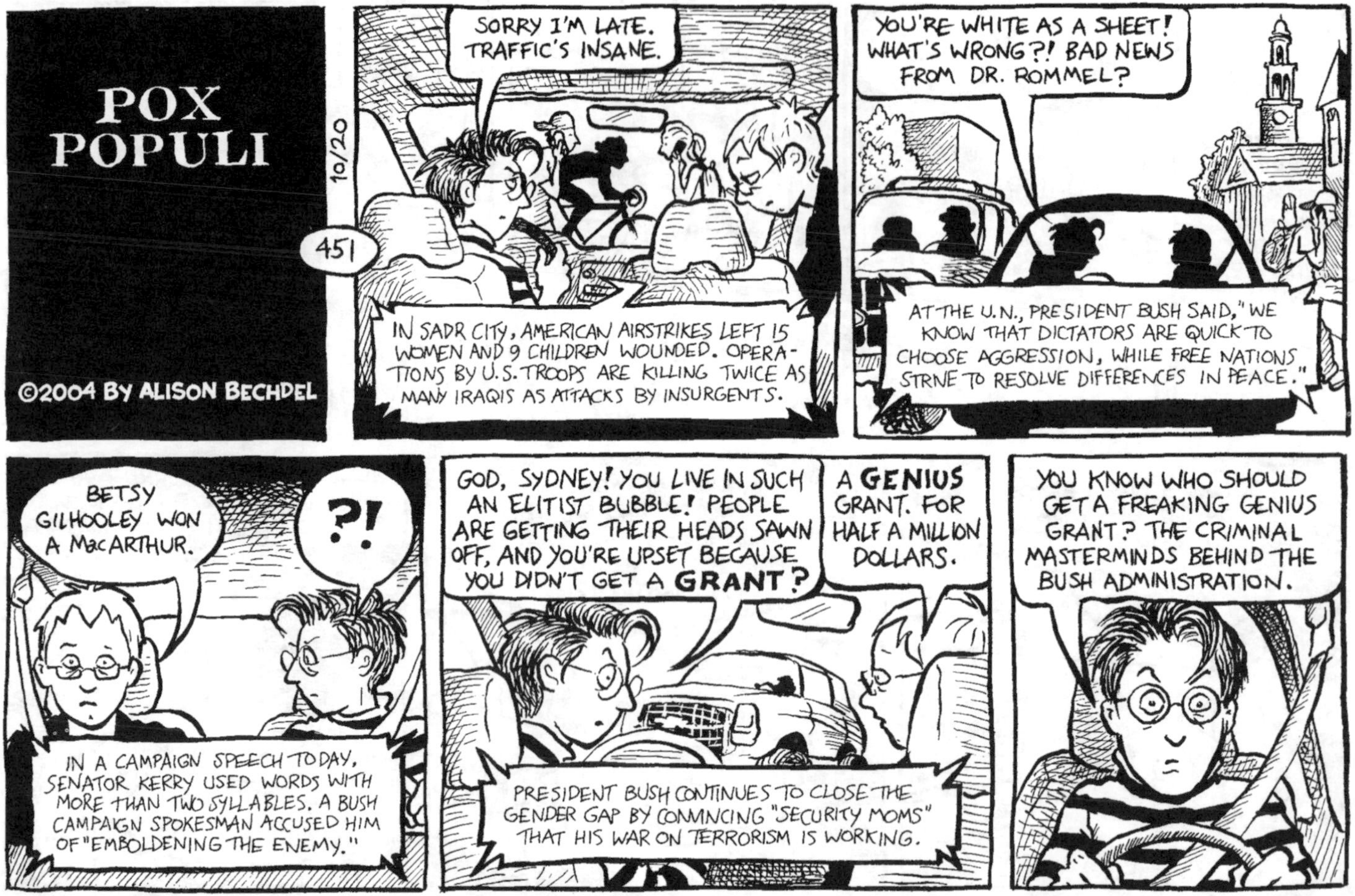
POX POPULI
©2004 BY ALISON BECHDEL
10/20
451
SORRY I'M LATE. TRAFFIC'S INSANE.
IN SADR CITY, AMERICAN AIRSTRIKES LEFT 15 WOMEN AND 9 CHILDREN WOUNDED. OPERATIONS BY U.S. TROOPS ARE KILLING TWICE AS MANY IRAQIS AS ATTACKS BY INSURGENTS.
YOU'RE WHITE AS A SHEET! WHAT'S WRONG?! BAD NEWS FROM DR. ROMMEL?
AT THE U.N., PRESIDENT BUSH SAID, "WE KNOW THAT DICTATORS ARE QUICK TO CHOOSE AGGRESSION, WHILE FREE NATIONS STRIVE TO RESOLVE DIFFERENCES IN PEACE."
BETSY GILHOOLEY WON A MacARTHUR.
?!
IN A CAMPAIGN SPEECH TODAY, SENATOR KERRY USED WORDS WITH MORE THAN TWO SYLLABLES. A BUSH CAMPAIGN SPOKESMAN ACCUSED HIM OF "EMBOLDENING THE ENEMY."
GOD, SYDNEY! YOU LIVE IN SUCH AN ELITIST BUBBLE! PEOPLE ARE GETTING THEIR HEADS SAWN OFF, AND YOU'RE UPSET BECAUSE YOU DIDN'T GET A GRANT?
A GENIUS GRANT. FOR HALF A MILLION DOLLARS.
PRESIDENT BUSH CONTINUES TO CLOSE THE GENDER GAP BY CONVINCING "SECURITY MOMS" THAT HIS WAR ON TERRORISM IS WORKING.
YOU KNOW WHO SHOULD GET A FREAKING GENIUS GRANT? THE CRIMINAL MASTERMINDS BEHIND THE BUSH ADMINISTRATION.

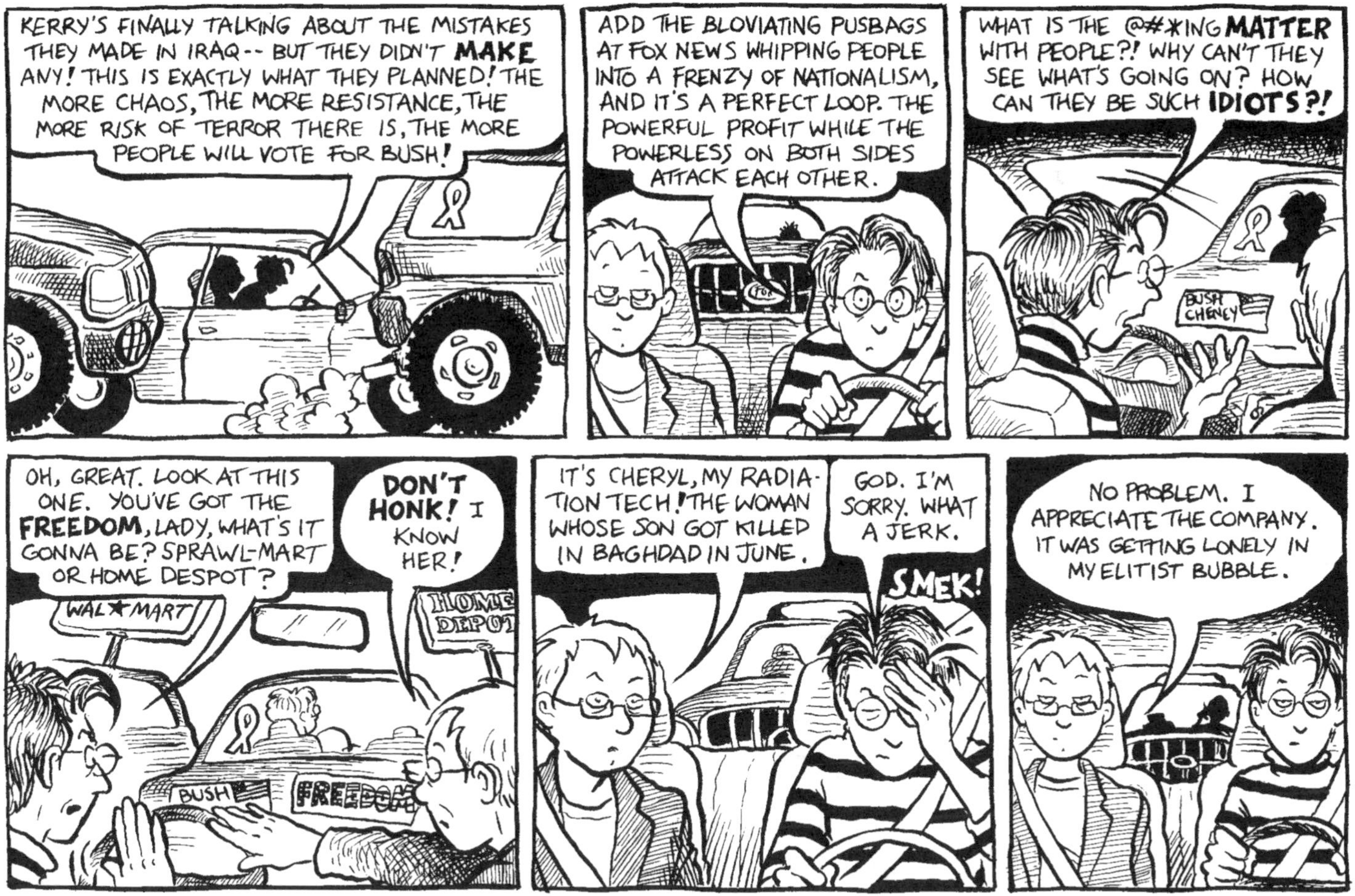
KERRY'S FINALLY TALKING ABOUT THE MISTAKES THEY MADE IN IRAQ-- BUT THEY DIDN'T **MAKE** ANY! THIS IS EXACTLY WHAT THEY PLANNED! THE MORE CHAOS, THE MORE RESISTANCE, THE MORE RISK OF TERROR THERE IS, THE MORE PEOPLE WILL VOTE FOR BUSH!
ADD THE BLOVIATING PUSBAGS AT FOX NEWS WHIPPING PEOPLE INTO A FRENZY OF NATIONALISM, AND IT'S A PERFECT LOOP. THE POWERFUL PROFIT WHILE THE POWERLESS ON BOTH SIDES ATTACK EACH OTHER.
FOX
WHAT IS THE @#*ING **MATTER** WITH PEOPLE?! WHY CAN'T THEY SEE WHAT'S GOING ON? HOW CAN THEY BE SUCH **IDIOTS?!**
BUSH CHENEY
OH, GREAT. LOOK AT THIS ONE. YOU'VE GOT THE **FREEDOM**, LADY, WHAT'S IT GONNA BE? SPRAWL-MART OR HOME DESPOT?
DON'T HONK! I KNOW HER!
WAL★MART
HOME DEPOT
BUSH
FREEDOM
IT'S CHERYL, MY RADIATION TECH! THE WOMAN WHOSE SON GOT KILLED IN BAGHDAD IN JUNE.
GOD. I'M SORRY. WHAT A JERK.
SMEK!
NO PROBLEM. I APPRECIATE THE COMPANY. IT WAS GETTING LONELY IN MY ELITIST BUBBLE.

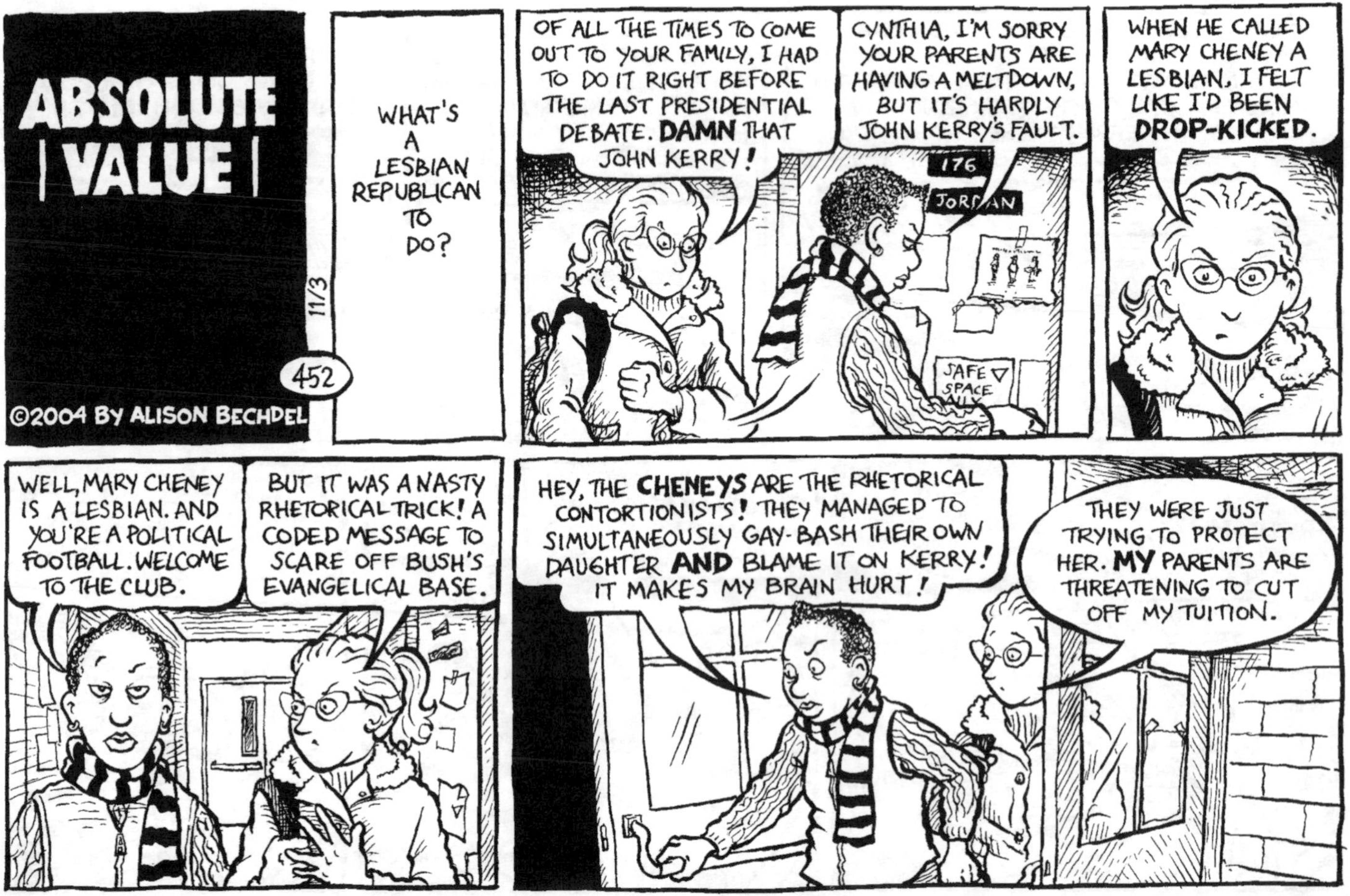
ABSOLUTE |VALUE|
©2004 BY ALISON BECHDEL
452
11/3
WHAT'S A LESBIAN REPUBLICAN TO DO?
OF ALL THE TIMES TO COME OUT TO YOUR FAMILY, I HAD TO DO IT RIGHT BEFORE THE LAST PRESIDENTIAL DEBATE. DAMN THAT JOHN KERRY!
CYNTHIA, I'M SORRY YOUR PARENTS ARE HAVING A MELTDOWN, BUT IT'S HARDLY JOHN KERRY'S FAULT.
176
WHEN HE CALLED MARY CHENEY A LESBIAN, I FELT LIKE I'D BEEN DROP-KICKED.
WELL, MARY CHENEY IS A LESBIAN. AND YOU'RE A POLITICAL FOOTBALL. WELCOME TO THE CLUB.
BUT IT WAS A NASTY RHETORICAL TRICK! A CODED MESSAGE TO SCARE OFF BUSH'S EVANGELICAL BASE.
HEY, THE CHENEYS ARE THE RHETORICAL CONTORTIONISTS! THEY MANAGED TO SIMULTANEOUSLY GAY-BASH THEIR OWN DAUGHTER AND BLAME IT ON KERRY! IT MAKES MY BRAIN HURT!
THEY WERE JUST TRYING TO PROTECT HER. MY PARENTS ARE THREATENING TO CUT OFF MY TUITION.

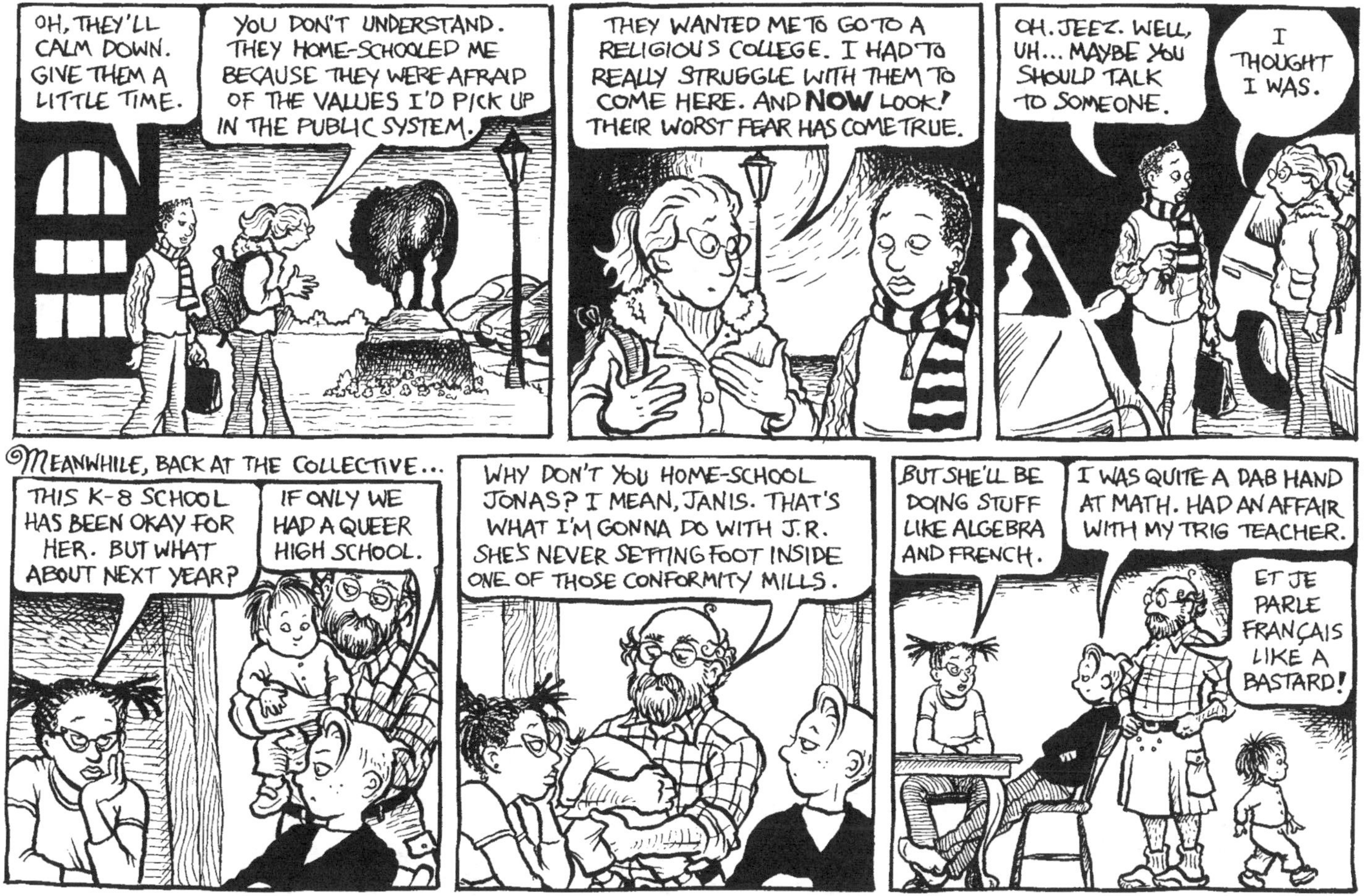

OH, THEY'LL CALM DOWN. GIVE THEM A LITTLE TIME.
YOU DON'T UNDERSTAND. THEY HOME-SCHOOLED ME BECAUSE THEY WERE AFRAID OF THE VALUES I'D PICK UP IN THE PUBLIC SYSTEM.
THEY WANTED ME TO GO TO A RELIGIOUS COLLEGE. I HAD TO REALLY STRUGGLE WITH THEM TO COME HERE. AND NOW LOOK! THEIR WORST FEAR HAS COME TRUE.
OH. JEEZ. WELL, UH... MAYBE YOU SHOULD TALK TO SOMEONE.
I THOUGHT I WAS.
MEANWHILE, BACK AT THE COLLECTIVE...
THIS K-8 SCHOOL HAS BEEN OKAY FOR HER. BUT WHAT ABOUT NEXT YEAR?
IF ONLY WE HAD A QUEER HIGH SCHOOL.
WHY DON'T YOU HOME-SCHOOL JONAS? I MEAN, JANIS. THAT'S WHAT I'M GONNA DO WITH J.R. SHE'S NEVER SETTING FOOT INSIDE ONE OF THOSE CONFORMITY MILLS.
BUT SHE'LL BE DOING STUFF LIKE ALGEBRA AND FRENCH.
I WAS QUITE A DAB HAND AT MATH. HAD AN AFFAIR WITH MY TRIG TEACHER.
ET JE PARLE FRANÇAIS LIKE A BASTARD!

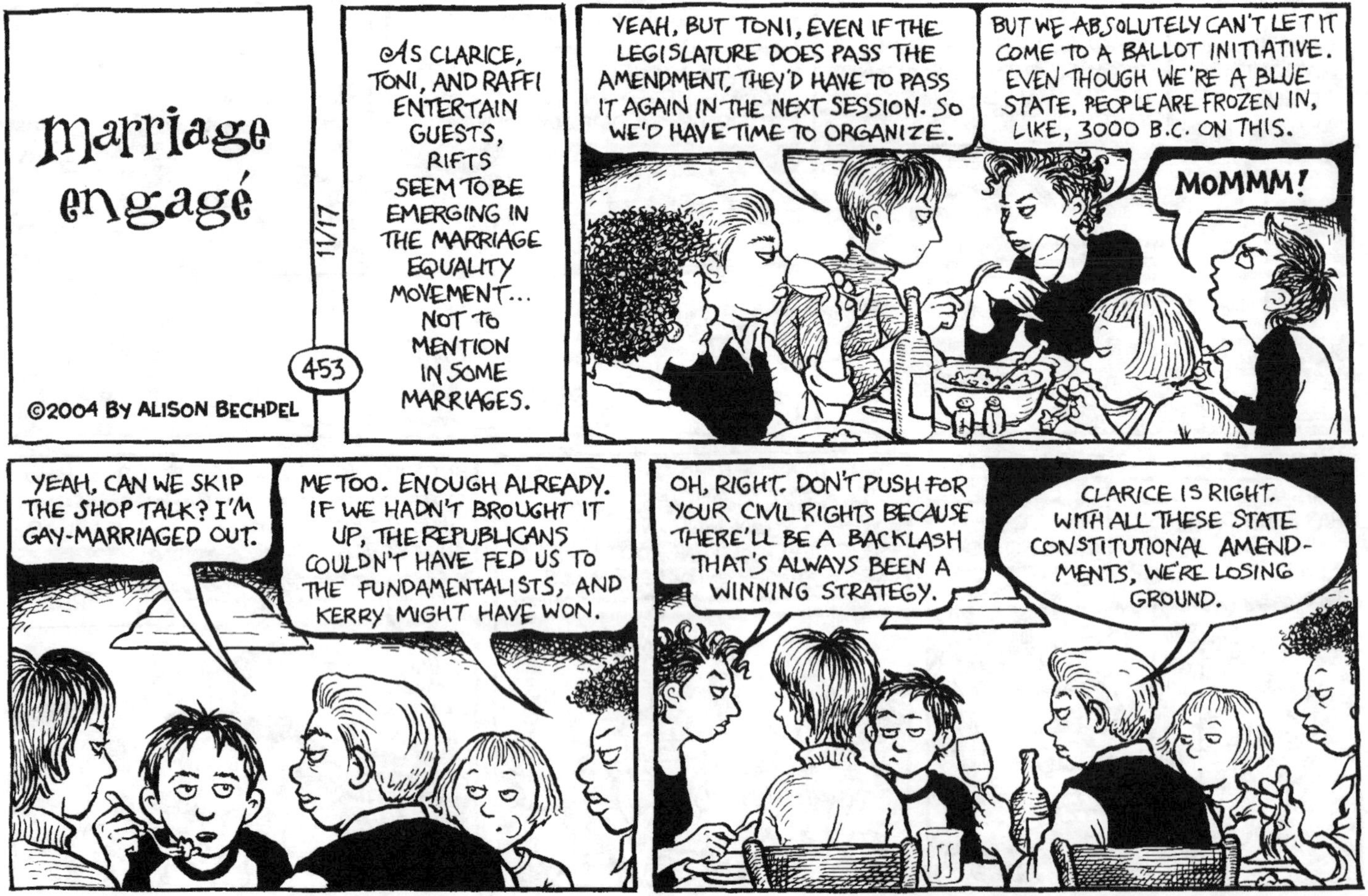
marriage engagé
©2004 BY ALISON BECHDEL
453
11/17
AS CLARICE, TONI, AND RAFFI ENTERTAIN GUESTS, RIFTS SEEM TO BE EMERGING IN THE MARRIAGE EQUALITY MOVEMENT... NOT TO MENTION IN SOME MARRIAGES.
YEAH, BUT TONI, EVEN IF THE LEGISLATURE DOES PASS THE AMENDMENT, THEY'D HAVE TO PASS IT AGAIN IN THE NEXT SESSION. SO WE'D HAVE TIME TO ORGANIZE.
BUT WE ABSOLUTELY CAN'T LET IT COME TO A BALLOT INITIATIVE. EVEN THOUGH WE'RE A BLUE STATE, PEOPLE ARE FROZEN IN, LIKE, 3000 B.C. ON THIS.
MOMMM!
YEAH, CAN WE SKIP THE SHOP TALK? I'M GAY-MARRIAGED OUT.
ME TOO. ENOUGH ALREADY. IF WE HADN'T BROUGHT IT UP, THE REPUBLICANS COULDN'T HAVE FED US TO THE FUNDAMENTALISTS, AND KERRY MIGHT HAVE WON.
OH, RIGHT. DON'T PUSH FOR YOUR CIVIL RIGHTS BECAUSE THERE'LL BE A BACKLASH. THAT'S ALWAYS BEEN A WINNING STRATEGY.
CLARICE IS RIGHT. WITH ALL THESE STATE CONSTITUTIONAL AMENDMENTS, WE'RE LOSING GROUND.

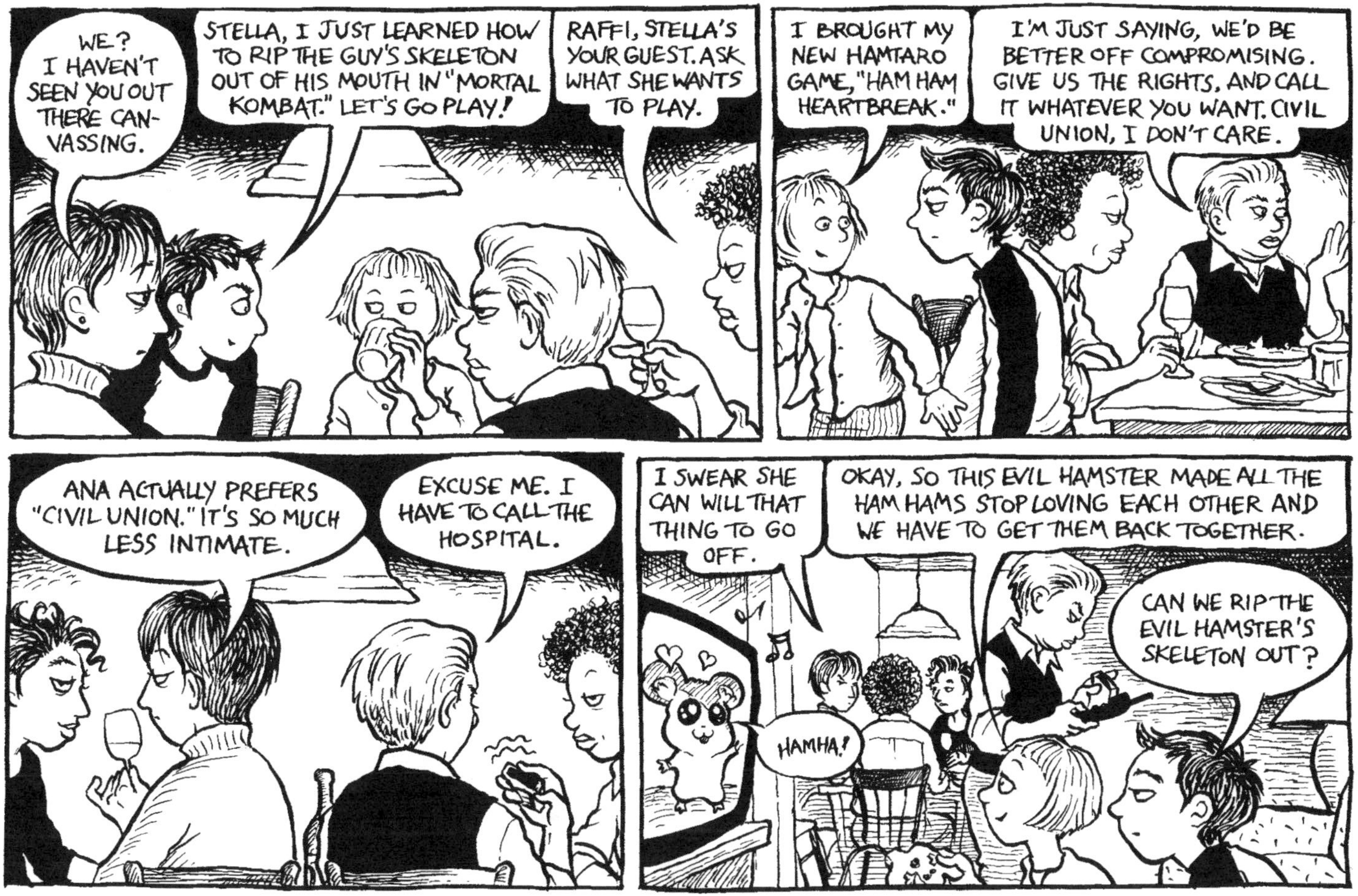
WE? I HAVEN'T SEEN YOU OUT THERE CAN-VASSING.
STELLA, I JUST LEARNED HOW TO RIP THE GUY'S SKELETON OUT OF HIS MOUTH IN "MORTAL KOMBAT." LET'S GO PLAY!
RAFFI, STELLA'S YOUR GUEST. ASK WHAT SHE WANTS TO PLAY.
I BROUGHT MY NEW HAMTARO GAME, "HAM HAM HEARTBREAK."
I'M JUST SAYING, WE'D BE BETTER OFF COMPROMISING. GIVE US THE RIGHTS, AND CALL IT WHATEVER YOU WANT. CIVIL UNION, I DON'T CARE.
ANA ACTUALLY PREFERS "CIVIL UNION." IT'S SO MUCH LESS INTIMATE.
EXCUSE ME. I HAVE TO CALL THE HOSPITAL.
I SWEAR SHE CAN WILL THAT THING TO GO OFF.
OKAY, SO THIS EVIL HAMSTER MADE ALL THE HAM HAMS STOP LOVING EACH OTHER AND WE HAVE TO GET THEM BACK TOGETHER.
HAMHA!
CAN WE RIP THE EVIL HAMSTER'S SKELETON OUT?

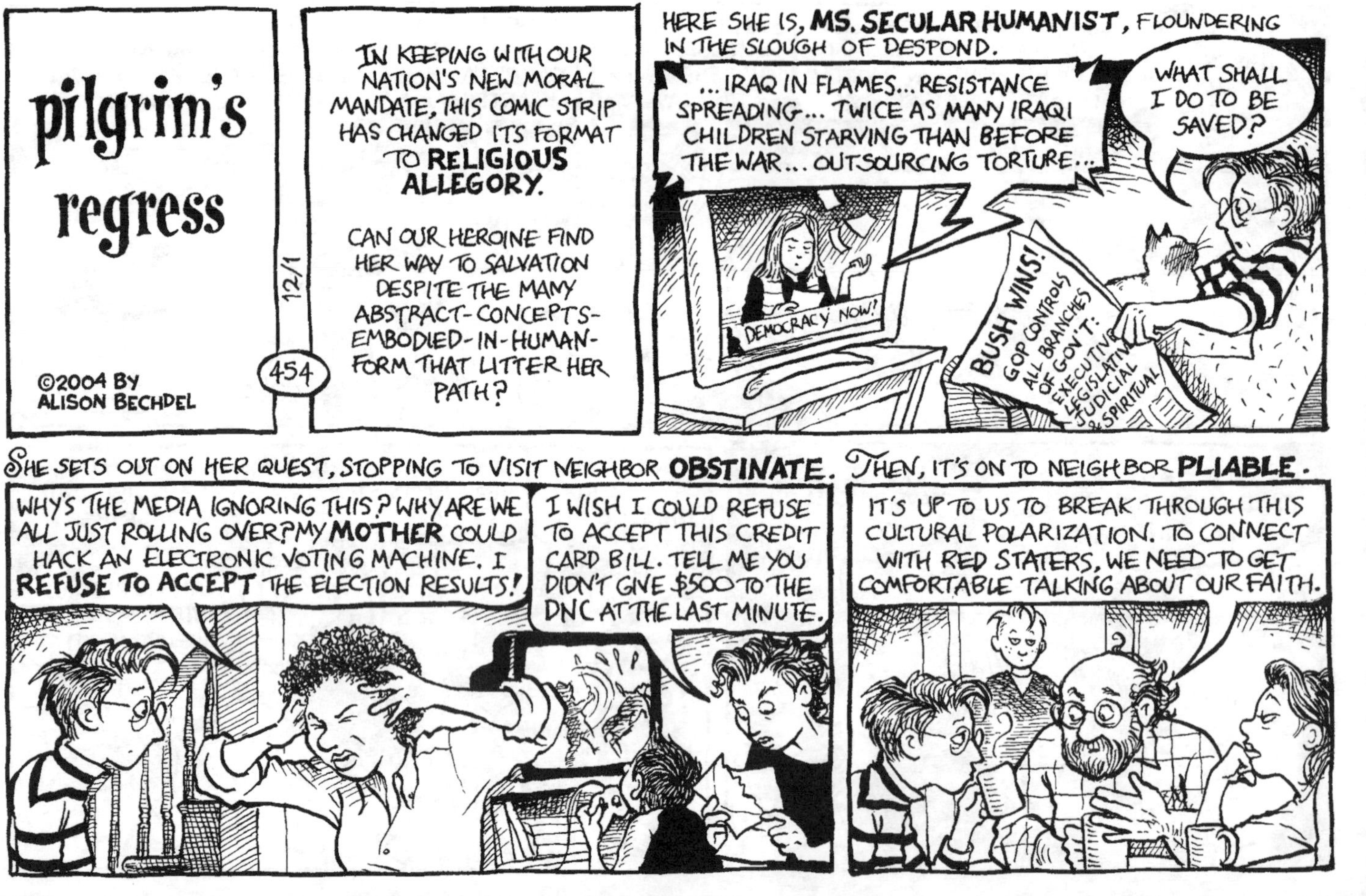
pilgrim's regress
©2004 BY ALISON BECHDEL
454
12/1
IN KEEPING WITH OUR NATION'S NEW MORAL MANDATE, THIS COMIC STRIP HAS CHANGED ITS FORMAT TO **RELIGIOUS ALLEGORY**.
CAN OUR HEROINE FIND HER WAY TO SALVATION DESPITE THE MANY ABSTRACT-CONCEPTS-EMBODIED-IN-HUMAN-FORM THAT LITTER HER PATH?
HERE SHE IS, **MS. SECULAR HUMANIST**, FLOUNDERING IN THE SLOUGH OF DESPOND.
...IRAQ IN FLAMES... RESISTANCE SPREADING... TWICE AS MANY IRAQI CHILDREN STARVING THAN BEFORE THE WAR... OUTSOURCING TORTURE...
DEMOCRACY NOW!
BUSH WINS!
GOP CONTROLS ALL BRANCHES OF GOV'T: EXECUTIVE LEGISLATIVE JUDICIAL & SPIRITUAL
WHAT SHALL I DO TO BE SAVED?
SHE SETS OUT ON HER QUEST, STOPPING TO VISIT NEIGHBOR **OBSTINATE**.
WHY'S THE MEDIA IGNORING THIS? WHY ARE WE ALL JUST ROLLING OVER? MY **MOTHER** COULD HACK AN ELECTRONIC VOTING MACHINE. I **REFUSE TO ACCEPT** THE ELECTION RESULTS!
I WISH I COULD REFUSE TO ACCEPT THIS CREDIT CARD BILL. TELL ME YOU DIDN'T GIVE $500 TO THE DNC AT THE LAST MINUTE.
THEN, IT'S ON TO NEIGHBOR **PLIABLE**.
IT'S UP TO US TO BREAK THROUGH THIS CULTURAL POLARIZATION. TO CONNECT WITH RED STATERS, WE NEED TO GET COMFORTABLE TALKING ABOUT OUR FAITH.

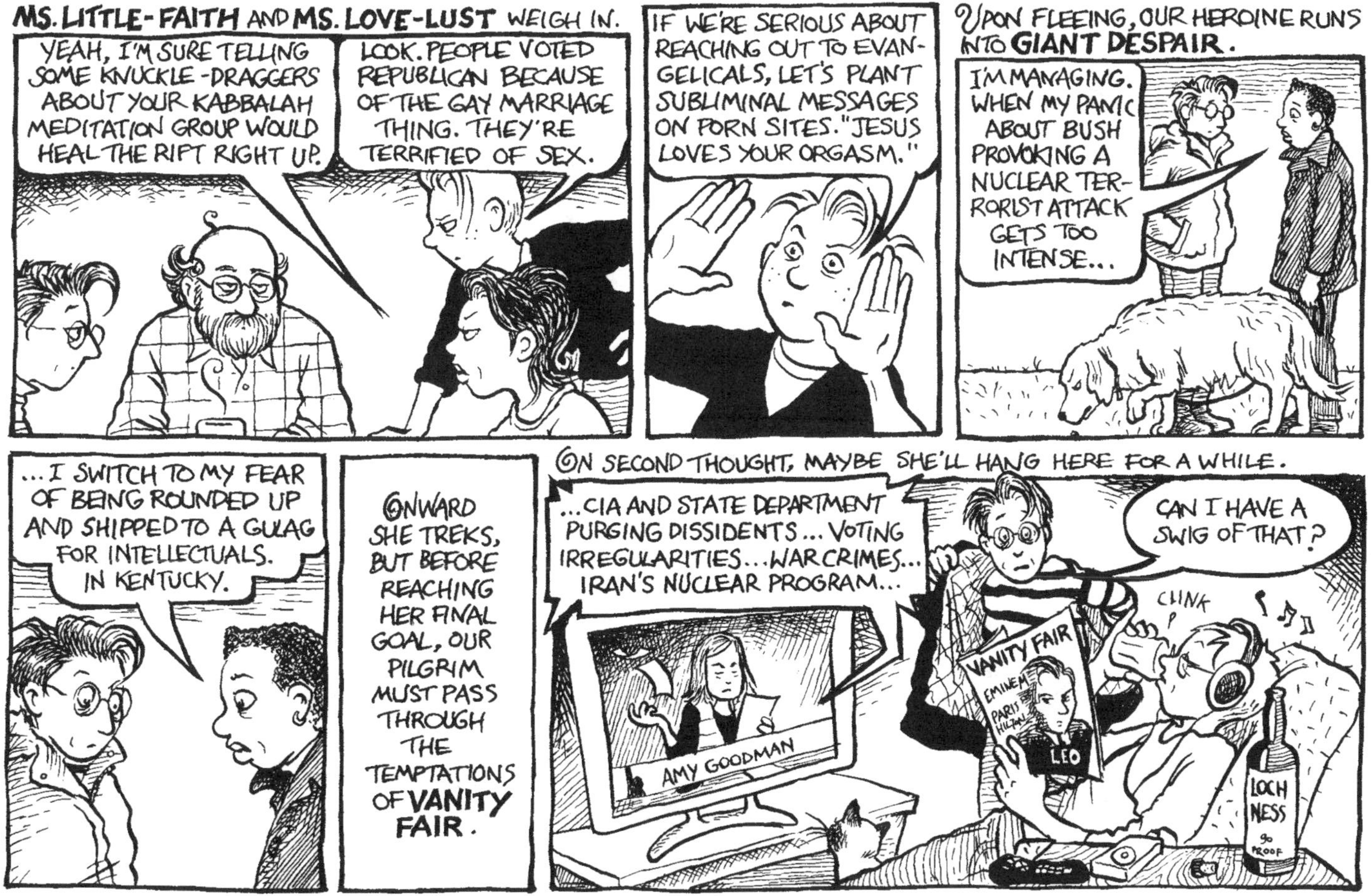
MS. LITTLE-FAITH AND MS. LOVE-LUST WEIGH IN.
YEAH, I'M SURE TELLING SOME KNUCKLE-DRAGGERS ABOUT YOUR KABBALAH MEDITATION GROUP WOULD HEAL THE RIFT RIGHT UP.
LOOK. PEOPLE VOTED REPUBLICAN BECAUSE OF THE GAY MARRIAGE THING. THEY'RE TERRIFIED OF SEX.
IF WE'RE SERIOUS ABOUT REACHING OUT TO EVANGELICALS, LET'S PLANT SUBLIMINAL MESSAGES ON PORN SITES. "JESUS LOVES YOUR ORGASM."
UPON FLEEING, OUR HEROINE RUNS INTO GIANT DESPAIR.
I'M MANAGING. WHEN MY PANIC ABOUT BUSH PROVOKING A NUCLEAR TERRORIST ATTACK GETS TOO INTENSE...
...I SWITCH TO MY FEAR OF BEING ROUNDED UP AND SHIPPED TO A GULAG FOR INTELLECTUALS. IN KENTUCKY.
ONWARD SHE TREKS, BUT BEFORE REACHING HER FINAL GOAL, OUR PILGRIM MUST PASS THROUGH THE TEMPTATIONS OF VANITY FAIR.
ON SECOND THOUGHT, MAYBE SHE'LL HANG HERE FOR A WHILE.
...CIA AND STATE DEPARTMENT PURGING DISSIDENTS... VOTING IRREGULARITIES... WAR CRIMES... IRAN'S NUCLEAR PROGRAM...
AMY GOODMAN
CAN I HAVE A SWIG OF THAT?
CLINK
VANITY FAIR
EMINEM
PARIS HILTON
LEO
LOCH NESS
90 PROOF

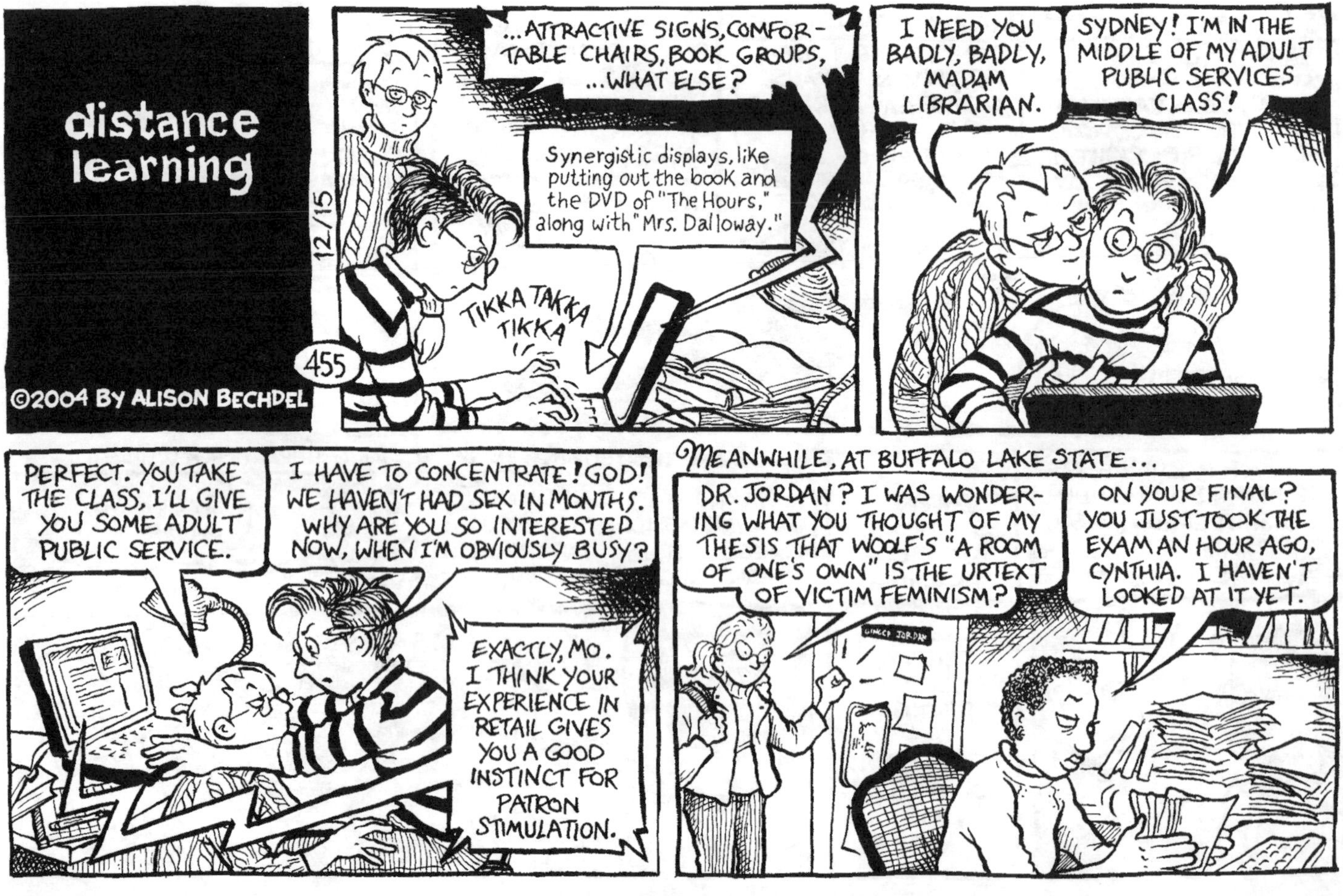
distance learning
©2004 BY ALISON BECHDEL
455
12/15
...ATTRACTIVE SIGNS, COMFORTABLE CHAIRS, BOOK GROUPS, ...WHAT ELSE?
Synergistic displays, like putting out the book and the DVD of "The Hours," along with "Mrs. Dalloway."
TIKKA TAKKA TIKKA
I NEED YOU BADLY, BADLY, MADAM LIBRARIAN.
SYDNEY! I'M IN THE MIDDLE OF MY ADULT PUBLIC SERVICES CLASS!
PERFECT. YOU TAKE THE CLASS, I'LL GIVE YOU SOME ADULT PUBLIC SERVICE.
I HAVE TO CONCENTRATE! GOD! WE HAVEN'T HAD SEX IN MONTHS. WHY ARE YOU SO INTERESTED NOW, WHEN I'M OBVIOUSLY BUSY?
EXACTLY, MO. I THINK YOUR EXPERIENCE IN RETAIL GIVES YOU A GOOD INSTINCT FOR PATRON STIMULATION.
MEANWHILE, AT BUFFALO LAKE STATE...
DR. JORDAN? I WAS WONDERING WHAT YOU THOUGHT OF MY THESIS THAT WOOLF'S "A ROOM OF ONE'S OWN" IS THE URTEXT OF VICTIM FEMINISM?
ON YOUR FINAL? YOU JUST TOOK THE EXAM AN HOUR AGO, CYNTHIA. I HAVEN'T LOOKED AT IT YET.

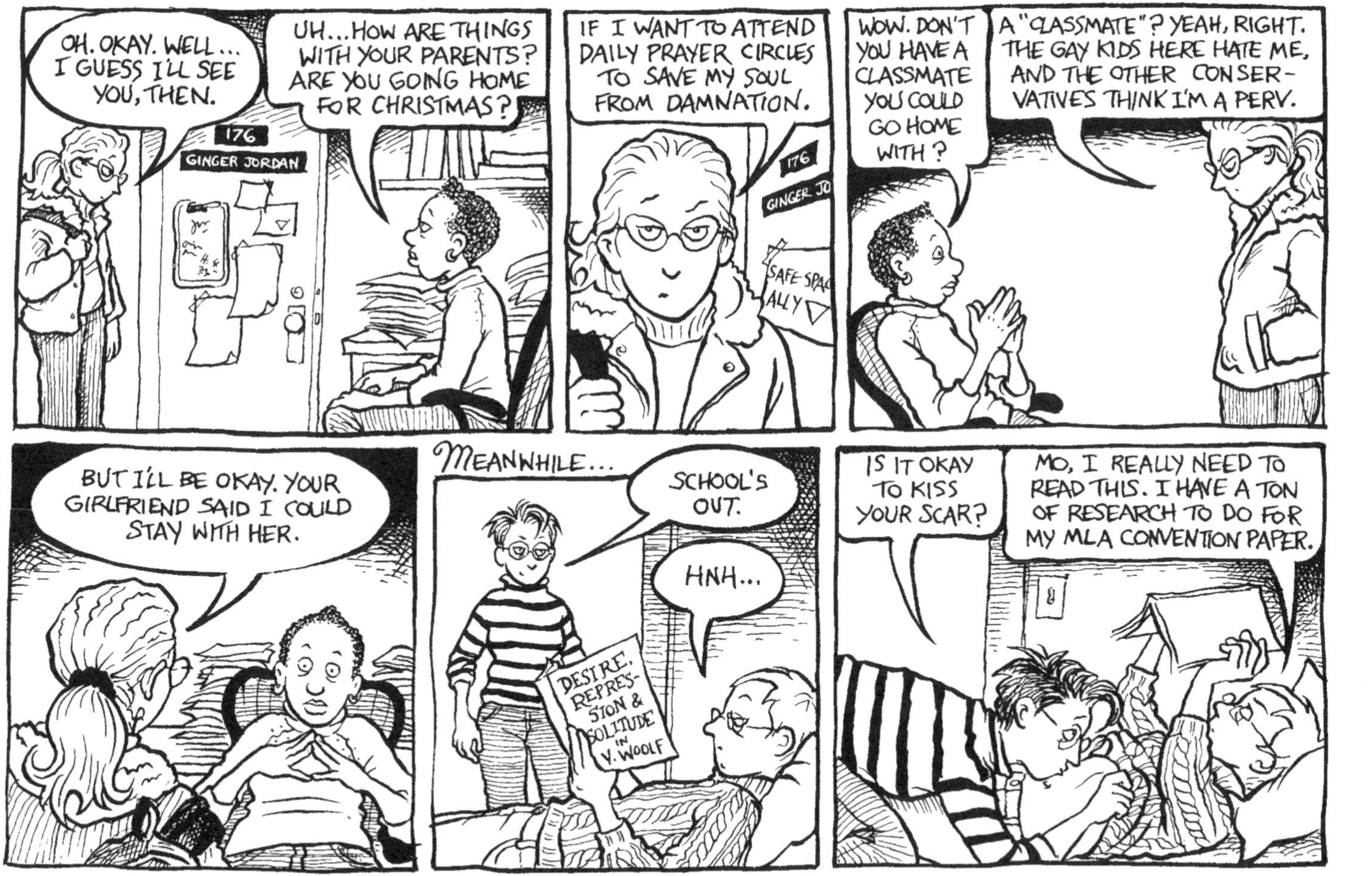
OH. OKAY. WELL... I GUESS I'LL SEE YOU, THEN.
176
GINGER JORDAN
UH... HOW ARE THINGS WITH YOUR PARENTS? ARE YOU GOING HOME FOR CHRISTMAS?
IF I WANT TO ATTEND DAILY PRAYER CIRCLES TO SAVE MY SOUL FROM DAMNATION.
176
GINGER JO
SAFE SPAC
ALLY
WOW. DON'T YOU HAVE A CLASSMATE YOU COULD GO HOME WITH?
A "CLASSMATE"? YEAH, RIGHT. THE GAY KIDS HERE HATE ME, AND THE OTHER CONSER-VATIVES THINK I'M A PERV.
BUT I'LL BE OKAY. YOUR GIRLFRIEND SAID I COULD STAY WITH HER.
MEANWHILE...
SCHOOL'S OUT.
HNH...
DESIRE, REPRES-SION & SOLITUDE IN V. WOOLF
IS IT OKAY TO KISS YOUR SCAR?
MO, I REALLY NEED TO READ THIS. I HAVE A TON OF RESEARCH TO DO FOR MY MLA CONVENTION PAPER.

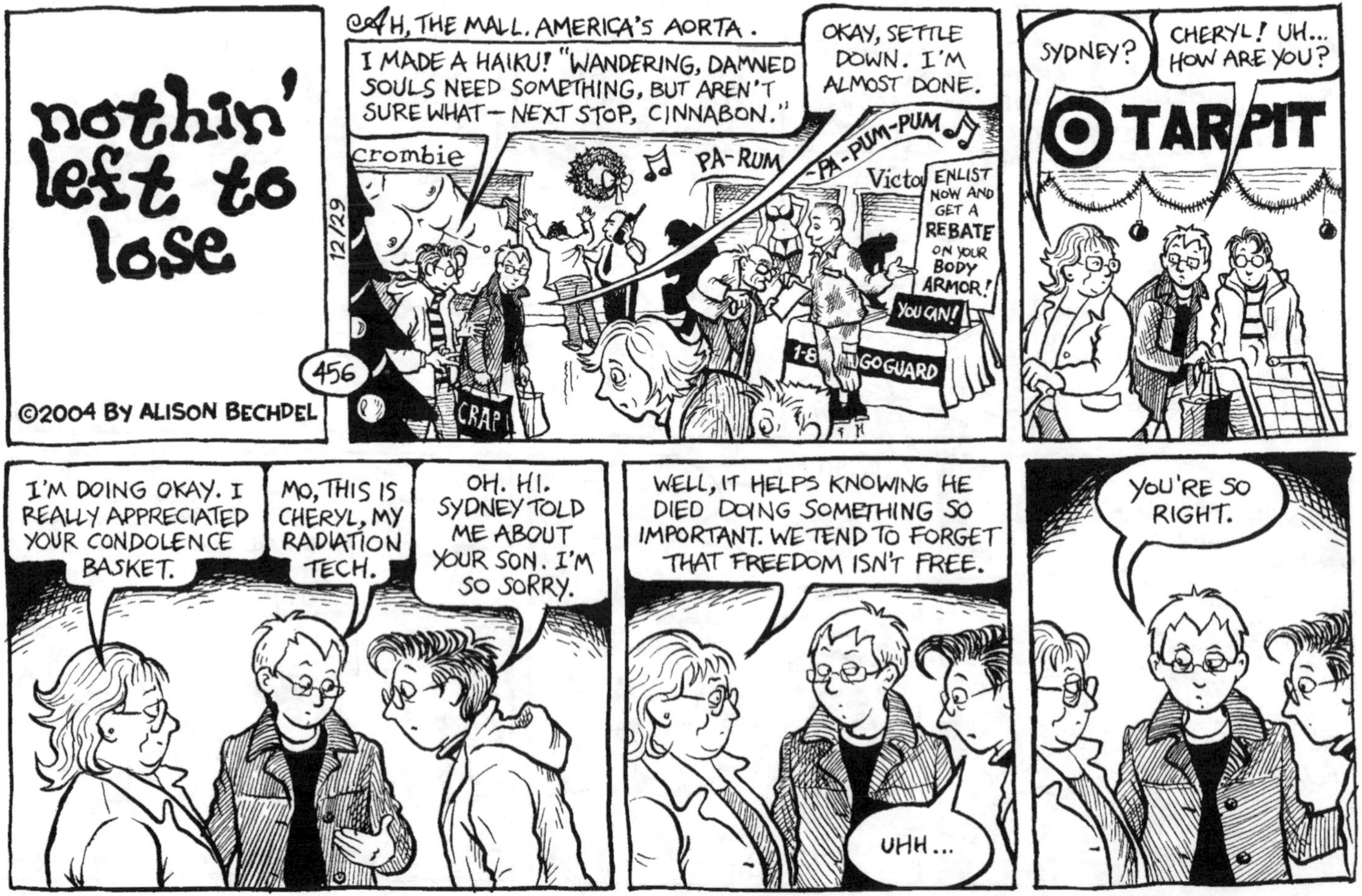
nothin' left to lose
©2004 BY ALISON BECHDEL
456
12/29
AH, THE MALL. AMERICA'S AORTA.
I MADE A HAIKU! "WANDERING, DAMNED SOULS NEED SOMETHING, BUT AREN'T SURE WHAT— NEXT STOP, CINNABON."
OKAY, SETTLE DOWN. I'M ALMOST DONE.
crombie
PA-RUM-PA-PUM-PUM
Victo
ENLIST NOW AND GET A REBATE ON YOUR BODY ARMOR!
YOU CAN!
1-8 GO GUARD
CRAP!
SYDNEY?
CHERYL! UH... HOW ARE YOU?
TARPIT
I'M DOING OKAY. I REALLY APPRECIATED YOUR CONDOLENCE BASKET.
MO, THIS IS CHERYL, MY RADIATION TECH.
OH. HI. SYDNEY TOLD ME ABOUT YOUR SON. I'M SO SORRY.
WELL, IT HELPS KNOWING HE DIED DOING SOMETHING SO IMPORTANT. WE TEND TO FORGET THAT FREEDOM ISN'T FREE.
UHH...
YOU'RE SO RIGHT.

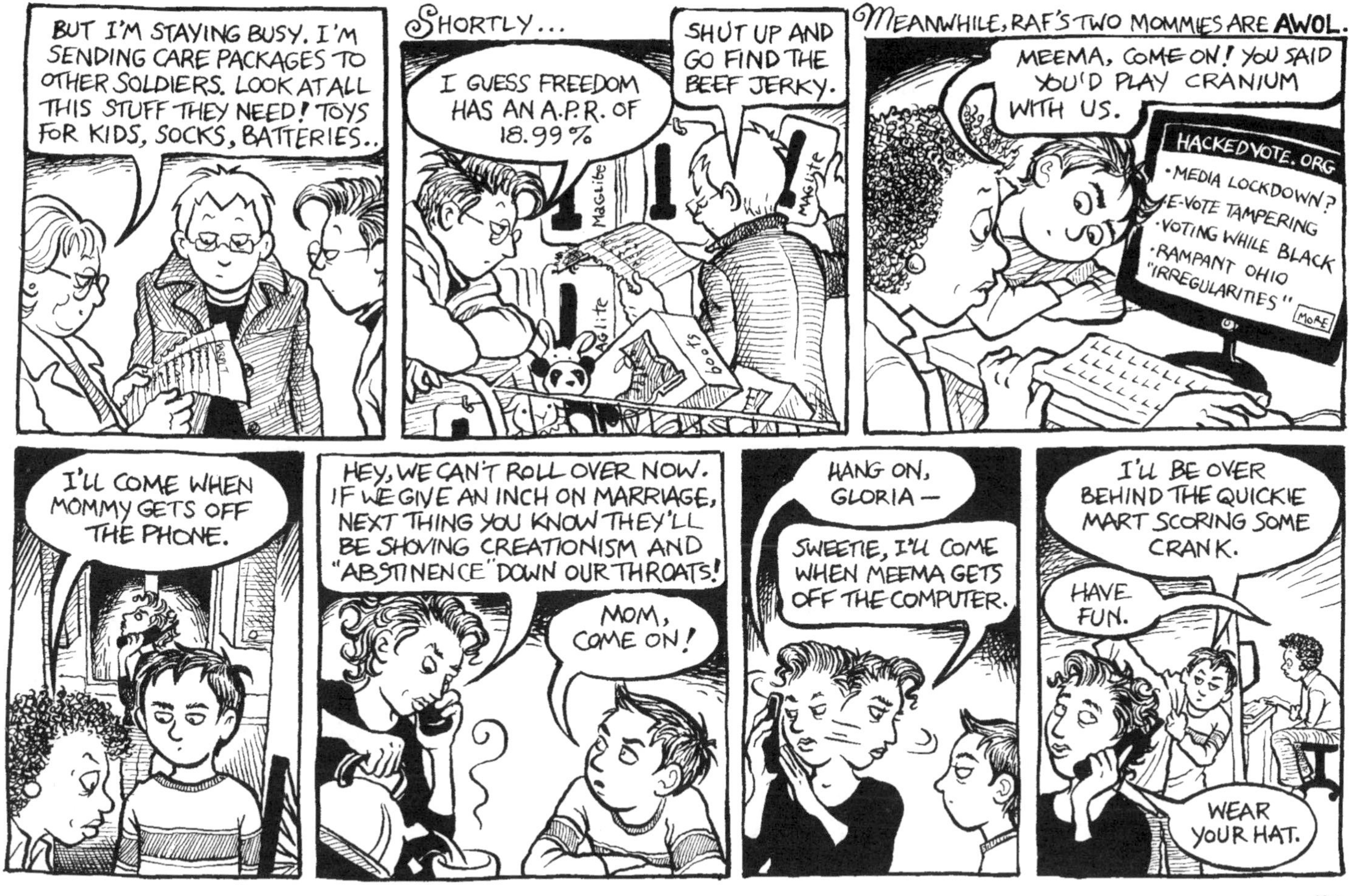
BUT I'M STAYING BUSY. I'M SENDING CARE PACKAGES TO OTHER SOLDIERS. LOOK AT ALL THIS STUFF THEY NEED! TOYS FOR KIDS, SOCKS, BATTERIES..
SHORTLY...
I GUESS FREEDOM HAS AN A.P.R. OF 18.99%
SHUT UP AND GO FIND THE BEEF JERKY.
MAGLITE
MAGLITE
MAGLITE
MAGLITE
books
MEANWHILE, RAF'S TWO MOMMIES ARE AWOL.
MEEMA, COME ON! YOU SAID YOU'D PLAY CRANIUM WITH US.
HACKEDVOTE.ORG
•MEDIA LOCKDOWN?
•E-VOTE TAMPERING
•VOTING WHILE BLACK
•RAMPANT OHIO "IRREGULARITIES"
MORE
I'LL COME WHEN MOMMY GETS OFF THE PHONE.
HEY, WE CAN'T ROLL OVER NOW. IF WE GIVE AN INCH ON MARRIAGE, NEXT THING YOU KNOW THEY'LL BE SHOVING CREATIONISM AND "ABSTINENCE" DOWN OUR THROATS!
MOM, COME ON!
HANG ON, GLORIA—
SWEETIE, I'LL COME WHEN MEEMA GETS OFF THE COMPUTER.
I'LL BE OVER BEHIND THE QUICKIE MART SCORING SOME CRANK.
HAVE FUN.
WEAR YOUR HAT.

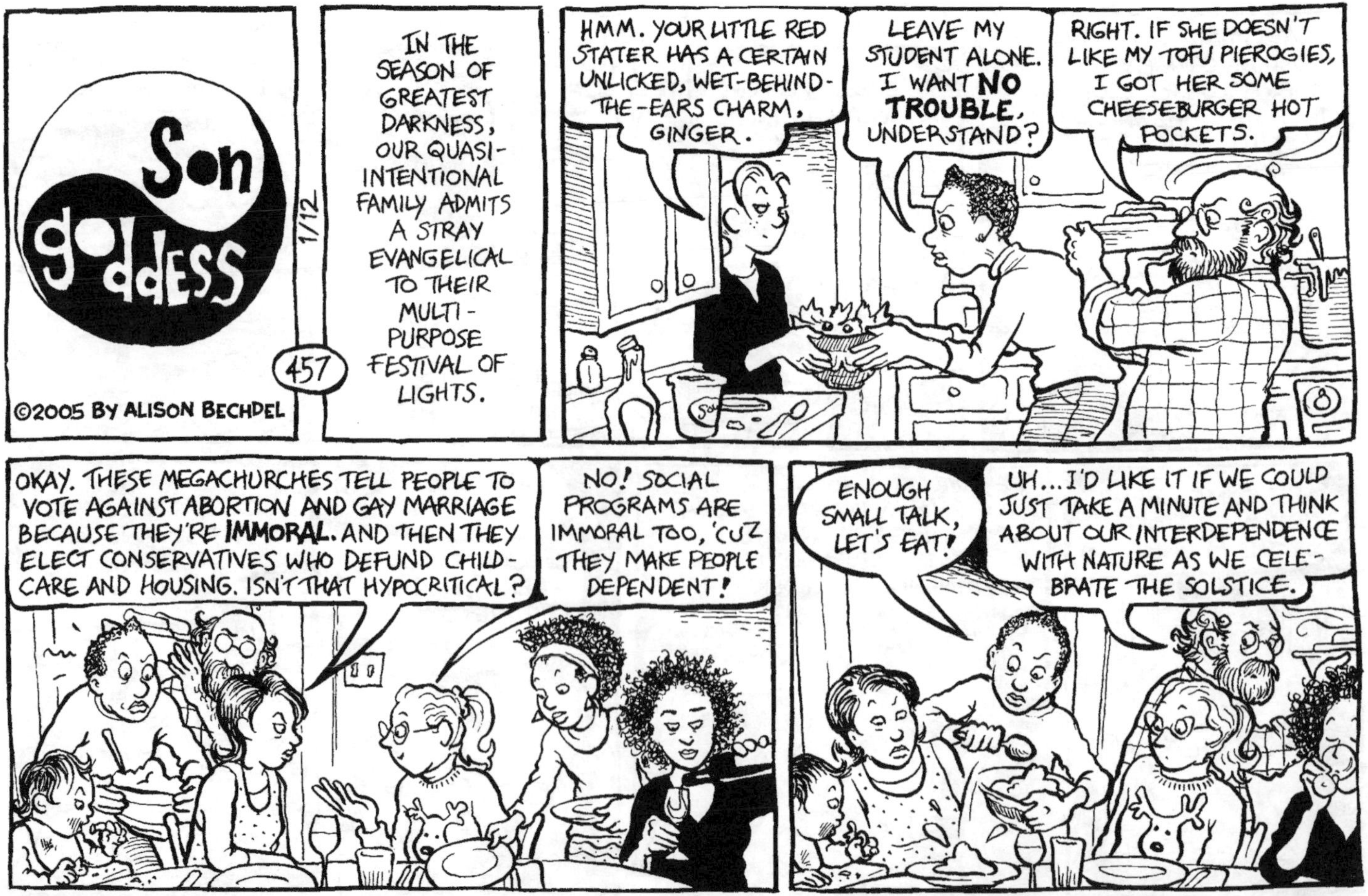
Son goddess
©2005 BY ALISON BECHDEL
457
1/12
IN THE SEASON OF GREATEST DARKNESS, OUR QUASI-INTENTIONAL FAMILY ADMITS A STRAY EVANGELICAL TO THEIR MULTI-PURPOSE FESTIVAL OF LIGHTS.
HMM. YOUR LITTLE RED STATER HAS A CERTAIN UNLICKED, WET-BEHIND-THE-EARS CHARM, GINGER.
LEAVE MY STUDENT ALONE. I WANT NO TROUBLE, UNDERSTAND?
RIGHT. IF SHE DOESN'T LIKE MY TOFU PIEROGIES, I GOT HER SOME CHEESEBURGER HOT POCKETS.
OKAY. THESE MEGACHURCHES TELL PEOPLE TO VOTE AGAINST ABORTION AND GAY MARRIAGE BECAUSE THEY'RE IMMORAL. AND THEN THEY ELECT CONSERVATIVES WHO DEFUND CHILD-CARE AND HOUSING. ISN'T THAT HYPOCRITICAL?
NO! SOCIAL PROGRAMS ARE IMMORAL TOO, 'CUZ THEY MAKE PEOPLE DEPENDENT!
ENOUGH SMALL TALK, LET'S EAT!
UH... I'D LIKE IT IF WE COULD JUST TAKE A MINUTE AND THINK ABOUT OUR INTERDEPENDENCE WITH NATURE AS WE CELEBRATE THE SOLSTICE.

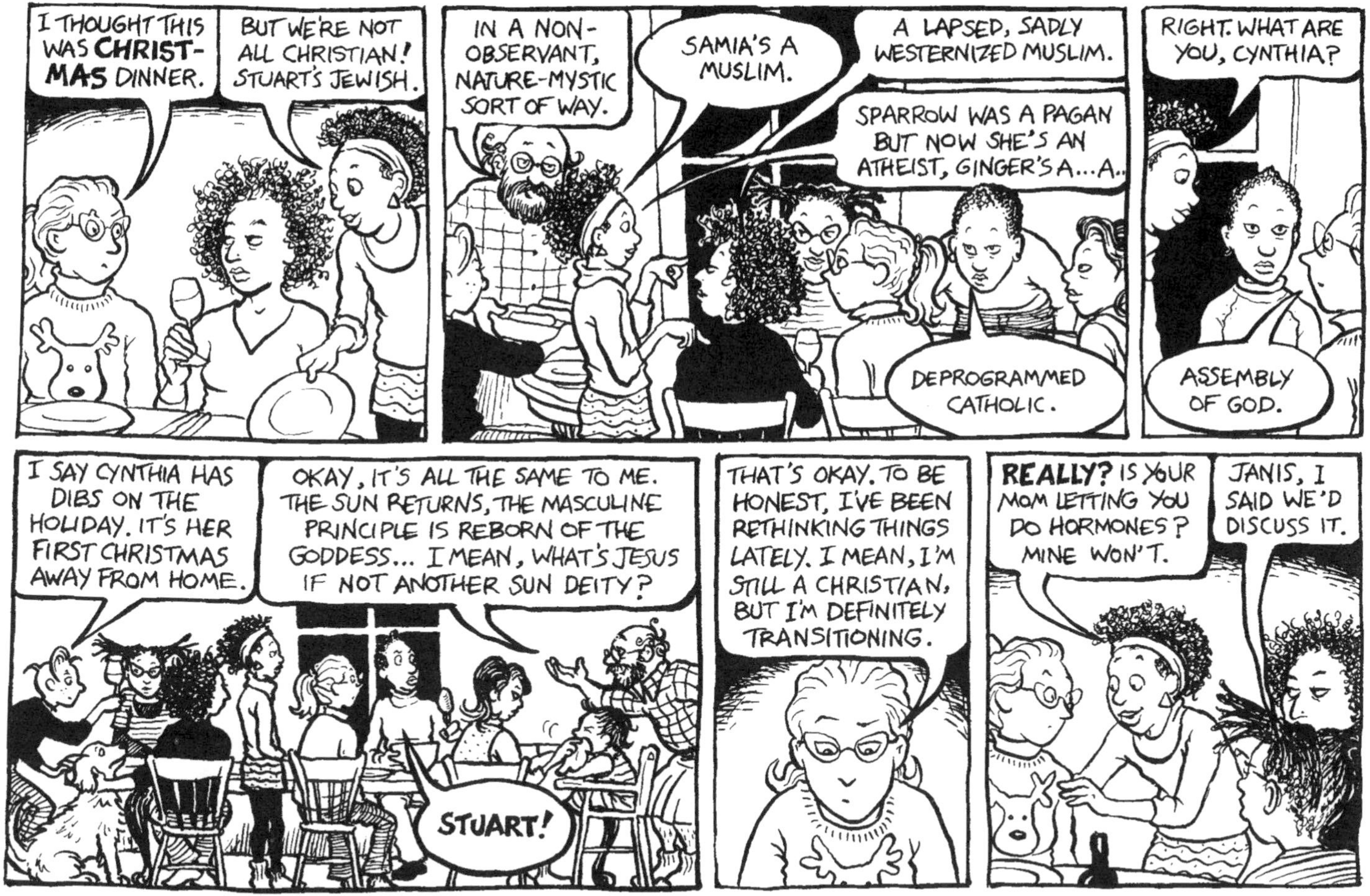

I THOUGHT THIS WAS **CHRISTMAS** DINNER.
BUT WE'RE NOT ALL CHRISTIAN! STUART'S JEWISH.
IN A NON-OBSERVANT, NATURE-MYSTIC SORT OF WAY.
SAMIA'S A MUSLIM.
A LAPSED, SADLY WESTERNIZED MUSLIM.
SPARROW WAS A PAGAN BUT NOW SHE'S AN ATHEIST, GINGER'S A...A..
DEPROGRAMMED CATHOLIC.
RIGHT. WHAT ARE YOU, CYNTHIA?
ASSEMBLY OF GOD.
I SAY CYNTHIA HAS DIBS ON THE HOLIDAY. IT'S HER FIRST CHRISTMAS AWAY FROM HOME.
OKAY, IT'S ALL THE SAME TO ME. THE SUN RETURNS, THE MASCULINE PRINCIPLE IS REBORN OF THE GODDESS... I MEAN, WHAT'S JESUS IF NOT ANOTHER SUN DEITY?
STUART!
THAT'S OKAY. TO BE HONEST, I'VE BEEN RETHINKING THINGS LATELY. I MEAN, I'M STILL A CHRISTIAN, BUT I'M DEFINITELY TRANSITIONING.
REALLY? IS YOUR MOM LETTING YOU DO HORMONES? MINE WON'T.
JANIS, I SAID WE'D DISCUSS IT.

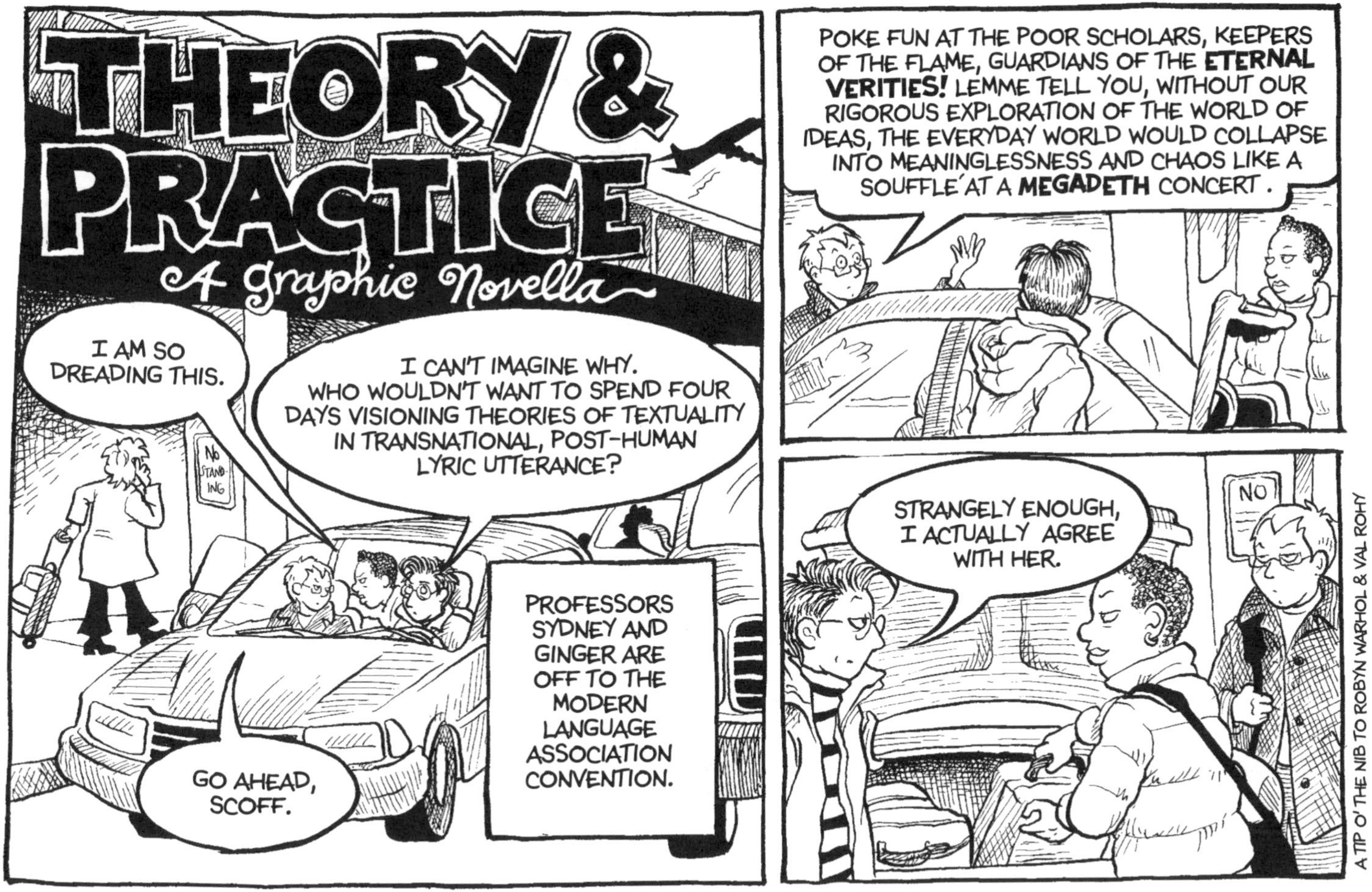

THEORY & PRACTICE
A graphic Novella
I AM SO DREADING THIS.
I CAN'T IMAGINE WHY. WHO WOULDN'T WANT TO SPEND FOUR DAYS VISIONING THEORIES OF TEXTUALITY IN TRANSNATIONAL, POST-HUMAN LYRIC UTTERANCE?
NO STAND-ING
GO AHEAD, SCOFF.
PROFESSORS SYDNEY AND GINGER ARE OFF TO THE MODERN LANGUAGE ASSOCIATION CONVENTION.
POKE FUN AT THE POOR SCHOLARS, KEEPERS OF THE FLAME, GUARDIANS OF THE **ETERNAL VERITIES!** LEMME TELL YOU, WITHOUT OUR RIGOROUS EXPLORATION OF THE WORLD OF IDEAS, THE EVERYDAY WORLD WOULD COLLAPSE INTO MEANINGLESSNESS AND CHAOS LIKE A SOUFFLÉ AT A **MEGADETH** CONCERT.
STRANGELY ENOUGH, I ACTUALLY AGREE WITH HER.
NO
A TIP O' THE NIB TO ROBYN WARHOL & VAL ROHY

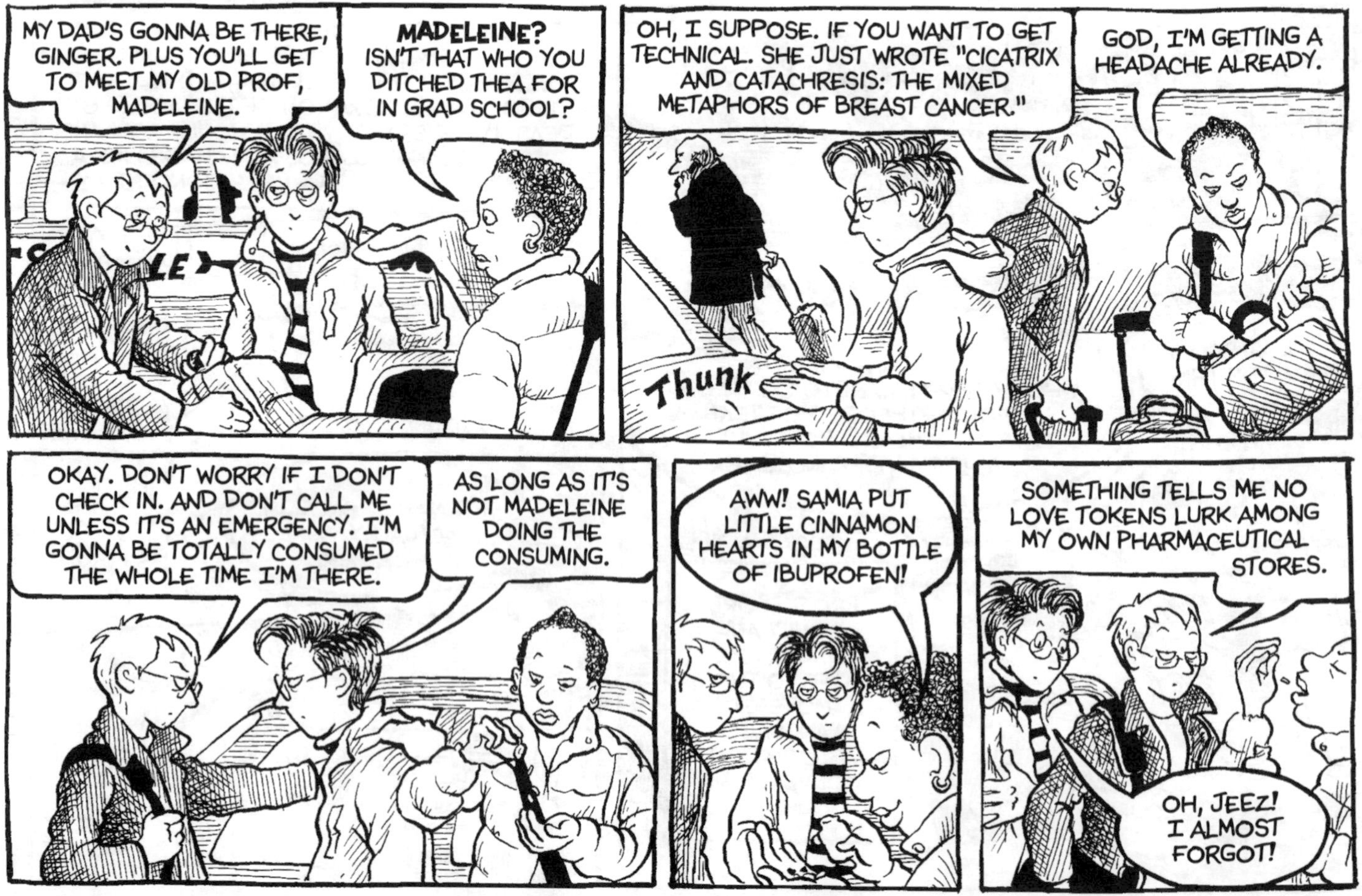
MY DAD'S GONNA BE THERE, GINGER. PLUS YOU'LL GET TO MEET MY OLD PROF, MADELEINE.
MADELEINE? ISN'T THAT WHO YOU DITCHED THEA FOR IN GRAD SCHOOL?
OH, I SUPPOSE. IF YOU WANT TO GET TECHNICAL. SHE JUST WROTE "CICATRIX AND CATACHRESIS: THE MIXED METAPHORS OF BREAST CANCER."
GOD, I'M GETTING A HEADACHE ALREADY.
Thunk
OKAY. DON'T WORRY IF I DON'T CHECK IN. AND DON'T CALL ME UNLESS IT'S AN EMERGENCY. I'M GONNA BE TOTALLY CONSUMED THE WHOLE TIME I'M THERE.
AS LONG AS IT'S NOT MADELEINE DOING THE CONSUMING.
AWW! SAMIA PUT LITTLE CINNAMON HEARTS IN MY BOTTLE OF IBUPROFEN!
SOMETHING TELLS ME NO LOVE TOKENS LURK AMONG MY OWN PHARMACEUTICAL STORES.
OH, JEEZ! I ALMOST FORGOT!

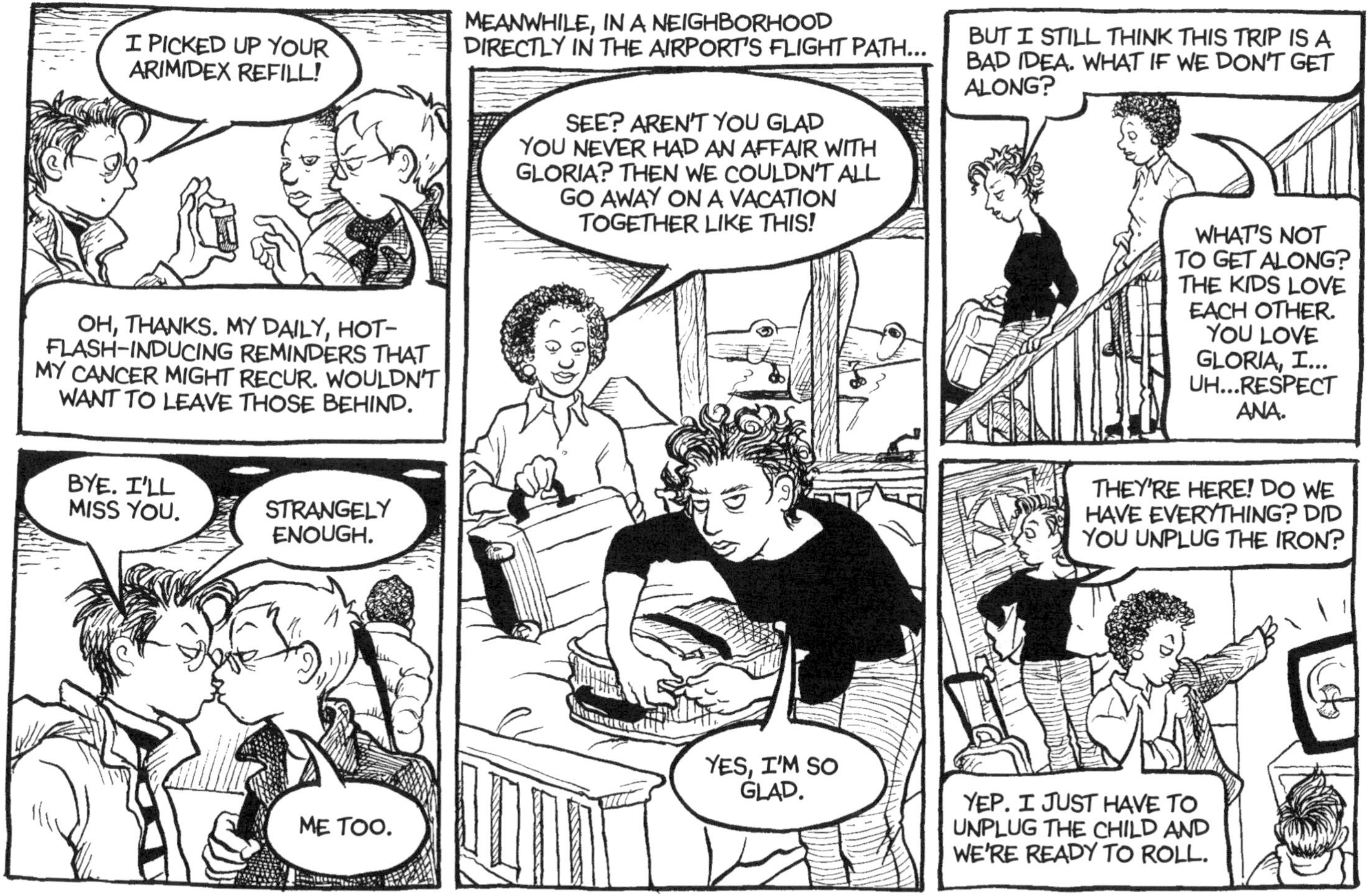
I PICKED UP YOUR ARIMIDEX REFILL!
OH, THANKS. MY DAILY, HOT-FLASH-INDUCING REMINDERS THAT MY CANCER MIGHT RECUR. WOULDN'T WANT TO LEAVE THOSE BEHIND.
BYE. I'LL MISS YOU.
STRANGELY ENOUGH.
ME TOO.
MEANWHILE, IN A NEIGHBORHOOD DIRECTLY IN THE AIRPORT'S FLIGHT PATH...
SEE? AREN'T YOU GLAD YOU NEVER HAD AN AFFAIR WITH GLORIA? THEN WE COULDN'T ALL GO AWAY ON A VACATION TOGETHER LIKE THIS!
YES, I'M SO GLAD.
BUT I STILL THINK THIS TRIP IS A BAD IDEA. WHAT IF WE DON'T GET ALONG?
WHAT'S NOT TO GET ALONG? THE KIDS LOVE EACH OTHER. YOU LOVE GLORIA, I... UH...RESPECT ANA.
THEY'RE HERE! DO WE HAVE EVERYTHING? DID YOU UNPLUG THE IRON?
YEP. I JUST HAVE TO UNPLUG THE CHILD AND WE'RE READY TO ROLL.

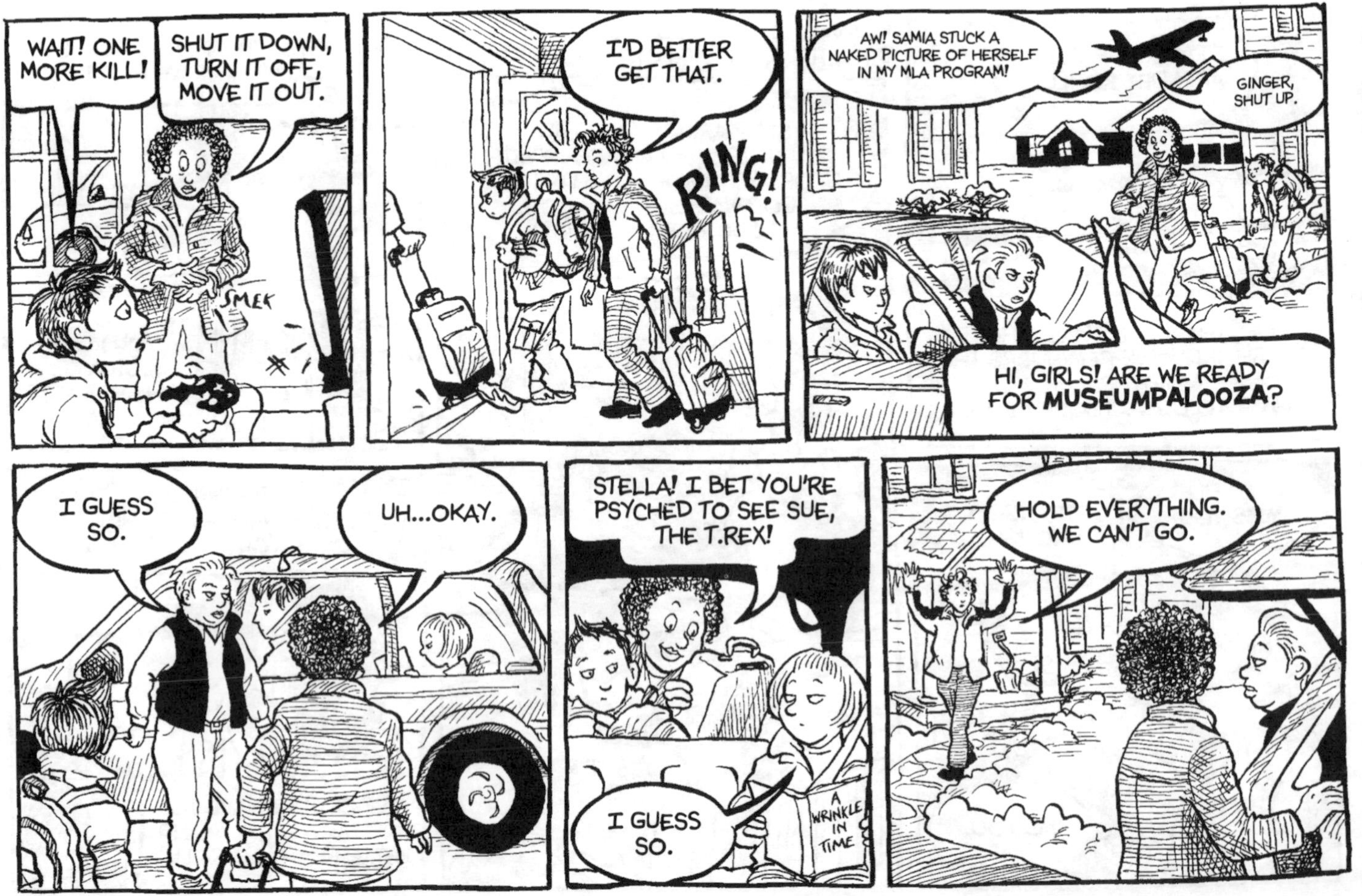
WAIT! ONE MORE KILL!
SHUT IT DOWN, TURN IT OFF, MOVE IT OUT.
SMEK
I'D BETTER GET THAT.
RING!
AW! SAMIA STUCK A NAKED PICTURE OF HERSELF IN MY MLA PROGRAM!
GINGER, SHUT UP.
HI, GIRLS! ARE WE READY FOR **MUSEUMPALOOZA**?
I GUESS SO.
UH...OKAY.
STELLA! I BET YOU'RE PSYCHED TO SEE SUE, THE T.REX!
I GUESS SO.
A WRINKLE IN TIME
HOLD EVERYTHING. WE CAN'T GO.

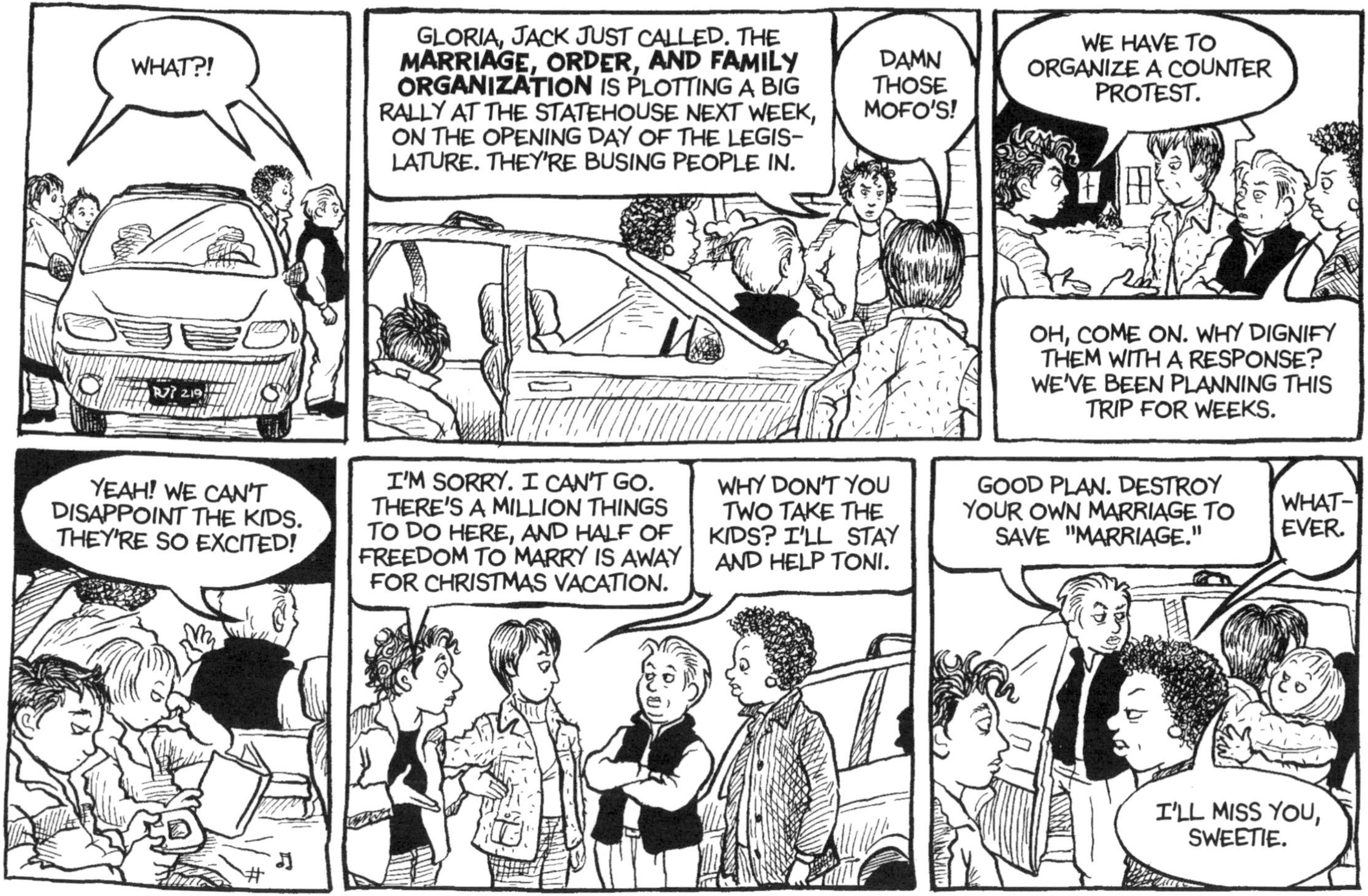
WHAT?!
GLORIA, JACK JUST CALLED. THE **MARRIAGE, ORDER, AND FAMILY ORGANIZATION** IS PLOTTING A BIG RALLY AT THE STATEHOUSE NEXT WEEK, ON THE OPENING DAY OF THE LEGISLATURE. THEY'RE BUSING PEOPLE IN.
DAMN THOSE MOFO'S!
WE HAVE TO ORGANIZE A COUNTER PROTEST.
OH, COME ON. WHY DIGNIFY THEM WITH A RESPONSE? WE'VE BEEN PLANNING THIS TRIP FOR WEEKS.
YEAH! WE CAN'T DISAPPOINT THE KIDS. THEY'RE SO EXCITED!
I'M SORRY. I CAN'T GO. THERE'S A MILLION THINGS TO DO HERE, AND HALF OF FREEDOM TO MARRY IS AWAY FOR CHRISTMAS VACATION.
WHY DON'T YOU TWO TAKE THE KIDS? I'LL STAY AND HELP TONI.
GOOD PLAN. DESTROY YOUR OWN MARRIAGE TO SAVE "MARRIAGE."
WHATEVER.
I'LL MISS YOU, SWEETIE.

AFTER CHECKING INTO THEIR ROOM, GINGER AND SYDNEY JOIN THE MLA MELÉE.

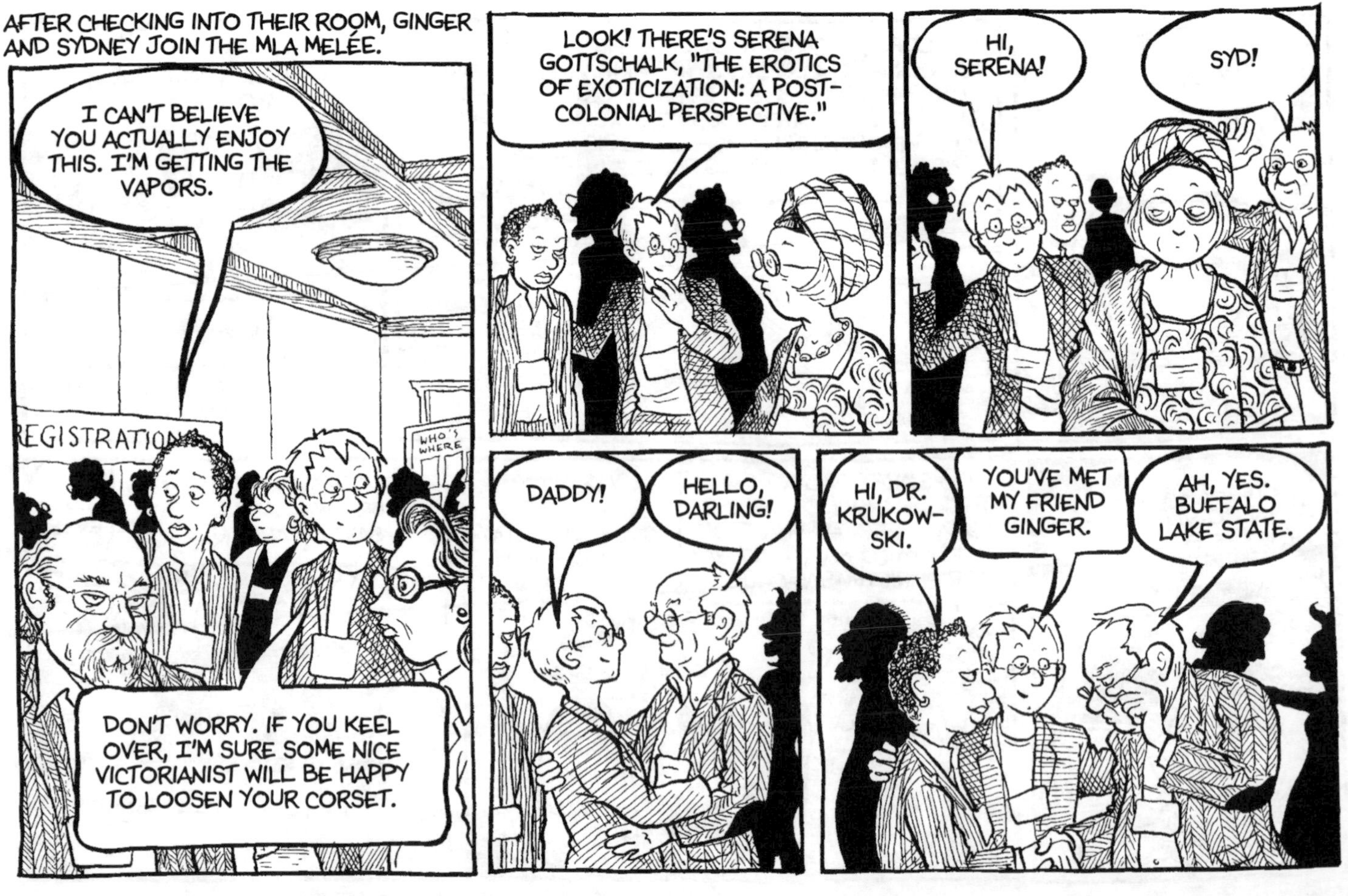
I CAN'T BELIEVE YOU ACTUALLY ENJOY THIS. I'M GETTING THE VAPORS.
REGISTRATION
WHO'S WHERE
DON'T WORRY. IF YOU KEEL OVER, I'M SURE SOME NICE VICTORIANIST WILL BE HAPPY TO LOOSEN YOUR CORSET.
LOOK! THERE'S SERENA GOTTSCHALK, "THE EROTICS OF EXOTICIZATION: A POST-COLONIAL PERSPECTIVE."
HI, SERENA!
SYD!
DADDY!
HELLO, DARLING!
HI, DR. KRUKOW-SKI.
YOU'VE MET MY FRIEND GINGER.
AH, YES. BUFFALO LAKE STATE.

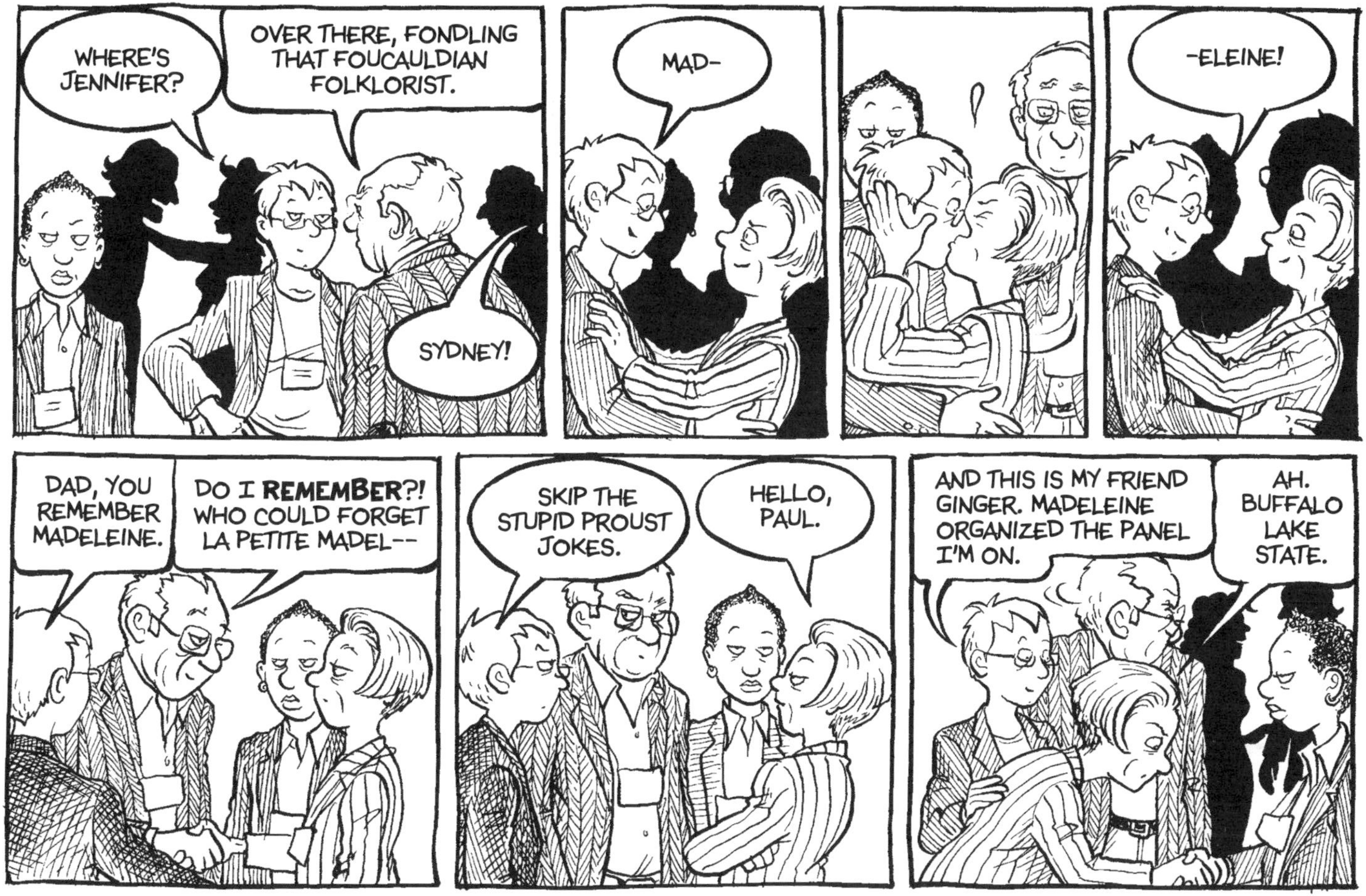
WHERE'S JENNIFER?
OVER THERE, FONDLING THAT FOUCAULDIAN FOLKLORIST.
SYDNEY!
MAD-
-ELEINE!
DAD, YOU REMEMBER MADELEINE.
DO I **REMEMBER**?! WHO COULD FORGET LA PETITE MADEL--
SKIP THE STUPID PROUST JOKES.
HELLO, PAUL.
AND THIS IS MY FRIEND GINGER. MADELEINE ORGANIZED THE PANEL I'M ON.
AH. BUFFALO LAKE STATE.

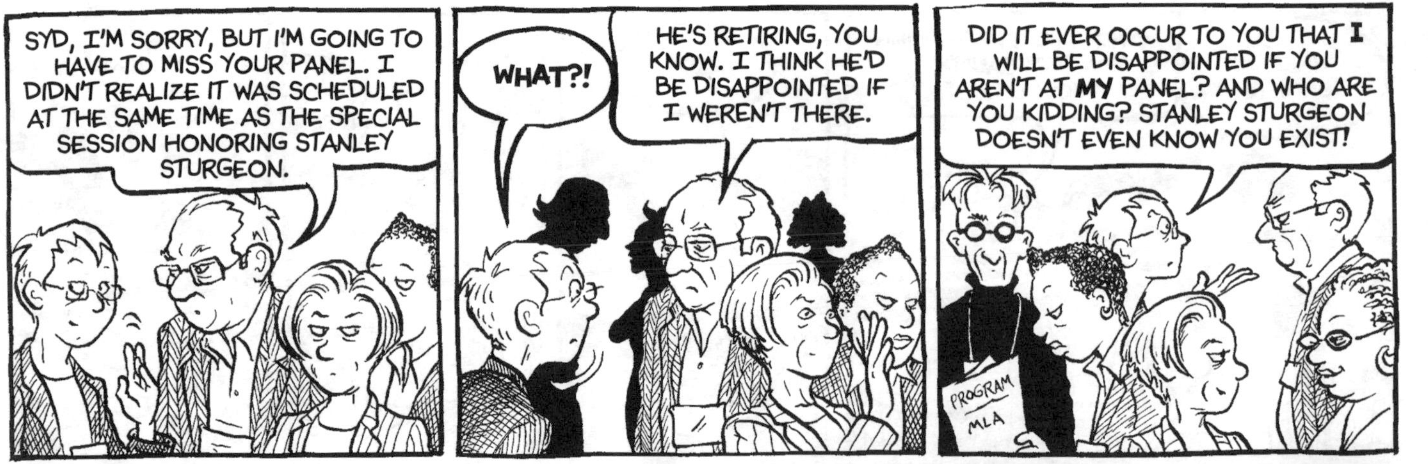
SYD, I'M SORRY, BUT I'M GOING TO HAVE TO MISS YOUR PANEL. I DIDN'T REALIZE IT WAS SCHEDULED AT THE SAME TIME AS THE SPECIAL SESSION HONORING STANLEY STURGEON.
WHAT?!
HE'S RETIRING, YOU KNOW. I THINK HE'D BE DISAPPOINTED IF I WEREN'T THERE.
DID IT EVER OCCUR TO YOU THAT **I** WILL BE DISAPPOINTED IF YOU AREN'T AT **MY** PANEL? AND WHO ARE YOU KIDDING? STANLEY STURGEON DOESN'T EVEN KNOW YOU EXIST!
PROGRAM
MLA

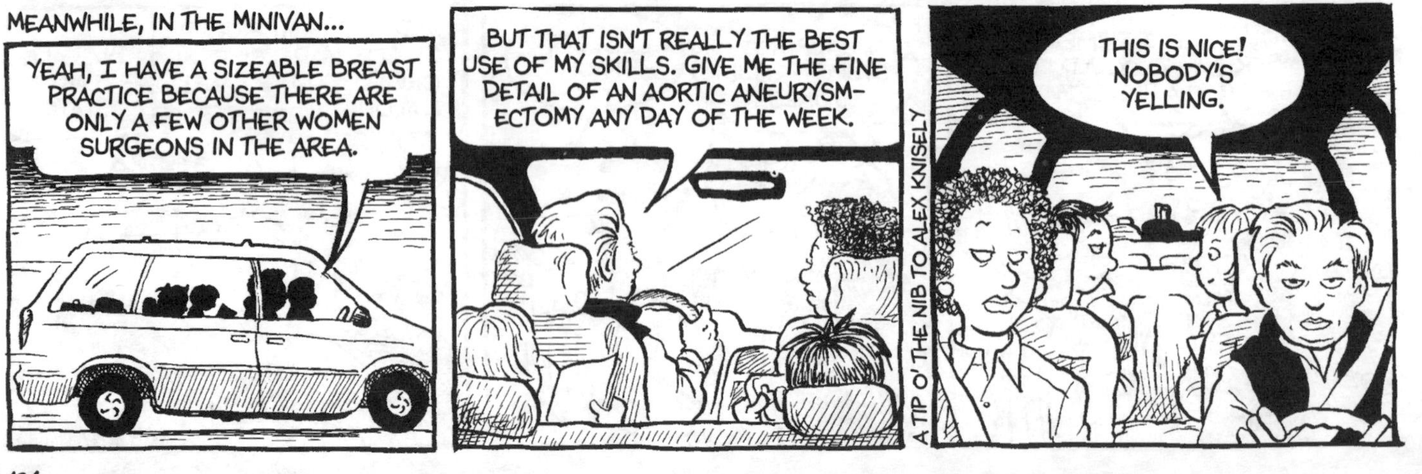
MEANWHILE, IN THE MINIVAN...
YEAH, I HAVE A SIZEABLE BREAST PRACTICE BECAUSE THERE ARE ONLY A FEW OTHER WOMEN SURGEONS IN THE AREA.
BUT THAT ISN'T REALLY THE BEST USE OF MY SKILLS. GIVE ME THE FINE DETAIL OF AN AORTIC ANEURYSM-ECTOMY ANY DAY OF THE WEEK.
THIS IS NICE! NOBODY'S YELLING.
A TIP O' THE NIB TO ALEX KNISELY

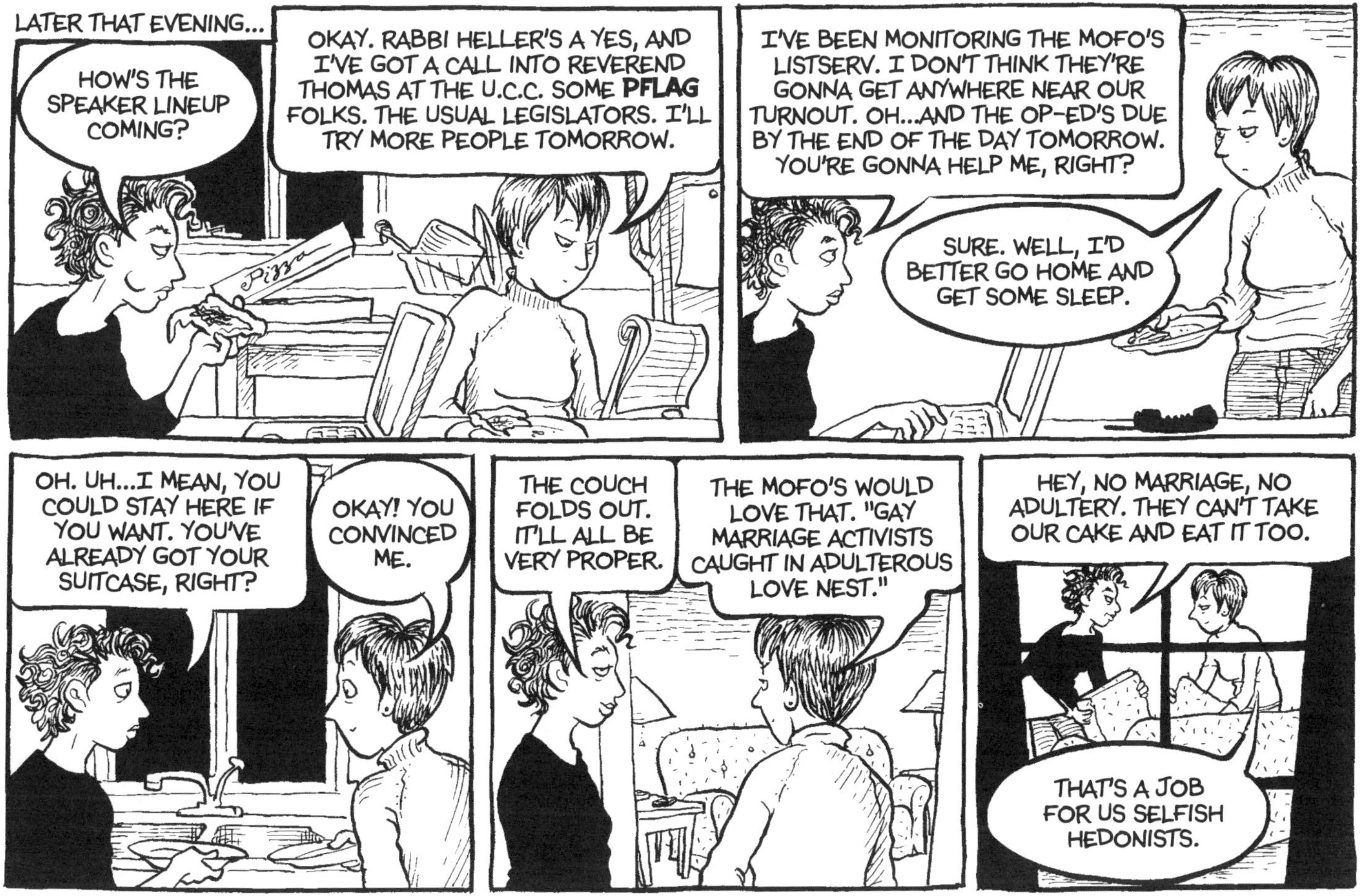
LATER THAT EVENING...
HOW'S THE SPEAKER LINEUP COMING?
OKAY. RABBI HELLER'S A YES, AND I'VE GOT A CALL INTO REVEREND THOMAS AT THE U.C.C. SOME **PFLAG** FOLKS. THE USUAL LEGISLATORS. I'LL TRY MORE PEOPLE TOMORROW.
Pizza
I'VE BEEN MONITORING THE MOFO'S LISTSERV. I DON'T THINK THEY'RE GONNA GET ANYWHERE NEAR OUR TURNOUT. OH...AND THE OP-ED'S DUE BY THE END OF THE DAY TOMORROW. YOU'RE GONNA HELP ME, RIGHT?
SURE. WELL, I'D BETTER GO HOME AND GET SOME SLEEP.
OH. UH...I MEAN, YOU COULD STAY HERE IF YOU WANT. YOU'VE ALREADY GOT YOUR SUITCASE, RIGHT?
OKAY! YOU CONVINCED ME.
THE COUCH FOLDS OUT. IT'LL ALL BE VERY PROPER.
THE MOFO'S WOULD LOVE THAT. "GAY MARRIAGE ACTIVISTS CAUGHT IN ADULTEROUS LOVE NEST."
HEY, NO MARRIAGE, NO ADULTERY. THEY CAN'T TAKE OUR CAKE AND EAT IT TOO.
THAT'S A JOB FOR US SELFISH HEDONISTS.

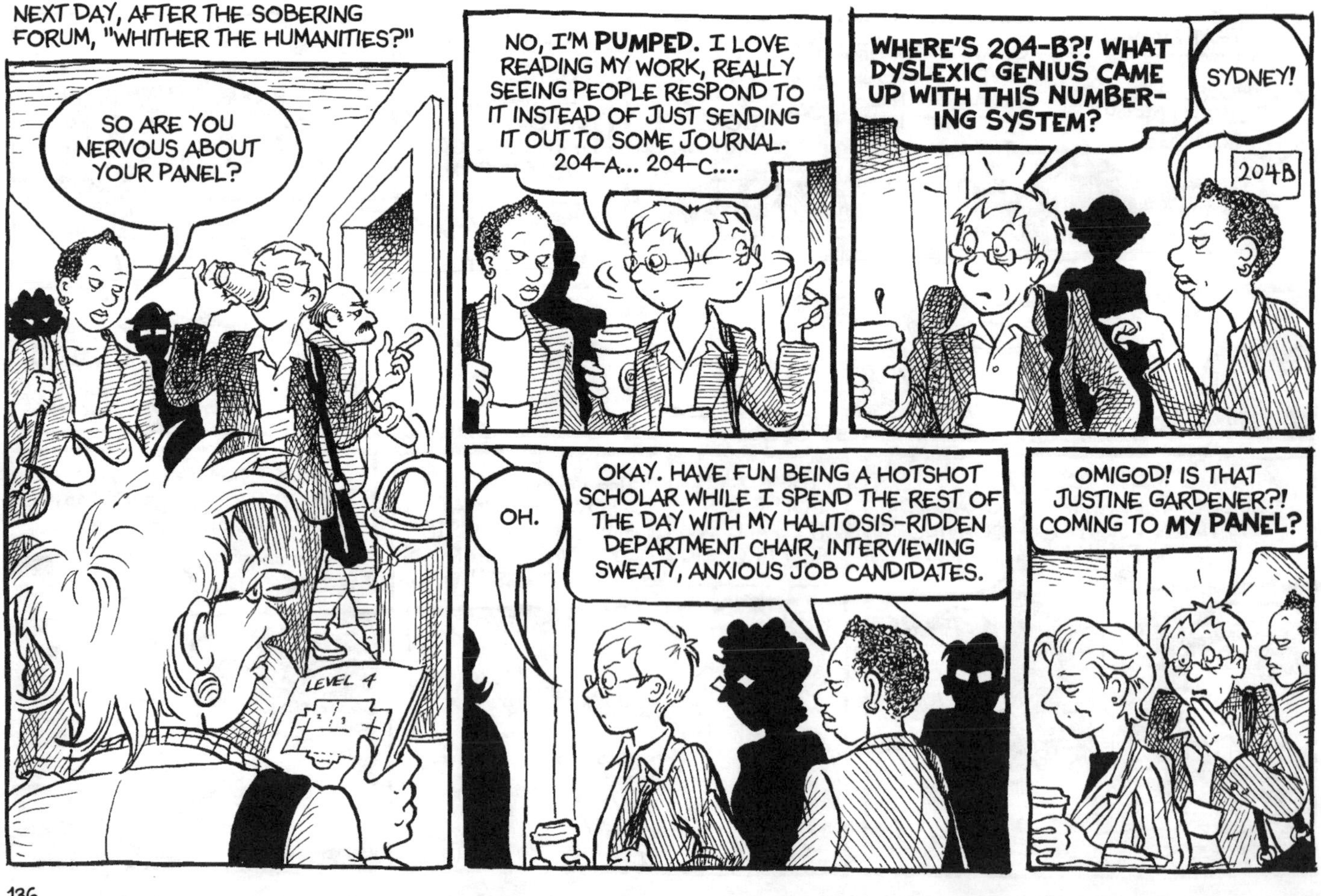
NEXT DAY, AFTER THE SOBERING FORUM, "WHITHER THE HUMANITIES?"
SO ARE YOU NERVOUS ABOUT YOUR PANEL?
LEVEL 4
NO, I'M **PUMPED.** I LOVE READING MY WORK, REALLY SEEING PEOPLE RESPOND TO IT INSTEAD OF JUST SENDING IT OUT TO SOME JOURNAL. 204-A... 204-C....
WHERE'S 204-B?! WHAT DYSLEXIC GENIUS CAME UP WITH THIS NUMBER-ING SYSTEM?
SYDNEY!
204B
OH.
OKAY. HAVE FUN BEING A HOTSHOT SCHOLAR WHILE I SPEND THE REST OF THE DAY WITH MY HALITOSIS-RIDDEN DEPARTMENT CHAIR, INTERVIEWING SWEATY, ANXIOUS JOB CANDIDATES.
OMIGOD! IS THAT JUSTINE GARDENER?! COMING TO **MY PANEL?**

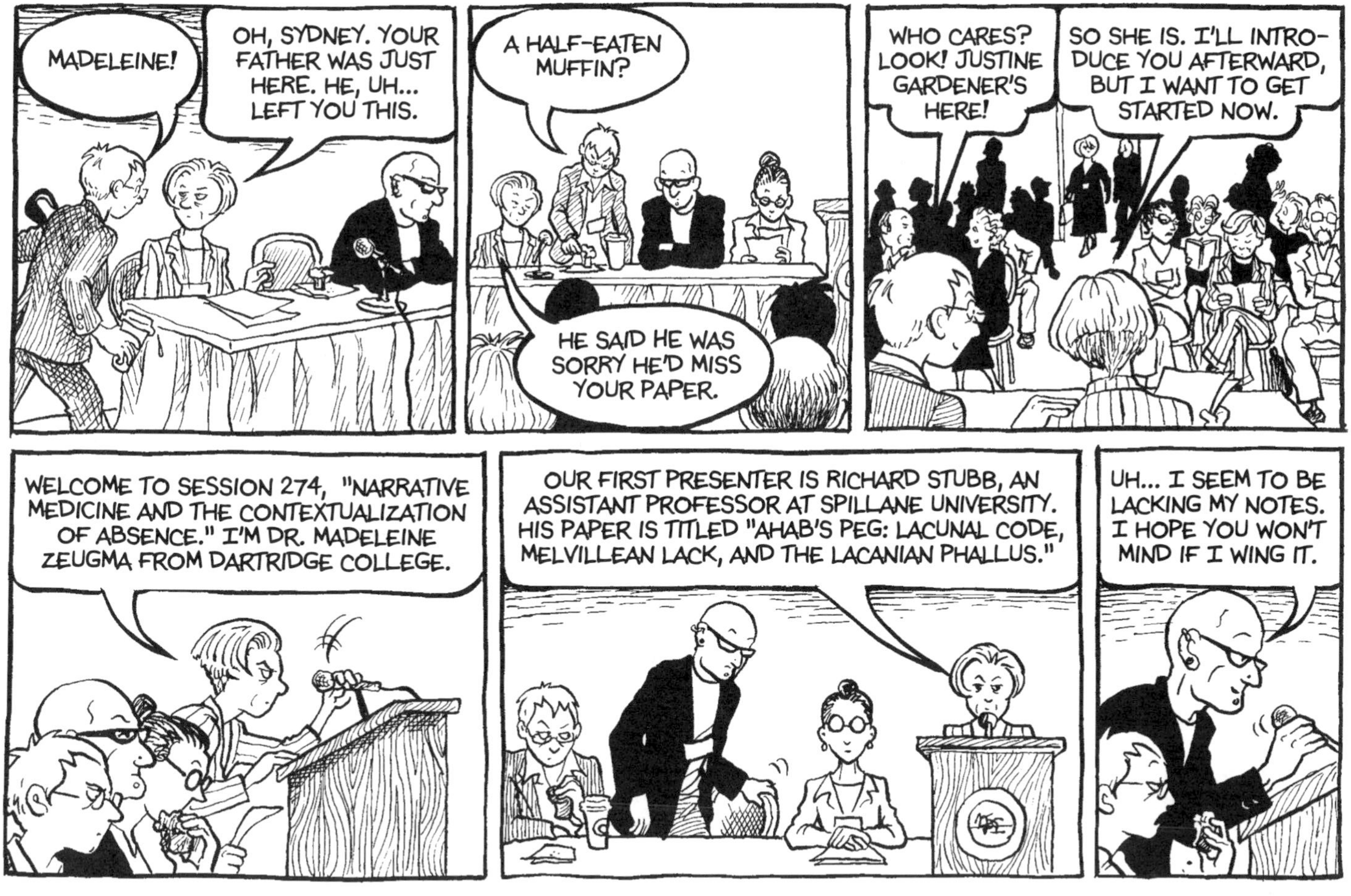
MADELEINE!
OH, SYDNEY. YOUR FATHER WAS JUST HERE. HE, UH... LEFT YOU THIS.
A HALF-EATEN MUFFIN?
HE SAID HE WAS SORRY HE'D MISS YOUR PAPER.
WHO CARES? LOOK! JUSTINE GARDENER'S HERE!
SO SHE IS. I'LL INTRODUCE YOU AFTERWARD, BUT I WANT TO GET STARTED NOW.
WELCOME TO SESSION 274, "NARRATIVE MEDICINE AND THE CONTEXTUALIZATION OF ABSENCE." I'M DR. MADELEINE ZEUGMA FROM DARTRIDGE COLLEGE.
OUR FIRST PRESENTER IS RICHARD STUBB, AN ASSISTANT PROFESSOR AT SPILLANE UNIVERSITY. HIS PAPER IS TITLED "AHAB'S PEG: LACUNAL CODE, MELVILLEAN LACK, AND THE LACANIAN PHALLUS."
UH... I SEEM TO BE LACKING MY NOTES. I HOPE YOU WON'T MIND IF I WING IT.

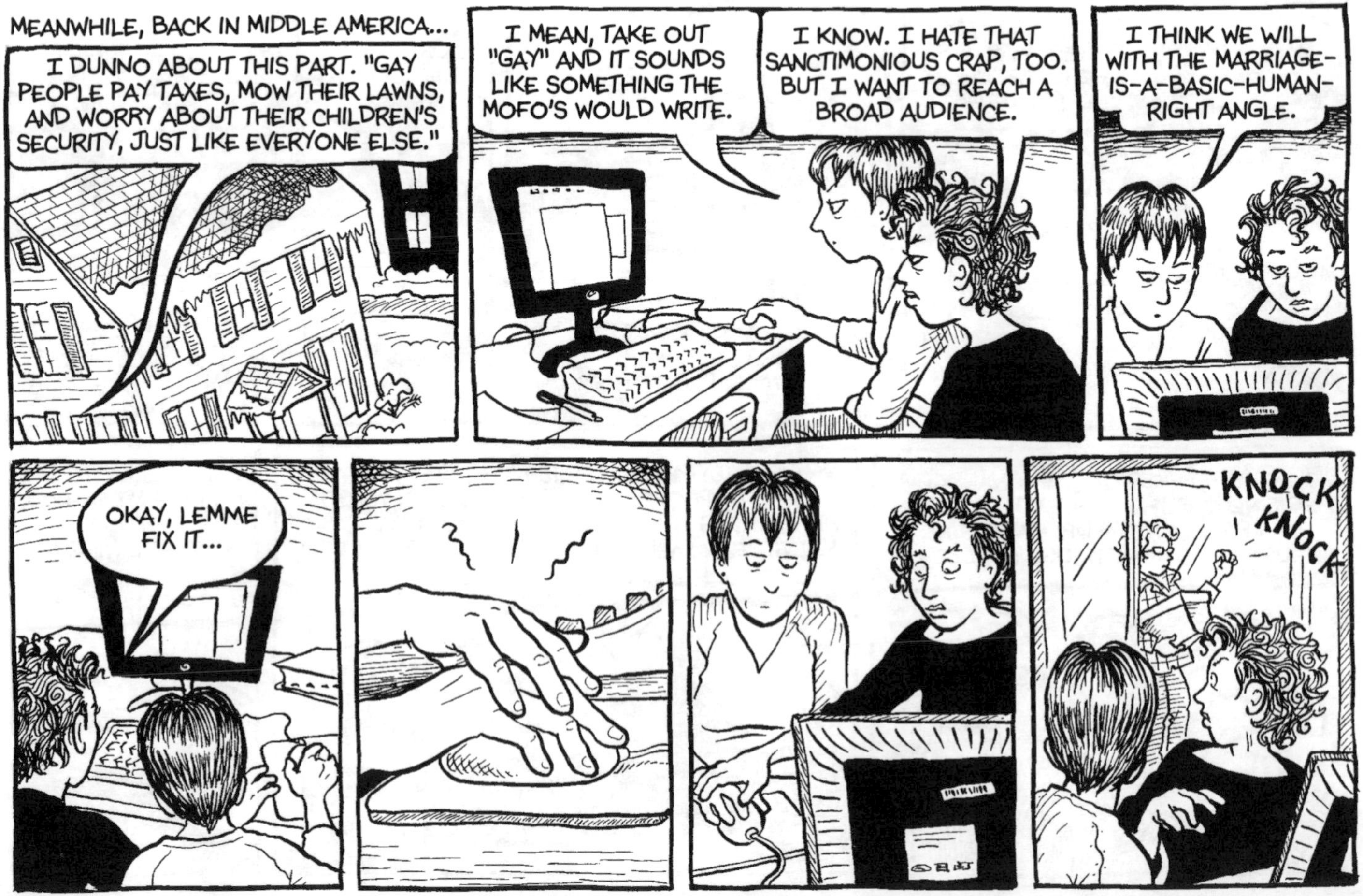
MEANWHILE, BACK IN MIDDLE AMERICA...
I DUNNO ABOUT THIS PART. "GAY PEOPLE PAY TAXES, MOW THEIR LAWNS, AND WORRY ABOUT THEIR CHILDREN'S SECURITY, JUST LIKE EVERYONE ELSE."
I MEAN, TAKE OUT "GAY" AND IT SOUNDS LIKE SOMETHING THE MOFO'S WOULD WRITE.
I KNOW. I HATE THAT SANCTIMONIOUS CRAP, TOO. BUT I WANT TO REACH A BROAD AUDIENCE.
I THINK WE WILL WITH THE MARRIAGE-IS-A-BASIC-HUMAN-RIGHT ANGLE.
OKAY, LEMME FIX IT...
KNOCK KNOCK

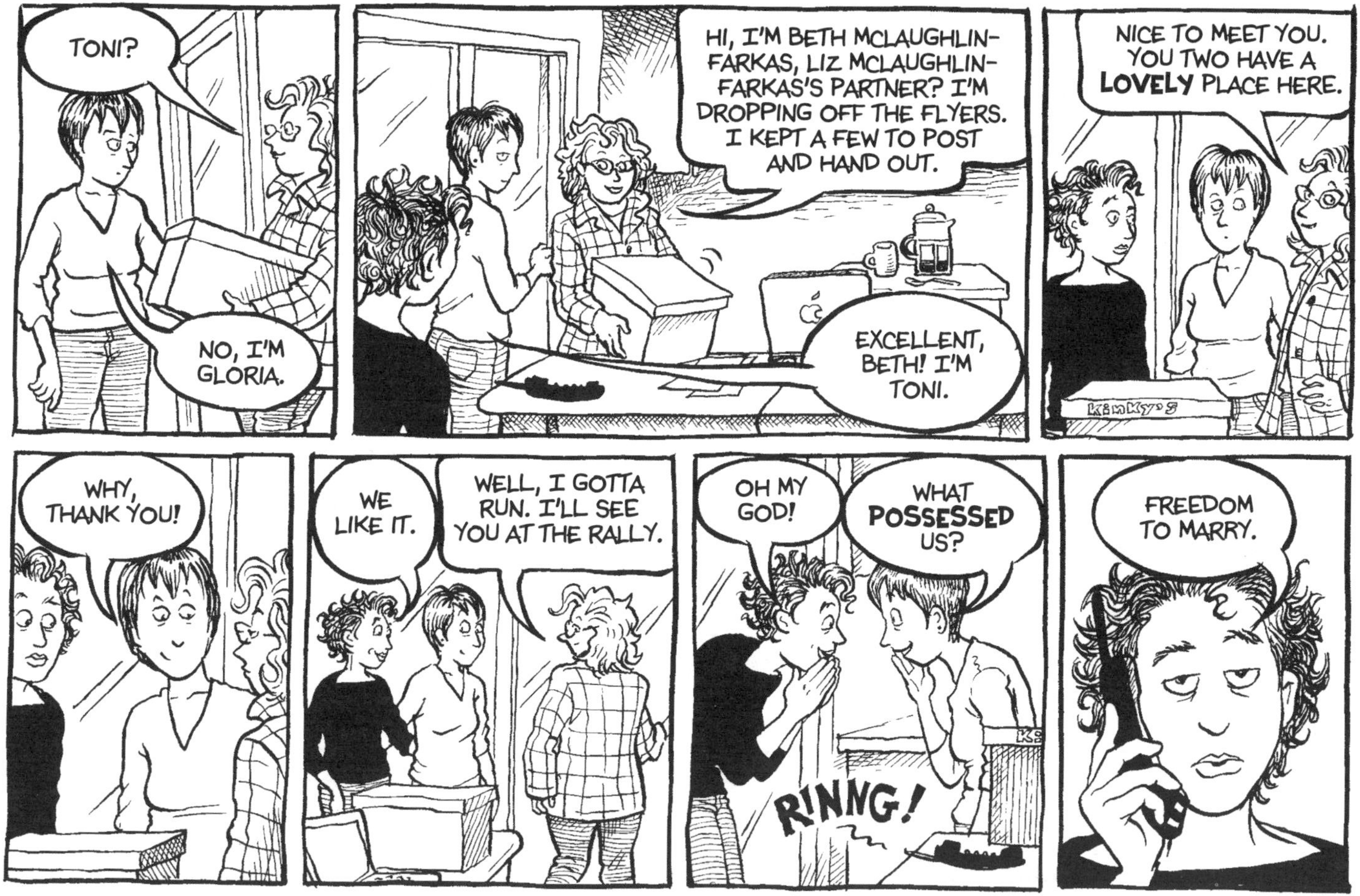
TONI?
NO, I'M GLORIA.
HI, I'M BETH MCLAUGHLIN-FARKAS, LIZ MCLAUGHLIN-FARKAS'S PARTNER? I'M DROPPING OFF THE FLYERS. I KEPT A FEW TO POST AND HAND OUT.
EXCELLENT, BETH! I'M TONI.
NICE TO MEET YOU. YOU TWO HAVE A **LOVELY** PLACE HERE.
KinKy's
WHY, THANK YOU!
WE LIKE IT.
WELL, I GOTTA RUN. I'LL SEE YOU AT THE RALLY.
OH MY GOD!
WHAT **POSSESSED** US?
RING!
FREEDOM TO MARRY.

ENDANGERED!
SPECIES at RISK

HI, SWEETHEART. HOW GOES THE STRUGGLE?

UH, FINE. BUSY. IS EVERYTHING OKAY?

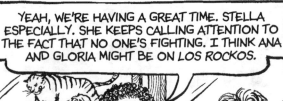

YEAH, WE'RE HAVING A GREAT TIME. STELLA ESPECIALLY. SHE KEEPS CALLING ATTENTION TO THE FACT THAT NO ONE'S FIGHTING. I THINK ANA AND GLORIA MIGHT BE ON *LOS ROCKOS.*

CHILDLESS N. AMERICAN LESBIAN
DYKUS UNDOMESTICUS

HUH. REALLY.

MEANWHILE, SYDNEY'S ON DECK...

...SUGGESTING THAT THE PROSTHESIS IS IN FACT A SORT OF PASTICHE, AN IMITATION THAT MOCKS THE VERY NOTION OF AN ORIGINAL. THE INTACT BODY IS SUBVERTED--REVEALED AS A FICTION, AND A DISJOINTED FICTION AT THAT. ABSENCE IS OMNIPRESENT.

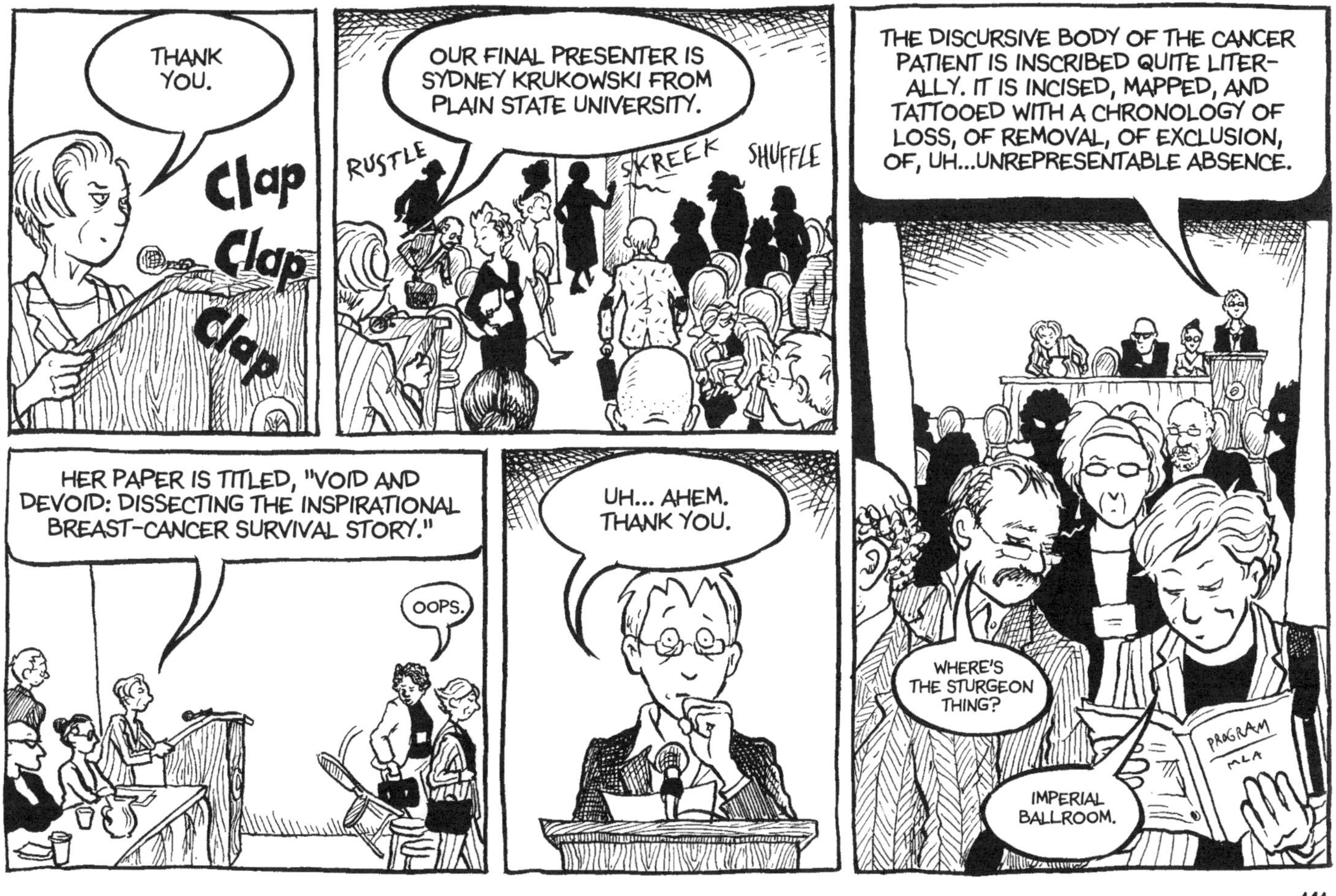
THANK YOU.
Clap
Clap
Clap
OUR FINAL PRESENTER IS SYDNEY KRUKOWSKI FROM PLAIN STATE UNIVERSITY.
RUSTLE
SKREEK
SHUFFLE
THE DISCURSIVE BODY OF THE CANCER PATIENT IS INSCRIBED QUITE LITERALLY. IT IS INCISED, MAPPED, AND TATTOOED WITH A CHRONOLOGY OF LOSS, OF REMOVAL, OF EXCLUSION, OF, UH...UNREPRESENTABLE ABSENCE.
HER PAPER IS TITLED, "VOID AND DEVOID: DISSECTING THE INSPIRATIONAL BREAST-CANCER SURVIVAL STORY."
OOPS.
UH... AHEM. THANK YOU.
WHERE'S THE STURGEON THING?
IMPERIAL BALLROOM.
PROGRAM
MLA

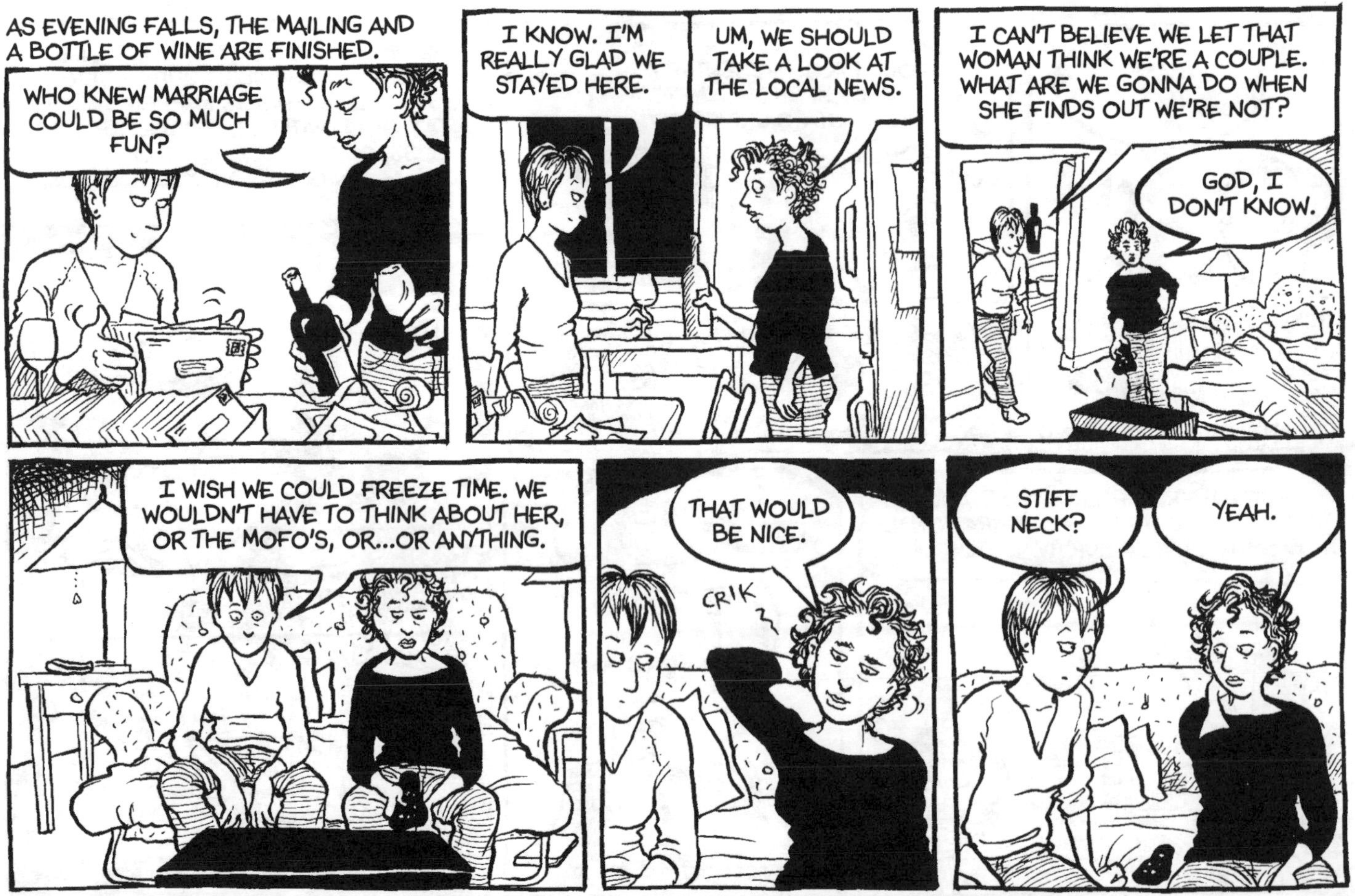
AS EVENING FALLS, THE MAILING AND A BOTTLE OF WINE ARE FINISHED.
WHO KNEW MARRIAGE COULD BE SO MUCH FUN?
I KNOW. I'M REALLY GLAD WE STAYED HERE.
UM, WE SHOULD TAKE A LOOK AT THE LOCAL NEWS.
I CAN'T BELIEVE WE LET THAT WOMAN THINK WE'RE A COUPLE. WHAT ARE WE GONNA DO WHEN SHE FINDS OUT WE'RE NOT?
GOD, I DON'T KNOW.
I WISH WE COULD FREEZE TIME. WE WOULDN'T HAVE TO THINK ABOUT HER, OR THE MOFO'S, OR...OR ANYTHING.
THAT WOULD BE NICE.
CRIK
STIFF NECK?
YEAH.

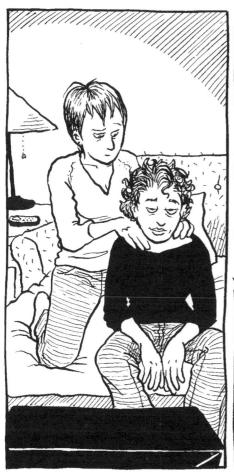

HELLO?

HI, MOMMY! WE SAW THE T. REX SKELETON!

MOM! WE'RE HAVING AN AWESOME TIME. I MISS YOU.

MEANWHILE, AT THE *THEORETICAL CRITIQUES OF CRITICAL THEORY* CASH BAR...

IT WAS LIKE SOMEONE ANNOUNCED A CLEARANCE SALE AT THE OVERLY FASHIONABLE **EYEGLASS** BOUTIQUE! COMPLETE MASS EXODUS! THEY COULDN'T GET OUT OF THERE FAST ENOUGH!

SYD, YOU CAN'T TAKE THAT SORT OF THING PERSONALLY. I WAS ON A PANEL WITH STURGEON ONCE. AS SOON AS HE FINISHED, **POOF!** EMPTY ROOM.

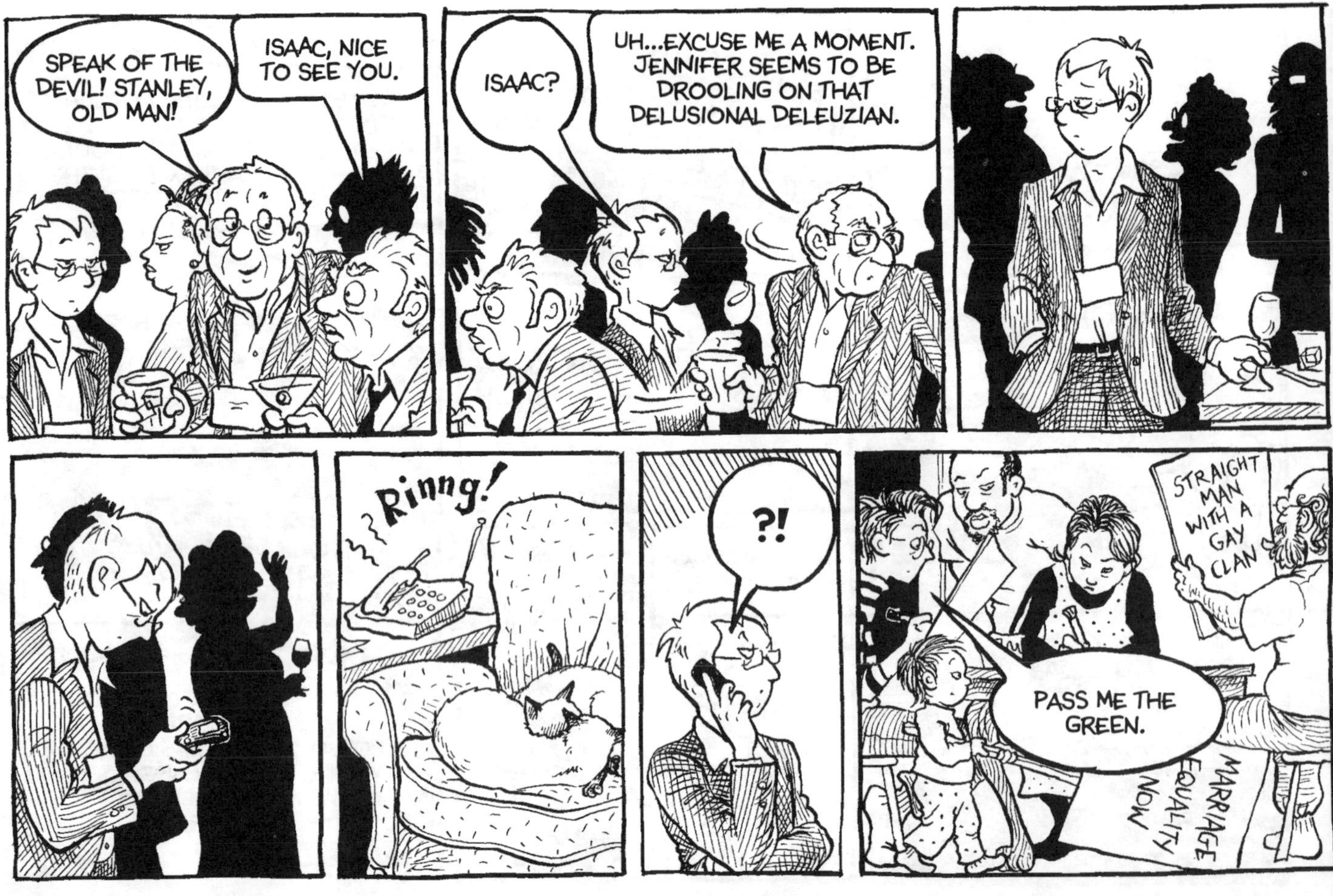
SPEAK OF THE DEVIL! STANLEY, OLD MAN!
ISAAC, NICE TO SEE YOU.
ISAAC?
UH...EXCUSE ME A MOMENT. JENNIFER SEEMS TO BE DROOLING ON THAT DELUSIONAL DELEUZIAN.
Rinng!
?!
STRAIGHT MAN WITH A GAY CLAN
PASS ME THE GREEN.
MARRIAGE EQUALITY NOW

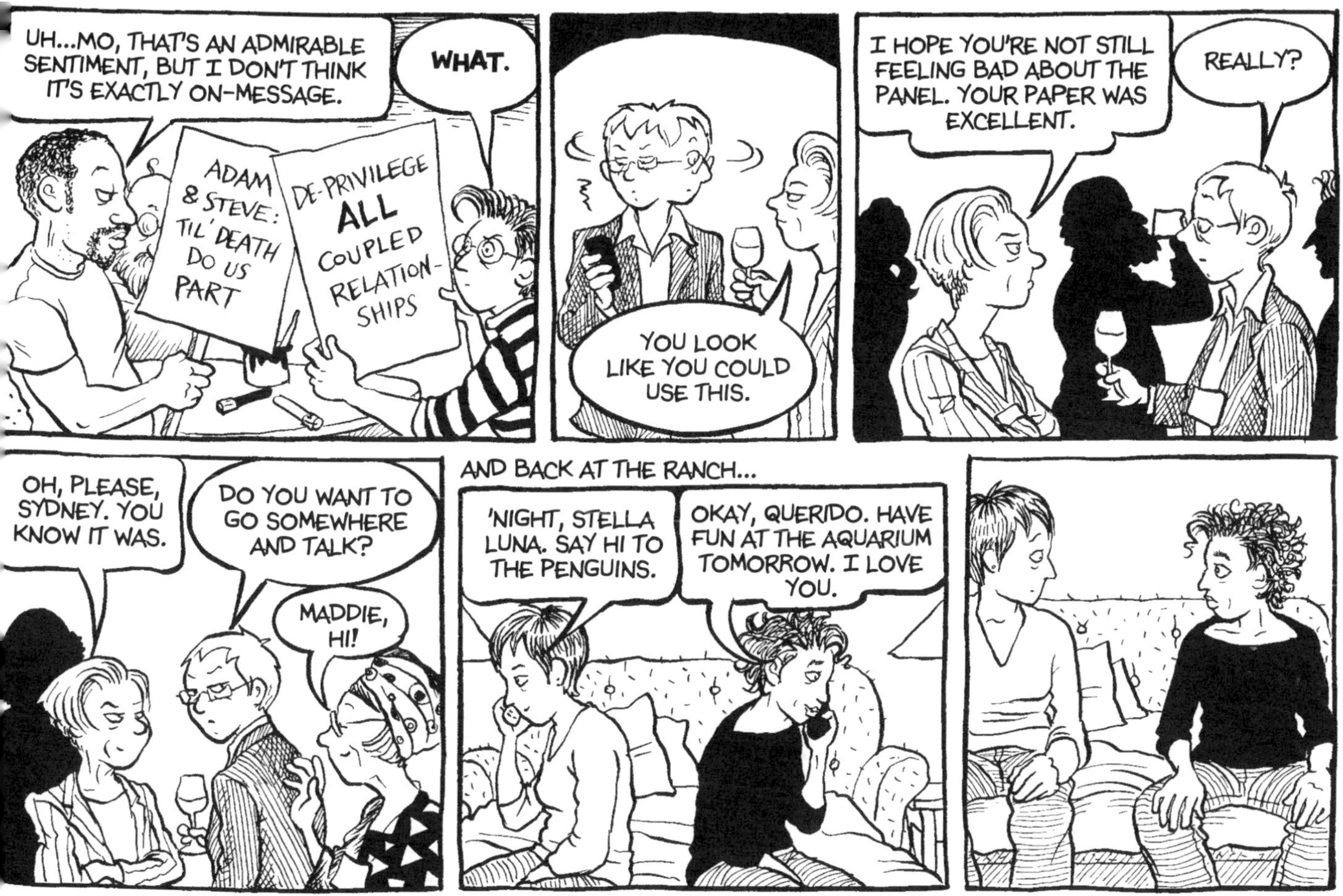
UH...MO, THAT'S AN ADMIRABLE SENTIMENT, BUT I DON'T THINK IT'S EXACTLY ON-MESSAGE.
WHAT.
ADAM & STEVE: TIL' DEATH DO US PART
DE-PRIVILEGE ALL COUPLED RELATIONSHIPS
YOU LOOK LIKE YOU COULD USE THIS.
I HOPE YOU'RE NOT STILL FEELING BAD ABOUT THE PANEL. YOUR PAPER WAS EXCELLENT.
REALLY?
OH, PLEASE, SYDNEY. YOU KNOW IT WAS.
DO YOU WANT TO GO SOMEWHERE AND TALK?
MADDIE, HI!
AND BACK AT THE RANCH...
'NIGHT, STELLA LUNA. SAY HI TO THE PENGUINS.
OKAY, QUERIDO. HAVE FUN AT THE AQUARIUM TOMORROW. I LOVE YOU.

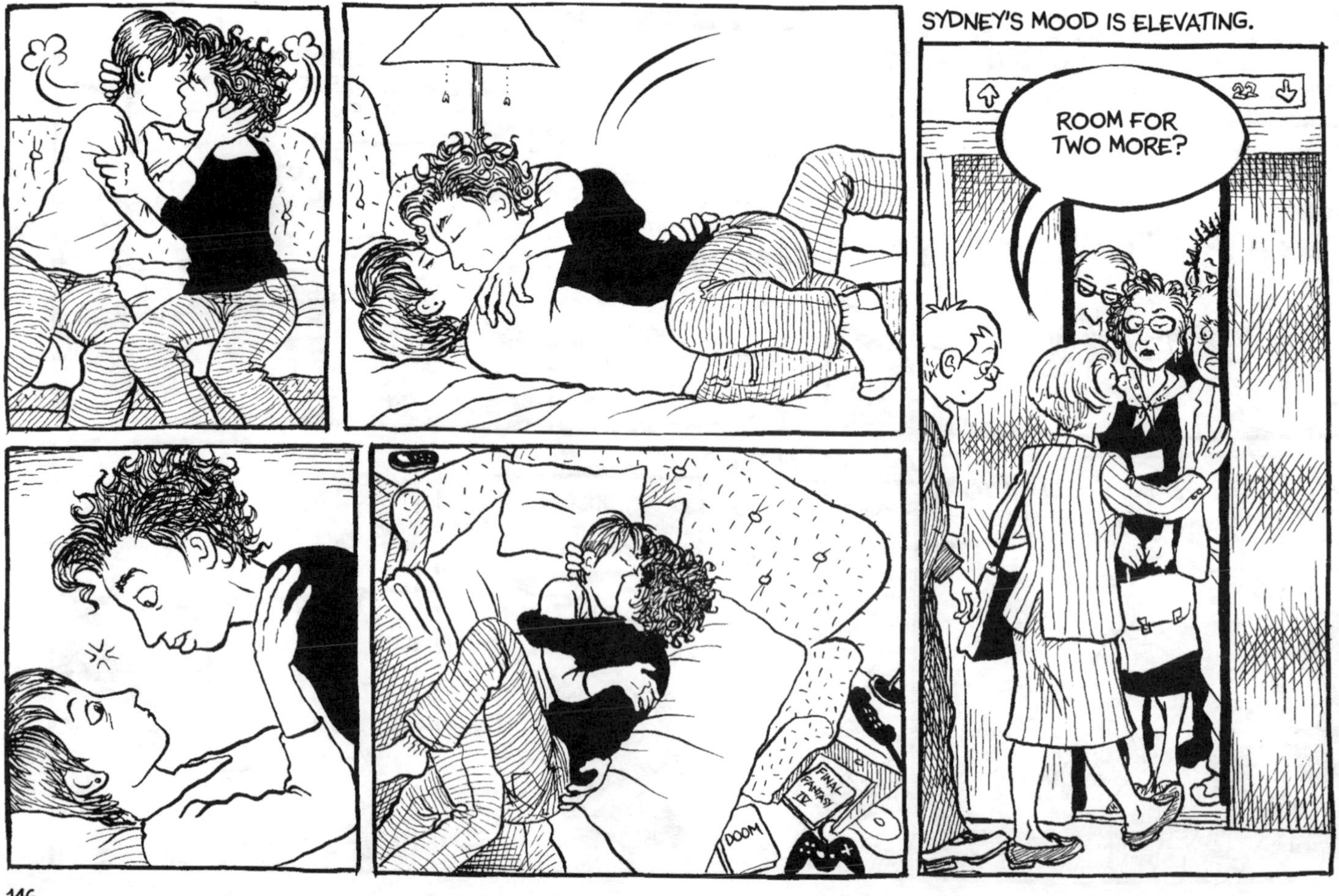
FINAL FANTASY IV
DOOM
SYDNEY'S MOOD IS ELEVATING.
22
ROOM FOR TWO MORE?

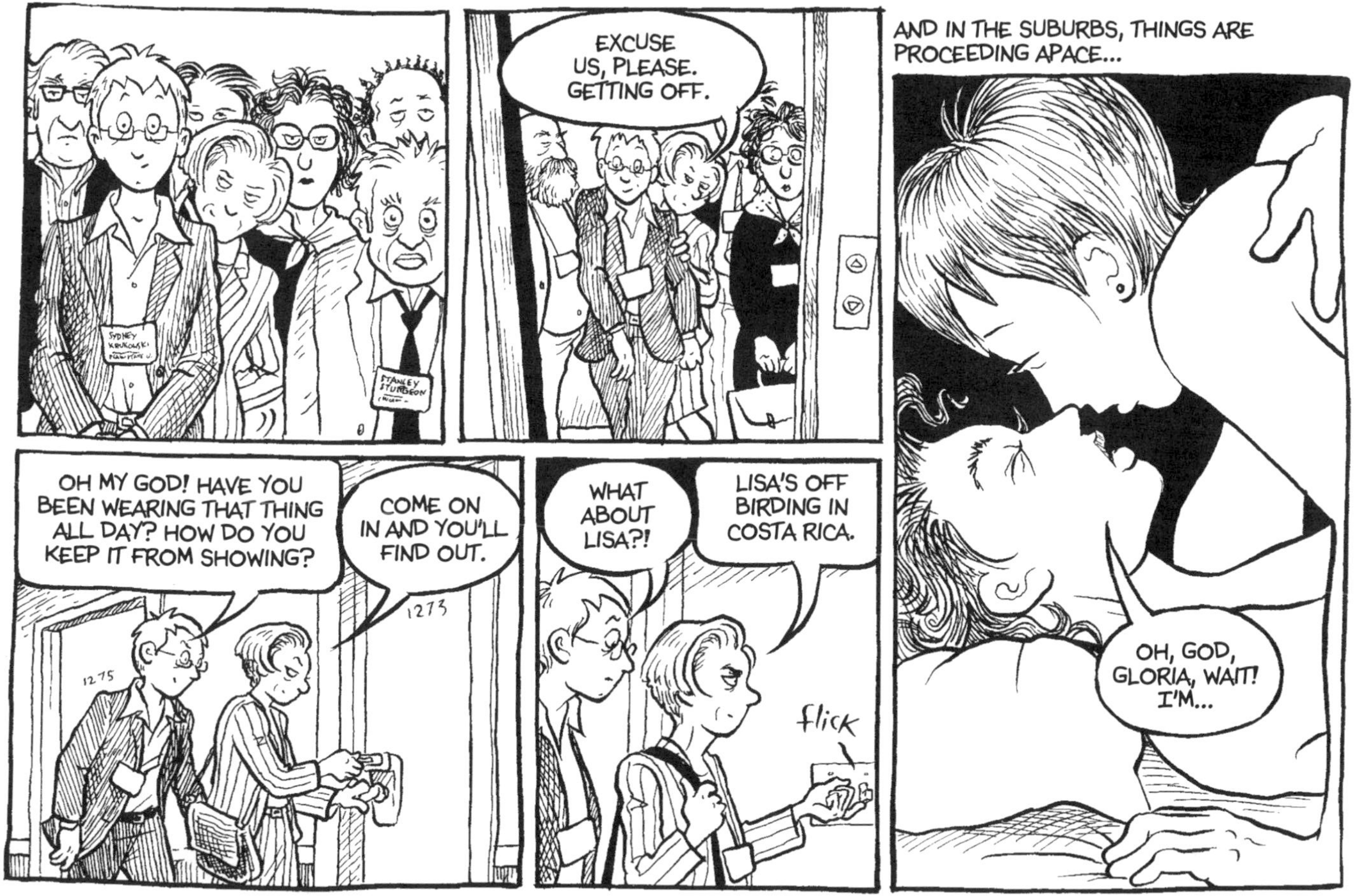
EXCUSE US, PLEASE. GETTING OFF.
OH MY GOD! HAVE YOU BEEN WEARING THAT THING ALL DAY? HOW DO YOU KEEP IT FROM SHOWING?
COME ON IN AND YOU'LL FIND OUT.
1273
1275
WHAT ABOUT LISA?!
LISA'S OFF BIRDING IN COSTA RICA.
flick
AND IN THE SUBURBS, THINGS ARE PROCEEDING APACE...
OH, GOD, GLORIA, WAIT! I'M...

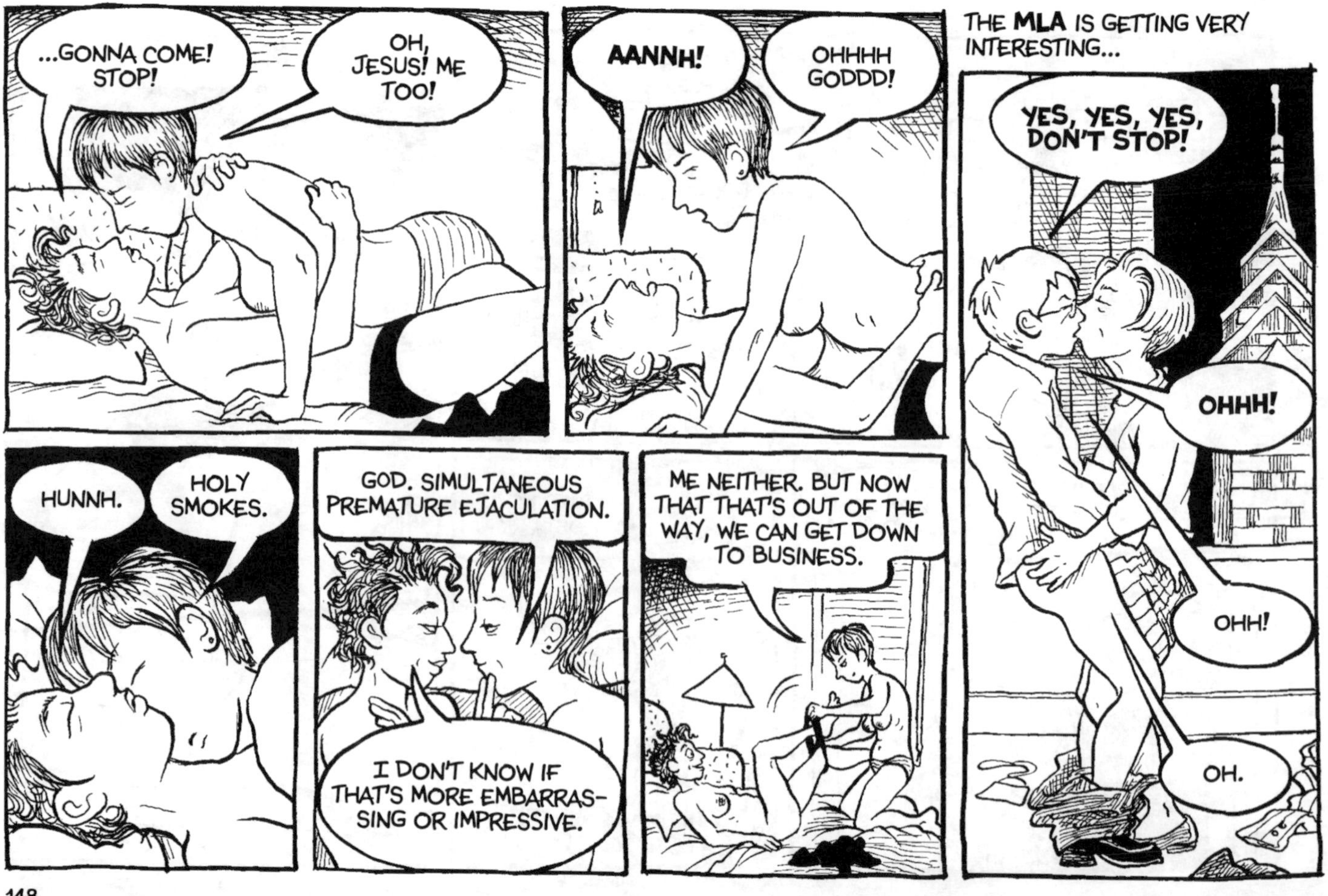
...GONNA COME! STOP!
OH, JESUS! ME TOO!
AANNH!
OHHHH GODDD!
THE **MLA** IS GETTING VERY INTERESTING...
YES, YES, YES, DON'T STOP!
OHHH!
OHH!
OH.
HUNNH.
HOLY SMOKES.
GOD. SIMULTANEOUS PREMATURE EJACULATION.
I DON'T KNOW IF THAT'S MORE EMBARRAS-SING OR IMPRESSIVE.
ME NEITHER. BUT NOW THAT THAT'S OUT OF THE WAY, WE CAN GET DOWN TO BUSINESS.

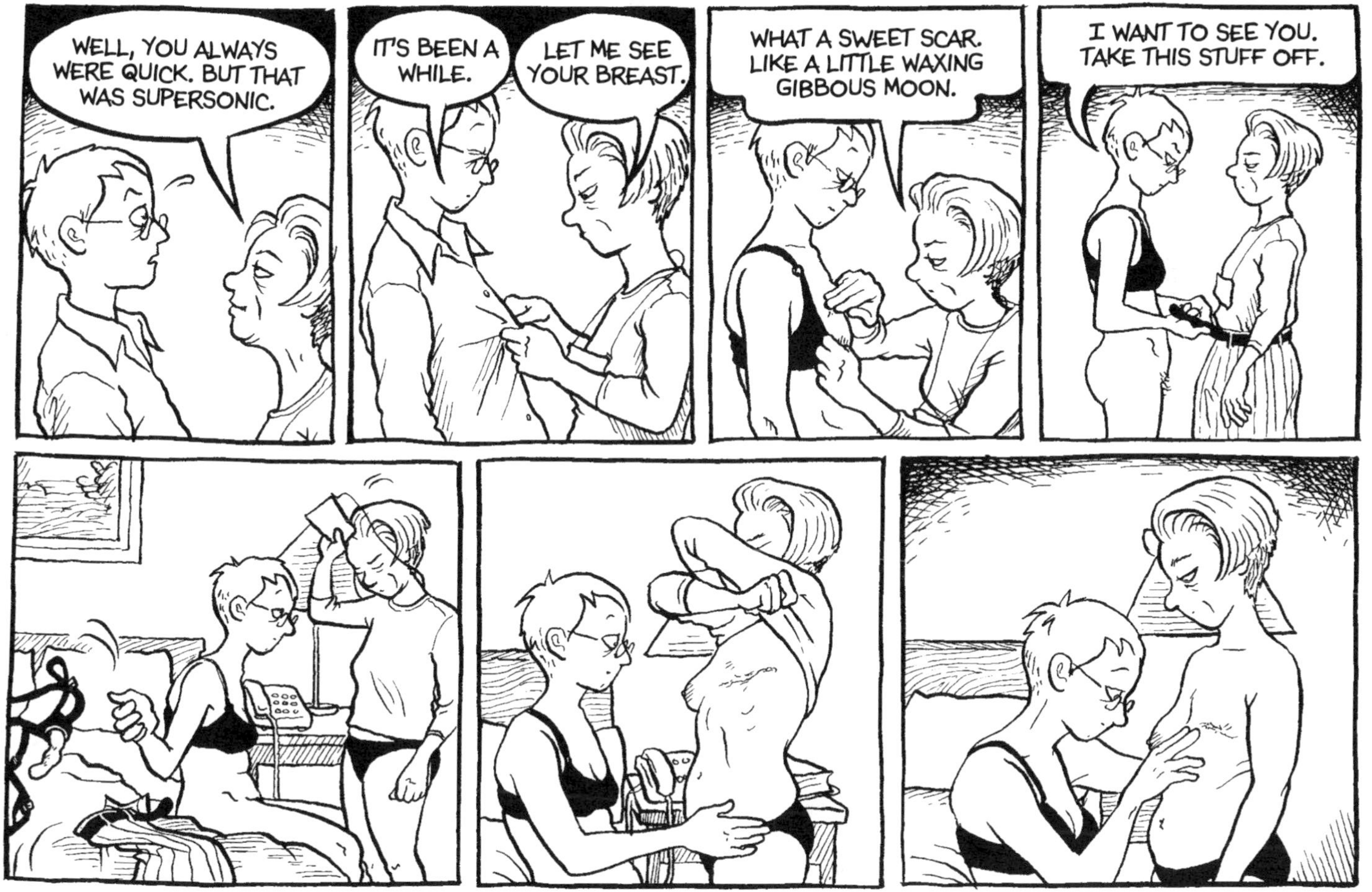
WELL, YOU ALWAYS WERE QUICK. BUT THAT WAS SUPERSONIC.
IT'S BEEN A WHILE.
LET ME SEE YOUR BREAST.
WHAT A SWEET SCAR. LIKE A LITTLE WAXING GIBBOUS MOON.
I WANT TO SEE YOU. TAKE THIS STUFF OFF.

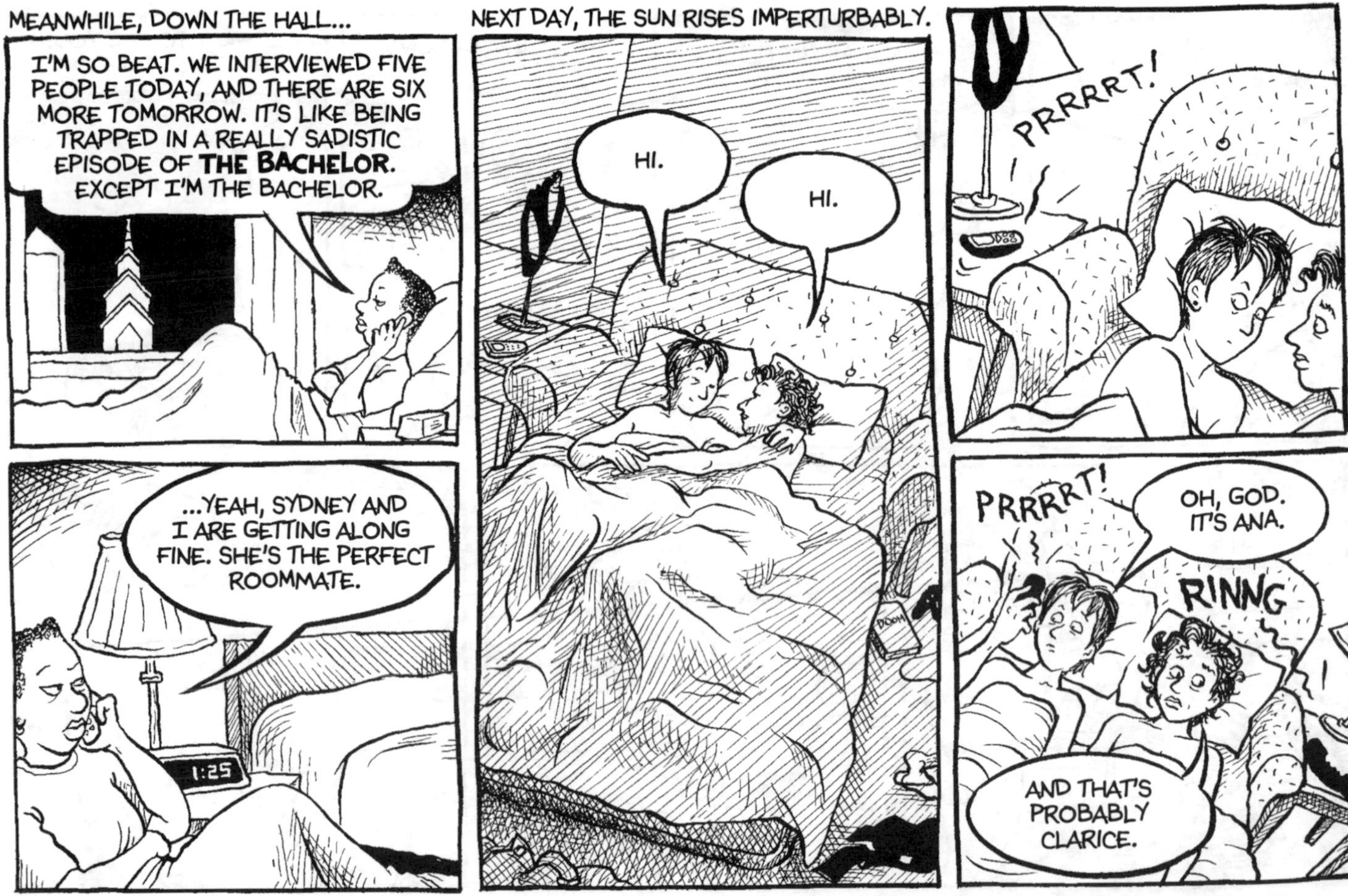

MEANWHILE, DOWN THE HALL...
I'M SO BEAT. WE INTERVIEWED FIVE PEOPLE TODAY, AND THERE ARE SIX MORE TOMORROW. IT'S LIKE BEING TRAPPED IN A REALLY SADISTIC EPISODE OF **THE BACHELOR**. EXCEPT I'M THE BACHELOR.
...YEAH, SYDNEY AND I ARE GETTING ALONG FINE. SHE'S THE PERFECT ROOMMATE.
1:25
NEXT DAY, THE SUN RISES IMPERTURBABLY.
HI.
HI.
PRRRRT!
PRRRRT!
OH, GOD. IT'S ANA.
RINNG
AND THAT'S PROBABLY CLARICE.

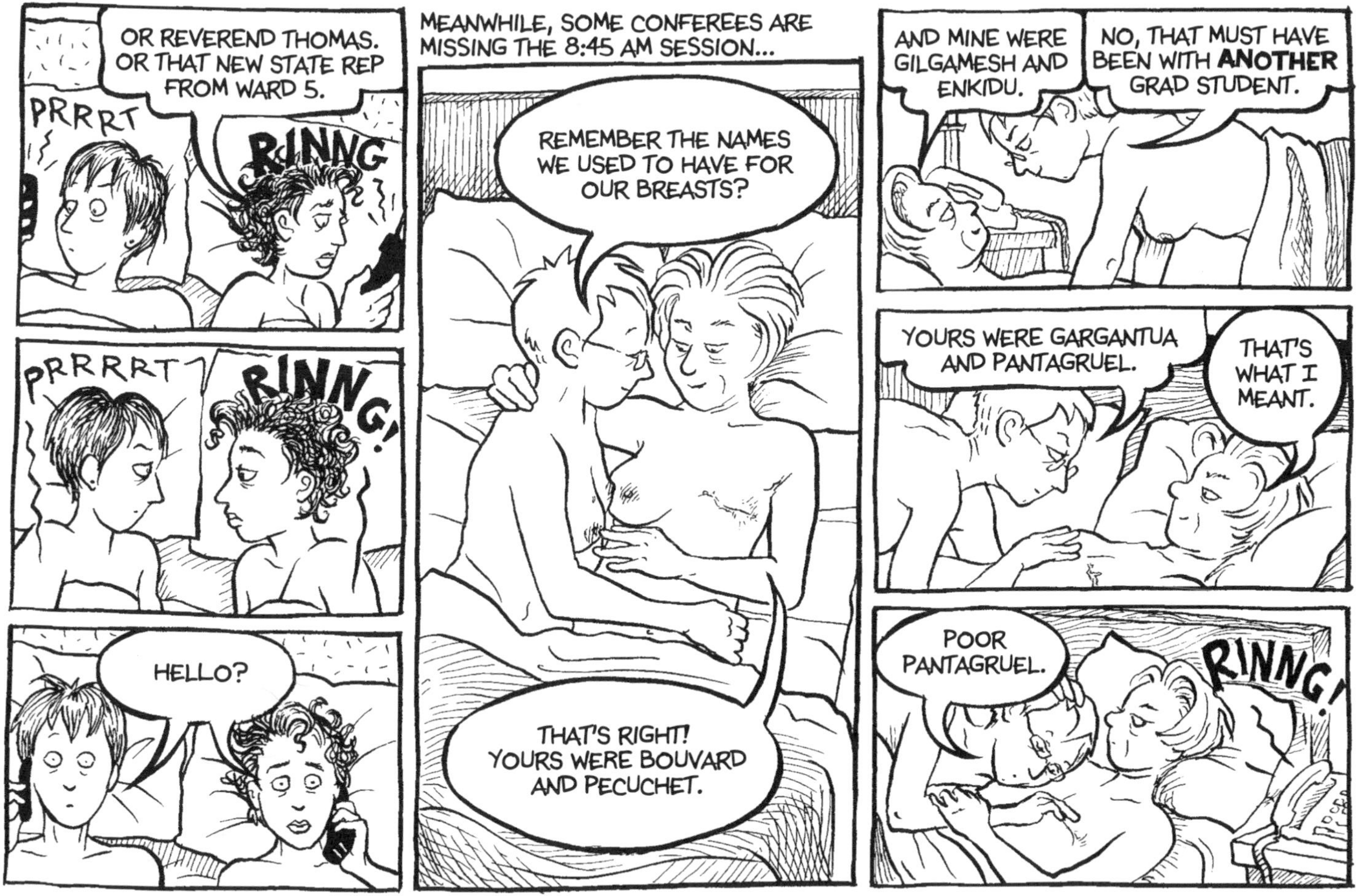

OR REVEREND THOMAS. OR THAT NEW STATE REP FROM WARD 5.
PRRRT
RINNG
PRRRRT
RINNG!
HELLO?
MEANWHILE, SOME CONFEREES ARE MISSING THE 8:45 AM SESSION...
REMEMBER THE NAMES WE USED TO HAVE FOR OUR BREASTS?
THAT'S RIGHT! YOURS WERE BOUVARD AND PECUCHET.
AND MINE WERE GILGAMESH AND ENKIDU.
NO, THAT MUST HAVE BEEN WITH **ANOTHER** GRAD STUDENT.
YOURS WERE GARGANTUA AND PANTAGRUEL.
THAT'S WHAT I MEANT.
POOR PANTAGRUEL.
RINNG!

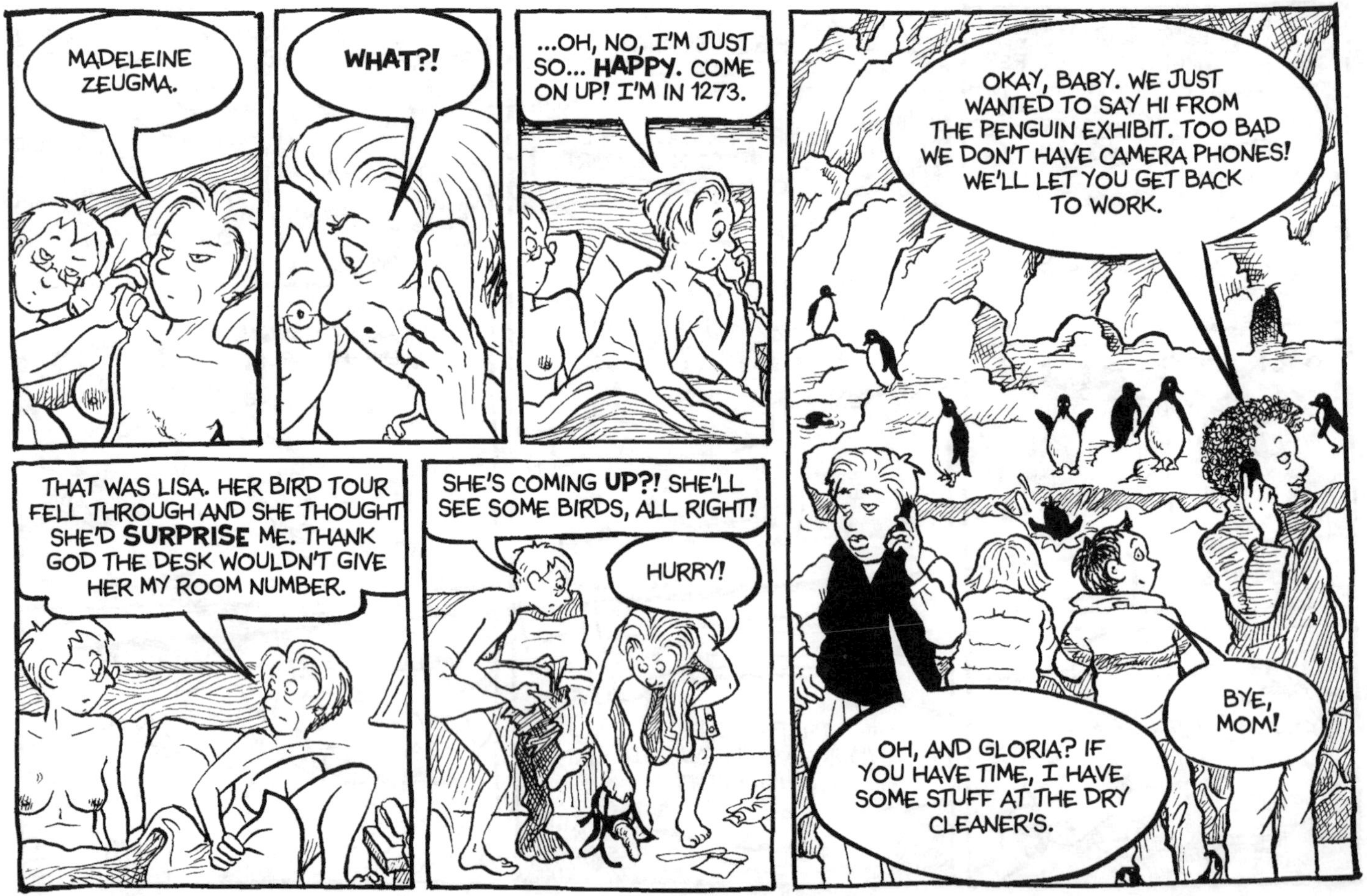
MADELEINE ZEUGMA.
WHAT?!
...OH, NO, I'M JUST SO... HAPPY. COME ON UP! I'M IN 1273.
OKAY, BABY. WE JUST WANTED TO SAY HI FROM THE PENGUIN EXHIBIT. TOO BAD WE DON'T HAVE CAMERA PHONES! WE'LL LET YOU GET BACK TO WORK.
THAT WAS LISA. HER BIRD TOUR FELL THROUGH AND SHE THOUGHT SHE'D SURPRISE ME. THANK GOD THE DESK WOULDN'T GIVE HER MY ROOM NUMBER.
SHE'S COMING UP?! SHE'LL SEE SOME BIRDS, ALL RIGHT!
HURRY!
BYE, MOM!
OH, AND GLORIA? IF YOU HAVE TIME, I HAVE SOME STUFF AT THE DRY CLEANER'S.

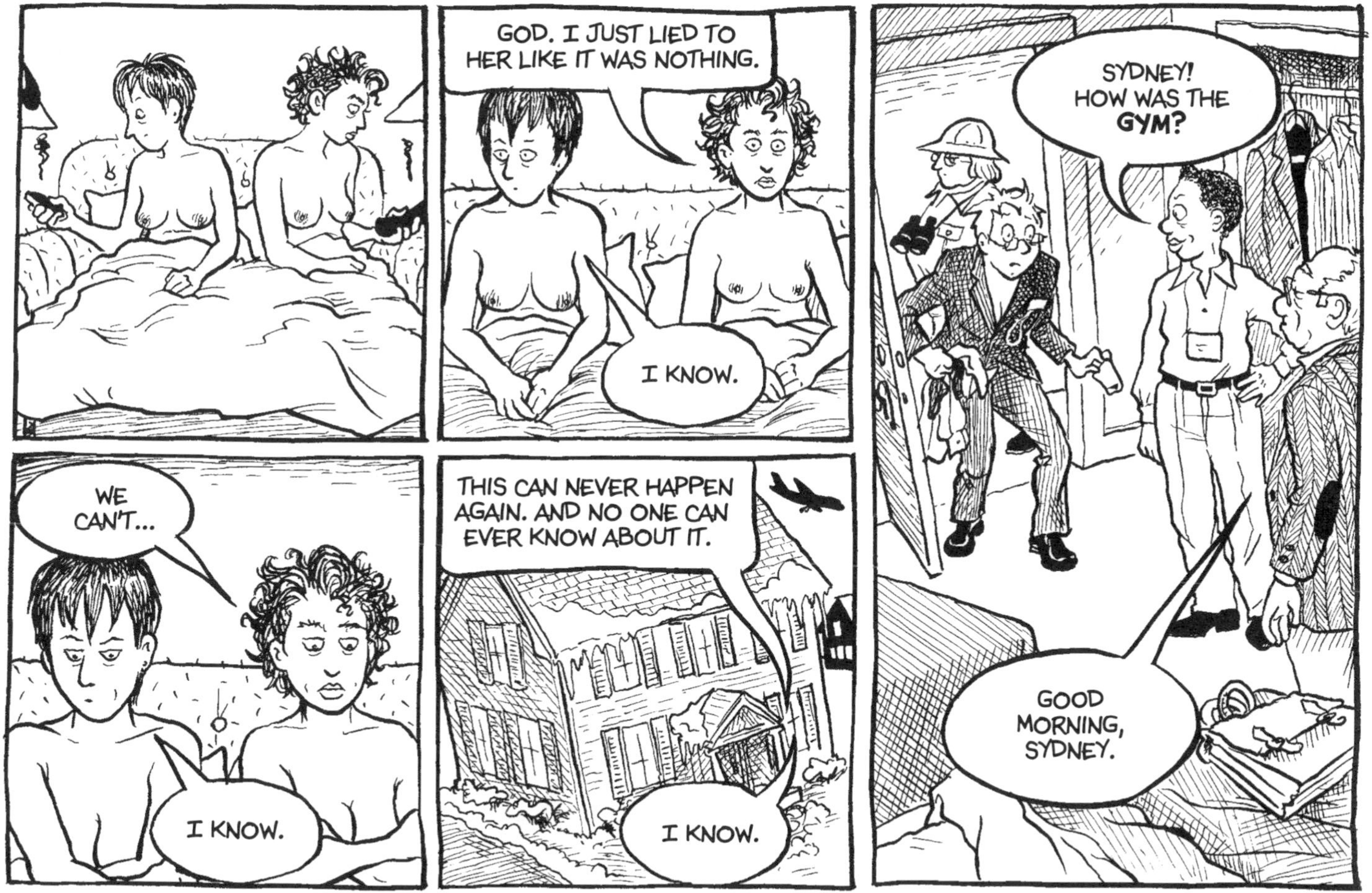
GOD. I JUST LIED TO HER LIKE IT WAS NOTHING.
I KNOW.
SYDNEY! HOW WAS THE **GYM?**
GOOD MORNING, SYDNEY.
WE CAN'T...
I KNOW.
THIS CAN NEVER HAPPEN AGAIN. AND NO ONE CAN EVER KNOW ABOUT IT.
I KNOW.

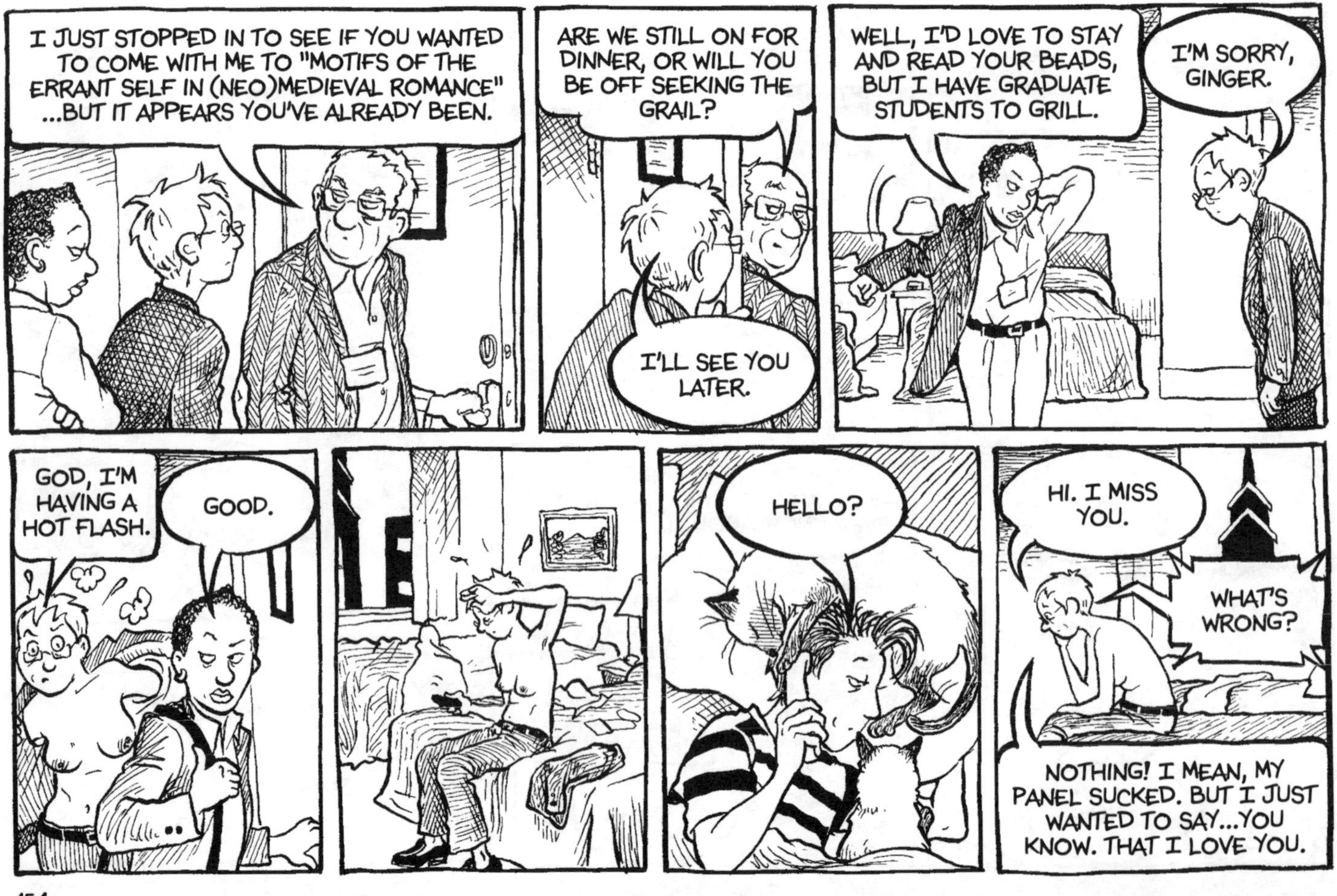
I JUST STOPPED IN TO SEE IF YOU WANTED TO COME WITH ME TO "MOTIFS OF THE ERRANT SELF IN (NEO)MEDIEVAL ROMANCE" ...BUT IT APPEARS YOU'VE ALREADY BEEN.
ARE WE STILL ON FOR DINNER, OR WILL YOU BE OFF SEEKING THE GRAIL?
I'LL SEE YOU LATER.
WELL, I'D LOVE TO STAY AND READ YOUR BEADS, BUT I HAVE GRADUATE STUDENTS TO GRILL.
I'M SORRY, GINGER.
GOD, I'M HAVING A HOT FLASH.
GOOD.
HELLO?
HI. I MISS YOU.
WHAT'S WRONG?
NOTHING! I MEAN, MY PANEL SUCKED. BUT I JUST WANTED TO SAY...YOU KNOW. THAT I LOVE YOU.

THAT'S GREAT, REVEREND THOMAS. YOU'LL GO RIGHT AFTER THE TACTICAL PUPPET SQUAD DOES THEIR ODE TO BERT AND ERNIE.
YEAH, FIVE MINUTES. WE'RE TRYING TO FOCUS ON THE EQUAL RIGHTS ANGLE.
YOU KNOW, HOW WE WANT THE SAME PROTECTION AND SECURITY FOR OUR RELATIONSHIPS AND KIDS THAT EVERY-ONE ELSE HAS BECAUSE WE'RE JUST LIKE EVERYONE ELSE, BLAH BLAH BLAH.
The End